28797

McKenzie's Hundred

McKENZIE'S HUNDRED

Frank Yerby

DOUBLEDAY & COMPANY, INC.

GARDEN CITY, NEW YORK

1985

Library of Congress Cataloging in Publication Data

Yerby, Frank, 1916–
McKenzie's Hundred.

1. Virginia—History—Civil War, 1861–1865—Fiction.
I. Title.
PS3547.E65M34   1985   813'.54
ISBN *0-385-27726-1*
Library of Congress Catalog Card Number 84-18804
Copyright © 1985 by Frank Yerby

McKenzie's Hundred

Chapter One

Rose Ann McKenzie looked at her brother Jeff, sitting—or rather lolling, with boneless and presumably aristocratic grace—on the seat opposite hers in the all but empty railroad car.

Well, we McKenzies are a First Family of Virginia, she thought wryly. For all the good it's going to do us now . . .

She flashed her brother one of those absolutely shameless Mc-Kenzie grins that were high on the list of the reasons that Tidewater people gave when they solemnly swore that the Clan's original ancestors had been a warlock and a witch who'd whooped and hollered and sashayed around a mite too lustily while celebrating a Black Sabbath's Mass down in Dismal Swamp a couple of centuries back.

"Be there soon, won't we, Jeffie love?" she purred. "By my reckoning, can't be very far by now . . ."

"Don't call me Jeffie love!" Geoffrey McKenzie exploded. "Lord God, Ramb! I'll admit we McKenzies are great hands at getting into trouble, but did you have to get into *that* kind? Sent down for scandalous behavior, of all things! How in the name of Old Ned are we ever going to be able to hold our heads up again? People, sister mine, aren't even going to start to believe that the schools in Boston close before the fifteenth of April. We aren't the only Virginia family who're blessed with Yankee kissing kin, y'know. Why, half of Richmond's got relatives up North. So, sure as shooting, a couple of those evil-minded old dames you've shocked spitless too many times by now are going to put their heads together and start figuring—"

" 'Til they come up with the right answer," Rose Ann said bleakly. "Or the wrong one. Only, in my case, the right answer may *be* the wrong one. As far as public opinion is concerned, anyhow. So—"

Geoffrey stared at his sister. His jaw dropped open. His normally ruddy face became a winter's landscape, bleached colorless by consternation. Even his lips went white.

"Lord Jesus, Ramb!" he whispered. "You don't mean to tell me that you—that you—"

"That I what?" Rose drawled.

"Are in the—well, in the family way, to say it straight out and ugly. Are you, Ramb?" Jeff quavered. He was, his sister saw, totally appalled.

"And if I were?"

"Jesus!" Jeff croaked prayerfully.

Rose looked out of the window at the smiling Virginia country-side, crawling slowly backward past them as the train snorted and puffed and clacked its way through it.

"If I were," she said flatly, "I'd have a perfect right to be, Jeff boy. After all, I married the oily little cuss. And I've got a nice, official damnyankee piece of paper complete with flowery script and ribbons and sealing wax to prove it. Not to mention a ring. Got it on a string around my neck. He stole it from his fat and greasy old-country *mamma mia*, so it keeps falling off my finger. But—"

"But what, Ramb?" Jeff moaned.

"But, as a matter of fact, I don't think I am. He wasn't very good at what men—especially husbands—are supposed to be good at. That is, if any of you ever really are. But then I wouldn't know, would I? There's no way for a highborn Virginia maiden to find out, is there? Not beforehand, anyhow . . ."

"Ramb, I swear to God—"

"Don't. Swearing's wicked, I'm told. And quit callin me Ramb, will you? Just because I wandered off and got lost a couple of times when I was small is no reason for people to go on calling me Rambling Rose McKenzie forever. Besides, I've got a much better nickname now. Girls at the school Aunt Cornelia sent me to, Miss Phoebe Bradstreet's School for Young Ladies—just the place for little old me, wouldn't you think?—dreamed it up the first time old Miss Frozen Phiz allowed us—properly chaperoned, of course!—to go to a ball. Lots of fine, upstanding Yankee lads there that night. So when those stiff and awkward Northern fillies saw me start in to operate, they called me—"

"What? Brazen Hussy, I'll bet!"

"Among other things. But actually the one they settled for was milder. You see, they'd already decided to call me by my second name, Ann, because they'd found out by then there was nothing sweet and flowerlike about me. So after that ball they rechristened me Rapid Ann. Pretty good, isn't it?"

"Fits you like a glove, anyhow. Lord God, Ramb, what on earth are we going to do now? Not only do you run off with a damn-yankee but you arrange things so that the Pinkertons A'nt Corny hired didn't catch up with y'all 'til noon of the *next* day. So there's no way we can claim that nothing happened twixt you two—"

"Well, nothing, exactly nothing, maybe not." Rose Ann sighed.

"Mighty little, though. Besides, I told you we'd stood up before a justice of the peace, and got ourselves a license to commit the poor excuse for matrimony we did commit. So quit worrying, will you?"

"I can't. Look at it, Rosie. Not only do you run off with a Yankee but said Yankee is a greasy foreigner. The son of an Eye-talian greengrocer by God! Why—"

"My pappy-in-law is nobody's grocer. He's an *entrepreneur* and the richest Roman Catholic in Boston. He owns twenty grocery stores, not just one. Why, do tell! This here little old choo-choo train is really picking up speed, isn't it? Looks like somebody really slipped a cocklebur under the engineer's saddle—"

"Yes, worse luck! I was kind of hoping we wouldn't get to Richmond 'til way after dark. That way I'd maybe have a ghost of a chance of getting you through town and out to the Hundred without anybody's seeing you, but now—"

"Why, blast and damn!" Rose swore feelingly. "Getting legally hitched in double harness may be a mistake, Jeff McKenzie—and in my case, I'll sorrowfully admit it sure Lord *was*—but it's neither a sin nor a crime! Giuseppe—that's Italian for Joe, love—was a mighty pretty boy. Maybe, given time, I'd have even taught him something useful. But there's no hope for that now. What I'm saying, Jeff, is that you can't expect me to feel ashamed of falling in love with the handsomest he-male critter I ever did see, and damned near the nicest. I'm only sorry that it didn't work out, that we weren't even given a chance to get to know each other better. Papa Giovanni has probably had the whole thing annulled by now, I'll bet, just like he was threatening to. On the score that I'm not of the One True Faith, a point not even worth arguing about; that dear little Joe-Joe, my boy baby doll, was under the age of consent —also true, 'cause the mannish little critter lied to me, swore he'd reached a hoary and respectable twenty, instead of being a wee bit shy of seventeen, as, in actual fact, he was; and that I'm a loose, designing Southern female, all of which except the geography and the gender is distinctly debatable. So don't you go pinning old Nat Hawthorne's scarlet letter on me, Jeffie love. I just won't stand for that, you hear?"

"Rosie," Jeff sighed, "a hell of a lot more women—and *men*— have been purely ruint for being stupid than for being wicked. That's your case right now. At the moment Clan McKenzie could get away with you creeping back home again with your wages of sin squalling away lustily in your poor deceived arms, while you, innocent—well, halfway innocent, anyhow—victim of Yankee dastardy—hang your wronged head in shame, bowed down in tears over the way that conniving bluenose has gone and treated you, a hell of a lot better than we can face the charges of moral treason involved in any Southern gentlewoman's actually going so far as to forget her place in this world and the high, chivalrous civilization from which she sprang to the extent of actually marrying a counterjumping, moneygrubbing Yankee!"

Rose grinned at her brother merrily. "In other words, bedding with the critter for fun and the hell of it would have been perfectly all right, the mistake consisting in making the rumpus legal?" she drawled.

"Exactly!" Jeff thundered. "We aren't talking about morals, Ramb—oh, hell, Rose Ann—but about strategy. Feeling is running mighty high down here, now that that shambling ape from Illinois is actually in the White House. And Virginia, our proud Old Dominion—sister, I could weep for her! Look at the picture! Seven Southern states—South Carolina, Mississippi, Florida, Alabama, Georgia, Louisiana, and Texas—*already* out of the blasted Union! And Virginia, our Virginia, mother of Presidents, natural leader of them all, holding back, hemming and hawing while as long ago as the ninth of January our friends in South Ca'lina had showed their mettle by treating Yankee reinforcements aboard the U.S. steamer *Star of the West* to a nice hot whiff of Southern grapeshot and cannonball, by cracky! Don't know what's happened in Charleston Harbor by now, but when I left to come after you, those Ca'lina boys, under that little Creole gamecock from New Orleans, Beauregard, were demanding the surrender of Fort Sumter . . ."

"Then there's a war on," Rose sighed. "Never did meet a Carolinian—North or South—who had a mite of sense . . ."

"Why—Rosie!" Jeff thundered.

"Jeff, honey—you've been up North visiting our Yankee cousins in Boston almost as many times as I have. So you know as well as I do we can't whip the Yankees. Setting aside the fact that a mighty heap of them are as brave as lions and gentlemen to boot, even if they *were* the cowardly counterjumping clerks you fellows like to sound off about and, more unlikely still, even if one gallant Southerner could really take three damnyankees with him when he went —beating them to death with singletrees and hickory sticks likely, for God knows there's not *one* gun manufactory in the length and breadth of the South—there'd still be three Yankees standing up and shooting after all of you are dead. Because they won't quit.

They're the stubbornest damn people anybody ever heard tell of. They'll lose every battle, maybe—except one. The last one. The one that counts. Oh, Lord! Don't sit there glaring at me like that and twitching! We've got to fight them, and I'm going to do my part. More than my part, maybe, for this crazy land I love. So let's change the subject. Tell me something, dear gallant, fire-eating orator—why'd Gwen send *you* after me instead of letting Caleb come fetch me home?"

Jeff stared at her bleakly. "Ramb, that there's purely a rhetorical question, and you know it," he growled. "Our sister's nobody's fool. And that's what throwing dust-dry tinder and a permanent spark together off all by their lonesomes is the act of. So, when we get back home to the Hundred, I want you to promise me to keep your hot little sweaty hands the hell off of poor Caleb. He's a good boy, but as far as you're concerned, he's mighty weak. And wrecking a going concern, which Gwen's marriage to Caleb Henry *is*, doesn't rightly fall under the heading of appropriate procedures, appears to me!"

"That's because you're a he-critter too," Rose chuckled. "Never did see a pants-wearing animule yet who could appreciate another fellow's virtues . . ."

"Cabe's *virtues*, Rambling Rosie, are the *last* thing about him that interests you!" Jeff growled. "Lord God! What did I ever do to deserve a loose-limbed, caterwauling she-catamount for a sister?"

"Made a mighty big mistake in choosing your parents," Rose said cheerfully. "You'll have to admit I came by my—inclinations —honestly, Jeffie boy. Runs in the family. Being stood up on pedestals and worshipped as pure Southern womanhood, while you fellows go scrambling round the quarters changing your luck with black wenches, has never been an avocation of McKenzie females, brother mine. You ought to know enough family history to realize that. It's Gwen who's the off horse in Clan McKenzie, not me. Swear to God that if we didn't look so much alike, I'd suspect poor Mama got even with Pa on that one occasion for all his helling around . . ."

"Rosie!" Jeff roared.

"He sure Lord had it coming!" Rose laughed. "But speaking of Pa, when we get to Richmond, I want you to buy him a bottle of rotgut. Get him drunk fast enough and he'll maybe forget about taking all the hide off me in strips . . ."

"Which ain't even half what you deserve!" Jeff said sternly.

Rose looked at him from under the heavy forest-fire-red eyebrows that were a McKenzie trademark.

"And you should be given a medal for good conduct and spotless purity both, I reckon?" she drawled.

"Lord Jesus, Ramb—I mean Rosie—I'm a *man!*"

"And I'm a woman. A condition that plumb scares little boys. Which is why you're always trying to make us over into china dolls. But you never stop to think that it takes *two* to sin, as far as the carnal variety is concerned, anyhow, and—" She stopped short, and her face, which, by the standards of her times, was robbed of perfect beauty because a spray of the McKenzie freckles had been splashed across it like droplets of molten gold, split into an introspective but decidedly mocking grin. "I'll come off that one," she sighed. "Let's say it takes two to sin *satisfactorily*. And all such poor substitutes oughtn't even be held in account if the good Lord is fair. Let's quit this, shall we? The arguments about the double moral standard have been going on ever since Aristophanes wrote his *Lysistrata* . . ."

"Since Aris—*who* wrote his *what?*" Jeff gasped.

"Greek to you, Jeffie love. Ancient, Attic, and pure. Part of my fine Yankee classical education, so forget it. Changing the subject, brother, tell me: Why is our place called McKenzie's Hundred? We've got a heck of a lot less than a hundred acres, appears to me. I've been meaning to ask Pa that half my life, but always something interesting comes up and I forget . . ."

"Something interesting in pants!" Jeff snorted.

"Or out of 'em. Preferably the latter. C'mon, Jeffie, why is it?"

"Don't know. There're two theories: first that the original royal companies sent over here to colonize the Tidewater were made up of a hundred men each. The second is that each member of said companies was automatically granted one hundred acres. I hold to the first theory. All the original Hundreds—Berkeley, Shirley, Flowerdew, and Bermuda—had up to ten or twenty times more acreage than that. Pa swears that the original McKenzie's Hundred had over a thousand . . ."

"Drawing the long bow as usual," Rose said disgustedly. "If we had all that back then, why are we so Lord-awful poor now?"

"Point one, Pa's—well, not exactly lying, but say consoling himself for present disappointments by calling up dreams of lost glories in the always golden past. That's natural enough, Ramb. I'd guess our Hundred originally had two, three hundred acres. Now we've got eighty—"

"And five Negroes—two of whom are women and all of 'em getting along in years—to work our somewhat less than magnificent spread. You never even got a chance to change your luck down at the quarters like all your fine-feathered friends, 'cause we never had any young wenches for you to change it with," Rose Ann said drily. "We've got a real nice old Georgian house, red brick, ivy-covered, and all the rest, but the roof leaks every time there's heavy *dew*, not to mention a rain, and the poor old tired mess is falling down, brick by brick. Y'know, Jeff, if I hadn't been a fool and got mixed up with my darling little Eye-tie, I'd have *stayed* up North. And when this big fuss you fire-eaters seem determined to get into is over, that's where you ought to go, lambie pie. Me, I'm going to light out for parts unknown soon as I get a chance to. California, likely. Heard they purely appreciate fallen women out there . . ."

"Rose Ann, for God's sake!" Jeff said.

"Damn!" she swore feelingly. "This here rambling wreck is slowing down again. Looks like we won't get to Richmond afore dark after all . . ."

"Ramb," Jeff said sternly, "you're going to have to watch that vile tongue of yours, y'hear? And in more ways than one. Folks not only ain't—aren't—going to cotton to your swearing like a light horse trooper with every other breath, but a young lady from a family in our position in life just can't get away with talking worse than a nigger field hand or a swamp-bottom redneck. You'd better watch your language and your grammar both, sister mine!"

"Our position in life!" Rose hooted. "But what position have we got, Jeff McKenzie? Sometimes I wish I were a high yellow quadroon wench, because then I could be sold down the river as a fun filly for some rich old planter with all kinds of interesting abominable vices, and *really* have myself a ball . . ."

"Rosie, I swear to God—" Jeff groaned.

"Don't," Rose said gently, aware that her brother's distress was genuine. "I was only plaguing you, lambie pie. In company, and around *Gwen*, I promise I'll talk like a lady—a Back Bay *Boston* lady at that. Want to hear me? 'Oh, I say, my deah fel-low, I simply cawn't stand the way you benighted Southerners drawl!' "

"Oh, Lord!" Jeff laughed. "You've really got it letter-perfect, haven't you? Anybody hearing you would swear you'd been brought up on baked beans and codfish, and that your nose was a lovely shade of blue. Say, it *is* getting dark, isn't it? Well, that's a relief . . ."

"Jeff," Rose said quietly, "don't try sneaking me through town, or hiding me out at the Hundred after we get there. I've been—for just one night—a healthy young fellow's *wife*. I don't think anything's going to come of it, but the truth is, I don't *know*. And I won't know until sometime next month. Never was any great shakes at calendar watching, because, as you ought to realize, Jeffie love, I've never *had* to, before now. All the talk about my scandalous behavior was just that: *talk*. Instead of listening so hard to all the pearls of wisdom that fell from my flip tongue, our local Association of Evil-minded Old Witches should have paid a mite more attention to what more than one dear little creature I know, whose eyes are *glued* to the carpet and whose mouth could be used for a springhouse 'cause butter sure Lord wouldn't melt in it, was actually sneaking around and *doing*. So let me face the world, will you? I may be a randy, red-haired McKenzie woman with an overdeveloped appreciation for the opposite sex, but a coward I'm not. As I said before, I don't think I'm going to make you an uncle out of season, but even if that should be the case, I can handle the situation. And *not*, Geoffrey McKenzie, Esquire, Virginia gentleman, by letting you or Pa find some scrawny old black scarecrow of a Negress to dose me with cottonmouth moccasins' heads boiled in swamp root and nightbane, or ram a knitting needle up me as a last recourse. I won't be ruined for life to avoid the scandal of having a baby who'd be perfectly legitimate anyhow, and whom I'd likely love like crazy, being me. So don't you or Pa or maybe even Caleb do *anything*, you hear? Specially not getting yourselves killed in a tomfool duel 'cause some lamebrained idiot has called me a whore. Promise me?"

Geoffrey McKenzie stared at his sister. All their lives they had been much closer than any other two members of the Clan. So now, slowly, solemnly, he leaned forward and kissed her.

"I'm with you, Ramb," he husked. "Damnit, I'm with you all the way!"

Before they even got off the train in Richmond, they heard the shouting: thousands of male voices united in one full-throated, roaring bull-bellow. When, after having secured the services of a couple of the free blacks who served as porters, and retrieved Rose Ann's assorted valises and her trunk, despite her delighted insistence that they let her frowsy old rags go to the devil and sally forth at once to find out what was causing such a divine and delightful rumpus, they came out of the station finally, they saw it:

the night was aflame with torches as a tight-packed mob of over ten thousand men and boys, by the most conservative estimate, marched through the capital's streets yelling their heads off, their deep voices punctuated here and there with shrill soprano—but just as excited—shrieks from the women of all walks of life who stood on the sidewalks and egged them on.

"Hang old Abe Lincoln from a sour apple tree!" a clear tenor sang out. In seconds ten thousand voices were roaring it as one man. "On to Washington!" another prospective Rebel bellowed; then: "Arms! For God's sake, give us arms!"

"To the arsenal! To the arsenal!" Some anonymous but enterprising Virginian raised the cry, and the mob turned, ponderously, took a new course, flooding, going on.

"Well," Jeff said, his voice gone grave and troubled suddenly, "looks like it's started, Ramb . . ."

"Yes, reckon it purely *has,*" Rose Ann said happily. "Just thrilling, isn't it, Jeffie love? Look! There's Caleb! Which *proves* we've got ourselves a war on, plus famine, fire, and flood, or else Gwen never would have let him come into town all by his lonesome, the jealous cat! And do tell! There's the answer to this here particular lovelorn, yearning maiden's prayer—*ex*-maiden's now, damnit!—Colin Claiborne with him! Now that there's a real hunk of long-tall pants-wearing sin I'm going to have to *do* something about one of these fine days . . ."

"Rosie, you're incorrigible!" Jeff groaned, but by then Rose Ann had already lifted up her folded parasol and waved it gaily as she fluted, "Cabe! Colin! Who let you two cypress-bottom swamp rats loose on the town?"

Where she stood with her brother Geoffrey, flanked on both sides by the handcarts of the porters piled high with her luggage—and, of course, Jeff's one lone carpetbag—was across the street and a good twenty yards away from Caleb Henry and Colin Claiborne. But her high, clear voice reached them effortlessly above the infernal din that tight-packed mob of would-be warriors was making.

"Lord God!" Colin Claiborne said. "If it ain't li'l Rambling Rosie in person! Cabe, you mealymouthed, lying old hound dawg. Didn't you tell me that that there toothsome bundle of mighty appetizing homegrown sin of a sister-in-law of yours was way up North in Yankee Land?"

"I did, and she *was,*" Caleb Henry said grimly. "Only, under the circumstances, it appeared to us wiser to bring her back home. So we sent Jeff to fetch her and—"

"C'mon!" Colin laughed. "To heck with the arsenal! That there's the sector I aim to lay siege to! And right now, boy!"

But Caleb clamped a lean, work-hardened hand down on Colin's arm, halting that tall young aristocrat in his tracks.

"Colin," he said stiffly, "I don't have to remind you that my sister-in-law is a decent girl, and under my protection to boot, do I?"

"Remind away, old hoss," Colin chuckled. "Fat lot of good it'll do you. I mean to put a crimp into your ambition to go on being the number one A-rab sultan of the Tidewater. Everybody knows that poor Gwen has put a double twist into your long, red neck by slapping you winding every time she catches you attempting to play footsie with sweet li'l Rambling Rose. Which is right pert frequent from all I hear tell . . ."

"Colin," Caleb all but whispered, "who the ever-loving hell told you a thing like *that?*"

"Nigger grapevine. Fastest means of communication known to man. If old Sam Morse had come down South and found out just how rapid our tell-a-nigger system is, he'd have stuck to painting pictures, sure as hell . . ."

"I'm going to have 'em whipped!" Caleb snarled. "Every living one of the lying, liver-lipped black bastards!"

"No you aren't, old hoss, 'cause your Gwennie won't let you. And like every married woman south of the Mason and Dixon line, and north of it too, I strongly suspect, she wears the pants in the family. C'mon, will you?"

"Colin, I'm warning you!"

"Save your breath. You're going to need it to run from the Yankees. For your information, Caleb boy: my intentions toward your sister-in-law are as dishonorable as old hell. But since, in spite of all the lying talk, she's a sweet girl-child, with the hardest roundhouse slap in the Old Dominion, one of these fine days I'm going to give plumb up and pop the question. In fact, the very hour those miserable old graybeards in the State House get around to calling a referendum on the Ordinance of Secession, and you and I march away to take Washington, I'm going to have to. Leaving your rearguard unprotected just isn't sound tactics, boy. Besides, the more I see of Rose Ann, the more the idea of her presiding over Fairdale appeals to me. So that boot's on the other leg, Cabe. If, after she consents to becoming my lawful wife, I find out you've really been sharecropping out there at McKenzie's Hundred instead of tending to your lawful husbandry, I'll have no other recourse but to call you out . . ."

"And throw Rosie over?" Caleb asked, a little worriedly. The Claibornes were listed only after the Byrds and the Carters among the wealthiest planters in the Tidewater. Playing dog in the manger, and spoiling Rose's chances at becoming mistress of Fairdale, was just too rotten, and Caleb Henry knew it.

"No. Fan her dainty seat of iniquity good and proper, then send her out to put some posies on *your* grave," Colin said. "Now, will you come on?"

They pushed their way through the turgid crowd until they got to the sidewalk where Jeff and Rose Ann waited.

"Howdy, Rambling Rose," Colin said. " 'Pears to me you owe me a couple of kisses. I count five extra jaw-busting slaps for the last one I stole . . ."

"You try it, and you'll be Virginia's first casualty, before the war even gets started!" Rose said wrathfully; then: "Well, Cabe—aren't you even going to say 'Howdy' to the poor lost lamb returned to the bosom of the family?"

"No," Caleb said grimly. "What I'm going to do is to hold you down for Father Dave to beat on. Then Jeff and I will spell him. Maybe after we get through tenderizing the place where you wear your brains, Ramb, you just might learn a grain of common sense!"

He was fairly seething—so much so that Colin Claiborne, who was anything but a fool, not only heard the anger shredding his usually pleasant baritone but easily guessed the reason behind it.

"Cabe," he drawled, "you're acting just like the injured party in an affair of honor involving the Unwritten Law. Under whose provisions you *aren't* included, in case you've gone and forgot just which one of the McKenzie girls you're wedded to. But in light of my semi, demi, kind of honorable intentions toward little Rosie here, don't you think you ought to tell me what this is all about?"

"Rose," Jeff said, a shade too quickly, trying to keep the nervous shake that had got into his voice from becoming too clearly audible, "has just got herself expelled from that flossy girls' school our A'nt Cornelia sent her to. Seems she messed up for fair the darling daughter of the Lord High Chief and Head of the Black Republican Abolitionists of the Commonwealth of Massachusetts over a small difference of opinion as to the virtues of the South's peculiar institution. At least that's what that old codfish in a gray Mother Hubbard told *me* . . ."

Rose Ann gazed at her brother fondly, lost in the purest admiration at this opportune piece of masterly barefaced lying. But Colin, who knew her only too well, grinned at her and drawled, "Bet my bottom dollar there was a lot more to it than that . . ."

"Sure Lord was, Colin sugar," Rose said, her green eyes alight with delighted mischief. "Of course I did have myself a living ball, kicking her frozen fundament, improving on her physiognomy with my fingernails, and yanking all that broom straw out of her head. But what really got those proper Bostonians wild was when I told 'em that since they loved niggers so, I'd gladly send 'em up our prize big black burly breeding stud from our nigger stock-raising farm to service the lot of 'em and—"

"Jesus God!" Caleb all but screamed. "Jeff, I vote we lock her up on bread and water for a month, *after* Father Dave has striped her seat for her with a nigger whip and washed her mouth out with lye soap!"

"Tell you two what," Colin said with mock gravity. "Suppose y'all send her over to Fairdale for a couple of weeks. I'm the greatest hand at breaking wild fillies to the saddle and the bit anybody ever heard tell of . . ."

"That's what *you* think!" Rose Ann hooted. "In half an hour I'd have you crawling around on your hands and knees begging for the privilege of kissing my muddy riding boots—"

"Now you're plain overworking my imagination and my curiosity both, Rambling Rosie," Colin drawled. "So begging the pardons of all those present and accounted for, including *yours*, honey child, I just can't resist asking you a mighty improper question: D'you make a practice of wearing riding boots—in bed?"

"I sure Lord do," Rose shot back at him. "Strapping *spurs* to bare heels is mighty unhandy, Colin dear!"

"Ramb," Jeff said sadly, "you promised me you were going to act like a lady—like the highborn Virginia gentlewoman you *are*, sister mine—from here on in. And now you're disappointing me."

"Oh, Lord, Jeffie love, forgive me!" Rose wailed. "But Colin *knows* I'm just funning. Don't you, Colin honey?"

"No," Colin said, even more solemnly. "I *don't* know it, my darling thorny Rose. I honestly think you meant every blessed word you said . . ."

"And I may have, at that," Rose said bleakly. "Oh, confound this wicked tongue of mine! C'mon, Jeffie, take me home before I say something else I shouldn't. Colin, I beg your pardon mighty humbly if I've offended you . . ."

"You haven't, baby doll. And I don't think you could even if you seriously tried to," Colin said, a note of real tenderness moving through his voice. "Jeff, don't bear down on her too hard. After all the vapid little milksops their fond mamas are always throwing at my head, you just don't know how downright *refreshing* this little wildflower is. And ask your pa to let me call on her the night *after* those old trembling grandpas of the Convention finally decide to put Secession to the public vote . . ."

"I'll do that, Colin," Jeff said quietly. "And you know—you *do* know, don't you?—that with Rosie it's all *talk?*"

"Of course," Colin said. "They say the Convention's set for tomorrow, the seventeenth, so—"

"Oh, Lord!" Rose said. "What's really happening? Please tell us! Jeff and I got stuck in Washington overnight because the trains weren't running. And there was the wildest kind of excitement there. Some people were saying there was a war on between the North and the South, and others swore that nothing was happening yet. But when we asked them for news from Virginia, they said all the telegraph lines had be cut—"

"They had," Caleb said grimly.

"Then?" Rose Ann breathed.

"Fort Sumter fell to the Confederate forces under Beauregard after two days of bombardment," Caleb said. "That was on Sunday, the fourteenth. I'm mentioning the exact dates so you'll get them fixed in your memory, Ramb—because they're the birth dates of our Southern Confederation! Yesterday, Monday, the fifteenth, old Abe called for seventy-five thousand men to be used in—and I'm quoting, Rose Ann—'suppressing the rebellion of the Southern states' . . . And he wants 'em for ninety days only. He's right. If those doddering old fools in the Capitol ever do get around to calling for a referendum on the Ordinance of Secession, we'll have burnt Washington to ashes, with that long, loose-jointed, apish-looking critter chained inside the White House to roast, inside a week!"

"More likely they'll have taken Richmond, and captured all your womenfolks, with me and Gwen heading the list," Rose Ann said sweetly. "Now wouldn't *that* really be a lovely fate worse than death! After poor little yours truly, with some slight assistance from your darling Gwen—who, after all, *is* a McKenzie female, and has her moments, I happen to know—got through *ruining* the Yankee army, the war would be over in a week, which is more than you wild Secesh boys will ever be able to accomplish . . ."

"Jeff," Caleb whispered through clenched and grinding teeth, "take her home right now. Or, by God, I'm going to forget I'm a gentleman and—"

"Don't worry," Jeff said. "That's just what I aim to do. And when I get her there, I'm going to sew her mouth shut with packing thread. After stuffing it with buckshot to hold her loose tongue down. Come along, Ramb. I should have known better than to leave my riding crop at home when I lit out after you!"

As they walked away, crossing the street to where the two black free—or freed—men waited with the handcarts on which Rose Ann's luggage was piled, ready to haul it to the nearby livery stable now that the street was finally clear of enthusiastic warmongers, Rose looked back at Colin Claiborne. He was following her with his gaze and smiling the bemused smile of a man who has totally accepted his own perdition. She had him now. After, through her own egregious folly, having made an honorable marriage between them at least temporarily, if not permanently, impossible. She lifted her gaze toward a somber, starless sky.

"Dear Lord, fix things up for me a little, won't You? You short-changed me something awful when You were handing out brains, so how about a little luck? That's all I'm asking. You grant me that, and I'll take care of all the rest myself. Thank You very kindly, Lord. Amen," Rose Ann McKenzie prayed.

By the time they had got within fifty yards of the Big House of McKenzie's Hundred, they could hear their father's voice.

"Our Southern Confederation," David McKenzie was proclaiming, "will be bound on the east by the Procession of the Equinoxes, on the west by Primeval Chaos and the Setting Sun, on the south by the Infernal Regions, and on the north by the Aurora Borealis!"

Rose grinned at her brother, although by then it was much too dark for Jeff to even see her face.

"Looks like Pa has been able to promote himself a bottle," she said.

"Which will maybe save your little tail for tonight," Jeff said grimly, "but tomorrow he's sure to be in a pea-green foul mood. Ramb, tell me something: Why'd you behave like that in front of Colin? He's the best catch in the Tidewater, and any fool can plainly see he's crazier than a snake-bit hound dog baying at the absent moon over you. Since you aren't really mentally retarded, why the devil were you deliberately trying to throw him off his feed?"

"Jeffie love, *think*," Rose sighed. "You can, if you really try. I can't let Colin propose right now. I'm a *married* woman, remember? I've asked A'nt Corny to notify me just as soon as my wedding to my boy baby doll, Joe-Joe, is annulled. That is, if this here Secession war you damn-fool fire-eaters are cooking up doesn't stop all mail from Yankee Land for the next ten years. After I know I'm free, I'll grab Colin with both hands and both feet, and get around to explaining to him that what he's surer than Old Ned going to find out on our wedding night wasn't caused by my riding Prince Rupert barebacked and seated astride over a steeplechase course for the heck of it, when we have our first real serious fight. No, not our first. That wouldn't be smart. He just might walk out on me, *that* soon. Say, our eleventh or twelfth. By then I'll have him so wrapped around my little finger that he'd shoot himself before giving me up . . ."

"Which would be a *way* of giving you up. Mighty rough, though. Lord! I'd plumb forgot about *that* problem. Here's hoping you don't compound it by going around looking like you've swallowed a half-grown shoat by August. C'mon now. Let's go beard the lion in his den . . ."

"You mean the lioness, don't you? Pa's no trouble really. But when she wants to be, Gwen can be downright *mean*. No help for it, though, now. All right then, come on," Rose Ann said.

When they came into the dining room, Dave McKenzie looked at his younger daughter—and youngest child—from under a hedgerow of bushy eyebrows so streaked with white that they rather resembled flame shot through with woodsmoke.

"Why—why—you look just like me little Rosie," he rumbled in a baffled tone of voice. "But you can't be, can you, child? 'Cause she's way up there in the frozen North, among them canting Abolitionist swine . . ."

"Papa," his daughter Gwen said, her clear voice quivering with disgust, "you've been drinking again! Oh, Lord! Why can't you give up that filthy, vile stuff?"

Rose Ann looked at her elder sister. And, as always, she was struck—more than a little enviously—by Gwen's perfect beauty. Unlike all the rest of the family, including Rose herself, who were redheads—"Made up of hellfire and brimstone, with just a whiff of the fumes of sulfur!" Dave McKenzie always said of his ancestors and his offspring as well—Gwen was the palest blond possible, escaping albinism by maybe a shade or two. And she was flawlessly, classically beautiful, so much so that Rose suspected that there was something obscurely repellent about the chiseled perfection of her face and form. Men, Rose knew with an absolute certainty that had not a drop of vanity in it, were tremendously impressed by Gwen, up to the exact moment that she, Rose, hove into view. Then poor Gwen was lost, for all her Nordic snow maiden's lissome lines and serenely lovely countenance. At that very moment, the images her mind had formed gave Rose a clue to what the problem was. She looks so—cold, she thought. And yet, she's not. At least Cabe says she isn't, and he sure Lord ought to know!

Thinking of Caleb made her smile, for it brought back to mind his candid explanation of what had happened. "You'd gone up North. Spent a whole year with your Yankee cousins in Boston. And you left here a wildwoods half-grown filly, all arms and legs— hell, all elbows and knobby knees and buckteeth and uncombed fox-fire hair and owl-sized sea-green eyes. Built like a fence post. Table-flat both fore and aft. So I got too hard up, and married Gwen, who sure as hell wasn't disposed toward charitable donations to a poor horny sinner. Then you came back, and I saw a miracle had happened. Pure living glory heaped up in extra helpings at just the right places, tucked in neat at others, and spread out wide just where it would catch the lewd, lecherous, and concupiscent eye of a sad old housebroke husband, kept on starvation rations of country comforts by his ever-loving, as the custom is down here . . ."

She'd been slapping her brother-in-law off ever since. And now, unless she was blessed with a miraculous amount of luck, she'd closed, by letting her heart—Now that's a nice, polite way of putting it! she thought sardonically—get ahead of her head, an absolutely splendid means of escape from the situation she found herself in, which marrying the richest and handsomest young planter in the Tidewater indisputably was.

But Pa was saying querulously: "Vile stuff! Good Bourbon and branch water is nectar from heaven, the cure for all the ills the flesh falls heir to, the liquid bulwark against the pains and sorrows and disappointments—such as being cursed with this viper's brood of offspring that the devil sent me—'How sharper than a serpent's tooth it is/To have a thankless child!' said the Bard, and rightly! Where was I? Oh, yes. This gift from the Olympian gods that you, pale whey-faced wench, call vile stuff! Why, Gwennie daughter, this here drinking whiskey of mine will conglomerate the vesicles of the aorta, phlogistify the phylacter maximus, hemstitch up the depatic ducts, insulate the asperifollus gland, deflagate the duodenum, and wilt all the buttons on me waistcoat!"

Pa really was in fine form, Rose saw. So she grinned at him and sang out: "Quit argufying, Pa—and come here and give your erring daughter a kiss! Aren't you even slightly glad to see poor little old me?"

"Rosie!" Dave McKenzie bellowed, and lurching forward, he swept her into his arms.

Which takes care of keeping welts off my southernmost promontory—for tonight, anyhow! Rambling Rose McKenzie thought.

Chapter Two

"Rose," Gwendolyn McKenzie said to her younger sister, "Colin Claiborne is downstairs in the parlor. In uniform. And since the Claibornes can afford it, that uniform is just about the finest one I've ever seen. A gold bar on his collar. Which means, he tells me, that he's a commissioned second lieutenant in the Army of the Confederate States of America. I suppose you know why he's here . . ."

"Know it, as a certain sure thing? No, Gwennie darling," Rose said sadly, "but I reckon he's come to ask me for my hand. And all the adjacent territory it's attached to, I can safely assume, knowing him, without being presumptuous hardly none—I mean *any*—at all . . . Oh, Lord, Gwen, what should I do?"

"That," Gwen said acridly, "is a decision only *you* can make, Rose Ann. But first, let's deal with the practical questions involved. The moral ones are simply none of my business, so I'll spare you a sermon. Besides, you might misinterpret my motives for raising them. In fact, my womanly pride forbids me to . . ."

Rose stared at her sister a long, slow thoughtful time.

"You mean," she whispered, "that because you—you were almost in love with him yourself, some time back, I could get the idea without even trying hard that you just plain don't want any other female's getting her claws into his long-tall handsome hide. Specially not *me* . . ."

"Exactly. And it's not 'almost.' I *was* in love with him," Gwen said evenly. "Maybe I still am. No—*surely* I still am. I only accepted Caleb because it was perfectly apparent that Colin's indifference toward me was complete. I'm not ill favored—"

"Lord, Gwen, you're beautiful!" Rose Ann gasped.

"But I obviously and noticeably lack the McKenzie fire. You, my panting lecher of a husband swears, could burn up a swamp-bottom cypress grove in the middle of a rainstorm by merely walking along a muddy path fifty yards from the nearest tree. So, even though I'm your elder by three years, I've had to play second fiddle to you practically all our lives. Oh no, I don't resent it; I prefer the even tenor of my way to your madcap existence, Rose Ann. But watching your antics, and those of some quieter, but more effective sinners among the women of our set, has convinced me of one thing—"

"Which is?" Rose whispered.

"That morality is mankind's projection of a rather wistful human desire for ethical order against or upon the hard facts of life," Gwen said bitterly. "I'm not sure it even exists; I am sure it serves for very little. An utter swine, by the exercise of sufficiently intelligent hypocrisy, can be canonized as a saint in this world we live in, dear. So let's examine your circumstances by the light of reason rather than by pious sentiment. Here in Virginia, only Jeff, Caleb, and I know your actual legal state. Communications between us and the North, never very rapid, or effective, have broken down completely now that we and they are theoretically at war. The only way, at the moment, that a letter could reach us from Boston would be for Aunt Cornelia to mail it to some friend in Canada, or England, and ask that friend to forward it to us. In either case, a matter of from three months to half a year. So there's practically no way at all that Colin could find out about your elopement with young Lucarelli. Nor you, that said marriage has been annulled. As it probably has, legally defective as it was, since you were indisputably guilty of the crimes of enticement, abduction, and probably even that of contributing to the delinquency of a minor, unless you're prepared to state that you didn't—dear God, how can it be said? At least without resorting to terms utterly abhorrent to any gently bred Southern woman, I mean. All right! That you, a reasonably adult young—well—female person of eighteen didn't indulge in gross physical intimacies with a male child a full two years your junior!"

"Now that's really putting it as sweet and soft as pudding and pie," Rose Ann sighed. "Apart from the fact that neither the law nor the Church finds anything gross about two people's making love *after* they've honestly given each other their pledged word before a minister of the Gospel, or a justice of the peace, I'll satisfy your nasty-minded curiosity on that particular point: Why, sure, Gwennie darling, I turned my boy baby doll every which a way but loose!"

Gwen's smile was infinitely pensive, inward-turning, mocking, lighted from within by the subtlest, purest, most feline of triumphs.

"Even so, I can't gainsay you," she purred, "for the objection's still merely moral, rather than pragmatic. An immediate, whirlwind honeymoon—would still all questions, wouldn't it? Or prevent them from ever being raised—especially since poor Colin is rather dark himself, and has a most exquisitely *quattrocento* cast of countenance, wouldn't you say?"

Rose Ann hung there, staring at her sister, until she couldn't see her anymore. Her sea-cave emerald eyes had gone too blind for that.

"Oh, damn you, Gwen!" she whispered. "Damn your evil soul from Bitter Creek to Vinegar Bend, plumb from hell to breakfast!"

Then, very quietly, she got up and went downstairs to the parlor.

Colin Claiborne, newly second lieutenant of the CSA, listened very quietly until she had finished, then he said, his voice flat, controlled, seemingly emotionless, "I see."

Rose Ann rushed recklessly on: "And that's not all, Colin honey. I—I might even be going to have a baby. I—I don't know for sure, one way or the other, and I won't 'til sometime next month, 'cause that's how us females work. So I just couldn't do that to you. I've been dreaming of becoming *your* wife and mistress of Fairdale ever since I grew up enough to realize what both conditions meant. I only gave up and got involved with Joe-Joe when it came to me that I didn't have any chance at all . . ."

"It came to you wrong," Colin said drily.

"I know. I was a fool. But then I've always been one. In my defense I can only offer the fact that I wasn't—I'm not—rotten enough to marry you under false pretenses, to keep my big, wide, perpetual-motion machine of a mouth shut, and let you think you'd be getting a sweet, innocent little old Virginia country girl instead of—"

"A damnyankee's leavings. A greasy macaroni's," Colin said.

Rose's hand flew upward, pressing itself, palm outward, against her half-opened mouth, as though he'd slapped her across it, hard. As he had, in a way. Then, very slowly, she let both her hands fall to her sides and stood up. So did he. As they faced each other, she heard the ticking of the grandfather's clock in the hall. That usually pleasant sound had transformed itself into a series of sledgehammer blows, crashing into her consciousness, almost unbearably loud.

"Goodbye, Colin. Goodbye—forever," Rose Ann McKenzie said.

But just before he turned and marched away from there, as stiffly as the soldier he thought he was, she saw his eyes. The recognition of what was in them made her slender body go rigid, halting her abruptly chilled blood, her breath, her life.

Why, she wailed somewhere within the awful, echoing desolation her mind had become, I—I've sent him to his death!

For the next three days, she did not leave her room, and spent practically the whole of them crying, until those matchless sea-green eyes that, throughout her life, awed many a man into trembling silence were swollen almost shut. Then, being the gallant, absurd, and tough-fibered red-haired McKenzie woman that she was, she quit that bloody nonsense completely. She started going out, joining the swarms of women who flocked to parties, teas, banquets being given at the hotels and boardinghouses to entertain the thousands of troops concentrated in and about Richmond. The capital had never been so gay. Life was aswirl with gold braid, nodding plumes, the strains of martial music, immaculate uniforms, prancing steeds, and oh so handsome officers! She stood on the sidewalks, in the company of a laughing, cheering host of girls of her age, many of them friends of hers, and waved her lacy handkerchief at the passing soldiers. She attended the presentations of new regimental colors to half a hundred companies of volunteers. She was elected sponsor and patroness of several such companies by their members, and officiated as such, handing out the new—as yet unstained by gun smoke and blood!—battle flags to their equally elected commanding officers, whereupon she was fervently kissed by all those fine young officers. She watched the graceful maneuvers of the Zouaves, the Rangers, the Rifles, her heart beating in tune with the drums, her blood stirred by the fifes' wild piping. The war was a party, a picnic, fun! The Yankees would never come, and if they did, why, she was prepared to chase them away herself, as she proved by attending pistol practice, along with a crowd of other fierce female Rebels, three times a week, under the instructions of one of those oh so handsome officers.

Strangely enough, the one major objection to her giddy gadding-about she had been nerving herself to beat down, was notably, even shockingly conspicuous by its absence. Now, old lion David McKenzie loved his gay, mischievous, sprightly younger female cub with a fiercely possessive paternal love. Usually he made thunderous fulminations, fueled and made sulfuric by pure, brute male jealousy, and hurled them at Rose's bright red head on the score that her fast, forward, advanced behavior was sure to bring down disgrace upon the family name. Yet now, turned astonishingly lamblike and benevolent, he actually encouraged his Rambling Rose to sally forth from his hearth whenever she took a notion to.

"Those boys—those fine and gallant examples of splendid young Southern manhood!—are going to march forth in defense of our native soil," he rumbled. "And an awful lot of 'em are going to die. For, unlike you, son-in-law Caleb, I don't hold to the mighty optimistic view that the Yankees are going to run like rats at the sound of gunfire. There were Yankees on both sides of my company at Monterrey, and Buena Vista, and Cerro Gordo. And you can take it from me they didn't run worth a good goddamn. I remember one young lieutenant—Grant his name was, Ulysses Simpson Grant, though he told me his name was really Hiram—riding like a Comanche, hanging on to his horse on the off side by the mane, through a hail of bullets on his way to ask headquarters to send us the ammunition we were danged nigh out of. And he was a Yankee. Mighty heap of fine young Northern boys like him who fought like a roaring pride of lions in Mexico. So since our boys are plumb going to face a foe worthy of their steel, it's the simple patriotic duty of our Southern belles to encourage and cheer 'em up all they can . . ."

"Well," Caleb drawled, "as long as Rosie provides that encouragement and cheer in a vertical position, with her skirt tail down and her lacy pantalets *up*, reckon there's not too much harm in it, after all . . ."

Gwendolyn McKenzie Henry lanced her husband through with the dead-still, ice-tipped twin blue spears of her gaze.

"There'll come a day," she said quietly, "when divorce will no longer be frowned upon in Virginia, Caleb. And under the appropriate circumstances, justifiable homicide never has been. So I'd suggest that you save your lecherous carcass for the Yankees, and refrain from giving me further excuse to invoke the Unwritten Law . . ."

In the dead-stopped hiatus that followed that gentle, loving matrimonial exchange, Rose, knowing all too well when not to throw coal oil on a smoldering fire, kissed her father quickly, and got out of there.

In June, the war finally began to snarl and splutter, and even flash a little, for by then men had actually died, gut-shot and bayoneted at places like Philippi, in what was already, since May, the new Union state of West Virginia, and at Big Bethel and Vienna, both well within the Old Dominion, and a sight too close to Richmond for comfort. Near the end of June, Rose attended one more ball. And Colin Claiborne was there. She was dancing with an engaging lout—up from Mississippi to "whup all them clinking, ding-dang black Republican Yankees plus a barrel o' wildcats 'n' a sore-haid b'ar o' two all by mah lonesome!"—when she saw how

Colin was watching her, his eyes turning into precision calipers as he measured her hand's span of a waist. At once, she stopped dancing.

"Excuse me, Johnny," she said to her dancing partner, "I'll be right back in two shakes of a jackrabbit's tail. Just you wait, 'cause I wouldn't want one of these fast Virginia belles to steal you from me, you hear?"

"Honey," the hayfoot-strawfoot buck private drawled, "ah ain't fixin' to budge from this heah spot 'til ah've got all that livin' glory in mah arms again, even if ah gits co't-martialed fur disobedience o' orders 'n' shot daid first thing in the mawnin'!"

Full steam ahead, Rose Ann plunged through the crowd of dancing couples until she got to the place where Colin stood, in a little group of Confederate Army and Navy officers that included both her brother and her brother-in-law.

"Take a good look," she said flatly; then, after a long, slow breath-stopped pause: "Satisfied?"

"Ramb, for the love of God!" Caleb Henry said, his voice high, tight, strangling. But Jeff, crisp in his spanking-new naval lieutenant's uniform, laid a cautioning hand on his shoulder.

"Leave 'em be, Cabe," he said in a grim undertone. "Let them work things out. It's none of your business, boy . . ."

"I asked you a question, Colin," Rose Ann said. "But I'll repeat it in case you didn't wash your ears this morning. Are you—satisfied? At the results of your observation of *my* salients, I mean?"

"Entirely," Colin said mockingly. "But this is hardly the place for us to air our differences, my dear—or the time. Except for Jeff and Caleb here, none of these other officers—and, presumably, gentlemen—has the faintest idea what you're talking about. Which is one of the many cases of ignorance's being bliss, wouldn't you think? What d'you say to our taking a stroll in the garden while we discuss matters? I'd much rather be at peace with you before marching off to war, Rose Ann . . ."

"You *are* at peace with me," Rose said bleakly, "so we don't need to stroll in the garden, for we haven't anything to discuss, Colin. Nothing that would interest me, anyhow. So, if you'll excuse me, I have a partner waiting and—"

She half turned, but Colin stepped forward and caught her arm.

"Nothing that would interest you?" he said, too low for the others to hear him. "Not even a renewal of—my offer, or rather my petition, Rambling Rose?"

"Not even that," she said flatly. "Or, maybe, especially not that. So—"

"Please!" Colin whispered, his voice rent and shaken with terrible urgency. "Hear me out, Rose Ann!"

Rose hung there. What she was doing was much more reacting than thinking. Colin was—so tall, and so handsome, and his eyes were so dark and troubled and—and abject. The feeling that stole over her was warm and soft and melting.

"All right, then," she sighed, "but only five minutes, you hear?"

"I—I just don't know, Colin honey," she said after she had heard him out, which, of course, took considerably longer than the scant five minutes she had conceded him. "I—I've been in love with you nearly all my life. But now, I'm scared. I've behaved badly and foolishly: I went and got myself married to a pretty boy too young for me, who wasn't all that much of a man, if that's any comfort to you . . ."

"It is," Colin said. "Go on, Rose Ann . . ."

"And now you say you're willing to forget the whole thing. You promise you'll never bring it up anymore, even when we have a knock-down-drag-out fight, as we're sure as Old Ned going to, like every loving couple born, because that's just plain human nature. But don't you see, Colin honey, darling sugar, love of my life, that none of that is even the point?"

"Then what *is* the point?" Colin said.

"That there's a war on. That among the governments we're getting set to fight is that of the state of Massachusetts. So how much good d'you think it would do me to petition the legislature of that state to grant me a bill of divorcement from Giuseppe?"

"Giuseppe? Oh, Christ!" Colin said.

"It's a nice name. Because you don't know the language doesn't change that. And he was a very nice boy—"

"But a trifle—effeminate, shall we say?" Colin mocked.

"No. Just—too young. And too—too inexperienced. Oh, Lord! Let's not go into *that*. It's no fit subject for a gentleman to discuss with a lady. Oh, damn! For a man to discuss with a woman he's not married to. What I'm trying to say is that I *can't* take the necessary steps to legally free myself to marry you, and if he or his papa does take 'em—as my somewhat less than loving father-in-law was threatening to—it won't do us a whit of good, since there's no way I can be notified now that those damn-fool South Carolinians just had to go and start themselves a war."

24

"We can wait, honey," Colin said. "This here small-sized squabble will be over within six weeks at most. Less. I'm betting it will be finished inside the first hour after that rabble of counterjumping dry-goods clerks finally get up nerve enough to face our steel . . ."

"Colin, that's not so. But I'm not going to waste my breath trying to convince you or any other pigheaded Southerner of that fact. I've made myself mighty unpopular too many times now by telling the truth about what's sure to happen. So forget that. The rock-bottom fact is that we *can't* do anything about each other 'til it's over. So, it appears to me that neither of us ought to make the other any promises. Besides, it strikes me as only fair to leave you free so that you can marry yourself a nice, sweet, little old 'Oh, I pray thee, kind sir, touch me not!' kind of a girl with nary a whiff of scandal attached to her name, and forget you ever *heard* of me. All right, all right! Don't look at me like *that*. Let's put the whole thing off 'til this big fuss is over. Then, if you come back alive, and not too crippled up to father the babies I'm purely longing to have, I'll go through with it. Marrying you, I mean. Now quit arguing and take me back inside before Jeff and Caleb feel called upon to defend the family honor. I've had my say, and taken my stand, from which I don't mean to budge. So take me inside, Colin, will you, please?"

"Without even having sealed our bargain—bad as it is!—with a kiss?" Colin said mournfully.

Rose Ann glared at him. Then her green eyes softened. He was, after all, marching off to war. She stiffened suddenly, clutching her slender middle, as an icy stab of very nearly physical pain and fear tore through her. But there was no denying the grim actuality of her thought: He might even find a hero's lonely grave. Who was she to deny him the comfort of a tender parting kiss? Quietly she stepped forward into his waiting arms.

But as kisses between two young people powerfully attracted to each other usually do, that kiss quickly got out of hand. Several long, long moments later, Rose Ann was clinging to Colin, and strangling and sobbing, and moaning such age-old stupidities as: "Oh, Colin honey, I *do* love you so!"

Never a man to let slip such evident and golden opportunities as this, Colin caught her arm in a flesh-purpling grip and snarled, "Come on!"

"Come on—where, Colin honey?" Rose Ann murmured.

"Over there. Where it's darker. Away from the door. There's too much light here!" were the phrases of poetic beauty and limpid

25

tenderness that fell from her lover's lips. Of course, he ripped them out with the speed and something of the staccato sound that the machine gun one Dr. Richard J. Gatling was almost at that very moment patiently putting together in Indianapolis, Indiana, would soon make on the battlefields of half the world. But poor Rose was far too bemused, lost, and swooning with desire to notice that. Obediently she followed Colin away from the doorway of the hotel where the ball was being held, deeper into the shadow of the massive trees in the garden surrounding it.

And—

Several small, inconsequential things went wrong. But as small, inconsequential things quite often do, they managed to completely spoil not only that lovely moment but practically all the rest of poor Colin's life. One of those was the almost impossibly difficult logistics of an unplanned seduction in June 1861. And the other was time. Item: while Rose Ann McKenzie had a hand's span of a waist that was the envy of all her peers among the belles of Richmond, she, being a woman, simply refused to believe it was actually small enough. So, that evening, while dressing for this ball, she had called in old A'nt Cindy to lace her into that diabolical instrument of torture the whalebone-stiffened corset. This operation required that the willing victim cling to one of the bedposts with all her might while the even more willing torturer—for it's a safe assumption, surely, that black slave women obtained a degree of vengeful, sadistic pleasure from the act of inflicting so noticeable an amount of pain upon their arrogant young mistresses—did her absolute damnedest to crush in said victim's rib cage. At which, it has been claimed, some of the stouter ladies' maids occasionally succeeded. Aunt Cindy, for instance, felt no compunction whatsoever about putting her bare, black, rusty, work-hardened foot against Rose Ann's delectable little pantalet-clad derriere in order to give additional support to her efforts as she yanked on those cruel thongs, drawing that corset, much too small to begin with, another impossible sixty-fourth of an inch tighter.

Item two: besides the corset, which her brother Jeff swore gave him the idea for the ironclads he afterward designed for the Confederate fleet, Rose Ann had on *six* flounced petticoats, the outer one of which was tucked and embroidered. And under the petticoats she wore *une cage américaine*, an advanced type of crinoline, that curious garment that assured women's being able to rather resemble inverted brandy snifters as they floated, on the arms of their gallants, to the strains of the waltz, across the ballroom floor.

At first the crinoline—a vast improvement, thermally anyhow, over the minimum of thirty petticoats that fashionable ladies had been forced to endure in order to achieve the desired aspect of a slender stalk protruding gracefully from half a pumpkin—had been given its gobletlike form by a series of whalebone hoops, but by 1861 those hoops were made of spring *steel*.

Apart from the quite serious danger of dying from septic uremia because visiting the chaste little temples dedicated to the goddess Cloaca out behind the hotels while clad in the ballroom costume of that epoch was just too damn much trouble, the chief result of all this fashionable armor was to provide a highborn maiden of the 1850s and 1860s with a modernized and considerably ameliorated version of the medieval chastity belt, the amelioration consisting in the fact that the 1850s and 1860s model was workable and real, while the medieval one was almost surely mythical.

Which was where the element of time came in. For as Colin discovered, to his aching, tumescent, and almost weeping disgust, it took him so long to even *find* the drawstring of those ankle-length ruffled, lacy, and sachet-scented pantalets, which was way the hell up *under* the corset, and hence practically impossible to get at anyhow, while those steel hoops kept dealing him unexpected and cruel blows in various parts of his anatomy, that Rose Ann had all the leisure in this world and to spare to have the second, third, fourth, fifth, and whatever continuous series of thoughts she needed to ensure her safe retreat from the disastrous brink of folly.

"No, Colin," she said firmly.

"Why not?" poor Colin, beside himself from the acutest, most agonizing physical anguish that a young, abruptly frustrated male can suffer, grated.

"Because this is *wrong*," Rose Ann whispered. "What's more—it's ugly. I—I just don't want to be—taken—like a female animal on the ground. That's too—too low. Besides—"

"Besides what?" Colin moaned.

"In another five minutes, Jeff, or Caleb, or both of them will come out here looking for me. You might be able to talk some sense into Jeff, but Caleb hasn't any. Not where I'm concerned, any-how . . ."

"Rose Ann," Colin got out, his voice doubly thick now, doubly strangled, "don't tell me that that horny swine has—has—"

"No," Rose sighed, "but only because I wouldn't—won't—let him. Not because he hasn't tried often enough . . ."

"I'll kill him!" Colin all but screamed.

"No, you won't. Not unless you're prepared to—to lose me forever," Rose Ann said quietly.

"Jesus God!" Colin whispered. "You're saying that—that you—"

"No, I'm not saying what you're implying now. The only man under heaven I *love* is you, Colin honey. But I like Caleb, so I don't want him dead. And Jeff's my brother, so I don't want him shot down in a stupid duel either. And as I said before, I love you. Which means that standing by and allowing any of the three of you to kill any other would—break my heart, Colin. And drive me stark, raving crazy, likely. Besides, instead of murdering—because that's all dueling amounts to!—each other over poor little old me, it would make more sense for y'all to shoot yourselves some Yankees, don't you think?"

"What I think," Colin said morosely, "is that you don't really love me. Or else you wouldn't—*couldn't*—stand there enwrapped in icy calm and let me march away to die without ever having known a moment's bliss!"

"Colin, you—you're wrong, you know!" Rose Ann whispered dolefully. "Like most men, you just don't know *anything* about women. Right now, I—I want you so bad I *hurt* . . ."

"Fine way you've got of showing it!" Colin snarled.

"Colin," Rose said then, her voice tombstone-granite bleak, "do you want me as your wife—or as your whore?"

"I," Colin said quietly, honestly, even humbly, "just want you, Rose Ann. Any way I can have you. Any way at all. Wait! Before you fly off the handle, my dear, hear this: I'd marry you tonight if I could. Must I remind you why—whose fault it is—I can't?"

Rose Ann stood there, staring at him. Her eyes were twin green seas awash with anguish, pain.

"All right," she said flatly, quietly, sadly. "I'll meet you anywhere you want me to, during daylight hours, tomorrow. And I'll —be yours. Let you have your way with me, as the common saying goes. But—"

"But—what, Rose Ann?" Colin got out thickly.

"If you march away and get yourself killed, leaving me with a child you can't give your name to, 'cause you're dead, I'll curse your name, and your memory, forever. And teach *him* to," Rose Ann McKenzie said.

Colin bowed his head, looked up again.

"I—I can guarantee that won't happen, Rambling Rose," he murmured.

"How? By playing the coward?" she flared. "Then I'd despise

you. What's more, I'd close my door to you forever, and accept public shame for the rest of my life. Or at least for as long as it would take me to teach your son to be—a man!"

Colin studied her, slowly, speculatively, thoroughly.

"You've misunderstood me," he rasped. "I mean to do my duty in defense of my country, up to and including giving my life to uphold our high civilization and sacred ideals, if need be. So I can't guarantee I won't be killed. No soldier can. What I referred to was the fact that I *can* make sure that you don't—well—conceive, until such time as it will be perfectly lawful for you to, and I am once more at your side to protect and support you, and our children . . ."

"How?" Rose Ann said with that terrible directness of hers.

"I can't explain it. No, that's not true. I could explain it, but I don't want to, for the very simple reason that I'd be forced—for want of any others!—to use terms scarcely fitted for a gentlewoman's ears. For the ears—of my *wife*, and the mother-to-be of my sons . . ."

"Ohhh, Colin!" Rose Ann wailed, melting again, lost again, and put out her arms to him.

Before he turned her loose this time, he murmured into her dainty, shell-pink ear, "You'll meet me in town tomorrow, then?"

Rose drew back, peered up at the shadowed outline of his face, etched clean against the distant gaslights' glow. Her voice was a ripple on dead-still waters as she said, "Yes. When, Colin? Where?"

"Miss Emma's Ye Olde Tea Shoppe. On East Clay Street. You know it, don't you? That ought be conventional enough to suit anybody . . ."

"It sure Lord is, but—"

"We have tea together, pointedly and publicly. Then we stroll out of there—and disappear . . ."

"Where will we go, Colin honey?"

"Tell you tomorrow. No time now. A bunch of people just came out of the hotel. Among them your brother and his current light o' love, Mary Sue Hunter of Hunter's Point. Tell me, Ramb darling —is that serious?"

"I should hope *not!* I can't stand that little snip!" Rose said.

"I strongly suspect that you won't be able to stand any blushing maiden who takes a shine to Jeff," Colin drawled. "Possessive tribe, you McKenzies. Anyhow, I suggest we stroll in their direction, especially since your much too beloved brother-in-law has just poured himself, mournful hound-dog countenance and all, through that door. We've agreed that discretion is the better part of valor, haven't we? Well, come along, my dear . . ."

"Lord Jesus!" Rose Ann whispered. "I sure don't like the way he's looking at us right now. Like he could eat us both alive. Just gulp us down, dog fashion, without chewing on us hardly none—any—at all!"

"He won't do anything," Colin said grimly. "Not now, anyhow. He hasn't got a pot to pee into— Oh, excuse me, honey, that slipped!"

" 'S all right." Rose Ann grinned. "I say that myself, all the time —and worse . . ."

"I can bet," Colin said. "But more politely, if Caleb didn't run the Hundred—at which he's pretty good, I'll freely admit—for your whiskey-soaked old man—"

"Why, Colin Claiborne!"

"He is, and you know it. Besides, I kind of like the old soak. As I was saying, if Caleb didn't run the Hundred for you-all, because Jeff is sure Lord no planter either, since all he wants to do is to invent useless machinery to do what we've got an oversupply of niggers to do already . . ."

"He's good at it!" Rose said.

"I know that too. And maybe this war will furnish him with ample opportunities to put his inventive talents to some use. But to get back to Caleb. Marrying Gwen, and taking over the management of your place, saved his hide financially. But what's got me worried is his temperament. You know he's been elected captain of our company, don't you?"

"No!" Rose Ann breathed. "Nobody told me a mumbling word about that!"

"Well, he has been. Which makes him my superior officer. And feeling the way he does about you, my dear, it comes to me I'd better examine mighty carefully any order he gives me while we're under fire, and even make damn sure he doesn't get in back of me too often . . ."

"Cabe's neither a sneak nor a coward," Rose said stoutly. "He'd never pull off a dirty trick like that!"

"Who knows what any man will do under the stress of battle?" Colin said gravely. "Hell, I don't even know what *I* will do once the chips are down. And Caleb's a Henry—a family not distinguished for furnishing heroes to the cause. Take his great ancestor, Patrick, in honor of whom, I suspect, the boys elected Caleb to the captaincy . . ."

30

"Mighty remote ancestor!" Rose hooted.

"Not all that remote. If the lines were traced correctly, these Henrys would be at least third cousins to the famous orator's direct descendants. Anyhow, take old Pat. You've read his speeches; they're in every schoolbook now—"

"Of course: 'Caesar had his Brutus; Charles the First his Cromwell; and George the Third ("Treason! Treason!" from the back benches) may profit by their example. If this be treason, make the most of it!' "

"Yes, that one. But more to the point, the truly immortal 'Give me liberty or give me death!' oration. Old Pat was thirty-nine years old when he delivered himself of that gem, during a war in which old granddads of sixty were serving. And what did he *do?* Besides talk, I mean. He practically hid. Certainly he never risked his eloquent tongue or his hairy hide when the going got to be really rough. So Caleb may not even have it in him to—"

"Stand up and face a charging foe the way the Claibornes have always done . . ." Rose said softly.

"Yes. Exactly that. Only I'm beginning to wonder whether I'll be able to muster up the ancestral valor when push comes to shove. Having *you* to come back to puts an awful crimp in my ambition to become a hero, y'know. Now, come on; we'd really better join the bunch if we don't want to cause talk," Colin said. And taking her arm, he led her—a little too quickly!—toward where the others were.

Sometime between 1793 and 1818, the great English mystic William Blake wrote these lines:

> What is it men in women do require?
> The lineaments of Gratified Desire.
> What is it women do in men require?
> The lineaments of Gratified Desire.

Which is why, perhaps, the intimate relations between the sexes have been one long, practically never-ending disappointment, and their ordinary ones a state ranging between an armed truce and outright, furious war. Everyone, in his heart of hearts, knows this, just as he knows that one day he is going to die. And yet hope, fond, foolish hope, constrains him to disbelieve the damning and damnable evidence that life hurls into his teeth every moment of the day and night. *He* will not die; he, somehow, will be granted immortality. *His* loves will be sensual, rapturous, beautiful, perfect. Betimes, his own particular convocation of politic worms awaits him, and untenanted heaven, having no ears, cannot attend his prayers. Betimes, his woman weeps, shamed, outraged, and—worst of all!—disappointed. Or turns to adultery, finding—sometimes—that sweet vengeance lends an additional fillip to the treacherous play . . .

So say, then, that after leaving Ye Olde Tea Shoppe, Rose Ann McKenzie and Colin Claiborne took a cab, driven by a Negro who almost surely knew neither of them and wouldn't talk if he did, to a certain dwelling on the outskirts of the city. In this place, a house of assignation run by an ancient and remarkably evil-looking black woman called A'nt Sukie, they became lovers. In the physical sense, anyhow. Or, at least, Colin Claiborne did.

Warm and relaxed and satisfied, he contemplated the lovely, naked nymph at his side with ever-deepening tenderness, sure that the purveyor of such exquisite pleasures would transform his life into heaven, paradise, perfect bliss. In his overwhelming contentment he swore—as men always do—eternal fidelity to her. He would—as men always do—break that meaningless oath before a year was out.

While she wailed in the utter darkness inside her mind: I wasn't even here. Not me, Rose Ann McKenzie, a real, live, honest-to-goodness girl. No, a woman. A person. What was it that Cleopatra said? "I have immortal longings in me!" But I wasn't here. Only my body was—only a sack of guts and fainting blood—and so much wanting, wanting, wanting—left high and dry to toss and twist all night—or indulge in solitary sin that won't even be kind enough to drive me crazy like people say. I wanted you to be—good to me, Colin. I wanted to you to be sweet, and slow, and tender. Instead you tore into me like a wild man, snorting and bucking and whistling like a stallion. Then—dead soldier! All inside of two minutes. No, less . . .

And that *thing* you used, that you put onto yourself. If that's how you men keep us women from having babies, I'd rather have 'em, and be disgraced. So—so dead, so lifeless. So—ugggh! My Joe-Joe wasn't like that. He was hot and hard and alive. Course he didn't even last as long as you did, but now I wonder whether any of you ever do, or can . . . He didn't have your experience, but he was better off without it, because that fine experience of yours was gained with stinking black wenches in the quarters, or filthy redneck whores . . .

You don't even know what a woman's like, do you? That given

half a chance we can set the night on fire, light the day with flame! But even so, there's more to it than that—more than just bodies, twisting and turning and grinding together on a sweaty bed in this dirty old place that smells—that stinks—of a million unlawful loves. More than that awful, ugly word you men—you male animals!—call it. Somewhere the mind's got to enter into it, Colin. Somehow you've got to sneak the soul in—or the child we'll make will be—soulless, Caliban, a monster!

Well, you've lost me now. I've fallen out of love with you. Maybe that—rejection—includes every horny, thoughtless male critter there is. But I won't tell you that. Not now. It would be too—unkind. Reckon—I expected *love* of you, instead of being used like a doll of flesh to satisfy your horniness. You know what you really *did*, Colin? You used *me*—my body anyhow—to play with yourself. And if there's anything worse than that, I sure Lord don't know what it is . . .

"Darling," Colin murmured slumberously, "you don't look very happy . . ."

"I'm not," she said drily.

"Oh, Lord, Rose Ann! Did I do or say something that offended you? If so, I'm sorry! But you know—you must know—I didn't mean to, and—"

Nor did you mean to—satisfy me, did you? she thought bitterly. To leave me warm, and soft, and—and happy. What you meant, you did. Had yourself an ever-loving ball, while leaving me completely out . . .

She lay there, looking at him, studying him really, with attention, with care, trying to see if there was anything behind that handsome face, that fine-sculptured masculine form. She decided, sadly, that there wasn't. Nothing at all.

"No, Colin, you haven't offended me. Don't worry about it—it has nothing to do with you—"

"Then?" he whispered tenderly.

"Just one of my moods, I guess. Come on, let's get dressed, and out of *here*," she said.

Chapter Three

Rose Ann McKenzie looked down at the pair of soldier's socks she was knitting. They were among the articles of clothing—winter long drawers and scarves being the other two items most asked for —that the Confederate government had formally requested the women of the South to patriotically contribute to the armies as it became clearer every day that while the Southern states, as a predominantly agricultural region, could feed her soldiers well enough, the almost total lack of any kind of industries, heavy or light, made arming, clothing, and shoeing them problems of night-marish proportions. The government, naturally and wisely, had established priorities: the creation of arms and munition manufac-tories came first. On that July day in 1861, all too many Southern boys were being sent to the front lines—somewhere north of Fred-ericksburg now—with nothing in their hands, in the hope that they would be able to capture rifles from the enemy. It had been seriously proposed in the legislature by a distinguished member of that august body that the troops there were no arms for be equipped with pikes, a weapon easily and quickly fabricated in any blacksmith's shop. Granted the magnitude of that problem, it was no wonder that the government pushed such lesser items as uni-forms, haversacks, boots, and other desperately needed accouter-ments off on any voluntary civilian organization as conceivably might have some remote chance of procuring or producing them. The result of this policy was not yet evident, but it soon would be: "Bolivar Ward," as the Southern soldier called himself, that "Johnny Reb" business being a Yankee invention, was going to go barefooted and bare-assed to the very end of the war.

Rose glanced at her sister, Gwen, who sat in the little parlor with her, busily knitting away, a good bit more quickly and a damned sight more effectively than she. Gwen was good at all the traditional feminine chores. She was an almost perfect housewife who kept the interior of McKenzie's Manor as nearly spotless as its badly decayed state and the maddening slovenliness of the two black slave women she had under her orders allowed her to.

Besides which, she's sweet and gentle and a perfect angel—most of the time, Rose Ann thought wryly. Only letting loose a touch of brimstone and bitters when Cabe, or I, or both of us get her wild. And beautiful on top of all that. While I—

She stared up at the ornate plastered ceiling, plentifully

splotched and mildewed by the water that seeped through a roof become practically a sieve every time it rained, blinking her eyes to clear them of the scald of tears that had blinded them suddenly.

Gwen reached out a hand and touched her arm.

"He'll be all right," she said consolingly. "The Claibornes know how to take care of themselves. He'll come back covered with glory, wearing every medal our government has to give. Then, after you've solved your legal problem, or time and the war itself have solved it for you—"

"You mean that Giuseppe just might enlist and get himself killed?" Rose Ann said. "He might. He's plenty brave enough to. Only he's still too young. Besides, I don't want to be freed that way. I want him to live. And to find somebody else. And be— happy. Very happy. He deserves that much. He's a very, very nice boy, y'know . . ."

"I sometimes wonder if you *want* your marriage to him ended," Gwen said quizzically. "Though, even if you don't, there's not much you can do about it, is there? But satisfy my curiosity about one thing: D'you *really* want your madcap elopement with young Lucarelli annulled?"

"Yes," Rose Ann said sadly. "I do. But only because we're— awf'ly unsuited to one another, not because I'm not fond of him . . ."

"And Colin's proposal—which Jeff tells me he's renewed, after getting over the first shock of your rather lurid confession," Gwen said, trying not quite successfully to keep an edge out of her voice. "That has nothing to do with it?"

"Nothing at all," Rose said flatly. She let the knitting needles and the half—and badly!—formed socks fall into her lap, lifted her left hand with her slender fingers spread wide. "See? I'm not wearing his ring. I mean to give it back to him when he comes home."

"Dear God, Rose Ann, why?" Gwen gasped.

"I don't love him anymore. Don't ask me why. I don't even know, and— No. That's a lie. I *do* know. Only I can't tell you—or anybody—*that* . . ."

"You mean—there's—somebody else? My Caleb, for instance?"

"No. There's nobody else—and your precious husband least of all! I just don't feel like getting married right now. Or maybe ever. Look at these damn socks, will you? They're Lord-awful, just like every womanly thing I try to do. I can't cook, I can't even do common sewing, let alone embroidery, and any kind of housework makes me want to scream. If they'd let me I'd join the Army—the cavalry, anyhow, 'cause I'm too blamed lazy to march. But I can ride as well as most men, and shoot even better than that. Can you see *me* with a passel of snotty-nosed brats all yowling at the same time and peeing their drawers and—"

"Rose Ann," Gwen said gently, "it's—the wrong time of the month, isn't it?"

"Yes," Rose sighed, "but I assure you that's got nothing to do with—my moods, call it. I don't get all cramped up and just plain *mean* like most women, Gwennie darling. The trouble is that, quite recently, I've been forced to take a good, hard look at myself—and I just don't like what I see. Reckon about the only things I'm fitted for is to be some real rich man's kept woman, or a whore. A high-class, expensive one, that is. But a sweet and loving wife like you, honey—Lord, no!"

"Rose Ann," Gwen said sternly, "you stop talking like that, you hear? Stop it, right *now.*"

"All right. Didn't mean to offend you, sister dear. Tell me something: Have you heard from Cabe since since the fighting started?"

"No. Not any more than you've heard from Colin. They're in the same company, y'know, so any letters from them would arrive practically simultaneously—that is, if either of them bothered to write. They probably didn't. Too busy playing soldier like the small boys they are at heart . . ."

"Gwen," Rose Ann said quietly, "what would you do if—if Cabe got—killed? You two really don't get along all that well, y'know. And you haven't any children, so—"

"I don't know. I truly don't, Rose Ann. I'd wear black for a year or two, because, after all, I *am* fond of Caleb. He's not the worst of all possible husbands, really. Let's say he's quite acceptable as married men go, down here. Would I marry again, you mean? Perhaps. After a respectable interval. If the right man were also free, and asked me. Who knows?"

"*Your* right man is going to be free," Rose Ann said grimly. "I'm going to see to that!"

Gwen stared at her sister. Her clear blue eyes, to the discerning gaze of the merry, mocking apprentice witch that Rose Ann was, became twin light-filled fields of battle across which—almost visibly!—hosts of angels, hordes of fiends waged war. The angels won.

"Rose," Gwen said quietly, but the intensity of her feelings played contrapuntal flute notes through her voice, "you can't do this to Colin. You simply cannot. In fact, I don't see how a woman could do such an abysmally filthy thing to any man—which is what accepting his proposal and letting him march off to face *death* in a thousand terrible ways, believing he has her to come home to, *is*. I don't even know the word for that sort of behavior. 'Abominable' comes close, but I need something else, something even stronger . . .''

Rose Ann stared down at the would-be socks in her lap, looked up again, her green eyes misty emeralds, walled out, blind.

"I know I can't," she wailed. "I haven't got it in me to. So now I'm going to ruin his life and mine on the basis of an honor I've already lost. And all because I'm just not brave enough to be—as cruel as I ought to. Oh, Gwen! Don't you see that, over a lifetime, that cruelty would sure as hell turn out to have been—a kindness?"

"No," Gwen whispered. "I don't see that. Especially not if you pledge to yourself, to Colin, and to God never to let him see or even suspect whatever doubts or hesitations you may have. A deception? Of course. But—a noble one. You will keep your pledged word to that dear, dear boy, won't you? Promise me?"

"I—I promise," Rose whispered, "but—oh, Lord, Gwen, how I wish I didn't have to!"

Two days after this loving, romantic sisterly exchange, the first major battle of the Civil War was fought, near a hamlet called Manassas Junction, because the tracks of two railroads met and connected there, and along a creek two miles east of it named— somewhat grandly!—Bull Run River. Which is why this unholy mess, among the worst-led, worst-fought battles in North American history, has two names. The North calls it "the First Battle of Bull Run," and the South, "First Manassas."

The South won it, for one excellent reason and two dozen crazy ones. The excellent reason was that the Confederate commanders had set up a system of signaling each other by a wigwag code of waving flags from one hilltop, tower, or other high place to another. They tried it for the first time at Manassas Junction/Bull Run River, and it worked like a charm. The crazy reasons are also worth study. The first of them was the heat. It was so damned hot that long before they reached the place of battle, the dead-green Yankee troops, irked by the cartridge boxes banging against their hips, quite often took said boxes off and threw 'em in the ditches, so they *arrived* at the fight almost out of ammunition. The New York 69th, "the Fighting Irish," stripped to the waist and fought the whole battle bare-chested—or "topless" as their descendants would probably call it. At that, although the miserable heat generally favored "Bolivar Ward," alias "Johnny Reb," over "Billy Yank," alias "Bluebelly," because the Southern boys were used to it and the Northerners weren't, the 69th were lucky, because their semi-nudity enabled them to tell their own company members from the foe and thus kept them from killing each other. For at Manassas/Bull Run, the damnyankees quite often had on gray while the Rebs were just as often clad in blue. It would have been a laughable comic-opera mess if it hadn't been so bloody. The New York Fire Zouaves sported red fezzes, bolero jackets, and baggy Turkish trousers. The Garibaldi Guards wore hats cocked up on one side with rooster-feather plumes in 'em. The 79th New York made a brave show in fillebegs and Highland plaids. Funny as all hell until Griffin's and Ricketts's batteries got themselves overrun and murdered by a regiment of Zouaves whom they hadn't dared fire on and who turned out to be Confederates.

Then the intangibles. At one point the entire Confederate left, under Evans and Bartow, had been outflanked, pushed in, and all but crushed, and were running like hell, knocking their officers over the head, and even bayoneting them as they tried to stem the rout back toward the old Henry House, at which point Rebel general Bernard Bee stood up in his stirrups, pointed with his saber, and sang out, exactly as in a Hollywood epic: "Look at Jackson, standing like a stone wall! Rally behind the Virginians, boys!" Whereupon a Yank sharpshooter blasted him out of the saddle to lie in the dust, bleeding to death beneath his horse's hooves.

Intangibles. Why was Thomas J. (forever after that idiotic and/ or glorious moment "Stonewall") Jackson stonewalling at that peculiar and unforgettable hiatus in the flow of time? Very likely because, being the solemn religious fanatic that he was, he'd fallen into one of the prayerful trances that often descended upon him before, during, and after a battle. At such times, he became unaware of his surroundings, and "talked real wild and crazy" as a contemporary witness put it. Let's hasten to concede he was also a first-class fighting man, after he'd prayed and meditated himself into the mood for action. Only that usually took him so long that thousands of Bolivar Wards were slaughtered in several later battles before the Lord finally convinced "Stonewall" he ought to get a move on. But those particular Rebs, not knowing that, rallied and chased the damnyankees, with a stampede of carriages full of congressmen and their gaudy ladies in the van, clear across the Potomac.

Intangibles: Union ones. Hiram Ulysses (alias Ulysses Simpson)

Grant was way out West somewheres, and likely drunk. And William Tecumseh Sherman, who *was* there, found himself so busy at the start of that bumbling affair keeping congressmen come down from Washington to witness "the Glorious Victory of Our Arms!" from wandering around, drunker than Grant ever was or would ever get to be, *within* his lines and getting in the way of his soldiers, that he couldn't do anything really effective.

So the Rebels won the Battle of Whatever You Want to Call It. The only trouble with that was the fact that they thought they'd won the war.

Even Dave McKenzie, who actually knew better and had honestly admitted his hardheaded estimation of the true situation, allowed himself to be carried away by the general rejoicing. He stormed into the little parlor where his daughters were sitting as usual—knitting scarves and socks and long johns for the Confederate soldiers by the mile, although it must be admitted that the ones Rambling Rosie made were more nearly Yankee secret weapons than anything else—waving a copy of the Richmond *Whig* under their nicely uptilted and presumably patrician noses.

"Listen to this, me sugarplums!" he crowed, and then read aloud in one long, whiskey-thickened, boar-grunting rumble: " 'We have met the roundhead bullies and given them their well-deserved thrashing! But what else could one expect from a clash between the gamecock and the dunghill?' Now that's putting it right on the line, ain't it, me darlings?"

Rose Ann stared at her father. She was, by then, bored into a state approaching petrifaction with all that knitting, and her rock-bottom conviction that—whatever the morality of the question!—getting married to a man whose abilities as a lover existed in a state of urinal poverty was either the heights or the abysmal lower depths of folly, wasn't helping her not exactly saccharine disposition much, if at all.

"Pa," she drawled, "that there's about the biggest piece of pure jackassery I ever heard tell of . . ."

"Why—Rosie!" Dave McKenzie thundered.

"It is, and you know it, Pa," Rose Ann went on. "Did our boys take Washington?"

"No, but only because President Davis ordered 'em not to!" her father growled.

"Wouldn't have made much difference if they had. Old Abe would have moved the Yankee government to Philadelphia or New York or even Boston and settled down to getting ready to really fight. Pa, you silly old sweetkins you—remember what you told me about bear hunting out in Kentucky when you were a young fellow? Now tell me one thing: What happens when you shoot a bear? If you don't kill him outright with the first shot, I mean."

"You've got yourself a mighty heap o' trouble, Rosie honey," Dave said wonderingly. "You mind telling your old pa just what the tarnation you're getting at?"

"Just that. Right now we've got ourselves a wounded bear. Meanest, stubbornest, fightingest critter there *is*. Wounded in his pride of manhood, to make matters worse. Pa, one more question: Did we wipe out General McDowell's whole army? Or take fifty thousand prisoners or so?"

"No," Dave rumbled, uncertainly now.

"Then we're in for it," Rose Ann sighed. "I'm glad we won the battle, but it's not going to count for much. The first one never does. It's the *last* one that—"

"Rose Ann, you shut up!" Gwen said suddenly, sharply. "Father, tell *me* something: Were—any of our boys—hurt? Or—or killed?"

"Yes," David McKenzie said lugubriously. "There sure Lord *was*. And a helluva lot of 'em too. Appears there was some real hard fighting early on, and there's a mighty ugly rumor going around that some of our troops panicked and fled the field, 'til Gen'l Bee and Brigadier Gen'l Jackson steadied 'em, turned 'em back—right in front of that house where Cabe's grandauntie lives. Poor Bee got his'n right there; but Jackson hung on 'til Joe Johnson and Beauregard come up. Then Jubal Early and Kirby Smith both got there, and them Yankee boys decided that enough of a thing was enough, specially after Major Jeb Stuart—that ain't his name, just his initials, J.E.B.—riding hell-for-leather with his cavalry, chased them Zouaves from in front of the Yankee guns, and our fine 33rd Virginia swept in and wrecked both batteries. Why, I tell you—"

"Father," Gwen whispered, her voice descending almost below the levels of audibility, "was—Colin—hurt? Or—or killed?"

"Or," Rose Ann put in solemnly, "our darling Cabe, whom his own ever-loving wifey has purely forgot all about?"

"Oh, Lord!" Gwen said with real exasperation. "You know better than that, Rose Ann! It's just that I—"

"That you were—establishing precedence, or maybe preference," Rose purred. "C'mon, Pa, tell us: Were Cabe and Colin among the casualties?"

"Don't know. Done sent Jeff to find out all he can, 'cause that real pretty uniform of his'n opens doors that are barred to a tired old ex-soldier like me. Says he'll drop by here t'night 'n' let us know what—if anything—he's found out. Still a lot of confusion up in town, y'know—"

"Jeff?" Rose Ann squealed. "But what's he doing in Richmond, Pa? He's stationed way down at the naval base at Norfolk, isn't he?"

"Yep. Sure Lord is," Dave McKenzie said proudly. "But they sent him and another mighty handsome young fellow named Brooke—Lieutenant John M. Brooke—up here on a secret mission. Didn't even want to tell his poor old Pa what that mission was, but I sort of wormed it out of him, after I give both of 'em my word of honor I wouldn't breathe it to another living soul . . ."

"Which word of honor you're hereby going to break," Rose Ann said gleefully, "and tell *us!*"

"Wal, now—" Dave hesitated.

"Father," Gwen said icily, "if you've given your word, don't break it. We really don't need to know."

"*You* don't, maybe, but *I* do!" Rose Ann hooted. "C'mon, Pa, you old sweetkins, tell your baby girl a thing or two!" Then she flung herself upon her father, and started in to kiss him, tickle his ribs, pull on his earlobes, ruffle his hair, and make an outrageous nuisance of herself just as she'd done since babyhood whenever she wanted to get something out of him.

Which, of course, melted Dave McKenzie's heart, as hard as rendered lard and tallow as far as his Rosie was concerned anyhow, in two minutes flat.

"Wal, now—reckon ain't much harm in my spilling the beans within the sanctity of me own home," Dave chuckled. "Specially since what them two young idjuts are aiming to do just ain't possible nohow . . ."

"But what *are* they planning to do, Pappy mine?" Rose Ann wheedled.

"Build a steam frigate made out of solid iron. Had a writ with 'em from Secretary of the Navy Mallory allowing 'em to order seven hundred *tons* of pig and plate from the Tredegar Works, right here in Richmond. Now it stands to reason that iron damned sure won't float, and any ship made out of it ain't going but in one direction—straight *down*. Told them young fools that, but they swore on a stack of Bibles that they've done found out how to *make* it float, and what's more, they aims to armor the sides and decks and cabin of their frigate—designed it themselves, between 'em, 'n' showed Secretary Mallory a working reduced-scale model, they *claims*—with plate so thick that the Federal Navy's heaviest solid shot will bounce right off it like goober peas. Them young fellows is plumb loony! This here terrible war has gone to their heads and addled 'em for fair!"

"Pa," Rose said solemnly, "if Jeffie says he can do a thing, he *can*. Just doesn't hold with lying or drawing the long bow either one, that boy. And if he can, the blockade's over—just think of that! I can buy some pins and some lace again, both of which are getting to be as scarce as hen's teeth nowadays . . ."

Gwen shook her head despairingly.

"Of all the empty-headed, flighty, frivolous creatures under heaven, you take the cake, Rose Ann!" she said angrily. "The man you're engaged to might be lying desperately wounded or *dead* this very moment, and you concern yourself with pins and lace! I just don't know what to make of you, I swear!"

"Don't try," Rose Ann quipped, in her letter-perfect imitation of a crisp New England accent. "I just might strain your capacity for comprehension beyond its permissible limits, old dear. If Colin has been hurt or killed—which God forbid!—I shall be sorry. But I shan't don widow's weeds or die of a broken heart, I assure you. As I've already told you, I *don't* love him, and I am incapable of that degree of hypocrisy. Therefore, I'll leave the weeping for you, my dear sister, though I just might join you in a tear or two, if need be —which, again, God forbid!—for Cabe . . ."

Dave McKenzie stared at his youngest child in utter bewilderment.

"Rosie baby," he said in a baffled tone, "what were you talking like a furriner for? So la-di-da, and using all them long, highfalutin words? Swear to God, I couldn't understand a blessed thing you said!"

"Not a foreigner, Pa—a damnyankee." Rose Ann laughed. "And I was only plaguing Gwen, who can be so sugar and spice and everything nice that sometimes I could bash her head in with a singletree. Gwennie honey, forgive me. I'm *not* in love, but I have been, so I know how it feels. So I'll say all the prayers you want me to that Colin comes back home alive. What I *won't* do is to pray that Caleb *doesn't*. For that would be— What was that word you used? Oh, yes, abominable. It really would be, dear. No, unspeakable. Even—excretable. See what a fine Back Bay vocabulary I've got?"

Gwen hung there, staring at her.

"No," she whispered finally, her voice a husk, a scrape. "You're not—frivolous, Rose Ann. What you are, is—vile."

Then she turned, very quietly, and with all the dignity she could manage, walked out of there.

"They're both all right," Jeff McKenzie said. "Only I'm sorry to say, Gwen honey, your Caleb is a bit the worse for wear. Took a saber slash across his upper right arm that has left him with a slight paralysis that the Army sawbones swear is only temporary, but, since he doesn't believe them, he's in the worst despairing mood you ever saw. Seems he covered himself with glory on the field, earned a citation for valor from no less than Brigadier General Thomas Jackson of the Army of Virginia. And since General Jackson was himself the outstanding hero of the day—the papers are all calling him 'Stonewall Jackson' for the stand he made before the old Henry house—a citation from him means an awful lot. Only General Jackson couldn't sign the citation because he'd got shot through his own right hand, so he ordered his adjutant to. At which point our Cabe, bleeding like a stuck pig and practically unconscious on his feet, saluted 'Stonewall Jackson' with his left hand and piped up: 'Sir, I'd esteem it as an honor if you'd withdraw the citation until such time as you can sign it yourself. Because with *your* signature on it, sir, that's one document I aim to hand down to my great-great-grandchildren!' The talk is that the general is going to request that Cabe be transferred to his own command. He was heard to say as they carted Cabe away, *'That's* the kind of young officers I need on my staff . . .'"

"And—Colin?" Gwen whispered.

Rose Ann stared at her. She saw at once that Gwen simply couldn't have refrained from asking that question; the longing and the need, the utter anguish in her sister's voice were slivers of ice, coals of fire, the vibrations of a caress treasured in the memory, bells plunged into the wind, drowned in moving air, death and hell, a brand.

As she studied her pale, fair sister, Rose remembered suddenly, oddly, the machine that old Professor Upjohn had described to her class in Boston. The old Greek playwrights, the prof had said, used that crazy contraption of pulleys and ropes to let one of the Olympian gods down onto the stage when they themselves couldn't figure out a way to write their imaginary characters out of the mess they'd written them into. So they swung a nice old white-bearded deity down to toss in a miracle and straighten everything out. Well, that was what poor Gwen needed now—a god from the machine to rearrange her life.

I'm not in your way, honey, she thought silently, through the sound of her compassion-riven heart's slow, dirgelike beating. I'd give you Colin on a silver platter if I could. But what about—Caleb? He's an awf'ly nice boy, y'know. No—he's more than that now. He's a hero—and a man. While Colin—?

"Colin," Jeff was saying, "is over at Fairdale. No, he hasn't so much as a scratch on him. They gave him two weeks' leave to—well—rest up, sort of . . ."

Rose Ann faced her brother. She asked him, very, very quietly, "But since he's *not* hurt, you just said, why on earth did they do that? The Claibornes are rich and influential, all right, but that shouldn't cut much ice with the Army, Jeff."

"It doesn't," Jeff said testily. "Only there's more than one way of being hurt, Ramb. I repeat, Colin hasn't a scratch on him, but his—his mind is kind of messed up. He was a sight too close to a bomb burst, and the explosion affected his hearing—right now he's as deaf as a gatepost, and well—his nerves. That's why he hasn't come to see you, sister. The docs say it will pass within a week or ten days. They call it concussion. They tell me they have dozens of cases of it after every battle—usually in high-strung sort of fellows . . ." His voice trailed off uneasily into silence.

But Rose Ann went on relentlessly, a tigress stalking with sure, destructive instinct.

"What you're giving me, Jeffie love," she murmured slumberously, "is a nice, polite definition of—cowardice, isn't it?"

"Oh, God!" Gwendolyn McKenzie grated. "How could you—how dare you!—even think, much less say, a thing like that?"

"I have to think it, and say it too, because Colin's my concern, Gwennie darling, not yours." Rose Ann sighed. "A point you've formed the bad habit of forgetting a sight too frequently here of late. I'm—or I *was*—supposed to marry him one fine day. To make him the father of the children I'm purely longing to have. And right there, sister, I run head on to a mighty tangled thicket of—of conflicting responsibilities, say. I'll give my pledged word to my husband to be a good, loving, faithful wife to him, the mistress and keeper of his home, the mother of his children. But that's just where the rub comes in, it seems to me. Those children are going to be *mine*, as well as his. So I'll have an awful responsibility toward them too. And not just to teach them to stand up straight and speak to the truth, to fear God, and keep His commandments, but to *be* real men and women, all wool and a yard wide, as the saying goes. To do that I've got to give 'em something to start with—a heritage of sound bodies and real bright minds. But also—guts in their bellies, grit in their craws, what it takes to never bow to anybody except the Lord God Almighty. Now we McKenzies have always had all that and to spare. But it takes two people to make a baby. So I don't think it's demanding too much of any prospective father to ask that he be—at the very least—a man . . ."

The silence in the little parlor when she finished saying that was palpable. It had thickness, texture, terrible weight. Geoffrey McKenzie broke it.

"I agree with you, Ramb," he said quietly. "There you're certainly within your womanly rights. Tell you what: I'll call for you and Gwen tomorrow and drive you into town to visit Cabe at the military hospital. Mary Sue's folks are letting me have their surrey this weekend, to squire her about in, since I have to go back to Norfolk on Monday. So I'll drive the two of you, and her, and Pa, if he wants to go, into Richmond to visit Cabe. How about it?"

"Of course," Gwen said tonelessly.

"Count me out," Rose Ann snapped. "I wouldn't ride from here to the river with that simpering little snip of a Mary Sue Hunter, 'cause if I did, I might get just too tempted to push her in!"

"Ramb," Jeff said sadly, "you're talking about your future sister-in-law, y'know . . ."

"Oh, Lord!" Rose wailed. "Jeff, you haven't! You couldn't!"

"I haven't or couldn't do *what*, Rambling Rose?" Jeff asked her with solemn mockery.

"Propose to a—a *thing* like Mary Sue Hunter!" Rose exploded.

"Mighty delectable little thing for my money," Jeff chuckled. "Oh, come off it, Ramb. I could bring home the Venus de Milo and you wouldn't approve of her. You're just a jealous, possessive, red-headed, freckle-faced McKenzie female, than which there is no worse. Come on, you will come with us tomorrow, won't you?"

"No," Rose Ann said sullenly.

At which Jeff caught her, none too gently, by the elbow and shoved her into the hall, calling back over his shoulder, "Word in private with this she-cougar, before I have to take my riding crop to her in public. Be back in a minute, Gwen . . ."

Outside in the hall, he bent swiftly close to Rose's ear.

"You've got to come," he whispered. "Caleb has something he swears is mighty important to tell you—"

"Where I can meet him in some dark and cozy spot, leaving my little lace pantalets at home?" Rose Ann said bitterly.

"Lord! He sure is one horny poor sinner, ain't he?" Jeff chuckled. "But no, I'm sure it's not his evil designs on your sacred honor this time, Ramb. Whatever it is, seems to be troubling him something awful. I suspect it has something to do with Colin and that famous bomb burst of his. But Cabe won't tell me a blessed thing about what's on his mind. Says, 'Rose Ann can tell you after I tell her, because it's strictly *her* business, Jeff boy. That is, if she sees fit to. But I purely can't. The bad part about it is, she's gonna hate my wormy tripes for even telling it to her. But I've got to. Just ain't fair to let her believe—' And there he shut his jaw like a spring-steel bear trap, and I couldn't get another mumbling word out of him. Doesn't sound good, does it?"

"No," Rose Ann murmured. "It sure Lord doesn't. All right, Jeffie love, I'll come along with y'all tomorrow. Reckon I can keep from strangling your dearest darling Mary Sue with my bare hands for *one* day, anyhow. But it's going to be mighty hard on me, I can purely tell you that . . ."

The little group who gathered around Caleb Henry's bedside— David McKenzie, his daughters, his son, and his son's promised— were confronted with a phenomenon that would afterward become a commonplace in American history but that their generation was to be the very first to witness: the psychological effects of having fought in and survived a major battle in a *modern* war.

"How does it feel to be—a hero, Captain Henry?" that little snip of a girl, Mary Sue Hunter, simpered. She seemed unaware that Rose Ann's green eyes, examining her with pitiless ferocity, had long since not only stripped her to the skin but bored through insipid flesh, watery blood, and fragile bone as well. At the moment they were dissecting the poor little creature's vapid mind, and her immortal soul—if any.

Caleb leered at her like a famished wolf. He was in considerable pain and was burning up with fever, for although, technically, the war he was fated to serve in was the first really modern one, introducing, among other things, the armor-plated battleship, the machine gun, aerial reconnaissance, and accomplishing at least one successful submarine attack, as far as medicine and surgery were concerned both the North and South lingered in the Dark Ages. So, since no one had ever even heard of asepsis, poor Caleb's saber-hacked arm had been repeatedly examined by doctors with filthy, blood-encrusted hands and dressed by medical orderlies who'd come straight from the unspeakable latrines of those times without washing theirs either, so the fact that, in the end, his badly infected arm finally healed before those bloodthirsty butchers got around to hacking it off at the shoulder was something of a major miracle.

"Don't call me Cap'n Henry, sugar!" he cackled. "Call me Cabe. With darling, honey, love of my life tacked on behind it. New law. Passed by special edict of the War Department: All pretty girls are hereby commanded, on pain of death for disobedience of the herein and herewith proclaimed, to fall in love with me!"

"Somebody," his wife said sweetly, "should equip the Yankees with spectacles, so they could see to aim better. Or give them anatomy lessons, explaining to them the difference between the arm and the neck . . ."

"You would look nice in widow's weeds, wouldn't you, Gwennie darling?" Caleb said solemnly. "But two can play that game! Sweet Rambling Rose, fairest of women, couldn't you feed her a little Paris green in her soup? Then you and I could depart for points unknown and—"

"Cabe," Rose Ann drawled, "I like my men tall and handsome. And not only are you the runt of the Henry litter, but not even a mother could love that mistake of nature you've got between your eyebrows and your chin. The only thing it looks like at *all* is the south end of a horse heading north."

"Granted. But I've got so many other sterling characteristics: I'm sweet, lovable, pure—"

"Oh, Gawd!" Jeff groaned. "Cabe, will you please be serious for a minute? You've got a set of first-class brains, so I'd like to pick 'em for a while. John Brooke and I have been given practically carte blanche to invent anything that might be even remotely useful to the Navy. Now there's always a lot of overlapping between the services. Tell me, from your experiences in battle, what do you boys especially need?"

"The cloak of invisibility," Cabe said flatly. "Bulletproof hides. Redesigned legs and feet that can retreat at better than fifty miles an hour. A sort of discriminating poison that poured into all the wells, lakes, and rivers would automatically kill off every blithering jackass who ever again dreams of starting another war . . ."

Rose stared at her brother-in-law with real interest now. Seeing, out of the corner of her eye, that her father was opening his mouth to protest, she cut him off with an imperious wave of a queenly little hand.

"Cabe," she said quietly, "those don't sound like the words of a hero. And from all I've heard, you were very brave . . ."

"I was a fool!" Caleb snarled. "I just got so goddamned mad at the sight of Southern boys running like rats from Bluebelly counterjumping Yankees that I forgot where the hell I was and tried to beat them—the members of my company, anyhow—back into line with the flat of my sword. I was, frankly, hysterical. I was crying and cussing and screaming like a woman, but, all right, I did my job. Let me tell you one thing, Ramb: In this here war a hero is an outmoded concept. I had some real brave boys in my company. D'you know how long they lasted when what looked like the whole codfish-bellied Yankee Army came foaming across the bridge and over Red House Ford? Thirty seconds. Less. I should have ordered those poor brave bastards to retreat! I should have—"

"Calm down, Cabe," Jeff said, his voice soft with pure compassion. "You did all right, and that's what counts . . ."

"Yes," Caleb sighed, "it does, doesn't it? What we've got to teach our boys is the happy medium, Jeff. Not to be so all-fired hip-hip-hurrah brave as to get themselves slaughtered in the first five minutes, and not so yellow-bellied as to fly the field, exposing their comrades' flanks to enemy infiltration. I've wept a bucketful o' tears for the valiant poor devils who died at their posts within seconds when that blue tidal wave came in. But I'm going to hate the white-livered cowards—one of 'em in particular!—who left 'em to die, for the rest of my life . . ."

"Colin?" Rose said then flatly, calmly.

"Tell you that later!" Caleb rasped at her. "In private, if possible. All right, Jeff: inventions! A *repeating* rifle with a magazine that holds six, eight, a dozen shots so you could stop an attacking wave like that one cold without getting yourself killed trying to reload . . ."

"He's got a point there, Jeff boy," Dave McKenzie growled at his son. "In our war with the greasers, I saw boys spitted on the points of the Mex cavalry's *lances*—would you believe *that?*—or lassoed and dragged over the cactus and the rocks, before they could reload them damned smoothbore muskets we carried. A repeater sure Lord would have come in mighty handy!"

"All right," Jeff sighed, "but you're handing me a God-awful chore, Cabe. Colt tried adapting his revolver principle to rifles as far back as '55, and d'you know what happened? When the troopers testing 'em pulled the trigger to fire the shot lined up with the barrel, *all* the bloody shots in the revolving magazine went off at the same time and blew off the shooter's arm . . ."

"Then a breechloader!" Caleb said feverishly. "A gun a fellow could load lying on his belly behind a goddamned *log*, for God's sake! What I saw along Bull Run Creek and in front of my poor grandaunt's house makes me wonder how anybody *ever* survives having to load a muzzleloader in battle . . ."

"You know," Mary Sue Hunter sighed, "I don't understand a *word* you men are saying!"

"That's evident," Rose Ann snapped, "but be quiet and let *me* learn something. Cabe, why do the men get killed reloading?"

"Have to stand up to do it, making a perfect target out of your poor trembling carcass for any halfway decent shot. Takes too long: you have to bite the end off the paper cartridge, pour the powder down the barrel, patch the ball with what's left of the paper cartridge, push it down the barrel with the ramrod, remove the ramrod, ear the hammer back to half cock, put a percussion cap on the nipple of the chamber, ease the hammer the rest of the way back into full cock, then pull the trigger to shoot—*once*. And all the time the whole randy Yankee Army is shooting at you. Of course, we try to do it by turns: some fellows shooting while the others are reloading, but even so, it's a wonder that anybody ever comes out alive . . ."

"And this new kind of gun you just mentioned would change all that? It would solve the problem?" Rose Ann asked.

"Yes," Jeff said. "A breechloader, Ramb, is a gun you load from the breech instead of from the muzzle. In other words, from the back end instead of the front. So you wouldn't need a ramrod, or have to do all the practically suicidal things we have to do now. You'd just open up the back end of the rifle, just above the trigger, drop in a cartridge, bullet and all, slam her shut, put a cap on the nipple, and bang away. It could be done three times as fast and, best of all, you could do it lying flat on your belly, making a mighty poor target for their sharpshooters . . ."

"Then why haven't we got one?" Rose demanded.

"Because we're Southerners," Caleb said bitterly. "Which means that we do everything either ass backwards or too late."

"And to make matters even worse," Jeff said, "the Yankees *have* a breechloader already. Christian Sharps invented his breech-loading mechanism in 1848, right here in Virginia, at the Harpers Ferry armory. But the military, being military, just didn't cotton to it. But now the Secret Service swears they're gearing up to produce. In Connecticut—Hartford, I think. Jesus! If somebody would steal me just *one* example of Sharps's breechblock—just *one* —I'd turn the tide of this war in our favor inside of six months. And permanently, at that. I don't need the whole gun—just the breechblock, a piece you could carry in your hip pocket or in a lady's handbag. But they've got that damned factory so closely guarded that they shoot sea gulls for flying over it. Not one of our agents has been able to get within five miles of it . . ."

"Jeff," Rose said breathlessly, "send *me!*"

"Whaaat!" Jeff gasped.

"Exactly what I said. Even if I couldn't steal you one of those whatever-you-may-call-its, I could draw you so perfect a picture of it that you could make it from that. Or a map of Hartford so you could send a raiding party from one of our gunboats to the very street. I won first prize in drawing at Miss Bradstreet's School, y'know. Besides, I probably could get you one. I've got a better than perfect aristocratic Yankee accent. I'm not too hard to look at. I've got more damn nerve than anybody you ever heard tell of, and I'm—female. Fix me up some fake papers, send me to Hartford to look for my runaway husband who's deserted me and our three kids, and inside a week they'll pour that breechblock into my dainty slipper along with some real first-class champagne . . ."

"Y'know, Jeff," Caleb said with a grin, "I'll bet the Rambler could do it at that . . ."

"You know what's wrong with that proposition, Cabe," Jeff growled. "We've half a dozen female spies working for the Secret Service right now, and every goddamned one of 'em is—a whore!"

"Why, Jeff!" Mary Sue Hunter cried.

"Sorry, honey," Jeff muttered.

"Send me," Rose Ann insisted with a mocking grin. "With the stipulation that any money I make on the side, I can keep. The world's oldest profession always did strike yours truly as a mighty pleasant way of making a living anyhow, and besides, some of those damnyankee boys really aren't half bad . . ."

"Pa," Jeff growled, "if you don't stripe her seat for her good real soon, I'm going to, so help me God!"

"Rosie," Dave McKenzie groaned, "swear to God, I just don't know where I got you from!"

"From under a cabbage bush," Rose laughed, "or out of a hollow log down in Dismal Swamp. Oh, come off of it, you old sweetkins! You know exactly where you got me from—and how. And if you start in trying to be mean to poor little old me, I'll treat the assembled company to a complete and unedited story of your younger days. Got it straight from the horse's mouth—'cause Aunt Corny does look something like a mare, doesn't she? Bet she even whinnies in her sleep. Let me see . . . Shall I tell 'em about the time you broke your leg jumping out of Martha Claiborne's upstairs-back-bedroom window? Maybe I shouldn't be engaged to Colin, after all, because— How does one put that nicely, Gwennie darling? Oh, yes! Because the degree of our consanguinity may be a sight too great?"

"Ramb, I'm going to *hit* you in a minute!" Jeff howled.

"Whereupon I'll entertain the dear little simpie pie here with a names, dates, and places recapitulation of your own excursions down that good old primrose path," Rose said merrily. "Starting way, way back—like, say, the night the widow Tolliver taught you mannish tricks the time Pa sent you off to her house with a note dunning her for unpaid rent when you were only thirteen years old. Sure paid her debts off handsomely that evening, didn't she? But Pa never even saw the interest charges . . ."

"Ohhhhhhh, Jeff!" Mary Sue Hunter wailed, and burst into bitter tears.

Gwen put her arms around the shaking shoulders of her prospective sister-in-law.

"You mustn't pay the slightest attention to *anything* Rose Ann says," she said, more than a little acridly. "You see, she suffers from hoof-and-mouth disease—an ailment common to jennies . . ."

"There you may have a point, Gwennie darling," Rose sighed. "Every time I open my mouth I do shove my own foot—hoof—into it, don't I? Mary Sue, I'm sorry! I was only plaguing Jeffie anyhow. He's been a real *saint* all his life. Fact is, if he were to convert to the One Truth Faith, they'd plaster him over, polychrome him, and stand him up in a niche in the cathedral. Don't believe the things I say, honey child. I'm a liar and a witch, and the truth just isn't in me!"

"The understatement of the year!" Caleb cackled happily; then he sobered. "But you just delivered yourself of one piece of rock-solid truth, Ramb. Offhanded. Thinking you were joking . . ."

"Which was?" Rose said.

"Well—" Caleb began, but Dave McKenzie cut him off.

"Lord God!" he roared. "These here wild young'uns of mine, with all their flighty, frivolous talk, have made me forget the main thing I was meaning to ask you. Your grandauntie Judith now: from what I remember about the lay of the land up there, her house ought to've been mighty close to the fighting. Right up above Sudley Road, ain't it? Can't get out of my mind that there house had to be right betwixt both armies. Reckon them big locust trees give it a mite o' protection, but—"

Caleb bowed his head, looked up again, the unashamed tears glittering in his eyes.

"She wasn't my grandaunt, or rather she was, but only by marriage," he croaked. "Her old man was the Henry. Served under Captain Truxton on the *Constellation*. She's—dead, sir. We—murdered her. We—and they. Us and the Yanks. She was eighty-five years old. Bedridden and helpless. That house—the old Henry house—was riddled. Most of those grand old locust trees were cut down by small-arms fire, shredded and splintered by shell bursts. That's the kind of war this is, you see: neither age, nor sex, nor the hard-earned honor of a naval hero, nor even the respect due his widow could be taken into consideration. There was no time. There'll never be any. This is—a *modern* war, sir. The old concepts —decency, chivalry, noncombatants' rights—don't count anymore. They don't count a good goddamn . . ."

He turned his face away from them, toward the wall. His thin figure shook convulsively. Which was too much for Rose Ann. She flew to his bedside, collapsed the steel hoops of her *cage américaine* upward, exposing her petticoat, and dropped to her knees beside his bed. Then she clasped Caleb in her strong young arms, crooning, "Oh, no, Cabe honey! You mustn't cry! 'Twasn't your fault! It wasn't at all! You were brave—a hero. You couldn't have—"

"Rose Ann," Gwen said quietly, "might I remind you that Caleb's *my* husband, and that consoling him is—or ought to be— my obligation. My prerogative—even my privilege. So will you be so good as to turn him loose before you strangle him quite?"

"Oh, Lord!" Rose Ann moaned. "Can't I ever do *anything* right? Gwen, forgive me! But you know blamed well I didn't mean . . ."

"Forget it," Gwen said wearily. "You never mean anything. There's no meaning in you, and scant sense. So there's nothing to forgive. Cabe, you shouldn't let your grandaunt's death affect you so. She was very old and—"

" 'She should have died hereafter,' " Caleb quoted bitterly. " 'There would have been a time for such a word. Tomorrow, and tomorrow, and tomorrow, creeps in this petty pace—' Oh, to hell with it. Do me a favor, will you, you-all? Get out of here. I'm tired and dog sick, and I've had my belly full of company. Being polite is killing me. What I feel like doing is howling like a rabid wolf and bashing my head bloody against this wall. So get out, damnit! All of you—except Ramb. Gotta have a word with you, baby doll . . ."

"Cabe—" Gwen said, drawing his name out, making of it a moaning sound. Or a mourning one. Or both.

"Oh, hell!" Caleb grated. "How stupid can a woman get to be? My dearest wife, I have no intention of throwing your little sister down and ripping her frilly pantalets to shreds in my fiendish haste to have my lustful way with her. But only because I hold it a blotch upon the honor of highborn Southern chivalry to disappoint a woman in a horizontal position. Were I up to it, I'd rape, violate, and what-have-you, her, gladly. But I'm not up to it. So— talk. Conversation. Warnings of doom. Premonitions of disaster. Fate's hideous cruelty, destroying a maiden's roseate—or is it rosy? —dreams . . ."

"Caleb, you're feverish!" Gwen said sharply. "You're—raving, you know!"

"When haven't I been, both feverish and raving, my sweet? Oh, Christ! Seriously, Gwen, I have to tell Rose Ann something that concerns her, and her only. That's none of *your* goddamn business, to make the matter entirely clear. Nor *mine*. Only I had this knowledge thrust upon me. In fact, the author of it damn near amputated my arm. But I've got to set Ramb straight, or try to. I'm duty-bound to—"

"You have," Rose Ann said with deadly quiet. "He was running like a rat, wasn't he? And you tried to stop him. So then he—"

"A mere supposition of yours," Caleb said sardonically. "That, as a Virginian, an officer, and a gentleman, I refuse to either confirm or deny before the assembled company. Suppose somebody had seen you and, of course, one of your all too numerous swains coming out of old A'nt Sukie's place here in Richmond—"

He caught the barely perceptible start she made, saw all the color—wine and roses and flecks of gold!—abruptly leave her face. But within the deeper fibers of his being, Caleb Henry actually was, to an extent adequate enough to order and control his life, give his existence symmetry, harmony, even a certain depth and dignity, what he had mockingly proclaimed himself to be: a Virginian and a gentleman, for his being accidentally an officer, and a really effective one—a fact that surprised him more than it did anyone else!—really hadn't much to do with it. So he merely murmured just below the threshold of audibility, "Holy Jesus!" and went on with his thought: "You wouldn't want it, or any questions touching upon your maidenly honor, discussed in public, would you?"

"No," Rose said in a strangled whisper, "I wouldn't . . ."

"So let us not put on display any imputations against the manly honor of another officer and, presumably, a gentleman in his absence, thus denying him his absolute right to defend himself. In short, will all the rest of you, including this small and dainty morsel of Jeff's—next time you visit me, honey, bring along a knife, a fork, and a napkin, so I can dine upon all your delectable little delectabilities *au naturel,* which is French for raw—get the unholy hell out of here, and let me tell Ramb what I've got to!"

"Come on, all," Gwen said then, quietly. "Let's leave this precious pair in peace, and give my dearly beloved husband time to undertake the demolition of the character, or at least the reputation, of a better man than he is, or ever will be . . ."

Caleb leered at her, his eyes alight with mockery.

"Better how?" he asked her solemnly. "In the hay?"

Gwen faced him then, and her eyes were cold and still.

"If I knew *that,*" she said flatly, "which—most unfortunately!—I don't, it would delight me to my soul to tell you, Cabe. And if ever I should find it out, you may rest assured I will!"

Then she turned on her heel and marched out of there. Somewhat sheepishly, the rest of the family, except, of course, Rose Ann, followed her.

"All right, Cabe," Rose Ann said, "speak your piece . . ."

"No," Caleb said, "not until you treat me to an exhaustive account, complete with all the feelthy details, of your visit—or visits —to A'nt Sukie's . . ."

"No," Rose Ann said.

"Why not? You aren't going to deny you've been there, are you? You'd make a piss-poor poker player, Ramb. When I mentioned that last refuge for horny and lonesome sinners, your face was a printed page. Page, hell! A whole goddamn volume. And that volume sure Lord wasn't the Bible . . ."

"You should read the Bible sometime," Rose Ann said. "You might learn something. Come on, Cabe!"

"Tit for tat. You tell me how carefully Colin—it *was* Colin, wasn't it?—removed your nether garments, 'cause a gentleman of high degree like Colin Claiborne wouldn't just rip 'em to shreds the way a rutting old boar hog like me would have without a second thought, and I'll spill my rancid beans in turn!"

Rose peered at him thoughtfully. Then she flashed him a grin that was mischief's pristine self.

"That problem didn't even arise," she drawled. "I took 'em off myself . . ."

"Oh, Jesus!" Caleb whispered prayerfully. "Ramb—you didn't! You couldn't! Not with that—that—" His face, Rose saw sadly, was truly stricken—wore, in fact, the expression of a man wounded unto death.

"I most impurely did," she sighed. "Oh, come off it, Cabe! After all, what's it to you?"

"Just—my life," Caleb whispered brokenly. "When you walk out that door, sweet, wild Rambling Rose, I'm going to lay back on my filthy cot—and die . . ."

He actually had, she saw, tears in his eyes. For which, of course, physical weakness and wound fever accounted, but Rose didn't know that. Oh, Lord, she prayed, teach me how to stop making such a terrible mess of things, will You, please?

"Cabe, I'm sorry," she said, "but it's my sister you're married to, not me. And if it's any comfort to you, the occasion was disappointing. Very. I think I was within my rights to find that out before tying myself for life to a man who—"

"Is a miserable, short-fused dud?" Caleb cackled sardonically.

"Exactly. You men go helling around all over the landscape, acquiring experience, as you call it, before you settle down with the girl who was just plain made for you. But we women are supposed to accept on the basis of pure guesswork, without any concrete knowledge to back it up, the first likely-looking man who asks our hand. 'Tain't fair, Cabe! And to make matter worse, you damn Southerners have got the tomfool idea that the feminine sex can be divided into two mutually exclusive groups: good women and bad ones. Which automatically rules any honest to God *normal* woman out. 'Cause women like me *want* to be loved, hell, bedded, Caleb Henry! And hot and hard and frequently at that. Which means that, according to you fellows, *all* women who *are* women are bad. Thus leaving you with simpletons like Mary Sue, or icebergs from the frozen North like Gwen—"

"Gwen's not cold," Caleb said soberly. "That's just the trouble—"

"Huh? Well, I'll be goddamned!" Rose exploded. "Cabe, for your information, that pedestal you chivalrous Southern gentlemen put your wives up on is a mighty cold and lonely place. Never figured *you'd* complain because Gwen doesn't give you chilblains in bed . . ."

"I don't. But being *used*—at rare and infrequent intervals—as a

55

substitute for the bastard she wanted and couldn't get, is a hell of a thing, Rose Ann," he said bitterly.

She stared at him. Whispered, "So you knew . . ."

"So I *know*," Caleb corrected her, "which is why I find myself constrained to add a preamble to my subsequent discourse, to wit: Ramb baby, no man knows how he's going to react in battle. And the difference between a hero and a goddamned fool is totally indistinguishable to the naked eye. I was scared shitless at Manassas, honey. Only, by a fluke, I was able to dominate my fear. That fluke being that such idiocies and insanities as regional pride and my conception of myself as lover, warrior, man caused me to get so goddamned mad at the sight of noble and superior Southerners— another idea that doesn't qualify a man as an intellectual giant!— running like sheep from supposed counterjumpers and cowards, that I reacted like a jackass, the exact definition of a courageous, valiant soldier, as my citation from old "Stonewall" proves. Baby, those Bluebellies were *shooting* at us. Using live ammunition, not duds. Aiming with rifled Springfields firing conical minié balls that can kill you *dead* from as far away as eight hundred to one thousand yards. Under those circumstances the only defensible reaction of a rational man is to run like hell. Which is why I'm asking you to forgive poor old Colin. When he chopped my arm damn near off to get me out of his way, he was out of his mind with a fear he had every right to feel. Besides, courage on the field hasn't one goddamned thing to do with a man's being a sweet and loving husband and a good father. If you don't believe me, ask Gwen!"

"Cabe," Rose whispered, "if you weren't married to Gwen, I'd fall in love with you right now. So help me, I would. 'Cause you really are—kind of noble, aren't you?"

"Then poison her!" Caleb chuckled.

"Shut up. You're wrong, you know. It does have something to do with it in one peculiar way that's mighty important to little steam engines with their safety valves tied down like me. Cabe honey, tell me this: You ever see a seed bull or a stud stallion who *wasn't* brave?"

Caleb stared at her. Then he threw back his head and roared. He laughed until the tears of his unholy mirth literally choked and strangled him.

"Oh, Lord!" he gasped then. "Why didn't You send her back home three months sooner—before I married Gwen?"

Never one to put off until tomorrow what needs must be done today, that very next morning, without, of course, telling anyone in the McKenzie household, even the slaves, where she was going, Rose Ann rode over to Fairdale, the great plantation that Colin's father, the late Creighton Claiborne, had had the wisdom to withdraw from the land-ruining cultivation of tobacco and turn to diversified farming, so that by 1861 its production of wheat, alfalfa, clover, corn, garden crops, and, above all, peanuts was very nearly the greatest of any single plantation in the state. She undertook that ride with the sober but unshakable determination to break her engagement to Colin.

She chose an extremely early hour to set out, with malice aforethought, because she knew that Martha Claiborne, Colin's mother —remarkably well preserved and still beautiful in her early fifties —never got out of bed before noon, lying in a darkened room with compresses of cotton soaked in cologne over her eyes, to delay the onslaught of wrinkles, and a thick mess of buttermilk plastered over her face, neck, shoulders, arms, and even her breasts to conserve the snowy whiteness of her skin.

Now Rose had long since arrived at the conclusion that having Martha Claiborne as her mother-in-law was one of those fates that could legitimately be considered worse than death, but she'd been prepared to put up even with that out of what she'd believed to be her overwhelming love for Colin. But now that love was dead and gone, done to death almost mercifully in so swift and final a way, and under such unequivocal circumstances as to leave her without even the need to shed a tear for it. So, as she rode down the long alley of oaks leading to the somber Georgian magnificence of Fairdale, her feeling, by and large, was one of very nearly pure relief.

Glad to be rid of dear Martha too, she thought. 'Cause she sure Lord doesn't cotton to me at all, nor to any McKenzie born. Reckon she thinks Pa told us he tumbled her, instead of our getting it from those eternal bearers of ill tidings, the niggers. And in her twisted way, she still blames Pa for old Creighton's death. Was it Pa's fault that the old fool got it all mixed up and challenged the wrong man when he found out that witch had been cheating on him? What would have been served by Pa's coming forward and admitting that he was the guilty party instead of Pierce Roldan? There'd still have been a duel, and since old Creighton couldn't hit the side of bright red barn at twenty paces, the result would have been the same. Besides, maybe he *didn't* get it wrong. I'll wager Pierce Roldan was just as guilty as Pa. Who knows how many men dear Martha warmed his bed with whenever Colin's dear old pappy—if he even was!—was out of it? No, I'll back quietly away from that one. Likely Creighton Claiborne did sire Colin after all. That's one way of accounting for my dearest darling ex-lover's, ex-hero's being so no goddamn good at what it's a man's basic obligation to be good at if he doesn't plan to head straight for the nearest cloister and devote his life to meditation and prayer!

She rode on up to the portico of the Claibornes' mansion. She had dreamed of becoming mistress of it one day, but now looking at its dark red brick, ivy-covered immensity, she suddenly felt almost glad that that was not to be.

She felt a small jerk and, looking down, saw that Jeremy, the Claibornes' head groom, had gently seized Prince Rupert's bridle.

"Howdy, Miss Rose Ann!" Jeremy beamed. "You sho is a treat for these heah tired ol' eyes, that you is, missy. Yessiree bobtail!"

Jeremy, Rose was complacently aware, adored her. Nearly all the black male slaves did, on all the plantations that she visited with any frequency. The wenches were another matter. Us females, she thought wryly, just can't seem to get along, no matter what color our hides may be . . .

"Howdy, Jeremy," she said pleasantly. "Is the young master at home?"

The Claiborne slaves still called Colin "the young master," though any need to distinguish between him and "the old master," his father, had been ended forever by Pierce Roldan's contemptuous, not even deliberately aimed, shot. "I was trying to miss the old fool," Roldan swore afterward, "but he got the twitches and the jerks and plumb moved into the path of my ball." Rose Ann didn't doubt the truth of that statement. The poor old jackass probably wanted to die, knowing what he knew, she thought.

"Yes'm, sho Lord is, Miss Rose Ann. But I jes' doan know how's you's gwine t'talk to him. He deef as a gatepost, y'know!"

Rose's eyes darkened with anger at hearing that. Caleb's voice, speaking slowly, sadly, came back to her: "Bomb burst? That there's purely a laugh, Ramb. Wasn't hardly any artillery fire in our sector at all. Not at first. The big guns opened up later, after poor Bee and Stonewall Jackson had rallied us, and even then Jeb Stuart took out their infantry support, and the 33rd fair murdered their gunners. By the time the cannons started blasting, Colin was out of sight . . ."

"Well," she said with a well-feigned cheerfulness that nevertheless had a bitter edge to it, "I can always hug and kiss him and pinch and tickle him and muss up his hair, can't I, Jeremy? After all, he belongs to me just as much as you do to him . . ."

"That there's purely the truth you's done gone 'n' spoke now, Miss Rose Ann!" Jeremy laughed. "Worse, 'cause you's got them fetters 'n' chains 'n' shackles wrapped tight around he heart!"

"And if he doesn't behave himself, I'll use my whip," Rose Ann said solemnly. "Go tell Junius to announce me— Oh, Lord! How can you people tell Master Colin anything, since he can no longer hear?"

"Ol' Junius kin read 'n' write," Jeremy said proudly. " 'N' his ol' woman, Bess, kin too. Us gotta tell the young master anything, us tells Junius o' Bess, 'n' they writes him a note. Things been working jes' fine thataway . . ."

"All right. Take care of Prince Rupert for me while I go wait in the little parlor. But be careful, will you? He's a good bit nervy and skittish, y'know . . ."

"I knows that, missy," Jeremy said, "but since he the fastest hoss in the state o' Virginny, reckon us kin forgive him he little tricks. You's done won the ladies' riding contest three years running, ain't you, Miss Rose Ann?"

"And I'm going to win it again this year. That is, if it's even held, with this awful war going on. The only thing that makes me mad is that the Saddle and Spurs Society won't let me ride against the men . . ."

"They's scairt to," Jeremy chuckled. " 'Cause they knows you'll beat all them young gentlemens all hollow, and then they be so shamed they hafta die!"

"And good riddance!" Rose Ann laughed. "No—just you take care of Prince Rupert. I'll go find Junius myself . . ."

When Colin came into the little parlor, he had a sheaf of paper in one hand and a pencil in the other. Making a rueful gesture toward his ear with the pencil, he held them out to her.

Dead still, unsmiling, Rose Ann stared at him, keeping her hands down at her sides.

"No," she said, slowly, softly, clearly. "I don't need to write you notes, Colin, for I have no intention of taking part in this shameful charade. You can hear me perfectly well, because the cause of your troubles isn't your ears, but the backbone you were born without. As well as certain other masculine attributes, I do believe. But, anyhow, we have scant need for words. We've already done all the talking we're ever going to do. But my meaning will be clear enough without them, Mama's baby boy who doesn't even know how to—love and cherish and—and satisfy a woman—least of all, how to—bed her properly. So here, take these. One of them was yours to start with. And the other's—a gift from me. A token, call it. The symbol of what I know you are. My estimation of just how much I think you're worth . . ."

Colin stared at leather-clad palms of her hands, for she hadn't even bothered to take off her riding gloves. In the left one lay the engagement ring he had given her. The magnificent solitaire caught the light like frozen fire, cold as the forever he was going to have to exist in without her, piercing as the anguish that tore through him at that moment, having the awful symmetry, the terrible completeness of—death. But what she had in her other hand was, in a way, even worse. In her right palm, downy and soft, snowy against the black leather of her glove, lay a small white feather.

Colin stared at her, his eyes appalled. He made wild, foolish gestures toward his ears, his lips.

"Oh, hell," Rose Ann said wearily, and inverted the position of her hands, letting the diamond ring fall, and the small white feather drift, to the floor.

Colin jerked foward like a cripple, a spastic, a man sunk beneath the terrible weight of years. He dropped to his knees, groped amid the fibers of the rug for the ring. He ignored the white feather. That was the only thing he could do with it, then, at that rarely awful moment, and for the rest of his life.

Half turning to go, Rose Ann let her gaze fall on the Oriental vase on its stand beside the chimney. She knew it well. It was dear Martha's most prized possession, brought back by her from her honeymoon voyage to the Near East. That some bazaar keeper had accurately judged the limitations of her culture, her intelligence, and her taste was obvious. It was absolutely horrendous, one of those gaudy fakes that Levantine traders made to sell to English and North American tourists. Rose hated it with all her heart. For months she had lived under the threat of Martha's delicate hints that she meant to pass it along to her son's bride as a wedding gift. So now, inspiration struck her. Or the blood she had inherited from the original McKenzies, the warlock and the witch, went straight to her sublimely wicked little head.

In two long strides, with a great swirl of the hooped skirt of her riding habit, she crossed to the chimney. With no hesitation at all, she lifted that hideous vase high above the crown of her absurdly feminine imitation of a man's tall stovepipe silk hat, and hurled it to crash into a thousand bright fragments against the floor.

Colin—stone-deaf Colin—leaped a full two yards straight up.

Rose Ann stood there, staring at him, her green eyes soft with sudden pity. Then she saw the tears that were flooding his face, the white foam of a babbler's saliva at the corners of his wildly trembling—and weak and foolish, her mind supplied—mouth, and her emerald gaze hardened, became suddenly leonine.

"Goodbye, Colin. Goodbye—forever," she said.

Chapter Four

She was, Rose Ann McKenzie admitted to herself, thoroughly out of sorts: sad, mixed up, so lonesome that she hurt, nervous—"jumpy as a sick cat!" was the way she put it. And—face it, she told the image in her vanity's mirror, brave Southern *heroine* who had the gall to give poor Colin the white feather—you're plain down-right scared!

On that Saturday morning, June 28, 1862, she had reasons and to spare for all those feelings. From fully one quarter of the compass —that is, from due north to maybe even a little south of due east— she could hear the thump and thunder of the guns. At times she could even make out the eerie, whining, whistling scream of a shell coming over, distinguish the shattering, crashing explosion it made when it hit from the belly-deep boom of the cannon that had hurled it over thousands of yards to reduce brave men into un-recognizable messes of tangled, blood-slimed guts, ragged slivers of splintered bone. The Yankee guns were that close now, five or six miles away—seven at the best. They awoke in her a desire to go down on her knees and pray to God—not for herself, who was clearly beyond all redemption, fallen woman that she was!—but for her three absent warriors.

She knew more or less where two of them were. Caleb—Major Caleb Henry since his transfer to Stonewall Jackson's staff at that peerless fighting man's own request—was with the general in the Shenandoah Valley, ready to ambush and smash any Yankee armies that came that way. Colin, still a second lieutenant, and likely to stay one—that is, if he didn't get "busted" back to sergeant major or even below that for his obvious lack of soldierly aptitudes—was with the Army of Northern Virginia, recently taken over by General Robert E. Lee, after its old commanding officer, General Joseph E. Johnston, had been severely wounded at the Battle of Seven Pines, near the hamlet called Fair Oaks, seven or eight miles east of Richmond, on the thirty-first of May. But, worst of all, she didn't even know where her brother, Jeff, was. Norfolk had been evacuated on May 9, though Jeff and John Brooke had stayed in the city until the eleventh, long enough to supervise the burning of their masterpiece, the ironclad *Virginia*. On his last visit home, in the middle of March, Jeff had despairingly declared that his and Brooke's dream of what a fighting ship had to be from now on was a terrible piece of junk. They'd built it out of what was left of the

Union steam frigate *Merrimac,* and it had drawn too much water—all of thirty-two feet—with all that iron plate piled up on it, while its rusty, wheezing engines had been enough to make an angel weep—or swear. But all the same, it had gutted the Union Navy's battleships *Cumberland* and *Congress,* and would have left the North without even a rowboat if that funny-looking demonstration of the vast superiority of Yankee engineering, John Ericsson's *Monitor—* "A damned cooking pot on a shingle!" Jeff snorted—hadn't arrived, exactly as if the plot of the action had been written by a cheap scribbler of bad melodramas, just in the nick of time to fight the *Virginia* to a clanging, iron-denting draw. "Draw, hell!" Jeff growled. "The *Monitor* won! All right, she couldn't damage, sink, or even beat our *Virginia,* but she damn well could and *did* prevent her from doing what we'd built her for, depriving the Bluebellies of a fleet and breaking the blockade forever so we could quit having to drink this puking mess!"

So now Jeff was gone, south and west probably. Pensacola, Mobile, the rivers of the Middle Border. But out there the damnyankees were winning all the time: New Orleans had been taken by their fleet on April 24, Pensacola on May 10, Memphis, Tennessee, on the sixth of this very month of June. She'd told everybody who would listen that the South couldn't beat the Yankees in the long run, but they wouldn't believe her, accusing her of having been tainted by her Northern education. Besides, General Jackson and General Johnston had won real great victories, but—

At Seven Pines, the fighting had been so close to Richmond that they'd been able to bring the bodies of the Confederate dead back into the city for burial—six thousand of them. She'd been in town, she'd heard the heartrending screams of mothers, sweethearts, sisters, wives, seen them fall out in rows in fainting fits. What kind of a victory was it when six thousand brave boys got killed winning it? The Yanks had lost only five thousand. But there were three to five damnyankees to each Bolivar Ward. So the Yankees didn't even need to win that last battle the way she'd said. They could even lose it and the war would still be over and the final outcome theirs, because all the Southern boys would have got themselves slaughtered beating them . . .

I mustn't think this way! she told herself fiercely. But she couldn't help it. She was steadily losing weight, because her nerves-clamped stomach wouldn't let her eat. So her breakfast that morning had consisted, as usual, of one scalding cup of what Jeff had called "this puking mess!"—not a half-bad description of imitation coffee made of parched peanuts, which was one of the various substitutes for the real coffee that was totally unavailable now that the Yankee Navy had gone and done what Jeff and his friends of the South's makeshift fleet had sworn the Bluebellies would never be able to do: blockade all the major Southern ports, seal them tighter than a drum. Last fall, before the war had been going on six months, all the Richmond newspapers, the *Whig*, the *Enquirer*, the *Examiner*, and the *Dispatch*, had had to cut the size of their pages in half, for lack of paper and of printer's lead for casting type. By that late June day of 1862, they were down to a quarter of their former dimensions. They were filled with the stories of the triumphs of Southern armies—what General Jackson had done in the Valley not two weeks ago, cutting to ribbons Yankee forces adding up to more than a hundred thousand men with a hard-bitten little army less than a quarter of their numbers, had been a miracle—or one of the purest exhibitions of sheer military genius ever seen in the long chronicles of human valor.

Only, Rose Ann was sadly sure, the North would go right on attacking and losing battles, at the cost of horrible losses, and the South would go right on counterattacking, and winning them, at the cost of even more horrible losses, because the North could replace her fallen and the South couldn't. The South, her beloved Southland, was covering itself with glory, winning every battle, and losing the dad-blamed war.

Richmond wasn't so gay anymore. All those handsome young officers in their splendid, showy uniforms were gone. Because there no longer was enough gray cloth left to clothe even commissioned officers, the Bolivar Wards went to war in what once had been called "nigger cloth" but now was known by the euphemism "butternut brown," a shade very close to what their descendants were going to fight two world wars in and call "khaki."

The women of Richmond and the country round about it were becoming a good bit less patriotic, not quite so fire-eating fierce. The bodies of their warriors, fallen on fields no more than six or seven miles from the center of the city, often arrived home in unpainted pine boxes before the official notifications of their deaths did. And considering the emotional impact of such a macabre event, inevitably compounded by those Lord-awful whalebone corsets and the diet city dwellers had to subsist upon, that the all but universal response to this sadly become commonplace occurrence was to faint dead away and, once revived, to spend the rest of the day and night screaming the house down, could not, by any fair observer, be held strange.

The hospitals were jam-packed with wounded heroes. And their women, setting out to visit them, didn't have to ask directions. All they had to do was to lift their dainty noses and sniff the wind, because the stench of those institutions of healing, a combination of the aroma of gangrenous wounds, the putrefying mounds of amputated limbs—which piled up faster than they could be hauled away to be buried, usually to be followed by the rest of poor Bolivar within a day or two—the mingled perfumes of unemptied bed-pans and slop jars, wafting through the windows of wards always pitifully understaffed, plus the natural effluvia of male bodies un-washed for weeks, made following one's nose the quickest and sur-est way of arriving at one.

The loss of a hairpin, a pin, a needle, had already become a minor disaster, the breakage of a comb, a major one. None of these articles plus—especially trying to women!—mirrors could be re-placed at all. Strangely enough, laces, silks, satins, Paris perfumes, and such luxuries could still be obtained—if you had the carpetbag ful of ten- and twenty-dollar *gold* coins that the blockade runners asked for them, because these patriotic gentlemen, "engrossers"—by which the Josephine Rebs and/or Bertha Wards meant "profiteers"—to the man, weren't having any Confederate "shin plasters." "No, ma'am, thank you mighty kindly!"

If there were only something I could do! Rose Ann moaned to herself that fateful June morning. She was perfectly aware that her sister, Gwen, would have icily informed her that there was enough to occupy her, and twenty more like her, for a hundred years if she'd only put a hand to it! Gwen had converted the big parlor of McKenzie's Manor into a miniature textile factory. She had had brought down from the attic their great-grandmother's spinning wheel, more than a hundred years old, and taught herself the deli-cate art of using it. Caesar, the oldest of the male slaves, who'd been trained as a carpenter, was sent over to Shirley Hundred, the Carters' place, not yet at that time within the lines of McClellan's advancing Yankee army, to study and make drawings of the loom that had been miraculously preserved there. The Carters' loom was very likely the only one left in the Tidewater, if not the whole state, in that day when the Yankee and British textile factories had long since relieved the Southern ladies of the onerous tasks of spin-ning and weaving the cloth needed to make clothes for the family and the slaves. Caesar, a highly intelligent man—a characteristic that made him somewhat suspect among Virginians who still remembered the brilliant Nat Turner and the revolt he'd led thirty years before—came back with a perfect set of drawings. Two months later, Gwen had her loom. Now it ran all day long and far into the night. But the clang of the batten, and the rustling whisper of the shuttle as it shot back and forth carrying the thread of the woof horizontally over and under the vertical ones of the warp, drove Rose Ann, who was anything but a quiet, peaceful, domesticated soul, almost out of her mind. Besides, it took so long! One thread at a time, in and out, over and under, crossing and recrossing the warp that had been laboriously and patiently set up by hand, usually by Venus, old A'nt Cindy's daughter, whose fingers, unlike her mother's, had not yet been so gnarled and twisted by work, age, and rheumatism as to prevent her from performing this exacting task. But the method that Gwen and her slave women had to use retained all its obsolescence though brought abruptly forward a hundred years in time, and guaranteed that to make even a single yard of cloth would take hours. That is, if they were lucky, and nothing broke, collapsed, or otherwise went wrong. When something did, which was nearly always—for that ungainly contraption, with a positively fiendish mind of its own, according to Rose Ann, took a perverse delight in finding ever newer ways of breaking down—a few square inches of rough cloth might take them half a day. Sitting there, doing something as plumb, downright *dull* as weaving was, naturally didn't suit Rambling Rose McKenzie at *all*.

So now, to avoid being dragooned into spelling poor, patient Gwen at that mind-numbing task, she beat a quick retreat to her own private patriotic war effort, which was her medicinal garden. The heart of her effort was the endless rows of poppies she had planted in order to supply the military hospitals in Richmond with desperately needed opium. First of all, she went down the rows, inspecting the buds. Those that were ripe enough, she immediately pierced with a large needle that was carefully tied around her neck on a long, stout thread that had been passed through its eye, since losing a needle with the blockade on was an entirely valid excuse for honest tears. After that, she examined the buds she had already pierced a day or two before. On several of them she found a rewarding quantity of poppy juice that had bled out through the holes she'd stuck into them and had thickened into opium gum. Or, to use the words of the pamphlet that the Medical Branch of the War Department had passed around to such sterling female patri-

ots as she, had "exuded" and become "inspissated by evaporation."
She scraped the thickened gum off into an ordinary teacup with a
dull knife and stood there staring at it. What would happen if I
chewed a little bit of this stuff? she thought, with her habitual
incautious curiosity. Or even made myself a little old corncob pipe
and smoked it? Folks say it gives a body some mighty lively dreams
—and Lord knows, a dream or two would come in handy when the
only he-male critters within reaching and grabbing distance are
cripples, graybeards, or—cowards . . .

She pinched off a bit of the raw opium gum and rolled it into a
ball between her thumb and forefinger. But inches from her wine-
red lips, her hand abruptly halted. She had remembered the
screams of the poor devils in the hospitals she had passed by as the
surgeons' scalpels and bone saws bit into them, while medical
orderlies held them down upon the operating tables. Chloroform,
nitrous oxide "laughing" gas, and ether were all known by then,
but in the blockaded South they were very simply unprocurable.
So the only recourse the Medical Branch had was to fall back upon
that ancient soporific, opium. Some of the better doctors already
understood that opium was addictive, but between that possibility
and the brutal fact that without it the badly wounded died of trau-
matic shock under the knife, the choice was no choice at all. They
used opium—and encouraged the women of the South to grow
poppies in their gardens.

No! Rose Ann told herself sternly. Don't be a jenny-ass, girl!
Those poor, brave fellows need this stuff, and you *don't*. Be a heck
of a thing to waste it giving yourself some wild and wicked dreams.
As if you needed dreams! Why, if what folks swear will drive a
body crazy really would, you'd be swinging by your heels in an
iron cage in bedlam right now!

From the poppy beds, she passed on to her little grove of dogwood trees. The dogwood berry, experiments had proved, when
boiled into a paste, had something of the same alkaloid properties
that made Peruvian bark, or rather the medicine extracted from it,
quinine, such a sovereign remedy against malaria. And Virginia
with her teeming, fetid swamps was malarial country. So Rose
Ann worked, and worked hard, at producing this substitute for
quinine, and several others: the bark of such trees as the willow,
the cherry, the Spanish oak, and not only the bark but the roots as
well of the chestnut, and that dwarf variety of it called the chin-
quapin. Farther south, the women also made and used cottonseed
tea as still another substitute, but the Tidewater was too wet a

clime for cotton to grow well. None of these home remedies, Rose Ann shrewdly suspected, were adequate substitutes for the terribly necessary quinine, or really did any good at all.

If you had any nerve, she told herself furiously, or any of the kind of courage you accused poor Colin of lacking, you'd go North and smuggle a few pounds of quinine in. You could do it. Put on your best Back Bay Boston accent and—

But she knew better than that. In the first place, where would she obtain money for railway fare? She'd have to take a train to get anywhere close to any of the various places where she could sneak across the ill-defined and often changing frontier on foot. And no member of Clan McKenzie ever had a red copper—except maybe Gwen, who, prudent and canny housewife that she was, always managed to save a little. But she could neither ask her elder sister for money nor steal it from her, as she would have from Pa without a second thought. Only Pa drank up what cash came his way faster than anybody could rob him of it, while Jeff and Caleb, who would willingly let her have a dollar or two whenever they had any— which wasn't right frequent!—were away heroically fighting this *awful* war.

Besides which, she had to admit that she was afraid to try it, not so much out of a craven terror of suffering physical harm to her creamy, golden-speckled hide as because of what she was sure her hair-trigger McKenzie temper, bursting like a bombshell crammed with grapeshot, would be sure to drive her to. For she knew what happened at the checkpoints, where vigilant Union officers set what were known as "Yankee women inspectresses" onto a body like ravenous bloodhound bitches. She had found that out because she'd made a point of visiting Maud O'Sullivan, the Irish girl from one of Richmond's slum quarters who'd tried smuggling quinine in to sell for cash to keep her family from practically starving. The Richmond papers had made something of a martyred heroine of poor Maud, going so far as to actually print, with a daring unheard of in those prim Victorian days, that the uncouth Yankee females had abused their authority to the extent of tearing her crinoline and other undergarments from the poor girl's quaking form and then "searching the most intimate parts of her body!" Or so the Richmond *Whig*, at least, had declared in horrified tones. Only poor Maud, lacking the *Whig*'s vocabulary, had put it less gently: "Tell a body this, Miss McKenzie," she had moaned. "How in the Holy Naime uv Our Blessed Mither be I iver gonna convince me Mike, whan he come marchin' hame from this 'ere cruel war 'n' marries me, that I ain't been bad, whan them Yankee bitches have gone 'n' *ruint* me wit' their filthy fingers?"

Which, Rose Ann thought, is an unanswerable question if there ever was one! But persisting in her not exactly unselfish and altruistic efforts to get useful information out of poor Maud, she'd learned the one detail that brought all her fine plans tumbling down about her head like a house of cards. The so-called Yankee women weren't Yankees at all, but Unionist *Southerners* from the western counties that had been made over into the new state of West Virginia, or from the mountains of Tennessee and Kentucky. Against them, her trump card, her carefully cultivated and impeccable New England accent, meant less than nothing. As Southern as she, or even more so, they wouldn't even have recognized it as such. So acknowledging the obvious fact—If one of those delicate mountain flowers were to poke me where a girl sure Lord oughtn't to be poked, at least not with a female finger—except, in dire straits of extreme left-lost-lonesomeness, her own!—I'd kill her and get my fool self hanged, that's for certain!—she'd given up smuggling as a feasible project.

The only other truly interesting and exciting patriotic chore she had been determined to undertake had been closed to her with grim finality by the very authorities to whom she had applied. "Take you on as a *nurse!*" the head surgeons at *all* the military hospitals had thundered to a man. "Why, Miss McKenzie, if I didn't know your father and your family so well, I'd be constrained to think most ill of you! No *decent* young women should ever *dream* of engaging in an occupation involving *daily* such intimate contacts with strange men as to make it unfit for a young *lady* to even contemplate!"

And that had been that, even after she'd stubbornly argued that no man who'd shed his life's blood for Virginia and the South was or could be strange to her, that he'd become, in fact, her brother. For one craggy old sawbones, an old friend of her father's, had growled: "That's not what people will think, and *say*, Rose Ann child. They'll claim he is your—lover . . ."

"Thus donating me three or four *thousand* lovers at the same time?" she'd hooted. "Why, bless your sweet little old generous heart, Doctor! What girl could ask for more?"

Whereupon he'd threatened to call the sentries and have her marched out of there under guard. And that, to repeat, had been that.

So that sparkling late June morning, she went on with her various tasks in her medicinal garden cheerfully enough, for although they weren't wildly exciting, they had the saving grace of keeping her out in the open air she loved, to the utter ruin of her creamy complexion.

Looking up from the little patch of palma Christi, the one plant she disliked, because castor oil is extracted from it, she saw Brutus, Caesar's son—her grandfather, a fine Latinist, had inflicted classical names on all his slaves—driving the herd of sheep Dave McKenzie had bought with a loan obtained from a bank willing to trust even a man so notoriously as improvident as he, once he'd presented proof, in the form of a signed purchase order, that he actually meant to remedy one of the South's lacks, a native source of the wool she had always imported from the North, Canada, Scotland, and Australia, but now because of the blockade was forced to grow at home. As Brutus, with the help of the trained sheepdog her father had also bought, brought the flock closer, she could see his black face was frowning and troubled. He kept turning his head toward the north and east, and his broad nostrils seemed to sniff the air.

"Lord God, Brutus, what's wrong?" she said.

"Them guns, Miss Rose Ann," Brutus said worriedly. "They ain't shootin' no mo'. Not none at all. Hit's so blame quiet my ears fair ache. Don't yourn, missy?"

"Why, bless my soul, they do!" Rose Ann exclaimed; then she stiffened. This was wrong. All wrong. If the Yankee artillery, the one arm in which their superiority in both skill and numbers, was overwhelming, had stopped blasting, it meant the Northerners were up to something. With any other general except that old McClellan at the head of 'em, she reasoned slowly, a body might think they're trying a flanking movement. But Caleb, on the day he'd left to join Stonewall Jackson's staff, had sworn that McClellan had about as much stomach for a fight as a newborn lamb, while, at the same time, being the best tactician in either army when it came to retreats and fortifying positions. "He just doesn't like to attack," Cabe had said, "but for Gawd's sake don't let him get his artillery set up behind a pile of mud and logs, where we've got to attack *him*. Then it's pure unmitigated murder. He'll shoot the bravest regiment, brigade, or even a division into bloody rags before you can sing the first stanza of '*Dixie*' . . ."

So they're retreating, she reasoned, but which way? It took her less than a minute to figure that one out. General Lee's Army of Virginia was now *north* of the damnyankees, spread out in a wide semicircle that extended from Meadow Bridge past Mechanicsville to Gaines's Mill and even beyond that almost to Old Cold Harbor. To retreat that way, McClellan would have to *fight* his way through, attacking the best infantry and riflemen on the face of God's green earth. And he wouldn't do that. He couldn't. That meant suicide for the whole blamed Bluebellied army. So he's got to come down this way! Slanting down along the banks of the York or the James. But if he does that, General Lee will send General Jackson or General Longstreet or General Ewell or—bless my soul!—Jeb Stuart to eat him up alive if he exposes his whole army like that . . .

She halted, her green eyes afire. There wasn't a man in the Confederate Army who knew that country the way she did. She'd earned the nickname Rambling Rose McKenzie, at least in part, by endlessly wandering through that marshy, scrub-choked backcountry from the time she'd been big enough to stay on her first fat Shetland pony until long after she'd become the best equestrienne in the whole Old Dominion. So she knew, with a certitude that left no room for doubt, what General McClellan had to do: He'd sneak his huge army through the depths of White Oak Swamp, which lay between the Chickahominy and the James and ran in the right direction, and break out of it near Long Bridge Road, sure as hell's a-burning!

I'll ride up to General Lee's headquarters—or better still, to Jeb Stuart's—if I can even *find* that handsome devil!—and . . . There she stopped dead once again. As fond as General James Ewell Brown Stuart was of her, he simply wouldn't believe her if she came to him with her own unsupported opinion. He'd laugh at her, try his damnedest to cup one of her breasts in a playful hand, and that only because pinching the bottom of a girl clad in a hoop skirt was a tactical impossibility, kiss her soundly, and advise her, once she'd got her breath back, to leave soldiering to soldiers, then lope away whistling "Jine the Cavalreee" a little out of tune. Rose Ann adored the gallant cavalry leader, a sentiment she was forced to share with every white female Virginian under the age of ninety-six. She'd seen him every time he was in Richmond, because Jeb considered her pretty enough—along with two hundred others, damnit!—to be invited to the parties he gave when momentarily in the capital. She didn't know whom she was fonder of . . . Stop that lying mealymouth talk right now, Rose Ann! she told herself with bitter, but absolutely honest mockery. Which of those two fighting rapscallions you've got the wildest yen to crawl straight into the hay with, if either of them would crook his little finger in your direction, Jeb Stuart or his *aide-de-camp*, Major J. H. Heros von Borcke . . . Or both of 'em at the same time! Ohhh, Lord! But I *would*. And so would every one of the prissy misses who swoon dead away every time Jeb or Heros smiles in their direction, only they're not truthful enough to admit it, even to their silly selves!

By then she was already racing toward the house, because it had come to her what she was going to have to do: serve as a one-woman cavalry scout, and report what she was absolutely sure she'd see if she headed in the right direction, instead of what would seem to any of those stalwart warriors the vaporings of a wild female imagination, even though—or maybe even because!—the almost universally held opinion among the younger Confederate officers was that "Rambling Rose McKenzie is the gamest little girl in the state of Virginia, if not in the entire South!"

Changing into a riding habit, in those days when the clothes of women riders were even more insane than their ordinary garments, which included a hoop skirt quite as wide as the dresses she wore for walking, was a monumental chore. Rose Ann was sorely tempted to borrow a pair of Jeff's pants and mount Prince Rupert astride. But she knew that if she did that, her reputation, shaky at best, would be entirely gone. So she struggled into that voluminous costume which gave her the look of one who is desperately fighting to halfway emerge from an army tent while riding sidesaddle atop her nervous and frisky gelding, and made necessary the use of a small stepladder, or the cupped hands and broad shoulders of Caesar, Brutus, or Cassius, the McKenzie slaves, to boost her up into the saddle. Worse still, the hemline of that riding skirt, designed to maintain the pious Victorian fiction that *ladies*, anyhow, didn't come equipped with such vulgar accouterments as legs, maddened Prince Rupert into near ungovernability by beating without letup against his flank at any pace above a slow walk. Which would have been a minor matter, except that Rose Ann's riding skirt had several *pounds* of buckshot sewn into its hem, to keep it down, even at a hard gallop, and thus preserve the modesty that she honestly didn't give a fig about.

Ready at last, she set out at a brisk trot toward the intersection of the Darbytown and Long Bridge roads, a mile or two beyond where this latter breaks free of the underbrush of White Oak Swamp. And, as it nearly always did, her red-headed McKenzies' luck held true. Or did it? For the rest of her life she was going to wonder. Had she been of a more philosophical bent, she might have established, then and there, the Second Law of Coincidences, which may be stated thus: Coincidences, hazard, blind accidentality, chance *never* serve for anything as far as *arranging* the problems of human existence is concerned, but when it comes to fouling matters up even more dirtily than they already are, the performance of coincidence, and all other such elements beyond human control, is nothing short of magnificent!

Witness the fact that the Union cavalrymen she encountered, encamped and busily cooking their lobscouse by the side of the Long Bridge Road at that exact point where it emerges from the swamp, were members of the Ninth Black Horse Troop, attached to the Eleventh Division, Commonwealth of Massachusetts Volunteers, and Bostonians to the man.

She didn't realize that at first, because her first contact was with the sentries, not readily identifiable regionally, being enlisted men, and working-class Irish to boot. After they sheepishly lowered the muzzles of the Sharps carbines they had pointed at her heart (those very breechloaders that Jeff wanted her, or somebody, to steal an example of, but Rose Ann, who knew absolutely nothing about firearms and cared even less, didn't know that then), she laughed at them merrily and said in her best Back Bay accent, "Oh, my! We really are most frightfully fierce, aren't we now? I say there, my dear fellows, would you mind pointing your artillery in another direction? It's making Prince Rupert nervous . . ."

"Prince Rupert?" one of the sentries said.

"My horse. Guns upset him terribly, the poor dear! Might I ask what it is you're cooking? Smells absolutely delicious! So stop being so warlike and stern, and invite me to join you. I am, I assure you, as hungry as a bear!"

"Pete," one of the sentries said with a grin that was lechery's pristine self, "this 'ere little Josephine Reb is as pretty as a picture! First Southern female I iver seen what don't look like the rear end of a horse. So since we's gone 'n' captured 'er, I votes we turn 'er over to the cap'n—day after t'morry. Le's tek 'er back into that 'ere bog we jist come out of, and see whether what they say about Reb wimmen is true!"

"Now one moment, my good fellow," Rose Ann said crisply. "Who has captured whom is distinctly debatable. And the only reason I'm not going to turn the fine pair of you over to General Lee right now is that it so happens I'm *not* a Reb. I'm from Boston,

Massachusetts, which you ought already know, if you had any ear
for talk . . ."

"Why, gol blimey, 'n' damn me fer a sinner!" the other sentry
said wonderingly. "She *don't* talk like no blinking Reb, Ed me boy.
Sounds 'zactly like them high-muck-a-muck fillies what lives on
Beacon Hill, 'n' looks right through a fella jist like he wasn't
there . . ."

"That's exactly where I do live. On Chestnut Street," Rose said
recklessly. She had her little derringer with her, but shooting a
couple of damnyankee sentries was obviously less than advisable
under the present circumstances, while talking her way out of the
situation seemed much more so.

"Then," the first sentry, seeing his not entirely facetious plans
for having himself one grand 'n' glorious time, by golly, going
glimmering, said sourly, "whot be ye doing down 'ere, Miss Beacon Hill?" .

"Business," Rose Ann said calmly. "My father owns a shoe manufactory at Lynn. And his chief clients for the rougher, cheaper
line of work shoes are generally Southerners, who buy them for
their Negroes. He came down here at the urgent request of his
chief agent in Richmond, who wanted to work out the details of a
massive order to be delivered before this dreadful war that everyone could see coming cut off all possibilities of my father's being
able to supply him. My father's not too well, so I accompanied him
on the trip. And the outbreak of the war caught us down here.
That's all. Except that the Johnny Rebs have been much more
polite and hospitable than you two. So if you don't mean to share a
bit of that lovely-smelling stew you're cooking with a hungry Yankee refugee, please get out of my way and let me finish my morning ride . . ."

The two sentries looked at each other.

"Can't do that, miss," the frustrated lecher said. "This 'ere's a
secret mission, kind of. And if wind o' it gits back to the Johnnies,
me 'n' poor auld Pete here will *be* tomorry's stew, 'cause the cap'n
will serve us up, hair, hide, uniform, boots 'n' spurs 'n' all as the
tenderloin in the noonday mess. So 'tis sorry I am, but ye've got to
come back with me to headquarters. Don't worry: the worse that
kin happen is he detains ye 'til tomorry, for by then we'll have this
'ere operation over wit', as the Johnny Rebs is gonna find out to
their sorrow . . ."

Rose stiffened a little, hearing that, but she kept a wholly admi-
rable control over her nerves. She smiled at the sentries and said

with honeyed sweetness, "Is your captain a handsome man? If so, I might even enjoy the occasion!"

The sentry called Pete grinned at her.

"Wal now, missy," he quipped, "you gotta remember that we be enlisted men. And to the ranks, any officer looks 'zactly like the divil's own hindquarters. But so far the younger ladies ain't fell out in faintin' fits at the sight o' him, so a game li'l girl like ye oughta be able to put up wit' a phiz what musta been a sore trial to his own auld sainted mither!"

The matter was further delayed while they argued over which of them should escort her to headquarters, since leaving their post entirely unguarded was an offense for which they could be court-martialed. Ed, who fancied himself a lady-killer, pulled rank on poor Pete. He was, it seemed, an NCO—a corporal, to be exact, one measurable grade above the buck private in the rear ranks that poor Pete was. So he escorted Rose Ann into the Ninth Black Horse's camp, flirting manfully with her all the way.

She, being her own undomesticated self, flirted gaily back, trying all the time to pry useful military secrets out of him. Which, of course, was an exercise in sheer futility: what the High Command has in mind may filter down the ranks far enough to be figured out on the basis of pure hard experience by a hoary old sergeant major with his sleeves covered with service stripes, but such a lowly form of military life as a squad's corporal was never informed of anything; he was merely ordered to do whatever his superiors considered necessary at any given moment, which quite often included getting himself and his squad killed outright, trying to hold some impossible point of dubious strategic value.

But, actually, Rose Ann needed nothing more than her sea-green eyes, her lively imagination, and an intelligence all the keener for its total unconventionality to discern at once what the damnyankees were up to. Besides, she had the additional advantage of having listened with unflagging attention—largely because she adored her wise old whiskey-scented hound dog of a father—to Dave McKenzie's tales of his adventures during the war with Mexico; more, instead of being bored by his endless armchair, after-the-fact theorizing about the failures of strategy in that conflict, which had been far from the picnic, romp, dress parade that all too many would-be historians make of it, she had been genuinely interested in them, going so far as to argue, pencil in hand, with her father over his rough hand-drawn maps of Buena Vista, Veracruz, Monterrey, so the truth was that the Confederacy probably lost the services of a first-class brigadier general, at the very least, by not enlisting her.

Therefore, while leading Prince Rupert behind her by his bridle, and gaily chattering away as she walked along beside the corporal, she was busily drawing a map of the surrounding territory in her mind. Where they were, at the intersection of the Charles City and Long Bridge roads, the huge Yankee army had to head south to reach the James. Once at the river, they could embark on transport steamers and flee southeastward to the sea. That was obvious. But what was wrong with it was exactly that: it was too blamed obvious; and McClellan, the poorest general in history when it came to attacking, was one of the finest strategists, General Lee himself stoutly maintained, as far as retreats and defensive tactics were concerned that this world of bumblers has ever seen.

So he wouldn't, Rose Ann realized, commit the suicidal folly of trying to embark an army as big as his with an intact enemy at his back, ready to slaughter his men like so many sitting ducks as they went aboard the transports. No. Before retreating further, General McClellan had to make a stand, had to *win* the next battle, or at least inflict such grievous losses on her beloved boys in butternut brown that they'd have to withdraw long enough to let him get his army away.

But—where? In the name of God, where? Rambling Rosie unrolled all that country across the magic-lantern screen of her almost photographic memory. Along one of the three roads leading northwestward toward Richmond? Nonsense! The Charles City, the Darbytown, and the New Market roads ran through flat country, where Jackson's troops, who marched so fast they were called "the foot cavalry," or Jeb Stuart's real cavalry, who two weeks ago had ridden a circle around the entire Yankee army and destroyed seven million dollars' worth of their stores to boot, would chew 'em up piecemeal, until Longstreet, and both the Hills, A. P. and D. H., arrived to swallow whatever there'd be left of the Bluebellies by then.

So—the river itself? Even worse from the Yankees' point of view. With their backs to it, at places like Chaffee's Bluff, Deep Bottom, Turkey Bend, they could only die—unless they placed their artillery out in front of their infantry and risked its being overrun. That country's so damn flat that— she began; then she stopped. Holy Jesus! Malvern Hill! They get their big guns on top of that and halfway up each side and they'll have themselves a living turkey shoot. It's the only thing they're good at. I've heard those poor wounded devils curse those Yankee gunners a million times by now. I've got to get out of here! Got to go warn Jeb, if I can find him. Or—General Lee himself. He's the politest, most gentlemanly man I've ever seen. I don't think he even *knows* a cuss word. So when I tell him I'm Dave McKenzie's daughter, and remind him that Pa fought at his side in Mexico—what was that awful place? Oh, yes, El Telégrafo Hill—he'll let me tell him what I'm sure of, maybe. He doesn't treat women the way most Southerners do—as play toys, idiots, or, worst of all, plaster saints to be stood up on pedestals. Folks say he listens to Mrs. Lee, and acts upon her advice when it seems to him good. Can you imagine Jeb Stuart or Heros von Borcke or Stonewall Jackson listening to anything in skirts? So now to get away from these damnyankees and—

But then suddenly, shockingly, the sentry's reply to an idle question of hers crashed like a canister burst into her consciousness: "Where're we from, miss?" he said cheerfully. "Why, from your own hometown, Boston itself. Don't doubt ye'll know all our officers, since they be jist the kind o' boys what sparks ye young leddies from Beacon Hill . . ."

And I will! Rose thought despairingly. If just one of them was at one of the balls Miss Bradstreet took us to, I'm lost! Because ten minutes after I got to one I was dripping my little old Southern drawl all over every real good-looking fellow there. In certain circles I was known as "the Dixie belle" from one end of Boston to the other!

"Ed dear," she said then sweetly, "I'm awfully tired. Help me back up on my horse, will you? Oh, no! I'm not trying to get away. I'll give you the bridle, so you can lead us in . . ."

With a lecherous grin, Ed obliged, quickly sweeping his big paws up under her crinoline and delightedly squeezing her thighs through her soft, ruffled nainsook pantalets before finally and reluctantly depositing her onto the saddle.

Whereupon Rambling Rosie hit him lightly, playfully with her riding crop, and said with a wrath so patently false that Ed stretched up ten feet tall, sure that, to borrow the language of his descendants, he had it made: "You naughty, naughty boy! I'm going to ask your captain to have you shot at sunrise, so there!"

"Gol blimey, but this 'ere's wan Black Irish sinner who's gonna die happy t'morry, then!" he chuckled. "Ye wouldn't consider lettin' me steal a kiss, would ye? For thet they kin shoot me twicet!"

With a dulcet smile, Rose leaned down and planted a soft, wet kiss upon his grimy, ill-shaven cheek.

"Now behave yourself, Eddie boy," she murmured. "Or I will complain to your captain, so help me!"

And treading a newly discovered path of rosy clouds, Corporal Eddie led her into the camp.

"Present for the cap'n!" he said with a shameless grin as he led his supposed captive up to the pair of logs on which the captain and two lieutenants were sitting, wolfing down the savory stew of meat, potatoes, and onions that was a New England invention, called—especially in Navy circles—lobscouse. All three of them leaped to their feet, swept off their black Kossuth hats that had their left brims pinned up Australian style with the brass badges of the Ninth Black Horse, and stared at her in purest astonishment.

Rambling Rosie shot a swift glance over the three astounded young faces. Like the aviators in later wars, cavalry officers were generally virtual infants, which made handling them child's play for Rose Ann, who was rapidly losing her amateur status as a witch. She saw, to her vast relief, that she knew none of them, and relaxed completely, for if there was any one attribute of hers she knew she could trust, it was her steel trap of a memory.

Which, on this occasion, played her completely false, and for a reason that any really feminine woman can readily understand. To remember a man, you have to *look* at him. Most unfortunately for Rose Ann, for himself, and for several thousand Johnny Rebs and/ or Bolivar Wards, the second lieutenant and third-in-command of the Ninth Black Horse wasn't the sort of man whom women ever look at it. They glanced at his dull, bullfrog-shaped face, at his mottled skin, pitted with the scars of an acne he was not entirely free of even in his twenty-third year, at his bulging eyes, magnified by the thick glasses that should have got him excused from military service, except that he was a volunteer, and by then neither side was refusing volunteers even when they had the aspect of slightly warm corpses before rigor mortis had irreversibly set in, and then looked away, yawning audibly, or even giving visible release to a quick, involuntary shudder.

Still more unfortunately, but quite naturally, the result of this completely unvarying reaction to him by the entire female sex was that Lieutenant Elliot Prescott had come to hate women with his whole poor, pitiful, miserable heart, a fact that made him practically immune to even so enchanting a sorceress as Rose Ann.

You see, the trouble was that he loved them. More than that, he adored them. He was consumed by love, his whole short, thickset body constantly aflame with acute and almost ungovernable desire —which was a tragedy so great that not even the supreme creative geniuses of world literature have ever attempted to depict it, though it is entirely worthy of their skill: the lifelong, intolerable, even unbelievable anguish of those who have learned beyond the faintest ghost of doubt, to the utter annihilation of their feeblest hope, that they are totally unlovable.

So now, peering at Rose Ann through those saucer-shaped spectacles, listening to her gay and accurate chatter about the Boston she had known, and truly loved, he remembered—seething!—her honeyed voice speaking in its own sun-warmed native drawl, saying, "Sorry, Froggie boy, but I just don't feel like dancing right now . . ." Then turning upon the spur of that same instant and slipping bonelessly into the embrace of one of those tall, cool, collected young Back Bay aristocrats whom he hated only a little less then he did women, and swooping away on the sweeping downcurve of the waltz . . .

So he waited until she paused for breath, and broke in harshly to Captain Sedgwick: "Sir, make her get down from there. Put her under arrest. She's a Reb spy, sir. I happen to have met her some time ago. Oh, she knows Boston all right, and can imitate our accent almost perfectly. She attended Miss Phoebe Bradstreet's School for Young Ladies on Court Street—until she was expelled and shipped back down here to her native Virginia for scandalous behavior . . ."

Captain Jonathan Sedgwick stared at him.

"Elliot, are you *sure?*" he said.

"Absolutely, sir! She eloped with the son of that rich Italian merchant, Giovanni Lucarelli. Signor Lucarelli had the marriage annulled because young Giuseppe was under legal age. So this lovely witch is both a cast-off wife and a widow, since poor Giuseppe, who was a friend of mine, finally managed to get himself killed at Seven Pines . . ."

Sinner that she was, poor Rose was not yet a hardened one. At that terrible news, the great tears burst, exploded from her eyes, went flooding down her cheeks.

"Oh, no!" she moaned. "Not my Joe-Joe! Not my sweet little boy baby doll!"

"Tom," Captain Sedgwick said gravely to First Lieutenant Thomas Meredith, "take the bridle of her mount. Young woman, I'm afraid I'll have to place you under arrest . . ."

Which was when Rose Ann came alive. Before Lieutenant Meredith's clawing fingers were within six inches of Prince Rupert's drooping bridle, she'd snatched it up and brought her crop whistling down across her gelding's flank. Totally unaccustomed to such treatment, Prince Rupert gave an enormous bound. Only such a horsewoman as Rose Ann was could have stayed on him, seated sidesaddle, which was a miserable way to have to ride. By the second bound she was beyond the campfire and almost clear, when Second Lieutenant Elliot Prescott did what quite possibly only he among the hundreds of thousands of men in the Union hosts was capable of: drawing his heavy service revolver, he coolly took aim, and shot her.

His marksmanship was either very good or very bad, depending upon where your sympathies lay. That .44 caliber slug from his 1860 model Army Colt tore into the small of her back, just left of her spinal column, smashed her lowest rib to hell and begone, but was deflected by its encounter with tough McKenzie bone and angled still further to the left, plowing all the way through her slender middle, but far enough out not to perforate her dainty pink guts.

What happened next legitimately became part of the McKenzie Saga. Of pure Celtic race, of a people whose women have nearly always outmatched their men as far as sheer valor is concerned, of bloodlines reaching back to Queen Boadicea herself, Rose Ann performed pure prodigies of iron-willed courage that day. And she performed them with almost groveling humility, not even knowing she was being brave.

What saved her, of course, was the fact that there was no pursuit. For Captain Jonathan Sedgwick and Lieutenant Thomas Meredith stood there in that little clearing glaring at Second Lieutenant Elliot Prescott with total contempt.

"Elliot," Tom Meredith said flatly, "a man who would shoot—or even shoot *at*—a woman is lower than a dog."

"I quite agree," the captain said. "Good thing you missed, or by God I'd bust you back to buck private and set you to cleaning out latrines!"

"But, sir!" Poor Elliot almost wept. "I couldn't let her get away! She'll go to the Rebs, tell them—"

"What?" Tom Meredith said disgustedly. "That she ran into a bunch of Yankee horse troopers on the edge of a swamp? How much attention d'you think the Rebel High Command will pay to that? If she even gets to *see* anybody of importance, which I doubt.

She'll be too busy fighting off the first line of corn-fed pickets, pretty as she is. They'll only start to listen to her, if then, when she finally convinces 'em she's not going to let 'em remove her frilly little drawers . . ."

"Captain, sir!" Elliot Prescott implored. "Send riders after her! She's a spy, I tell you, a spy!"

"Elliot," the captain sighed, "you've been reading too many penny dreadfuls, and seeing too many melodramas. Now shut up, will you? And that, damnit, is an order!"

Which, of course, helped Rambling Rosie not all, because she didn't know it. Half a mile from there, she pulled Prince Rupert up.

I'm hit, her mind wailed. I'm—shot. I'm bleeding something awful. I'm going to die. Goodbye, Jeffie love. Goodbye, Pa. I'm sorry. Don't—grieve. Specially not you, Pa. Jeff's got his Mary Sue, but you've got—nobody. But don't—please don't grieve, Pa. Stay drunk a week, a month, a year—then forget me, huh? Never was any good, anyhow. Bad, wicked, immoral, and not—fit to be a wife and mother.

But You hear even the wicked when they're dying, don't You, Lord? So I ask only one thing: Give me an hour—two. Let me do some good before You take me. Let me get to Jeb, tell him to General Lee tell him to General Jackson to Cabe even to poor Colin to anybody I can tell where *they* are, what they're getting set to do— all those cannon, those awful terrible cannon up there on Malvern Hill, where they can—

No! Not the roads! Back. Back into the swamp. They can't follow you there, you know every damn path, every trail, and they— they've got to saddle up first 'cause they were eating their rations, but even so, out in the open they could catch me easy but in here in here in here—

She sat there on Prince Rupert and explored her middle with trembling fingers. Found both the entry and exit holes that the ball had made. Thought, slowly, quietly, carefully: Gut-shot. Pa says not one in a million survives being hit this way. So all right, I won't survive it I don't have to survive it all I got to do is stay alive until I get to where the army is. My petticoat. Tear some strips. Stuff 'em into these two holes give the blood something to clot on slowly now carefully now it doesn't hurt too bad yet just numb 'cause the shock hasn't worn off yet but when it does it's going to be plumb awful but I mustn't moan or cry or scream because this damn swamp is full of damnyankees and—

That's it. Even—feels better, doesn't it? Get going, Rambling Rose! This way—toward Richmond. Pa sent a whole lamb up to General Lee with a note—"In memory of Telegraph Hill, Dave McKenzie"—and he told Cassius to take it to take it—where? To Mechanicsville. Ohhh, Lord! That's so blamed far! Seven whole miles north of Richmond and I've got to get to Richmond first. Even then I can't go through town 'cause they'll grab me and put me in the hospital and nobody will believe me and the Yankees will get to Malvern Hill and fortify it and then—

She rode on grimly through the swamp. She ripped off more petticoat and tied it around her waist and looped the free end down through one of the cinch rings of her saddle and tied it there so that even if she fell off, Prince Rupert would bring her in, dragging her poor carcass in, which would maybe warn her beloved corn-fed boys even if she'd be dead by then and couldn't tell 'em—

But she didn't fall off. She kept right on riding. She was hurting now, hurting worse than she had ever believed it was possible for a human being to hurt and not die of it, and she couldn't even scream because she could hear the Yankees crashing through the underbrush like elephants on a rampage and she—silent—hurting bad, so bad, praying, saying, "Colin, forgive me. You were right to run. Nobody ought to be made to face this. I'm scared of the hell-fire we've both plumb earned with the sin we did together that wasn't even any fun, that was its own punishment maybe, so now—

"Gwen. Forgive me too, honey. You're an angel and I've been an awful sister to you flirting with Cabe and plaguing you and making you do all the work while I—"

Much of the time she was semi-conscious, slumped in that saddle, willing herself beyond the will's possibilities not to fall. Riding on, hurting on, praying, imploring, humbling herself, saying, "Take me. Send me down to hell to burn forever but first let me get there let me get there let me get there— Oh, Jesus! I hurt. I hurt. I hurt hurt hurt hurt and I can't won't will *not* scream. Our Father which art in heaven have mercy upon me a sinner a poor dying bedraggled sinner but let me get there—Lord!"

She got there. Thus demonstrating what? That life is an absurdity. Without reason, meaning, truth. But maybe that when a body rides through the bottom pits of hell on the basis of sheer guts, propped up by naked will, standing tall amid the torn and shattered rags of her flesh, she can lend it some mighty convincing substitutes. Like self-sacrifice. Like dignity. Like valor. Anyhow, she got there, maybe because too many lives depended on hers, so she couldn't let it slip away too soon accept the comfort of not hurting anymore the final relief of blessed nothingness the surrender of her sweet flesh to the Bard's convocation of politic worms—

When she rode into the yard of that house on the Mechanicsville Road it was Sunday morning, the twenty-ninth. She had been riding all night long, and yet she was both alive and conscious—sort of. She said, "General Stuart. Take me to him. I've got to tell him, to say—"

The sentry grinned at her. Her riding habit was black. He couldn't see that it was one solid board-stiff mass of dried blood or make out that she was burning up with fever, or that her tiny waist was swollen drum-tight and threatening to burst through that whalebone corset that she didn't need at all but this time had served to keep her guts from falling out of her middle, maybe.

"Honey," he said, "who the hell knows where old bright-eyed and bushy-tailed Gen'l Stuart is? Now tek me, fer instance. All the fillies sez I'm a reel prutty boy. 'N' you jes' doan know how sweet I kin be, when you gits t' know me . . ."

"General—Lee?" she whispered.

"Three houses down the road. But aw shucks, honey, Gen'l Lee is a sight too old for you and—"

He stopped still. Said in the strangled tones of total awe: "Lord God Awmighty!" Dropped his Enfield. Put up his two arms and caught her as she fell.

"Does anyone *know* who this young woman is?" General Lee said.

"I do, sir," a voice from the crowd of officers said, or rather croaked.

"Step forward, then," the General said; then: "You're Major—"

"Henry, sir. Caleb Henry. General Jackson's staff . . ."

General Lee stiffened.

"Tears, Major?" he said quietly. "Hardly the sort of behavior to be expected of one of General Jackson's aides . . ."

"Yes, sir. I know, sir. But hell yes, I'm crying. And if she dies I'm going to bawl like a yearling calf. I'm never going to stop . . ."

"She's—a relative of yours, Major?" the general said.

"My sister-in-law, sir. The gamest female human on the face of God's green earth. The daughter of a man who claims he served with you in Mexico, sir. But I won't push that one. My pappy-in-law's mouth bears no relationship to the Book of Common Prayer . . ."

"His name? This young woman's?" the general said.

"Dave McKenzie, sir. Of McKenzie's Hundred. And that game little critter in there is his daughter Rose Ann—"

The General smiled. "Well, Dave did part company with the truth some time ago," he said pleasantly, "but not in this case. He and I lay behind a pair of logs all night long, back of the hill the Mexicans called El Telégrafo, while most of Santa Ana's lancers rode all over us. And I don't know which of us was the scareder . . . Dave's daughter, eh? Explains a lot. Tell me, Major, have you any idea who shot her up like that?"

"No, sir. I'd guess—Yankee sentries. Trying to stop her from doing what she *did* do, sir: riding all night long, bleeding like a stuck shoat the whole time, to come here to you, sir. To tell you something—"

"That's obvious, Major," General Lee sighed, "but what?"

"Gen'l," a deep voice boomed, "I had that sentry who brought her in questioned. And he says—"

"What, General?" Robert E. Lee said.

"That she just kept repeating over 'n' over: Malvern Hill, Malvern Hill—and mumbling about cannons, guns—" "Prince" John Magruder said.

General Lee stood there, turned to stone. Become a statue. Only his eyes were alive. They took fire.

"Malvern Hill! But of course! Somebody bring me a map!" he said.

All the great generals, Lee and his lieutenants, Prince John Magruder, Stonewall Jackson, Longstreet, B. Huger, the two Hills, A. P. and D. H.—except, of course, J. E. B. Stuart, who was off raiding White House Station and burning Yankee stores—were poring over that map when the Surgeon General of the Army of Northern Virginia came out of that back room.

"Well, General?" General Lee said.

"Bad, sir," the Surgeon General sighed. "Appears to me the poor little thing hasn't a hope nor a prayer, but—"

"Oh, Jesus!" Caleb all but screamed.

"Control yourself, Major!" General Lee said, not unkindly. "You were saying, General?"

"That there's one hopeful sign, sir. She ought to have been dead since yesterday, and she's not. People that tough quite often live when all the chances are against it. If she had careful, devoted nursing, maybe . . . But that would mean pulling one of the matrons out of the hospitals or enlisting the services of one of the Catholic nursing sisters. Up here, all we've got are male medical orderlies, and that simply wouldn't do!"

General Lee turned to Caleb.

"What about—your wife, Major?" he said. "She's our little heroine's sister, isn't she?"

"Yes, sir. And she'll be a widow by her own hand if I don't fetch her up here to nurse poor Rose Ann. Your permission, sir?"

General Lee was noted for his unvarying observance of every nicety of good military form. He turned to Stonewall Jackson.

"Well, Tom," he said gently, "d'you think you could spare this young fellow for a couple of days?"

"Of course. It's a worthy cause, General. Permission granted, Major. Get going now!" Stonewall Jackson barked.

"Me little Rosie!" Dave McKenzie blubbered. "Me own poor little darlin' Rosie! Laying there a-dying! 'N' for what, I ask you Lord, for what?"

"Father, will you please hush?" Gwen said tiredly. "I'm sorry I ever brought her home. Of course, that house was just plain awful, but at least I wouldn't have had *you* underfoot up there . . . Oh, hello, Mary Sue! I reckon the Negroes' grapevine brought you the news?"

"Sure Lord did," Mary Sue Hunter said. "Gwen, have you got a room where you could put me? I've come to stay. To spell *you*, honey. You do have to sleep sometime, y'know. And just like Mama says, you just can't leave a body as bad off as poor Rose Ann is to the tender mercies of nigger wenches. Oh, I know she doesn't cotton to me none at all, but she *is* Jeff's sister and—"

"That's very sweet of you, my dear," Gwen said, "and the truth is, I really do need some help. You can bunk with me now that Caleb isn't here . . ."

"That's what *you* think, Gwennie," that all-gone, bone-weary voice from the doorway said. "But don't let that fret you, my sugarplums! I'll sleep in the middle, and you girl babies can roll them ol' bones, as the darkies say, to see which one of you gets a whack at me next!"

"Cabe," Gwen said sweetly, "isn't there any way I could meet a Yankee sharpshooter? I've got a twenty-dollar gold piece all saved up for the philanthropic person who brings me home your mangy hide so I can nail it to the stable door . . ."

"Howdy, Cabe," Dave McKenzie rumbled. "They give you leave?" Then: "Holy Jesus, son! You—you're hurt! You're bleeding!"

"A scratch," Caleb said contemptuously. "A spent and ricocheting ball. Creased my jaw. All it'll do will be to give me an interesting scar for all the patriotic li'l darlings like Mary Sue here to kiss . . . How's about it, honey? Doncha want to be the first to reward the wounded hero?"

"That's Gwen's job, Major," Mary Sue said, "but you had better let me tend to that there nasty cut. I'll clean it up and bandage it too, before it gets all infected up on you . . ."

"Later," Cabe sighed. "Right now what I could do with is a shot of your drinking whiskey, Father Dave. I'm so wore out and beat up that it feels like I'm walking on the bleeding gums of my back eyeteeth."

"Coming up!" Dave exulted, glad of this excuse to have a snort himself. "But tell us, boy—what's a-happening? Mighty heap o' artillery fire yistiddy!"

Caleb bowed his head, looked up again. Nodded in the direction of the half-open bedroom door. He could see the slight, elongated mound that Rose Ann's figure made, lying there still—too still.

"How is she?" he croaked.

"Holding her own, I think," Gwen said. "And I'm going to pull her through this, Caleb! I'm a McKenzie too, and as stubborn as they make 'em. Rose Ann has always been an awful pain in that part of the anatomy on which one sits, but she's my baby sister, and the truth is, I love her."

"She is—adorable," Cabe said with quiet bitterness. "And you've got to save her, Gwennie honey. Be just too rotten to let her die— for nothing . . ."

"For nothing?" Mary Sue piped up. "But everybody's calling her the greatest heroine of this war! They say she rode twenty miles while badly wounded to save General Lee's army and—"

"Twenty-five," Caleb rasped. "And not 'badly wounded'— butchered. Gut-shot. Her poor little pink tripes made into hash by a heavy-caliber ball. I couldn't have stood the pain of jolting over that first-class imitation of hell on a horse. I'd have screamed my guts up. But she didn't scream. She couldn't. There were Yankees all around her, and she had to get through to warn us . . ."

"Wal, didn't she?" Dave rumbled.

"Yes. Only she reckoned without the military mind. Old Cabe Henry's Second Law. The First Law states: You can never expect a nigger to do anything worth a damn, because any nigger smart enough to do anything worth a damn will apply that intelligence to finding the shortest route to Canada . . ."

"And the Second?" Gwen said quizzically.

"That there ain't no sich animal as a good soldier, because any man smart enough to be a *good* soldier is too damn smart to be any kind of a soldier. Any reasonable degree of cogitative ability would immediately discern the advisability of hauling ass in the direction where the whispering of the gentle breezes through the grass and the twittering of the birds are not drowned out by heavy gun-fire . . ."

"There's a point in all this mockery of yours, I reckon," Gwen said, "but I really wish you would get to it . . ."

"All right. Marse Robert was warned. Our darling Ramblin' Rosie warned him—at the cost of her own sweet life, maybe. So great military mind that he is, he came up with a plan for dealing with the situation that was a beaut—on paper. First the Yankee rear guard had to be taken out. Classic tactics, Father Dave. So he sent Prince John a-hopping straight east along the Williamsburg Road. Us, the sterling heroes of Jackson's foot cavalry, and D. H. Hill's boys were to come swarming over the Grapevine Bridge and mash the damnyankees up north of White Oak Swamp. Longstreet and A. P. Hill were supposed to backtrack up the damn Chickahominy again, cross the Meadow and Mechanicsville bridges, sweep all the way around Richmond and, with old B. Huger backing 'em up, cut McClellan off before he could get to Malvern Hill from the south end of the swamp—"

"Sounds all right to me," Dave rumbled. "Don't see a damn thing wrong with tactics like them, boy . . ."

"Too pretty. Too neat," Cabe snarled. "Took no account of the natural ass-backwardness of human nature. First, it was already Sunday, so old Jack Jackson wuz standin' in the need o' prayer. So that's what he did: prayed. And set us to rebuilding the Grapevine Bridge that we didn't need worth a good goddamn, 'cause we could have waded that little stream without half trying. And Prince John Magruder crept along. Didn't get to Savage's Station 'til way after midday, where those wild Irishmen of the New York 69th counterpunched him dizzy and got into the swamp without any real trouble at all. So one whole day, that poor little Ramb had shed her goddamn gallant blood to give us, was blown away that way, wasted . . ."

"Jesus!" Dave said prayerfully. "But surely that next morning—Monday, wasn't it?—y'all . . ."

"Did nothing. More bridge building. North of the damn swamp when we should've been on the *south* of it to stop the Yanks from getting to that murderous hill. And Longstreet and Hill—A. P. that is—who *were* in the right place, piddled around waiting for Huger to come up. Only Huger couldn't. The damnyankees had felled trees across all the swamp roads, and us lordly Sothorons, who are always fresh out of something, jist happened to be a wee bit shy o' axes . . ."

"Lord!" Dave groaned.

"And Ca'lina General Theophilus Holmes, marching his troops up or down the river road to beat McClellan to Malvern Hill, exposed their left flank to the Bluebelly Navy's gunboats on the James. Those bombards and mortars started tossing those long slim shells that our boys call 'lampposts' at them—'real careless like,' according to those Ca'lina Crackers. They were just about to panic when old Holmes, who's as deaf as a gatepost, turned around and sez, 'Didn't I hear firing?' So they started laughing instead of running, and actually did get to Malvern Hill. But McClellan's advance guard got there first. And started shooting the—well—masculine attributes off those rednecks, 'til old Holmes howled for help. Longstreet sent Prince John to bail the old fart out. But after he'd let Magruder go, old Jim started attacking the Yankee flank that was still sliding toward that bloody hill that poor little Rosie had tried to make us a present of, but the damnyankees have plain done quit getting scared of us sterling warriors anymore, so they turned right around and mauled old Jim Longstreet so bad that he sent riders flying to call Prince John Magruder back. And there we had old deaf-'n'-dumb Holmes waiting for Magruder, and Magruder marching back to help out Longstreet, and Longstreet fighting—and winning, sort of—the Battle of Frayser's Farm or Glendale, but taking so long to do it, even with Hill to help him, that the bulk of the Bluebellies got to Malvern Hill by dark. And another day that poor darling lying there had got her poor little pink tripes perforated to give us was gone—"

"And on Tuesday?" Gwen whispered.

"When I saw that hill, honey, I writ you a farewell note and pinned it in my buttonhole," Caleb said quietly. "The whole Army of the Potomac was up there, with two hundred and fifty of those guns they can call their shots with by now pointing down at us tier upon tier. And then, figuring, I reckon, that McClellan hadn't any you-know-whats, Marse Bob sent us in to charge that hill. Armistead's corps, out of Huger's division, didn't even get started. The Yanks murdered 'em like sitting ducks where they stood. So we charged 'em and charged 'em and charged 'em, and they killed us and killed us and killed us—seven thousand poor brave bastards all told. 'Cause McClellan's got balls all right. He just likes to keep 'em warm behind breastworks. So if that poor child dies it will have been in vain, 'cause there ain't no gen'l born what's got a lick o' sense, not even Marse Bob . . ."

"Oh, Lord!" Gwen moaned.

"Tell you one thing, though. You've got your lover boy back, sugar. Old Colin has got his million-dollar wound, though ain't nobody ever going to make me believe it wasn't self-inflicted. A shot-off kneecap, and if that ain't a reeel fancy Dan way of doing it, I'll eat my boots, spurs and all. That business of shooting a nice round hole through your foot doesn't work anymore. You come up with that one and your cap'n will growl, 'C'mon, you incestuous diddler of all your close female relatives, limp! But clear clean out that shit trench—'scuse me, Mary Sue! I meant latrine—and haul these here mules some more hay whilest you're at it . . .' "

"Caleb," Gwen said, her voice tight with almost visible fury, "this is shameful. This is unpardonable, and you know it! The Claibornes have always been heroes, in every war we've fought so far, and yet you *dare* stand there and say—"

"That his balls are crowding his tonsils for wiggling space," Caleb drawled. " 'Cause that's how high they've done gone and crawled by now, sugar. That sweet li'l three-quarters-dead child in there knows the truth, after having had it out with him in private. But, being a real lady—hell, a real *woman*, a quality you don't even understand, Gwen o' my heart—she refrained from telling you that the apple of your longing eye damn nigh chopped my arm off at the shoulder at Manassas, to get me the hell out of the way when I tried to impede his departure for points unknown . . ." He paused, grinned at her like a tired, wickedly mocking wolf, and went on: "So let me tell you one thing, honey chile: When I leave here tonight, I'm likely to be gone a long time. But because this here outsized squabble twixt us and the Yankees has cured me of any lingering taste for turd I may have had, I'm not asking you to make me any promises. Specially not since the one you made me before God, and in the sight of men, you've broken ten thousand times by now in your treacherous little heart . . ."

"Ten *million*," Gwen corrected him with icy calm. "So?"

"So hear this: When—and *if*—I come back, I don't aim to stage a court of inquiry into your doings whilst I wasn't here. And I'm hereby formally requesting that you button them sweet, kissable, shell-pink lips of yourn, and not volunteer me any information I just plain don't need to know, and might have more than a mite o' trouble handling. That's fair enough, ain't it?"

"Quite," Gwen said.

"But don't you *ever* let me find out accidental-like it was *him*. Reckon I could forgive you most anybody else, the hard facts of time and distance and female human nature being taken into consideration. I'd merely tenderize your tail for a week o' two and then forget it . . ."

"Caleb," Gwen seethed, "I will *not* listen to this! You're implying that I'm—"

"A potential adulteress and a whore? As what woman *ain't*, the pressures being great enough? Even my sainted prim 'n' proper li'l old mama up in heaven, I reckon . . ."

"Jesus God!" Dave McKenzie bellowed.

"Sorry, Father Dave, but that's so, and as a grown man what ain't no fool, for all the rotgut you've cooked your brains in by now, you know it. Anyhow, Gwen darling, if you foul your—hell, *my*—nest with that white-livered, ball-less wonder, I'll kill him. Dead. And break every bone in *your* body, starting with your dee-lightful 'n' delectable little estival tuberosity, and working both ways, north *and* south . . ."

He stood there grinning at her, quietly, peacefully. Then: "How's about that snort you promised me, Father Dave?" he said.

Chapter Five

"Where is she?" Colin Claiborne grated.

Gwen looked at the leg, thickly bandaged and supported by splints, he had sticking straight out past the dashboard of his buggy, one half of which had been cut away to accommodate it. He would never, she already knew, be able to bend that leg again.

"In there," she said, nodding her head toward the decaying bulk of McKenzie's Manor. "Wait. I honestly don't think she's dying, in spite of what Dr. Hendricks said. She was only hit once, with one lone revolver bullet. And that's not enough to kill a McKenzie. An ancestor of ours once came walking home after a battle with his claymore in one hand and his head in the other. He made signs to his wife that she was to sew that severed horror back in place atop his bloody neck. A couple of weeks after she'd done so, he was as good as new. But then, she was a witch, like all the McKenzie women . . ."

Colin stared at her. His eyes were very bleak.

"Are *you* baiting me too, Gwen?"

"Yes, come to think of it, I suppose I am," she said bitterly. "I've had many a disappointment in my life, but none more cruel than learning you'd played the coward, Colin. Unless you're going to tell me that you've been traduced, defamed . . ."

He bowed his head. Looked up again.

"No," he said harshly, "I'm not going to tell you that, because I haven't been. I am a coward. I just wasn't aware of it before. No occasion to test the matter, I suppose. A pity. Because if I had known it, I wouldn't have gone to war. A fine example of poltroonery like me is too dangerous to have around. Puts other men's lives in jeopardy when he panics and leaves a hole in the line where his worthless carcass should have been. But enough of this! Where are your Negroes? Climbing down from a buckboard is another of the many things I can't quite manage these days . . ."

"I'll help you down," Gwen said sweetly. "Unlike you lordly Claibornes, we dirt-poor McKenzies only have three blacks, who are about their far-flung chores at the moment. Don't worry, I am very strong—or does it offend the wounded hero to have to accept assistance from—a woman?"

"Gwen, stop it!" Colin said sharply. "That poor little creature lying in there has every right to rebuke, even bait me, if she sees fit. *You* haven't."

" 'Oh, what fools we mortals be!' " Gwen quoted bitterly. "You're perfectly right, of course, Colin. I haven't, have I?"

He stared at her then, a long, slow time. Afterward it came to him that that was the first time in both their lives that he had ever really *looked* at Gwendolyn McKenzie Henry.

By, God, she's—breathtaking! he thought. Then why haven't I noticed it before? Because, he reasoned slowly, I don't think I've ever seen her with such high color flaming in her cheeks until this very moment. Born of her anger, her disgust—her abysmal contempt for—a coward. But *why* should she feel that way about it? What's it to *her?*

It didn't take him very long to figure that out. Cowards, as a class, generally escape dolthood completely, an intelligent perception of the realities of this life being one of the root causes of pusillanimity. But once he had, he rejected his all too accurate estimate of the situation. It was—too disturbing. He wasn't sure he could handle it.

Quietly he reached behind him and drew out his crutches. He passed one of them over to Gwen. The other he extended downward until its tip touched the graveled drive. He put his right hand on the padded armpit crossbar of the crutch, and his left hand out to her.

She took it. And upon the spur of that same instant, he knew. Very quietly, and soberly, and perfectly, he knew. He could feel the nerves crawling like a nest of tiny vipers beneath the warm flesh of her palm. But he didn't exult in that knowledge. Rather, it troubled him—badly.

Are you, he snarled at himself in the bitter clarity of his mind, now going to add swinehood to cowardice?

He swung himself down out of the buggy, lurched clumsily as his good foot, the left one, struck the drive. He would have surely fallen if she had not swept both slim arms around him, clutched him with almost swooning tenderness to her breasts.

She didn't release him at once, as she should have. She couldn't. That was the simple, the appalling fact.

He hung there in her arms, staring down into her pale blue eyes, seeing the tide of primrose mounting ever higher in her cheeks. He bent willessly toward the wild flutter of shell pink her lips had become. But at the last agonizing instant, the final hairsbreadth from her mouth, he halted. Sighed. Said, "You'd better let go of me, my dear. We're making rather a bit of a spectacle of ourselves, y'know . . ."

"Oh, God!" she moaned. "Colin, you mustn't think, believe that meant—"

"Anything?" he said quietly. "Of course not, Gwen. I am still—a coward who fled the field, shot his own kneecap off in order never to have to go back into that horror or to face his country's foes again. And you are the wife of a brave and gallant soldier who deserves everything you have to give. Come, my dear, let's go in and see Rose Ann. If—which God grant!—she's not dying, why'd she send for me?"

Gwen bent her silvery-blond head, said sharply, "One moment, Colin!" she shuddered convulsively. Straightened up. Dashed the sapphire and liquid crystal, and pearls gone suddenly molten, from her eyes.

"I—I'm all right now," she said gaily, and gave his arm a little squeeze. "And I hereby promise to keep my—somewhat unpredictable—reactions—under better control in the future. Why'd Rose Ann send for you? Because *she* thinks she's dying. And she's not. Or rather she wouldn't be if she weren't willing herself to. It's all, dear boy, in her weird and wonderful little mind. She seems to believe she's done you a terrible injustice. She cannot, it also seems, rest quietly in her grave until she's rectified matters. And—d'you know what, Colin?—I'm all but certain that once you've set her mind at ease, she'll bounce back from her slough of despond like an India rubber ball . . ."

"Then come on!" Colin got out, hope become a pair of white-hot tongs tearing at his heart, his mind seething. Oh, God, if she'll only forgive me I'll march out on this gimpy leg, catch cannonballs in my teeth, and capture Washington single-handed! Which was, of course, so much mental bombast, and he knew it.

When they came into the bedroom, Colin's heart very nearly stopped beating. While always slender, Rose Ann had been, up until the moment he had last seen her, nicely rounded and sweet-curving, though not to that fine excess that Southerners called "pleasingly plump." Now she was emaciated, skeletal. In fact, she weighed on that early August day an ounce over sixty-three pounds, having lost a full forty-two from her normal weight.

Colin hung there. His eyes went scalded, blind.

"Oh, my God!" he moaned.

Rose Ann opened one bright green eye, then the other. They quite eclipsed what was left of her face. She put out a claw that would have disgraced a starving sparrow, made a horribly macabre grimace that was supposed to be a soft and winning smile.

"Come here, Colin," she murmured. "Can't talk—loud. Can't even talk, really. So kneel down here beside my bed and—"

"Rose Ann!" Gwendolyn gasped.

"Ohhhh, Lord!" Rose wailed, and started to cry. Terribly, bitterly. Colin realized that he would rather have charged up Malvern Hill into the muzzles of the Yankee sixty-four-pounders twenty times than hear her cry like that.

"You see?" she moaned. "I'm bad, wicked, thoughtless! Didn't even remember 'bout your poor leg! Come close as you can. Sit down beside me on the edge of the bed. You can do *that*, can't you?"

"Of course," Colin said, and lurched forward on his crutches. "Oh, Rose Ann, honey, darlin', my own—"

Gwen whirled at that, started for the door.

"No!" Rose Ann shrilled. "Please stay, Gwen! I *want* you to hear what I have to say to Colin. Specially the part I've got to tell him about—you . . ."

"Please, my dear," Colin said to—he reminded himself again!— his best friend's wife.

Gwen turned, came very slowly back into the bedroom, sank down into a chair. Her face was ghost white.

"Colin," Rose Ann whispered, "I want to beg your pardon, mighty humbly. If I could, I'd go down on my knees before you and ask you to—forgive me. I was—a fool. When I—called you a c-c-coward, g-g-gave you the white feather, I had no idea what— getting shot felt like . . ."

"And now you do," Colin said bitterly.

"And now I do. Nobody—ought to be asked to face that. Man who won't run when folks are shooting at him is a swaybacked spavined jackass of a fool. Only people sillier than that are the men who start wars in the first place. 'Cause nothing's worth killing people over! Or shooting their guts out of 'em and leaving 'em to hurt like that and—"

"Ride like that," Colin said gravely. "Twenty-five terrible miles watering all the earth with gallant blood. Teeth locked shut so that never a whimper would escape you to save—"

"Nothing. Nobody. I messed up as usual. Took so long to get to General Lee that those damnyankees had time and to spare to get all those big guns up on Malvern Hill! D'you know what that *feels* like, Colin? Not just to get your stupid guts shot out but to have s-s-seven *th-th-thousand* good, sweet-loving Southern boys *dead* and on your soul?"

"Oh, my God!" Gwen gasped. "So *that's* what you've been thinking! Rose Ann, you're wrong! Oh, my darling, you're so terribly wrong! You—"

"Got there in plenty of time," Colin said quietly. "Only men, stupid *men*, including General Lee, mucked up, as usual. We ought to quit, turn the world over to you women, so it would be run with a little decency, a little sense. You saved those seven thousand boys, Rose Ann. And then men, damn-fool men—and cowards like me— turned right around and lost them for you all over again. So don't blame yourself for that, my love . . ."

"I don't believe you!" Rose Ann said.

"I'll prove it to you," Colin said flatly. "Later. By tomorrow, or the day after. Now what else did you want to tell me?"

"About—Gwen. Look at her, Colin! First and last time you're ever going to get a chance to—gaze upon an angel . . ."

"Now, Rose Ann!" Gwen admonished her.

"An angel. Who worked 'til she dropped, taking care of me, who's never done anything but make her un-un-unhappy. Even that li'l snip of Mary Sue Hunter is better'n me, 'cause she pitched right in and helped out all she could. But Gwen—whom I'm never going to be able to pay back for what she did. For bathing me and combing my hair and feeding me with a spoon and—and yes, I will say it!—wiping my poor little old stinky behind like a baby's! That's pure—goodness sitting there, Colin, the best sister any girl could ever ask for, and all I've ever done is foul up her life for her. So I want you to promise me two things—"

"Which are?" Colin said.

"That if poor Cabe doesn't come back alive from this cruel war, you'll marry her, and make her happy. Don't shut me up, Gwen! Let me run off at the mouth as usual. 'Cause she loves you, Colin. She always has, and maybe always will . . ."

"Oh, my God!" Gwen gasped.

"But if Cabe does come back, I want you to promise me to get clean out of the state of Virginia. Go out to California or even to Australia. Give 'em the chance that with you still here and underfoot they won't even have. 'Cause I'm betting that when this war is finally over, if Cabe quits being so damn-fool brave and comes back alive, they'll stop fighting like cats and dogs and sort of cling to each other."

"Rose Ann," Colin whispered, "couldn't I, in that second case, just stay here—and marry—you?"

"No, Colin," Rose Ann said sadly. "And not 'cause you ran from the battle. I don't care about that anymore. As I said, I think now you were maybe smart. But—I don't love you. I grant you that love's not that all-fired important, but not loving a person the *way* I don't love you, *is*. I—forgive me, Gwennie!—just don't want you to touch me, Colin. I like you. I think you're a nice boy who's going to get his guts unscrambled one fine day and grow up to be a man. But I just don't want you to touch me, which isn't an insult, believe me, 'cause I just might *like* being touched by a fellow who couldn't even hold a candle to you in any way that counts. Say I'm just—female, and bitch-kitty perverse. Why doesn't Gwen love Cabe, and does love you? That's even more perverse from where I sit . . ."

"I can bet it is!" Gwen said bitterly.

"Gwen sugar, don't turn bitchy mean on me. If I ever get up from here, I'm going to light out for parts unknown too. What I've seen of Cabe these last few weeks makes him stand sixteen hands high as far as I'm concerned, so I don't mean to take any chances. Now both of you get out of here. Send Mary Sue to sit with me, and y'all go hold hands someplace . . ."

"No," Colin said. "I don't mean to hold hands with Gwen, as long as she has a living husband, and him a man—I admire and respect. I have other things to do, and at least one of them seems to me much more important . . . Walk me to my buggy, Gwen?"

Gwen got up with boneless grace and with her heart in her pale blue eyes. She walked with Colin to the buggy, steadied him as he began the tedious business of getting up into it with that board-stiff leg.

"Colin," she whispered as he took the reins, "you—you rather despise me, don't you?"

"No," he said quietly. "I'm simply trying not to do anything that will make me loathe myself any more than I do now, Gwen. Falling in love with you would be all too easy. But—let's give ourselves time, shall we? We need that—and a space empty of such giants in the earth as Caleb and Rose Ann. Then maybe us poor, ordinary critters will be able to breathe a little. You understand that, don't you?"

"Perfectly. And you're right. Goodbye, Colin," Gwendolyn Henry said.

That same afternoon, Colin Claiborne drove up to the Mechanicsville Road and asked if he could speak with General Lee. The sentries, being Southerners, or as they put it in those days, Sothorons, discerned at once that a man dressed in the kind of clothes Colin had on was "mighty high cotton!" And his bandaged leg lessened some of the abysmal contempt they felt for young male civilians. "Busted?" they asked him. "Took a header going over a stone wall after a fox?"

The question was barbed, and Colin knew it. Yeoman farmers, from which class these sentries came, hated fox-hunting aristocrats in pink coats with all their simple, stubborn hearts.

"No," he said quietly. "A minié ball took out my kneecap. And since a man whose leg isn't going to bend again as long as he lives can neither ride nor march, I've been invalided out. So go ask if the general will see me. It's important, or I wouldn't even ask him to spare me a little of his precious time. Tell him a grave injustice has been done . . ."

One of them went away. Came back.

"You've got five minutes, mister!" he said.

General Lee, with his habitual courtesy, took the time to ask Colin about his leg. Colin told him, drily, the established lie: "A spent ball, sir. Ricocheted and took out my kneecap. So my military service is over. Which is just as well, I was no great shakes as a soldier, sir . . ."

"I see—Lieutenant, I believe you said? Now, what can I do for you, young sir?"

Colin told him, finishing with: "So the poor little thing has been eating her heart out, believing she failed to get to you in time, and blaming herself for all our casualties at Malvern Hill. Sir, couldn't you write her out a citation? Her brother-in-law, Major Henry, told me you saw the state she was in when the sentries picked her up and—"

"I didn't expect her to live," General Lee said. "Nor did the Surgeon General, for that matter, and his opinion is worth far more than mine. That young woman, Lieutenant, is the bravest single soldier this war has produced so far. I've been meaning to call on her in person to see how she is faring. But war ends all things, even simple courtesy. Of course I'll write her a citation— here and now. If you'd care to wait, you can take it back to her yourself . . ."

"Sir," Colin said, "could you extend the favor you're doing me a little further, and send it to her by one of your aides? The—most imposing-looking one you can spare? Of the highest rank possible, short of a brigadier general, of course. Say, a lieutenant colonel. Look, sir, I know this sounds strange, but entrusting your citation to me to take to her would ruin the whole effect, rob the gesture of much of its value. I want her up from that bed she's wasting away in, sir! I want her—alive!"

General Lee stared at Colin with real interest now. Like all really great men in any field, even the utterly barbaric one he was a past master of, he had a deep and genuine vein of subtlety in his makeup. He knew perfectly well that a young man could be simultaneously a number of contradictory things: As tall as the one before him. As handsome, obviously aristocratic, well bred, rich. And —as utterly damned.

"Tell me, Lieutenant—Claiborne, I believe you said?"

"Yes, sir. And not Lieutenant anymore, please! I was—a rotten soldier, sir; I never deserved the title. Just call me—Claiborne. Or Colin, for—"

The general made a quick, almost brusque gesture toward Colin's wounded leg.

"Self-inflicted?" he asked quietly.

Colin bowed his head. Stared at the bitter earth while what he called his soul made three complete tours of duty through death and hell. Looked up again. Faced the general squarely.

"Yes, sir," he said. "It was."

The general stretched out his hand and let it rest on Colin's shoulder.

"And now you've already learned that staying in line, even dying, would have been easier," he said gently. "God pity you, my boy. The road back to self-respect is the longest, loneliest, roughest one there is. But you'll make it, I think. You've—truth in you, and that helps. All right, I'll send little Miss McKenzie her citation for valor by Lieutenant Colonel Bryant, of my staff, tomorrow afternoon. But satisfy my curiosity on one point, young Mr. Colin Claiborne. Just what is your connection with that gallant young lady?"

"I'm—in love with her, sir," Colin whispered. "We were—engaged. But one of the things those green eyes of hers can do, is peer into a man's soul. So—she gave me back my ring. *Before* I did this. Knowing that I was going to. Then shamed me past any conceivable hope of redemption by demonstrating to me—to all the world —exactly what valor is . . ."

"Amen to that," the general sighed. "Tell her one thing for me: The next time she sees fit to give me a hill, I promise, on my honor as a soldier, to take and keep it . . ."

He put out his hand to Colin. Because there was nothing else to do, Colin took that august hand, shook it briefly, turned so fast he almost fell, unwilling to let the general see how much that gesture had unmanned him.

"Sentry!" the general called out. "Help this gentleman—one of our wounded veterans—up into his buckboard, will you?"

"There are," Theodore McKenzie, Rose Ann's grandfather, who'd taught—or tried to—the classics to several generations of young officers at West Point, always said, "only two deities who have any influence at all upon human existence, man's fate. The first is Ananke, necessity, to whom even Zeus the Thunderer must bow, and the other is Hazard—blind chance . . ."

Which Rose Ann McKenzie and what happened to her next proceeded to abundantly prove. Of course, that little goddess Ate, mischief, whom old Professor Ted McKenzie seems to have forgotten all about, almost surely had a hand in the matter as well.

Witness the circumstances: By that time, Rambling Rosie's heroism had more or less slipped from the public mind, especially since it had produced no spectacular results. The Confederacy had won the Seven Days series of battles, but by margins so uncomfortably close that people were beginning to sense they had been Pyrrhic. Worse, the South had lost the last of those battles, the one at Malvern Hill, and suffered horrible casualties in the distinctly tragic bargain. The Richmond *Whig* was grumbling: "We had much praying at various headquarters and large reliance on special providence, but none was vouchsafed, by pillar of cloud, or fire. The campaign was nothing but a series of blunders, one after another and all huge!"

But in that long lull between the Malvern Hill battle on July 1 and the beginning of the second Bull Run campaign on August 23, the newspapers had precious little to write about. So when Lieutenant Colonel Hilaron Bryant, a vain and talkative man, on his way back to headquarters after the mission that Colin Claiborne had sort of pushed off on him—namely, delivering General Lee's citation for valor (the one you can still see, in a handsome mahogany frame, hanging above the fireplace in the grand salon of McKenzie's Manor, now that the Virginia Historical Society has declared the old house a Confederate shrine and restored it to a splendor it never knew when the McKenzies lived in it) to Miss Rose Ann McKenzie—stopped off at a barroom in Richmond to have himself a snort, he felt no compunction against proclaiming to the congenial company he found there: "Greatest heroine in the history of the South. 'Pon my honor, she is! And pretty! Gentlemen, I assure you that even wasted away as she is at the moment by her wounds and terrible suffering, Rose Ann McKenzie is *the* most beautiful girl upon whom I ever had the pleasure to feast my eyes! And her sister, Gwendolyn, Mrs. Henry—Major Caleb Henry's wife—is only a little less so . . ."

"Henry? One of *the* Henrys, I suppose?"

The question was shrewd; the man who had put it, shrewder. Anthony Collins of the Richmond *Dispatch* was what was known in those days as a "demon reporter." Tony Collins had the reputation of being willing to go to any lengths to get "an exclusive" (the racier term "scoop" had yet to be coined) for a paper whose journalistic standards weren't all that fastidious either, taking on, at times, a distinctly yellowish tinge.

"A descendant of the Great Orator himself," Colonel Bryant said. He wondered momentarily whether that statement was true or not, but warmed by that good Bourbon and branch water, and even more so by all the attention he was getting from a group of men bored past all endurance by the tedium of life in almost any city in the blockaded South, he dismissed the scruple as unimportant. It sounded great, made a good story; that, like nearly all good stories, it wasn't true, simply didn't bother him. "Close friend of mine," he went on, which was a half-truth at best. To Caleb, with his quick intelligence, his deep sardonic bent, suffering fools like Hilaron Bryant came more than a little hard. "Member of General Jackson's staff, to which he was transferred at the general's own request after witnessing the then Captain Henry's magnificent exhibition of valor on the field at Manassas . . ."

This, Tony Collins decided at once, was dross. Heroic soldiers were a dime a dozen in the Confederate ranks. But a BEAUTIFUL HEROINE—he set the words up in black boldface type inside his mind—was pure reportorial gold. Of course, he'd heard something about the McKenzie girl's feat. Two months back, wasn't it? About the time of the Seven Days . . . But he was a newcomer to Richmond, being actually a Georgian up from Savannah, where the Yankee frigates, tossing on the horizon in plain sight, had made life even more miserable than it was here in the capital of the Confederacy, so the name McKenzie had meant nothing to him. At the time, he'd been exploring the ramifications of what he called "a real spicy item!"—distinguished lady, from one of the First Families of Virginia, equally distinguished husband, somewhat less distinguished but younger and better-looking lover, winged by outraged husband's shot as he departed the dear lady's boudoir via a window and a drainpipe—so he'd let that "war heroine" business slip out of his mind. Besides, he'd already had one soured experience with "heroines." He'd interviewed that Irish lass—what was her name? Maud O'Higgins, O'Riley, O'Sullivan! That was it— who'd tried smuggling in quinine from Yankee Land, and she'd turned out to be a bedraggled, working-class slattern, whose aroma, proclaiming her membership in the great unwashed from a full two yards away, had instantly quelled his intention to personally explore the damage the Yankee women border inspectresses' probing fingers had done to her sacred honor.

So now he said, offhandedly, "But these McKenzies—who're they?"

And had been rewarded by a circle of outraged stares, and a "Holy Jeee-sus!" or two. But, born actor that he was, "demon reporter" Collins arranged that contretemps easily enough.

"Sorry, gentlemen!" he said with a rueful grin. "But I happen to be a lowly clay-eater from Georgia. I was sent up here to Ol' Virginny by my paper, the Savannah *Blade,* on a story, and sort of —well—fell in love with the graciousness of Old Dominion life, so I decided to stay. Now I work for the *Dispatch.* So if y'all will pardon the ignorance of a poor Jawgiah boy, I'd purely admire to be enlightened on the subject . . ."

Whereupon he was. The McKenzies, he learned, had been a clan of Border lairds in Scotland, who, though Protestants, had unaccountably supported Mary Stuart against Queen Elizabeth, and had therefore had—in the 1570s or thereabouts—to flee Scotland for the New World, by way of Holland at first, for at that early date there was no English colony in North America for them to flee to. But McKenzies were aboard the *Sarah Constant,* the *Goodspeed,* or the *Discovery,* though on which of the three ships of the tiny flotilla that landed at Jamestown on May 14, 1607, they were actually on has been a matter of dispute among their descendants ever since. In sober colonial Virginia they'd become notorious for brawling, wenching, drunkenness, and riot. They'd fought in the War of Jenkins's Ear, Bacon's Rebellion, the French and Indian War, the Revolution—and distinguished themselves for valor in them all. Early on, their women had acquired the reputation for being "a mite bold, a wee bit fast 'n' forward . . ." But McKenzie fillies had always been so slick that nobody had ever been able to pin concrete sins upon them, so they'd married well, with the result that most of the First Families of Virginia were now kissing kin of the Clan. There'd been a not entirely jesting charge of witchcraft made against the McKenzie females. "Their black arts consistin'," a member of the assembled company told Tony Collins, "o' charming a fellow right out his breeches and his small-clothes in two shakes of a jackrabbit's tail!"

In the War of 1812, finding poltroonery and pusillanimity rampant in the Army, they'd gone to sea. McKenzies had died aboard both the *Constitution* and the *Constellation.* Nearer in time, Dave McKenzie, father of the gallant heroine General Lee had seen fit to honor with an official citation, had fought in Mexico, shoulder to shoulder with General Lee, Beauregard, Longstreet, Prince John Magruder, Stonewall Jackson, President of the Confederacy Jefferson Davis, and such Union shining lights as Virginian George H. Thomas, Meade, McClellan, and Ulysses "Unconditional Surrender" Grant . . .

As they talked on, "demon reporter" Collins began to see that they were handing him, on a silver platter, what could easily be the greatest story of his whole career. Still, he needed "an angle." This story was, after all, two months old, so how could he give it the necessary "bite" that would make the *Dispatch*'s editor dance a jig from joy and grant him a much-needed raise in pay without his even having to ask for it?

Almost immediately Lieutenant Colonel Hilaron Bryant provided him with enough "bite" to, as he gleefully put it in his mind, "dismember a bear!" The trouble was that Colonel Bryant, while not a bad officer, and even competent enough within the limits of his intelligence and his talents, had your small man's exaggerated opinion of his own capacities. Robert E. Lee, who had known Hilaron Bryant all his life and was genuinely fond of him, hadn't the slightest intention of promoting him to general's rank anytime soon, or entrusting him with any task that called for quick thinking, decision, brilliance. Courage, Colonel Bryant had, and to spare, but the valor of a second- or even a third-rater is one of the most perilous things that the rank and file have to face, because it can get more good men killed than an outbreak of the bubonic plague. Intelligent cowards, such as Colin Claiborne, are far less dangerous to their own cause than vain, pompous, too brave idiots, of which species Hilaron Bryant was at least to some degree an example. He was, at the moment, harboring bitter resentments against his lifelong friend Bob Lee, and even more so against such fame-laureled officers as Stonewall Jackson, cavalry leader Jeb Stuart, and a host of others. He, with that matchless brilliance of hindsight, had pinpointed all their mistakes, and it never occurred to him, since humility is seldom a characteristic of little men, to ask himself what *he* would have done had he been in their places and had had to make their split-second decisions on the basis of information that, in the heat of battle, is generally insufficient, erroneous, or just plain nonexistent. No! They were fools and bunglers one and all, while he, the greatest military genius of the age, was being held back, for all sorts of inconfessable reasons, instead of given his rightful chance to flash like the sword he was, stand tall in thunder!

So when the reporter said, "What I don't understand is exactly what this young lady *did*—aside from getting herself shot full of holes by some jittery damnyankee sentry—that was so all-fired important . . . I've heard it said she saved Lee's army, but after the Seven Days, they were burying our dead in carload lots. And McClellan stayed right there at his base at Harrison's Landing on the James, in the very midst of the homes of your greatest families, until the third of August, and nobody so much as shot a child's popgun in his direction."

"Naturally not, young sir!" Colonel Bryant snarled; "that young lady—that beautiful young girl—was shot by those sentries on Saturday, June 28. And she rode all night long, bleeding, almost dying, to get to General Lee's headquarters in time to warn him that the Union forces were coming out of White Oak Swamp and heading for Malvern Hill—*the* most perfect natural formation for setting up defensive artillery batteries in the state of Virginia. She *got* to General Lee, young man, on Sunday, June 29. And *when* was the Battle of Malvern Hill fought?"

"Jesus God!" Tony Collins whispered. "On Tuesday, July the first!"

"Exactly," Lieutenant Colonel Bryant snapped. "So I still say that little Miss McKenzie is the greatest heroine in the entire history of the South, young Mr. Newspaperman. Is she to be blamed because military incompetents threw away the priceless advantage she shed her gallant blood and almost died to give us?"

So "demon reporter" Collins had his story. And, to use his own expression, he "did it up brown!" He visited McKenzie's Hundred three times, for the simple reason that Gwen wouldn't let him tire Rose Ann out by staging an inquisition that the Holy Office might have envied. He would have talked to "sweet Rambling Rose," as he publicly described her in his article, all day and all night long, if Gwen had allowed him to. His description of Rose's beauty was lyrical, of Gwen's own, equally so. He magnanimously forgave the elder sister in print before all Richmond for her vigilant concern for the still-feeble state of her heroic sibling. He called her "Guardian Angel," quoted Rose's paeans of praise for her tender care— "largely responsible for saving our heroine's life!" He described gruff Dave McKenzie, "invalided hero of a former fray . . ." which was a gross exaggeration, because if Dave's slight limp, caused by a ball through his left leg at Chapultepec, was sufficient excuse for his staying out of the present conflict, his age (he was ten years older than most of his former comrades-in-arms in the Mexican War) and a liver hors de combat from rotgut were even better ones. Collins mentioned Jeff's contribution to "Our Holy Cause," his able assistance to Lieutenant Brooke in the creation of the ironclad *Virginia*. But his description of "sweet Rambling Rose McKenzie's heroic ride" was a true masterpiece of florid Victorian sentimentality. One passage suffices to show its quality:

"So nightlong our gallant Heroine rode, watering all the earth with her precious blood! And if where each ruby drop of her fading strength, her departing life touched earth, a scarlet blossom did not that very instant spring up, there is, we swear it! no Justice in Heaven . . ."

So even though "demon reporter" Collins viciously attacked, in words of distilled venom, the "general incompetence" of a High Command that tossed away as useless "our darling Rambling Rose's matchless sacrifice"—quoting as his source a "distinguished officer of rank" who "naturally prefers to remain unidentified"— its effect upon the public mind was overwhelming. Other papers picked it up, not only all over the state of Virginia but as far away as St. Louis, Natchez, and New Orleans. Reporters besieged General Lee, who courteously confirmed the story as "essentially accurate." Both Gwen and Mary Sue Hunter were driven to distraction and despair by the swarms of newspapermen who descended like locusts upon McKenzie's Hundred. Delegations of Virginia ladies appeared with flowers and fruit for "our heroine." President and Mrs. Davis felt constrained to call, with whom, since old Jeff had absolutely no gift for small talk and the First Lady rather a bit too much, poor Rose passed a horrible hour. Dave McKenzie, naturally, ballooned up to twice his normal size with paternal pride. And Jeb Stuart, learning for the first time of "darlin' Rosie's" feat through the newspapers, staged a cavalry raid on the flower gardens of all the plantations for miles around, then appeared with twenty horsemen, covered from the crowns of their black slouch

Kossuth hats to the hooves of their mounts with roses, and proceeded to literally bury Rose Ann under them.

All of which, of course, helped Rambling Rosie's morale no end. But the chief result of Colin Claiborne's playing *deus ex machina*, or, perhaps, of grim Ananke's combining forces with laughing Ate and the drunken, ribald gods of mocking chance, was that a new element was introduced into Rose Ann's life, capable of distorting it out of all recognition, possessing the power to actually destroy it.

That element came marching into her bedroom the very day after Jeb Stuart and his wild troopers had buried her under roses. He was, her stunned mind realized, the most beautiful man she'd ever seen.

So struck was she that it wasn't until Heros von Borcke, Jeb Stuart's imported aide-de-camp, burst into a huge bull bellow of gusty laughter that she noticed he had accompanied the stranger. Now, overlooking Heros von Borcke took some doing, for the Pomeranian volunteer to the Southern cause was actually a physical giant. He was close to seven feet tall. And he wasn't skinny tall, as most men over six feet six inches generally are: he was barrel-shaped, tremendously muscular, and as fat as a well-scrubbed Prussian pig. He was also jolly to an extent that made his presence an unfailing joy. In addition to all that, he was very, very handsome. Ninety-seven percent of all white Virginia females under the age of ninety-six were hopelessly in love with him. The *same* ninety-seven percent who were also in love with J.E.B. "Jeb" Stuart. Which, considering the prevailing currents of mid-Victorian morality, must have troubled many a blushing maiden's conscience. Few of them were either as earthy or as candid about such delicate matters as Rambling Rose McKenzie.

"Ho!" Heros roared. "Do not gaze upon Zizi so, my little love! He is a *Schweinhund*. He is a pig-dog. It is thus you say it, don't you?"

"Heros," Rose Ann said, "you stop that right now. You speak better English than I do. And you only use 'dot Cherman accent' to amuse silly girls. Only I'm not a silly girl, or any other kind of a girl, anymore. I had my girlish dreams blasted out of me with a bullet. If you had any eyes, you'd see I even look like an old hag."

"Good Lord!" the beautiful, beautiful man said softly, smiling, Rose noticed even then, with his lips only, not his eyes. "And may He repopulate the world with such old hags as you, my dear!"

He turned imperiously to Heros von Borcke, said in an icy, ripping snarl of *Hochdeutsch*, "You may go now, Heros. As I suspected, she is perfect for my purposes. So be a good fellow and leave us, will you?"

"Thunderclaps and lightning bolts!" Heros roared in German. "Who the devil d'you think you are, Zizi? Why, confound it all! I—"

"Stop it!" Rose snapped. Then from the heights, or the depths, of that supremely arrogant conviction that all the world damned well ought to speak English for their blissfully lazy convenience that has made North Americans the worst linguists on earth, she went on, "Either stop barking at each other in German or go home!"

"I am so sorry, love!" Heros rumbled. "But this blockhead—"

"There you go again!" Rose Ann said severely. "Why are you so mean to your real nice friend?"

The beautiful man lifted his head and loosed a peal of pleasant baritone laughter. "Heros," he chuckled, "who is in excellent form today, calls me a blockhead. But he fails to mention that I dragged him through the University of Leipzig by his ears, which aren't as long and hairy as they ought to be or he never would have graduated. He's a dear fellow, but he really hasn't any brains, my dear. I've been wondering for years if that huge dome of his is perfectly solid or perfectly hollow. Which does it seem to you, my lovely Valkyrie?"

Rambling Rosie looked wonderingly from one to the other of them.

"Do y'all always fight this way?" she demanded.

"Always," Heros said cheerfully, "from the very day we met. Old Zizi here is a capital chap, but he has some peculiar ideas. You see, he wants to be a German. And why should *anyone* want to be a German? I am a great big lummox of a German, but I want to be a slim and polished Frenchman, with a leetle moostache so that I could seduce all the pretty girls the way those devilish Frenchmen do!"

"You do all right in that department," Rose said drily. "All the babies they find on the church steps these days are great big bouncing blonds and look just like *you*, Heros. But, by the way, aren't you *ever* going to introduce your friend?"

"With the deepest regrets, and the most profound sorrow," the huge German sighed. "For, as I told you, Zizi is a pig-dog. But you haf not such a word in English, do you? How then can you call *ein Schweinhund* like Zizi the pig-dog that he is?"

"Well," Rose laughed, "if he really is *awful*, we call him the first part of that word and leave off the second. And if he's worse than that, we call him a son of the second part of your terrible jaw-breaker of a word—female gender, naturally!"

"A whoreson?" Heros asked her eagerly, using, of course, the German *Hurensohn*, which sounds much the same.

"I don't know what that means, but it sounds terrible, so I'm sure it's a bad word," Rose Ann said primly. "Come on now, introduce me to your friend . . ."

"Thunder and gale storms!" Heros sighed. "Oh well—since there's no help for it—this whore-hopper is Count Sisimond Kurt Radetzy, *und* he is a Bohemian—"

"Oh!" Rose said. "You mean one of those wild, artistic fellows who go around painting pictures of naked women, and drinking wine, and singing, and starving to death?"

"*Ach, so!*" Heros guffawed. "Precisely that, my leetle luf!"

"He is jesting as usual," Count Radetzy said with his icy, mirthless smile. "Actually, I'm Austrian, but my native province is part of the ancient Kingdom of Bohemia. I was born in Prague, the city of the great martyr John Hus, whose story all the world knows . . ."

"Except me," Rose Ann sighed. "I'm a terrible ignoramus, Count. Oh, that's not right either, is it? I should say 'milord,' shouldn't I?"

"No," Heros chuckled, "for he is no longer a count, but only a no-count, as we Southerners say, don't we, sweetkins? He was bereft of his title, and his lands confiscated, when he was kicked out of the Austro-Hungarian Empire for killing a rich old Jew. So now he doesn't count, this no-count—not none a-taaaall, honeychile. There! Did I get my Southern accent right this time, *mein* leetle luf?"

"Heros, you're impossible," Rose sighed. "Is any of the terrible things he says about you true, Count Radetzy?"

"Yes, I'm afraid they are," Radetzy said. "I was much too impulsive as a youngster. I've learned to study matters much more coolly and at length before taking action. In the case of the Jew Steinermann, if I'd troubled to find out that it was not to him but to all his hooked-nose avaricious cousins that the Prince owed money, I should have chosen one of them instead for my target practice. Whereupon, instead of being exiled, I should now be sporting a decoration. The Swastika, likely . . ."

"You mean," Rose Ann whispered, "you actually killed a rich old man, in peacetime, because—"

"He was a Jew?" Radetzy said calmly. "Of course. A perfectly reasonable procedure when dealing with 'the Chosen People' it seems to me . . ."

Rose stared at him, her green eyes wide.

"You—you're horrible!" she said.

Radetzy threw back his head and laughed, making a low, purring, pleasant sound.

"So I've often been told," he said. "Especially by female sentimentalists. What I am, my darling little Valkyrie, is practical. Since it is obviously the destiny of the German peoples to rule the world—"

"Germany Above All Others, eh?" Heros growled. "What this one really is, is mad, sweetkins. As a hatter. He has read too many books, written by idiotic philosophers. That is one thing. The other is that he *wants* to be a German, *und* that is the root of his madness . . ."

"But isn't he?" Rose Ann said wonderingly. "All right, he's from Austria, but the Austrians *are* Germans, aren't they?"

"Some of us are, others aren't," Radetzy sighed. "Depends what part of the Empire one hails from mostly. An Austrian can be a Croat, a Balt, a Czech, a Slovene, a Hungarian, even a Slav if he's born too far east. Just as this huge oaf, dearest Miss McKenzie, ought by right to be a Pole, since Pomerania, his native province, had always been a part of Poland, until we Germans stole it from them a century ago . . ."

"*We* Germans!" Heros snorted. "Look at him, *und* carefully, my little love. See his hair, which is as black as the night, and as straight as the tails of the ponies his barbaric ancestors from the steppes of Asia rode when they invaded Europe hundreds of years ago. Note his skin—a yellowish gold, inherited from his Hun forebears, or from his Magyar ones. Look at his eyes! See how they slant—"

"But they're blue," Rose Ann objected.

"Gray," Radetzy corrected her, "an inheritance from my mother, who was as blond as this huge, miseducated *Kerl*—that means low fellow, my dear!—and from a family from Wien—Vienna, to you—itself. But in part, he is right. My father was Hungarian, largely Magyar. And the Magyars actually were—God pity them!—Orientals. But many of this gross Polack's forebears were —ugh!—*Slavs*. The people from whose name is derived the word 'slaves'!"

"Zizi, old boy," Heros von Borcke growled then, meaning it,

Rose was suddenly sure, "remind me to kill you, one day soon. *Tot.* And that, my sweet, means dead!"

"Oh, stop it, you two!" Rose Ann said. "Heros, you didn't bring your friend Count Radetzy here just to give me a headache arguing about things I know nothing about, and don't even understand, did you?"

"No, gracious Miss McKenzie," Radetzy said smoothly. "I asked —or rather begged—him to bring me here, present me to you. For one point in that newspaper account of your brilliant exploit struck me most forcefully—and that was the skill with which you deluded those Yankee sentries by assuming a Northern accent. So I said to myself, Kurt, old boy, this young lady can be of unparalleled service to our noble Southern cause—"

"*Your* noble Southern cause!" Rose Ann exploded. "But you are—"

"A foreigner?" Radetzy said. "Not any longer, my dear. I am a naturalized citizen of the Confederacy, and of the state of Louisiana, since New Orleans, as the greatest port in the South, was the one I had the readiest access to after I was exiled. When I saw the South wasn't going to be able to hold it under the onslaught of the North's overwhelming naval strength, I made my way here, and offered my services, and my special skills, to your—our—government . . ."

"Special skills, horse droppings!" Heros snorted. "He means that he was a spy for the Imperial government. A member of the Death's-Head Squad of the Austrian police, whose mission it was to make people disappear—pouf!—like that!"

"Not always—pouf!—like that, Heros, dear boy," Radetzy said with an icy smile.

"I should say not," Heros snapped. "More often it was—slowly, and most unpleasantly. But they always disappeared afterwards, anyhow, when your Death's-Head Squad had finished with them. Or what was left of them did. But all you had to do with *that* was to carry it out in a slop bucket and pour it into the drains, eh, Gruesome Kurt, as they called you in those days?"

"My God!" Rose Ann whispered. "And you came over *here* and offered those kinds of services to our government and—"

"Had them welcomed? Of course not, dear sweet little girl! I'm all too aware of how deep Anglo-Saxon sentimentality runs. I offered, merely, to apply my matchless experience to the reorganization of the Secret Service. Which was accepted at once. In fact, I was immediately commissioned as a full colonel, and given carte blanche to do all that was necessary. But then, I talked to the right man: your then Secretary of War, who has since been transferred to heading the Secretariat of State, the Jew Judah Benjamin. An immensely able and intelligent man. Most—subtle. Almost a European, in fact. He and I got along famously. With this new man, General Randolph—George W. Randolph, who was placed at the head of the War Department when our fine Jew lawyer was shifted over to State—less so. But he seems to realize he's beyond his depth, and has left me strictly alone, so far. Which is all I ask—"

"But—but you said you *hated* the Jews," Rose Ann whispered, "and now—"

"No, I merely despise them. They aren't important enough to hate. Such extra-special ones as Benjamin I may even keep alive, to help me deal with the great problem of disposing of the rest. Dear God, there are so many of the grubby beggars! And when to them is added all the teeming swarms of the ever-breeding, hopelessly inefficient Latin races, dress and perfume makers like the French; spaghetti and bambino manufacturers like the Italians; mule-driving bandits like the Spanish and the Portuguese, I fear our task shall be difficult indeed!"

"And *us?*" Rose Ann whispered. "We Scots, and the Irish. We aren't big blond Nordics, appears to me."

"Your ancestors were," Radetzy said pleasantly. "The Jutes, the Picts, and the Scots were all fine, invading Viking tribes. Besides, look at that skin of yours, that flaming hair! You're perfectly fitted to be the mother of lusty Teutonic warriors, my splendid girl!"

"Haven't *I* anything to say about that?" Rose Ann demanded.

"Not one word!" Radetzy laughed. "Kitchen, children, and the church are the roles for the woman, my dear!"

"Well, I'll be damned!" Rose Ann said feelingly.

"You will be, my poor little maiden, if you pay any attention to this madman," Heros said. "Come along, Zizi! You haf tired our heroine out enough for one day!"

"No!" Rose Ann said. "Please, no, Heros! Or at least not yet. I have to lie here all day long with nobody to talk to, most of the time. Besides, I find him fascinating, to tell the truth about it. Tell me, Count Radetzy—"

"Kurt, to you, my darling, please!"

"I'm not your darling, but I will call you Kurt, because you're too crazy to be a count. Tell me a few things, will you, please? First of all, why'd you come over *here?*"

"Your charming Confederacy was the obvious place for a man of my ideas and my ideals to go," Kurt Radetzy said gravely. "All Europe is caught in the grip of muddleheaded liberalism—that is, when, which is even worse, the people of my continent aren't paying too much heed to the ravings of that crackpot Jew Karl Marx and his toady, Friedrich Engels. So your splendid South, which knows, by instinct, it seems, the proper order of things. For the Negro, the whip! What else are those mindless apes fit for except to serve us as two-legged beasts of burden?"

"And the woman?" Heros said sardonically. "You've always advocated a leaded lash as the finest present possible for a new bridegroom, Zizi. Are you going to be diplomatic and deny that now, old chap?"

"Of course not," Radetzy laughed. "But such a remedy is only necessary for stupid females. Intelligent ones, such as our heroine here, will be able to keep their dainty seats unstriped—quite easily . . ."

"How?" Rose Ann asked him flatly.

"By obeying us, your lords and masters, implicitly," Kurt said with a charming smile. "One doesn't enjoy applying corrective force, y'know, my dear. How much simpler, then, for you darling girls to never make it necessary?"

"I see," Rose said, too quietly.

"Go on with your questions, my sweet!" Radetzy said gaily.

"Why are you so down on the Jewish people?" Rose said evenly.

"Various reasons. But chiefly because they've succeeded in perverting our noble Teutonic civilization by introducing the creeping poison of that bastard offspring of Mosaic law, the Christian religion, among us."

"Then you don't believe in Jesus or the Christian faith?" Rose Ann asked him wonderingly.

"Of course not! More than that, I reject them utterly. I have returned to the gods of my fathers: Wodan and Freya and Thor and Tyr, and such a very beautiful Valkyrie as you, lovely *Fräulein* McKenzie, to bear me up to Vahalla when I die!"

"Daft," Heros rumbled. "Stark, raving—"

"But amusing, I think!" Rose giggled. "But tell me one thing, Kurtie boy, aside from educating my poor little feeble mind on the subject of just how wonderful you Germans are, why'd you make Heros bring you here to see me anyhow?"

"Precisely for that, first of all," Kurt Radetzy said. "To *see* you. But more than in the sense of merely looking at you, sweet maiden, though that is, I'll freely confess, an exquisite pleasure. But to per-ceive what you are, to discern the qualities of mind, of spirit, that make you unique. I haven't been disappointed. It seems to me I've found a treasure. May I call upon you again frequently?"

"God in Heaven!" Heros von Borcke whispered prayerfully.

Rose Ann stared at him.

"Why?" she said.

"It would save time. I've already talked to your doctor, who tells me you must remain in bed another two, three weeks, a month, perhaps. During that hiatus, I could easily teach you a goodly part of all the things you'll have to know."

"But *what* things, Kurt?" Rose Ann demanded. "And *why* do I have to know 'em?"

"General polish, of course. Deportment. I mean to transform you into a highborn European lady who would pass muster anywhere. And I'm already convinced that no Pygmalion was ever presented with finer materials to create a Galatea who will be a masterpiece! I'm going to be very proud of you, my dear!"

"But for *what*, Kurt? Tell me *that?*"

"So that you'll be perfectly prepared to join my group. To become, in fact, *la prima diva* of my organization. Number one! Whom forevermore the Confederacy will call blessed!"

"Number one, you say?" Heros growled. "But of *what?* Your suicide squad, Zizi?"

"Good Lord!" Rose Ann said.

"Look, Rose Ann—you'll permit me to call you thus so quickly? —let me confess at once that the risk is high, for both of us. We may die. That's the simple truth. But if we do, it will be as soldiers, in the service of a noble cause. What I'm proposing is to make you, whose courage is beyond all dispute and whose gifts as an actress almost equally so, the first and foremost female agent of our new, reorganized Secret Service."

"Jehoshaphat!" Rose whispered.

"You'll travel throughout the Northern states. You'll be supplied with unlimited funds. Your contacts will be already listed, and letters and other, subtler means of introduction provided for you. With the program I have planned, you'll be able to do the South more good in a couple of months than all her armies have in two years of war. Come, my dear, what d'you say?"

"That I don't know," Rose Ann whispered. "I don't think I'm that brave anymore, Kurt. A bullet hole through your middle takes an awful lot out of you, y'know."

"I do know," he said in a gentle, understanding tone of voice.

"I've been laid up that way twice now, and I'll admit it's rather awful. But the danger of that sort of thing isn't very great for you. Up until now, the Yankees have done no more than to imprison for a few months, and then quietly exile South all our women spies they've caught. It's we men they shoot, or hang. Besides, on your first few trips, I'll go along with you. We'll pose as husband and wife and—"

"Whaaat!" Rose Ann gasped.

"Your usual dirty tricks with women, eh Zizi?" Heros said, too quietly.

"No," Kurt said mockingly, "I have no intention of playing fast and loose with this dear child, as you so gently put it, Heros. Of course, if she should happen to feel in a tender mood one night, it would be ungentlemanly of me not to oblige her, but—"

"Of all the insufferably egotistic, vain, impossible—"

"Scoundrel," Heros supplied. "Blackguard. Rascal."

"Yes!" Rose cried. "All those!"

Kurt smiled.

"Well," he said, "I have been all of those unpleasant things upon occasion, but only in the service of the glorious state. For, my dear, even the great Hegel held that ethics and morals of the conventional sort are irrelevancies before the needs of the Greater German Reich and her heroes . . ."

"*Und der alte* Kant, what did he say?" Heros said mockingly. "You've read *The Critique of Pure Reason,* haven't you, *Herr Philosoph?*"

"Immanuel Kant was a humbug! Pure reason, bah! Pure excreta! The physical existence of things *a priori* to their perception by human senses, why—" Kurt stopped short. A curiously charming smile illuminated his much too handsome face. Charming, all right, Rose Ann thought, but it gives me the shivers all the same . . .

"Aha!" he said to Heros. "I see your game, my friend! You'd sidetrack me into a deep philosophical discussion, and thus make me forget the matter at hand! Rum show, old boy. I won't be diverted from my objectives. Rose Ann, you must consider it! You love the South because it is your homeland, and I, because it seems to me the hothouse in which to nurture the seeds of world dominance by, if not we Germans solely, at least by the blond, white, superior races, reducing all others to our servitors, our slaves, or in the case of such extremely pestilent growths as the Jews, exterminating them. All right, all right! I know that you don't and cannot

113

agree with me fully. Your gentle heart forbids you such rude hardi-
hood of spirit. But we can travel part of the road together, my
sweet. Achieve your rather limited objectives first. Mine can wait.
We members of the super-race can quite easily possess our souls in
patience, since our triumph is ultimately inevitable!"

"If," Rose Ann said impishly, "you propose that we travel together, stopping in hotel bedrooms as man and wife, we aren't
going to get even as far as my garden's footpath, Kurt honey! And
if you think you're going to call on me two or three times a week in
order to make me over into a grand duchess or something without
giving my father some mighty convincing reasons, you're even crazier than you sound. Pa's one crack shot, I can tell you that, and
fellows who come messing around his daughters with intentions
that won't stand the light of day have a peculiar way of winding up
dead. Or *tot*, as Heros calls it."

"Then marry me!" Kurt burst out, with no perceptible pause for
breath, not to mention cogitation. "You insist upon that stupid
convention? Very well. It's a small enough sacrifice to make for the
good of the cause. What sort of a ceremony would you like? Catholic? Protestant? Civil? I'll waive my own beliefs. 'Twould be too
difficult to find a parson or a priest who'd ever heard of the Twi-
light of the gods in this benighted country!"

Heros shook his huge head in aching wonder.

"Zizi," he groaned, "don't you know *anything* about women?"

Kurt threw back his head and laughed aloud.

"Apart from the evident fact that they should shut up and do as
they are told in order to keep the hide on their delectable little
seats intact, what is there to know?" he said cheerfully. "Oh, come
now! We're wasting time. When shall I arrange to have the ceremony performed, my beloved wife-to-be? And—oh, if that's what's
troubling you, I wouldn't insist upon my husbandly rights . . ."

"But I most certainly *would* insist upon my wifely ones," Rose
told him solemnly, her green eyes become twin emeralds, lighted
from within and ablaze with delighted mischief. "In fact, on our
wedding night, I'll stipulate that you make violent and vicious love
to me all night long in twenty-seven different positions. What's
more, I demand that you get me in the family way that very first
night. And last but not least, I want a *big* family. Six boys, six girls.
An even dozen at the very least, though fourteen or fifteen would
be even nicer . . ."

Kurt Radetzy smiled at her peacefully. And now she saw that
Heros's description of him hadn't been off the mark at all. His

mist-fog gray eyes *did* slant. Very definitely. His cheekbones were high, and the cast of his whole truly handsome countenance was decidedly Oriental. At the moment it bore an expression rather like that of a Mongol archer peering speculatively across the Great Wall the Chinese emperors had built to keep just such barbarians as he out. Or that of a sleepy tiger.

"Done," he said calmly. "Anything else?"

"Oh, Lord!" Rose Ann laughed. "Called my hand that time, didn't you, Kurt sugar? All right. Let's be serious for a change. Kurt, I like you very much. It would be hard for any normal girl not to like a fellow as good-looking as you are. But I don't love you. And I'd never marry a man I didn't love. I wouldn't even marry one I *did* love unless he could convince me of one thing beyond the faintest ghost of a doubt . . ."

"And that thing is?" Kurt murmured.

"That he loved and worshipped me past madness and despair!" Rose said with total conviction.

Again Kurt smiled. "Not an insurmountable difficulty, it seems to me," he said, and getting up from his chair, crossed to the bedside. Very calmly, he put his right hand, long-fingered, spotlessly clean, and smelling of a woods-and-heather kind of cologne or toilet water, under her chin. Lifting her face toward his, he bent and kissed her mouth.

She heard, from across the ocean maybe, from some far-distant shore, Heros's "Oh, dear God!" But after that, her mind shut out the world, as Kurt Radetzy went on about the enterprise at hand.

He wasn't at all rough about it. He kissed her very gently. Only he took his own sweet time, molding her lips beneath the slow, soft tactile pressure of his own. Rose Ann's first impulse, to tear her mouth violently from his and pretend a maidenly indignation at his presumption, died abruptly out of time and mind. Her lips bloomed under his, thickened like the blood-gorged petals of some carnivorous tropical flower, in some steaming jungle somewhere below the wind, went softer still, sweet-sighing, slackening, parting.

And then, to her vast astonishment, he slid a scalding tongue tip, as busy as a hooded cobra's when the snake charmer's flute lifts up its piping cry, between them. Her astonishment lasted a split second too long; before it could release her into reactive anger, her senses—what she sadly called her "baser nature"—had taken over. She discovered with no particular surprise that she wanted him to go on kissing her like that, forever. She realized with that bedrock

honesty characteristic of all McKenzie females, including even her
much more cautious sister, that she actually didn't want him to
stop, but to commit with her the sin that neither the highborn
Virginia maiden she no longer was, nor the recent widow she had
become since her darling Joe-Joe's death at Seven Pines, had any
right to contemplate, even in the darkness of her mind. But she did
contemplate it. She wished Heros von Borcke would get the clinking ding-dang hell out of there and give her and Kurtie pie a little
privacy so that they could—

Only I'm so weak! her mind wailed. And I wouldn't want him to
see I've got two belly buttons now, 'stead of just one like other
girls, thanks to old Froggie boy's bullet. And besides, it's wrong,
wrong, wrong, and I did it once with Colin and it wasn't any good,
no fun at all, but this here Hungarian Austrian German wild Chi-
nee-looking pig-dog swine with ghost-gray eyes sure Lord ain't—
isn't—Colin! Oh, Lord, oh, Jesus, I—

He drew his mouth away from hers. Then pensively, lost in
deepest thought, with the expression—it afterward came to her,
for in that rarely awful moment, nothing did!—of a scientist im-
mersed in a new and absorbing laboratory experiment, he pushed
his hand around under the back of her neck, amid the darkling
flames of her sunset hair, and began to finger her vertebrae, one by
one, working downward, murmuring softly, abstractedly to himself, in German: "*Ach, so*—it must be about here. In the majority of
women, it's—let me see—one, two, three, four, five—Yes, here!"

She felt his straying fingers touch that spot. Near the fifth verte-
bra below her collarbone in her back. And she stiffened. Grew
rigid as the ultimate bone, as death. Then—her insides exploded.
Turned into a Gatling gun. Fired off round after round after round
of the most hurtful terrible crippling murderously sweet exquisite
divine unbearably *good* feelings she had ever felt in all her life. As
long as he kept his hand there with his fingers pressing that magic
spot they wouldn't stop, and if they didn't stop she was going to
die, but—oh, sweet Jesus!—if dying felt like this she was perfectly
willing to pass on to her reward in heaven, or much more likely,
her just deserts down below, every day in the week and three times
on Sundays!

She realized what it was, though she didn't know the clinical
name for it. It was what happened when people made love *right*.
She'd heard the nigger wenches talking among themselves too
many times not to know that, saying awful terrible phrases like:

"Then he ol' long rusty black thing hit bust 'n' my soul it flew plumb up to Glory!"

He took his hand away—and that tidal wave, that volcano, that scalding lava flooding in her middle ceased—snap! Like that. Her mind took over. But this is wrong all wrong! it wailed. He didn't do anything at all only touched me a couple of miles from down there, from what most fellows are always pawing at, or trying to, anyhow, and still and still—ohhhh, Lord! How aw-ful! He must think I'm a terrible poor starved left-lonesome bitch, and now he can't he won't there's no way he can ever respect me again, as long as I—as the two of us—shall live!

But he was smiling at her now, gently, tenderly.

"Now I must go seek your father. To ask him for your hand—with all the rest of you attached to it, of course! Till we meet again, my love! Come, Heros! I've a devil of a lot of things to do still, y'know," Kurt Radetzy said.

Chapter Six

Emitting squeaks of delight remarkably like those of the small white mouse she rather resembled, Mary Sue Hunter came flying into the little sitting room of McKenzie's Manor. But just inside the doorway she stopped, and an expression of purest awe stole over her tiny, heart-shaped face.

"Ohhhhh, Lord!" she breathed. "It's—divine! Why, it's just too lovely for words!"

From where she knelt beside Rose Ann, Gwen smiled at her prospective sister-in-law; then, taking some of the pins out of her mouth—for she was busy about the task of taking up the "it" in question, Rose Ann's wedding dress, enough so it wouldn't fall off the mere wisp her younger sister had become before she got to the altar—she said, "Yes, it is, isn't it? It was our grandmother's. Mama's was hopeless. When she married Father, Mama was pleasingly plump, while Rose Ann—"

"I don't exist," Rose Ann said morosely. "I'm dead. That damnyankee killed me. When I walk into St. Paul's in this circus tent, all the great ladies of Virginia's most exalted circles of high society are going to fall out in rows with laughing hysterics. That is, if any of 'em even bother to come. We McKenzies are nothing much anymore, y'know . . ."

"That's where you're wrong, Rose Ann," Mary Sue said. "Lord, are you McKenzies ever in trouble!"

"I don't see how that's even possible, Mary Sue," Gwen said calmly. "But tell us, my dear, just how is Clan McKenzie in trouble *this* time?"

"Y'all are just too popular!" Mary Sue squealed. "Since folks know I'm engaged to Jeff, everywhere I've been in the last few days I've been besieged! All my girlfriends and their mamas are fairly panting to find out if they've been included on your invitation list. And if you've forgot one grande dame among the FFVs—just *one*, Gwennie darling—you've made yourself an enemy for life. Everybody *knows* President and Mrs. Davis are going to attend, and Mrs. Lee, anyhow, even if the general can't. And since all the sweet young things of our circle are certain sure that Jeb Stuart will come along in honor of the best man, Major von Borcke, every drugstore in town is plumb out of smelling salts, since they're all aiming to faint dead away at the sight of Jeb, or the major, or both of 'em!"

"Surely both," Gwen said with a smile. "Heros is an awfully handsome great big strapping man, isn't he? Only I really don't follow you, Mary Sue. What really does this problem of ours amount to?"

Mary Sue stared at her. Said fervently, "Gwen, the problem is *serious.* Specially when you add to it the fact that *every* female creature in Richmond is *dying* to get a look at this *foreign nobleman* that Rose Ann's marrying! Why, every time I *mention* that I know him, they pounce on me like chicken hawks diving into a barnyard full of pullets!"

"And what do you tell 'em, may I ask?" Rose Ann said tiredly.

"That is he *ever* the handsomest thing! Tall, dark, and—and mysterious, kind of. With slanty eyes like a Chinaman's, only blue—"

"Gray," Rose Ann corrected her, even more wearily.

"Light-colored, anyhow," Mary Sue gurgled on. "And anytime he looks at you all steady and slow, you don't know your right hand from your left anymore, or which end is up."

"Just what *nice* little old Southern girls just *ain't* s'posed to do?" Rose Ann teased her solemnly. "Good! Tell you what, Mary Sue: *You* marry him. Run off with him anytime twixt now and my wedding day. I'd appreciate it. 'Cause you'd sure Lord be doing me a favor. And Jeff too, likely . . ."

"But, Rose Ann!" Mary Sue gasped. "How can you talk that way about the man you *love?* Whom you're going to marry?"

"You divide those last two statements up into their individual parts, and you'll be getting somewhere," Rose Ann sighed, "a mite closer to the truth, maybe. You're right about one thing: I'm going to marry Kurt Radetzy. All the hosts of hell plus the Yankee Army couldn't stop me from doing that. But I don't love him. He's—awful. No, 'horrible' fits him better. Most of the time, I hate his crazy, cruel guts. But—"

"But—what, Rose?" Gwen whispered.

Rose looked at her. At Mary Sue.

"What would happen if the truth were spoken?" she said gravely. "The whole truth. Be something like taking the lid off of Pandora's box, wouldn't it? The world would never be the same again. Not the warm, soft, *safe,* and cozy world us females inhabit, anyhow. Don't you agree, Gwennie darling?"

Gwen looked at her sister. Rose to the challenge. Faced her deadliest foe, her dearest friend, her sister, alter ego, almost second self. Said, with a bitter honesty as close to the sublime as human qualities ever are, "Perfectly. You're entirely right, Rose Ann."

"I just don't know what y'all are talking about!" Mary Sue fumed.

"Naturally you don't, snippie pie," Rose Ann said to her quietly, gently, almost tenderly. "But the question is: Do you even want to? And could you stand it if you did?"

"Stand what?" Mary Sue cried.

"The truth. Mighty unhandy thing, the truth. It is, folks say, the mirror of the soul. Only the soul isn't necessarily a lovely object either, snip. I'd just as soon not gaze at mine, too often. Don't enjoy getting the shudders . . ."

"Oh, Lord! Quit plaguing me, Rose Ann! I'm as much of a woman as you are. And I *can* stand the truth, you hear? So start telling me some, right now. F'instance, why are you going to marry Count Radetzy if you don't love him?"

Rose looked not at her, but rather at Gwen. Their gazes locked, twin ruler-straight parallel beams steady now, unblinking.

"Because," she said, her voice become ashes, sand, the taste and the feel of both, she thought, "I want him so goddamn bad I hurt . . ."

"Ohhh, Lord!" Mary Sue wailed. "I—"

She wasn't looking at Gwen, so she didn't see what was flaming in the pale blond elder sister's cheeks, her eyes.

"Forgive me, Gwennie darling," Rose Ann said contritely. "And you too, snippie pie. That's the kind of thing we females have been taught to not even *think*, much less say right out loud. Reckon I'm a natural candidate for number one in the lineup in a parlor house, but—"

"No," Gwen said quietly. "You're just honest—and indiscreet. A bad combination, as far as maintaining one's reputation is concerned. Pious hypocrisy aside, every woman who is precisely that —a woman—has felt that way at times. But is it, sister mine, suffi-cient reason for marrying a man you don't even *like?*"

"He's not going anywhere," Rose sighed. "He will be stationed here in Richmond for the duration, it appears. And I can't just haul off and leave. Where would I go? So, feeling the way I do about him, marriage is—safer, Gwen honey. 'Better to marry than to burn,' the Bible says . . ."

"The Bible says thaaat?" Mary Sue Hunter gasped.

"It sure Lord does, honey," Rose sighed. "Let's change this sub-ject, shall we? It's making us all doggoned uncomfortable and—"

"No!" Mary Sue said sharply. "Not 'til I've had my say anyhow. The main trouble is that us women are plain scared to speak up and tell the truth about—our problems. So while we're holding this old-fashioned, down-home, country-camp-meeting confession session, hear mine! If Jeff weren't such a perfect gentleman that I've often been tempted to hit him over the head and change his mind about being so blamed sweet and *respectful* toward me even when we're way off by our lonesomes before he came to again, I'd have been a fallen woman twenty times over by now. And on our wedding night, he's going to be the most flabbergasted little old pure and innocent Southern boy anybody ever heard tell of. 'Cause, so help me, Hannah, I mean to turn him every whicha-way but loose!"

Rose Ann crossed to where Mary Sue stood. Bent and kissed her tenderly. Straightened up, smiling.

"Welcome to the Sisterhood of Howling Horny Hard-up Bitches, snippie pie," she chuckled. "You just proved one thing to me, anyhow . . ."

"Which is?" Mary Sue whispered.

"That my brother isn't half as dumb as I thought he was. Now, c'mon. You've got a couple of things to tell us, as I recall . . ."

"I do. But I already told y'all one of 'em. Gwen honey, what d'you mean to *do* about all the folks who're expecting invitations to the wedding? 'Cause if you forget anybody who's the least bit important hereabouts, you'll have bought yourself a bushel and a peck of trouble for the rest of your natural life. You know how Tidewater people are . . ."

"Don't I, though!" Gwen sighed. "And to make matters worse, we'd thought of making this a rather small and quiet wedding. Of course, we *had* to invite the President and his wife, considering how kind they were to call on Ramb while she was laid up. Which meant we also had to invite Mrs. Lee, so we wouldn't seem to be slighting the military. Of course, she probably won't come, because she's practically an invalid, and never goes anywhere, except to church, but—"

"But Varina Howell Davis *will*, 'cause she just plain *loves* socializing, and making a show. And that means the fat is really in the fire," Mary Sue said. "And, anyhow, even without *her*, everybody would still want to attend the 'wedding of the century,' as they're calling it. 'Cause can't *any*body recall a Virginia girl's marrying a foreign nobleman before *now*, honey. Every time Major von Borcke comes into town, a crowd of girls waylay him—primed by their mamas, naturally, to ask him *all* about Count Radetzy. And he tells 'em the most *awful* lies! One time, Rose Ann honey, he says

121

your fiancé is the illegitimate half brother of the Austrian Emperor, and the next he says he's a morganatic son of the King of Hungary. Then he jokes that your Kurt is the Buddha from Buda, and the Pest from Pest. Or he swears that he isn't even here, that your lover is a figment of their wild imaginations, because he was boiled down years ago to make the goo they put in Hungarian goulash."

"Say, Gwen sugar, why don't we just put an announcement in all the papers? Invite everybody en masse. The butcher, the baker, the candlestick maker, the slum Irish, the free niggers, the—"

"D'you know, Ramb, that's an excellent idea! Shorn of all your wild exaggerations, of course," Gwen said. "Just wait a minute. I'll write it out right now. We'll excuse this unorthodox method of inviting people on the score of wartime shortages, caused by the blockade, which made it impossible to procure enough invitations to send out to all our gentle friends, and—"

"No!" Rose Ann said gleefully. "Let's say we *refused* to, not wanting to be so unpatriotic as to use up paper, ink, and type the newspapers need to print their reports about the war. And that's only half a lie, Gwennie darling. They *are* awf'ly short of damn nigh everything, y'know . . ."

"The McKenzie talent for barefaced lying again, Rose Ann? Oh, well, there is some truth in that, so let me see—"

She dipped her quill from the tail of their oldest, toughest rooster—steel pen points were another of the commodities unavailable by then—into an ink made of pokeberry juice and charred willow bark, and began her first rough draft on the back of one of Dave McKenzie's numerous unpaid bills. Her final effort, a little masterpiece of social diplomacy, read as follows:

"Due to the current difficulties in procuring paper, type, and ink that all our fair city's job printers are suffering because of the cruel blockade imposed upon us by our barbaric enemies, the McKenzie family, holding it unpatriotic to divert to such a private use materials so necessary in disseminating the news from our far-flung battlefronts, take this means to cordially invite all our friends, and as many of Colonel Radetzy's fellow officers as will be on leave Sunday, November 5, 1862, to attend the wedding of Miss Rose Ann McKenzie to Colonel (Count) Sisimond Kurt Radetzy, of the CSA, at St. Paul's Episcopal Church, at eleven o'clock in the morning, as well as to the general reception to be held in the ballroom of the Exchange Hotel, from 6 P.M., onwards . . ."

"That ought to do it," Gwen sighed. "Will you take it into all the papers tomorrow, Mary Sue? You're much closer to town than we are. Tell them to bill me, not Father, and assure them they will be paid . . ."

"Good!" Mary Sue said. "That's purely a relief, Gwen darling. 'Cause I was fearing we'd find ourselves mixed up in a female Civil War on top of the one with the Yankees we've already got. So now for my *big* news! Girls, I've heard from Jeff!"

"Oh, Lord!" Rose Ann moaned. "Where is he? Tell me so I can send him a *bomb* with the fuse all lit to blow him sky high! All this time without a word! Scaring me like that! Driving me crazy—"

"Not much of a drive," Gwen snapped. "Ramb, if you don't quit crying like a fool you're going to spot your wedding dress beyond redemption. Besides, carrying on so over good news is likely to put you back in bed. You know the doctor says that the principal thing you need now is rest, some light exercise, and *calm* . . ."

"But c'mon, Mary Sue! Tell me all about my Jeffie love! Where *is* he? What's he doing? Besides making the local belles at wherever he's at swoon dead away when he passes by . . ."

Mary Sue stamped a dainty foot. But no longer could that foot be called "well shod." Small as it was, when it struck the sitting room's floor, it made a tremendous clatter. For one thing, that floor was bare, its carpets having been confiscated by Gwen, so that their materials could be used for more pressing purposes—to replace the handbags whose leather had gone to make the uppers for such shoes as Mary Sue Hunter wore. But the second reason that little Miss Hunter's somewhat less than dainty slipper made such a noise was that its sole was made of wood. The South had always bought its footwear and other leather personal articles from New England manufacturers. The war had cut off that source of supply; the blockade, all others. What Southern belles wore on their hands, their feet, their bodies, and their heads by late October 1862 would have been comical, if it hadn't been so pitiful.

"You quit that, Rose Ann!" Mary Sue cried. "I'm jealous enough as is, without your adding to it! I know I'm not p-p-pretty, b-b-but—"

Again Rose Ann wrapped her arms about "that simple little snip of a female critter," as she habitually thought of Jeff's promised.

"But you're sweet and loving and good, and Jeff couldn't find a better wife," she said, meaning it. "You and Gwen practically saved my worthless life, so how could I be against you? Fact is, any straying female who looks at that there little old brother of mine with the idea of taking him away from you will have *me* to face, simpie sugar. And I'm a lot rougher and meaner than you'll ever be. So dry those pretty eyes of yours before you spoil 'em crying, and ruin my wedding dress into the bargain. C'mon, snippie dear, tell us what Jeff said in his letter . . ."

"Th-th-that h-h-he's stationed at Charleston, South Ca'lina," Mary Sue began, the very thought of her red-headed, freckled-faced lover rapidly drying her streaming eyes, "and that he's working on all kinds of projects under the direction of a man named Hunley—who's a real brilliant inventor, Jeff says. And that he's due for leave the last week of October. They're giving him all of fifteen days 'cause he hasn't had any time off in so long and—"

But by then Rose Ann had caught her by the shoulders with almost maniacal force and whirled her around to face the door.

"Simp, you precious idiot baby!" she howled. "All you've got in your cute little noggin is hominy grits! Get out of here! Ride into Richmond, right now!"

"But what do I have to ride into Richmond for, Rose Ann?" Mary Sue said a little fearfully.

"To send Jeffie love a telegram, you silly goose! Telling him about my wedding. Demanding that he ask his commanding officer for travel orders and a pass to Richmond, Vee-Ay! Alleging that I'll die of a broken heart, and you will too, if he doesn't come! Most higher officers are as sentimental as all get-out about weddings and suchlike, out of their stupid exaltation of 'pure Southern womanhood'! Lord, if they only knew what we're *really* like—"

Mary Sue Hunter loosed a clear, girlish giggle.

"Good thing they don't, or they'd all be hightailing it for the nearest woods, trying to escape from our hot little hands!" she laughed. "All right, I'm on my way . . ."

"No, wait," Gwen said. "Mary Sue, do you have enough money to pay for a telegram *that* long?"

"Lord, no! But I'll stop by home and Papa will give me some—"

"I'll give you enough right now," Gwen said quietly. "Or at least before you go. Because there's no need to go rushing off like a wild woman. The telegraph office stays open 'til ten o'clock at night these days. Later, sometimes, when there're a great deal of important messages to send. Richmond *is* the capital of the Confederacy, remember. Besides, Jeff will get it early tomorrow morning, no matter what time we send it today. So let's not get ourselves into a dither, shall we? What d'you two say to a nice cup of something hot? What'll it be, girls? Sassafras tea or imitation coffee?"

"Ugh! Ugh!" Rose Ann said. "And in case you haven't noticed,

Gwen sugar, that's two ughs. One for each of those thick, hot, sickening gut twisters. My poor little bullet-scrambled intestines just aren't up to handling the Lawd-awful stuff we have to drink nowadays. Besides, we're plumb out of sugar, so we'd have to sweeten 'em with sorghum, and sorghum, in case you haven't been told, turns the teeth *black*."

"It sure *does*," Mary Sue sighed. "Gwen honey, you don't have to play the perfect hostess. *Everybody's* out of delicacies these days. Even the Harrisons and the Carters are cutting back, I've heard. Let's just sit and chat awhile . . ."

"About what?" Rose Ann said morosely. "Not about Kurtie pie, 'cause I'm plain shamed to admit how much about him I just don't know. And all I do know, I wish I didn't."

"Oh, Lord, Rose Ann, he can't be *that* bad! Or else how could you even *dream* of wedding him?"

"I don't. I dream of *not* marrying him. Fat chance! Once a Mc-Kenzie woman's female instincts get ahead of her head, she's lost."

"Rose," Gwen said quietly, "I'm not going to try to deny that what you're saying is true. But not exactly in the way you're implying. We *are*—entirely too passionate. Even—much to my shame and sorrow—*I*. But all down the Clan's history, we—our ancestresses, anyhow—have only got into trouble, under—well—unforeseen circumstances, in—difficult situations, call them. Upon sudden impulse. And then only after having been subjected to weeks, months, even years of overwhelming temptation. But I swear to you that I've *never* heard of any woman of our family who coolly and calmly decided beforehand that she just had to do something she shouldn't. That's the very definition of inexcusable immorality, it seems to me."

"And to *me*," Rose said sadly. "But there you have it. 'Cause Kurt is an unforeseen circumstance, a one-man difficult situation all by himself, overwhelming temptation given flesh, packing all those weeks, months, years you mentioned, Gwennie darling, into five minutes flat. And around him, all my impulses become sudden. Explosive. Irresistible. And dead goddamn *wrong* . . ."

"Ohhh, Lord!" Mary Sue breathed. "That sounds *awful*. And—and—just thrilling!"

"Simpie baby, you sure had me fooled," Rose Ann said with a weary chuckle. "But now that we've exhausted the not exactly edifying subject of my promised, what *will* we talk about? I vote we skip the war. We've lost it already, or very nearly . . ."

"Why, Rose Ann!" Mary Sue squealed. "How can you say a

thing like that? Our brave boys have won plumb nigh every battle they've fought so far and—"

"Simpie pie," Rose Ann sighed, "you're a sweet child and I love you dearly, and aim to be a loving auntie to all two dozen of your red-headed, speckle-tailed McKenzie offspring, but you really aren't right bright, y'know. When you were a smart little girl baby at school, didn't anybody ever teach you to spell Pyrrhic?"

"No. What's pie-rick?" Mary Sue said.

"Oh, Jesus. Skip it," Rose Ann said. "Gwen, help me out of this gorgeous circus tent. I'm getting the cold sweats again. And I sure wouldn't like to stain the armpits of it . . ."

"But how *can* you perspire—cool as it is?" Mary Sue said wonderingly.

"It's a sign of weakness," Gwen sighed. "Ramb, I think maybe you'd better go lie down awhile . . ."

"All right," Rose said, "but only if you two will come sit with me. Lying there all by my lonesome gives me the horrors . . ."

"Rose Ann," Mary Sue said plaintively, "why d'you think we've lost the war?"

"Don't think it. I know it. We have. Unless every woman in the South, married *and* single, can figure out a way to have a boy baby every other day, and force-feed him so he'll grow up to rifle-toting size in a couple more. Look, snippie dear, while I was lying here deciding not to die, Marse Bob Lee and Company won the second Bull Run campaign. Then our private and personal hero, little old Cabe Henry—who's another reason I've got to marry Kurt, 'cause this here yaller-headed old meanie plain refuses to share her darling husband with me!—took Harpers Ferry, and eleven thousand damnyankee prisoners, with some slight assistance from Stonewall Jackson, of course. In the meantime, Marse Robert had invaded Maryland, thinking, maybe, that the population was going to rise to the man and join our noble cause. Only the population wasn't having any, thank you. They took one look at our brave boys, barefooted, ragged-assed, louse-infested, and stinking like billy goats—"

"Rose Ann, I do declare!" Mary Sue burst out.

"Simpie sugar, you've already declared. And your allegiance to the truth, at that. Well, this is it. When our boys marched through Frederick City, one dear old lady, with tears streaming down her face, called out to 'em: 'The Lord bless your dirty, ragged souls!' So nobody rose to join us. Those Marylanders decided that an army in which one third of the men had to be excused from keeping up with their companies because their poor bony, blistered feet were as bare as their tailbones wasn't going to win anybody's war . . . ."

"But we did win in Maryland!" Mary Sue cried.

"Yes'm, we sure Lord did. Our army was led by a military genius named Robert E. Lee, and he had back of him the bravest soldiers known to history, with the possible exception of the goddamn gallant boys in blue they were fighting against. And both of 'em, the boys in blue and ours in butternut brown, filled up that sunken road in front of the old Dunker church with so much blood that it was actually getting into the shoe tops of them as had shoes. Result —Bloody Antietam. Twelve thousand brave Yankee lads dead in their boots. Which *they* had. God bless 'em, and accept their unshriven souls. *And* eleven thousand of our super-gallant corn-fed heroes—likewise. Only barefooted. And bare-assed. Same prayer. Ditto and amen!"

"Ramb," Gwen whispered, "the papers didn't print—the casualties. Nor, as I recall, *any* of the details you're talking about. So how on earth could *you* know them? I'll admit you sound awfully positive, but—"

"Kurt. Whose job it is to know things like that. Got most of 'em from Heros, who was *there*, remember. So we won. And marched back out of Maryland, *without* taking or even seriously threatening Washington, without invading Pennsylvania, which was what Kurt kind of thinks Marse Robert had in mind, without accomplishing one blessed thing except cutting down twenty-three thousand fine, brave, sweet, loving boys in the full flower of their manhood. So when you go home, look up that word Pyrrhic in your papa's dictionary. Or have Gwen explain it to you. She's the *smart* McKenzie sister, y'know . . . ."

"Gwen, what *does* that awful word mean?" Mary Sue asked plaintively.

"Later!" Gwen said sharply. "Ramb, I follow your reasoning as far as you go, but aren't you being unduly pessimistic? After all, General Lee saved our army and—"

"And nothing. That same night, fourteen thousand reinforcements joined the Union forces. And the *last* man, who is just that, who's got guts in his middle, brains in his head, and something else in his pants besides his legs, is *already* in our armies. There ain't no more, sugar. All that's left are boys like your darlin' Colin—"

"Rose Ann, I've told you—"

"All right, Gwennie dear. I'm just a wee bit deaf and a mite skeptical about the infinite perfectibility of female human nature. Specially the McKenzie variety. So let it pass. Besides, I can prove my point, on the basis of what the newspapers *have* printed. What happened right here in Richmond on April 16 of this very year, Gwen o' my heart?"

Gwen thought about that.

"Oh," she said, "that was the day Congress passed the first Conscription Act, wasn't it?"

"Go to the head of the class, honey! That act provided that a conscript could hire a substitute to get what he hadn't any of *nohow* shot off in his place. Now one of you real intelligent female corn-fed patriots tell me this: What was the going price for a prime, first-class substitute by August?"

"From fifteen hundred to three thousand dollars!" Mary Sue said bitterly. "All the rich cowards were putting announcements in the papers offering that much and more to any poor devil who'd march out and—"

"Aha!" Rose Ann said merrily.

"Rose, Colin volunteered. All right, maybe he did lose his nerve in battle, but you yourself said—"

"That I don't blame him. And I don't. A bullet in your guts feels real *bad*, honey. But let's pass over that. Very few cowards were rich. But a hell of a lot of 'em suddenly developed a burning call to preach, since ministers of the gospel were exempted. Likewise schoolmasters with at least twenty pupils. So down here where ain't nobody never give a cuss 'bout no book larnin' nohow we had schools and academies and what-have-yous springing up like mushrooms. Ditto apothecary shops, since pharmacists were exempted too. And the number of fellows who discovered that their folks plumb forgot to put their names down on those naturalization papers when they brung them over from the old country as tiny tots would astonish you. That is, if you've got any astonishment left, which I *ain't*. Every consular office in these here Confederate States of America has been swamped with stalwart lads swearing allegiance to foreign flags. And because like everything we do, that damn-fool law just wasn't made right, it has one loophole you could drive a team of Missouri mules through: A fellow can't be inducted in a state he's not a permanent resident of. So, sister mine, the itch for travel suddenly became an epidemic. All it adds up to, I reckon, is that we Sothorons are natural extremists. We've got the bravest, fightingest bunch of boys on God's green earth in our armies. Only we're using 'em up at a fearful rate, trying to do what can't be done: beat the Yankees. And we've got *the* most miserable bunch of lily-livered, yellow-bellied, sniveling polecats of cowards ever heard of in human history. Bar none. And to hell with 'em!"

"I've heard a little of all that," Gwen sighed, "but I dismissed it as unimportant. And, knowing *you*, I'm sure you're exaggerating as usual . . ."

"The corn-fed government, with Marse Jeff at the head of it, don't think so, Gwen sugar. So let's go on with our lessons in recent history. What happened on September 17, a little over a month ago? C'mon, honey child, tell me *that!*"

"The second Conscription Act was passed," Gwen said grimly, "providing—"

"That all subsitutes have become liable for induction and service on their own account, thus leaving the poltroons who bought and paid for their miserable hides as bulletproof armor plate, to cover the yellow streak they've got down their own spinal columns, without any protection whatsoever. Result: *Every* court in the length and breadth of our so gallant Southland has a backlog of cases it'll take ten years to try, suits brought by our Knights of the High and Holy Order of Pusillanimity in defense of the bona fide contracts they made with the government, and/or the crowd of rustic wiseacres they hired to save their skins, ninety-seven percent of whom deserted two hours after having been sent to camp. Which is where the matter stands at this very moment. Of course, to make up for having been real *mean* to the wearers of the white feather, the government turned right around and was absolutely generous with new exemptions . . ."

"Among them being," Gwen said acridly, "the one granted to factory owners, their mechanics, and other employees engaged in the manufacture of arms and munitions. But, Ramb, if you had a fair bone in your body, you'd have to admit that Colin opened his little arms and ammunition plant *after* his wound—self-inflicted or not!—had removed any possibility whatsoever of his being conscripted!"

"And I do admit it, gladly," Rose Ann said. "Now that you've told me that Colin's gone into the gun-making business. Honey, will you believe me when I say that I didn't even know that? I've been kind of poorly here of late, remember. And nobody, not even you, bothered to tell me the good news. I wasn't being sarcastic about Colin, Gwen. From where I sit, he's got an awful lot in his favor. He volunteered, went, and did the best he could. He found out in battle, and under fire, that he was a coward. That's a heck of a lot better than the perfect horde of dastards who made up their minds on that exact point beforehand, and pulled off every trick in the books to 'bombproof' their arrant hides. Tell me: Is old tall, dark, and stiff-legged going to make his own explosives?"

"No, I don't think so," Gwen said. "Most munitions factories don't, I believe. They merely order their gunpowder from the chemical plants who do make it, and use it to fill small-arms cartridges, artillery shells, naval torpedoes, and the like, I've been told . . ."

"A pity," Rose Ann sighed. " 'Cause I was going to be first in line to present him with my little old chamber pot, brimming over with some nice homemade pee-pee, piping hot. Lord, wouldn't he ever turn as red as a beet, and start in to splutter when I gave him my personal contribution to the cause!"

"Rose Ann, I do declare!" Mary Sue snapped. "If you didn't say something outrageous with every other breath, reckon you'd curl up and die. That's *real* embarrassing, isn't it? I mean, the War Department's coming right out and asking for *ladies* to save all the urine of their families and contribute it to the Niter Board to make gunpowder out of. Good thing we've all got nigger wenches to take it in for us. 'Sides, I just don't understand how they can get gunpowder out of *that*, anyhow . . ."

"Human urine," Gwen explained patiently, "has a high nitrogen content. And nitrogen is the basic material in the manufacture of explosives. So it seems to me that our feminine modesty about a natural bodily function ought to be waived in this case. Anyhow, Rose, Colin's hired a first-class engineer to run his little factory for him. A Swede named Lindsholm, who learned gunsmithing in his native country. Colin tells me that they aren't even going to try to compete with the big manufacturers, but will concentrate on new and highly experimental arms, such as the breechloaders and repeating carbines Cabe and Jeff suggested as being the weapons our troops most need . . ."

Rose Ann grinned at her sister mockingly.

"And just *where* did your darling Colin tell you all that, Gwen honey?" she purred. "At A'nt Sukie's?"

"Who's A'nt Sukie?" Mary Sue asked wonderingly. "Sounds like a nigger's name to me . . ."

"It is," Gwen said quietly, coolly. "Aunt Sukie is an old witch of a free Negress who runs an establishment whose precise nature is better left unspecified, it seems to me. And for your sweet, innocent information, Mary Sue—for I couldn't care less what Rose Ann thinks about the matter, and will charitably refrain from reminding her how little right she has to question *anyone's* personal behavior, beyond, of course, wondering just how *she* found out about that horrible place—"

"From frequent visits to it, with all my scads of lovers," Rose Ann said solemnly. "And 'tain't horrible, sister mine. Quite cozy in fact. So now, tit for tat. How did *you?*"

Gwen stared at her younger sister. Studied her, really. Then she gave a sigh of patient resignation.

"I only hope you're joking, Ramb," she said, "and even more that that wasn't one of those truths spoken in jest. With you, one never knows! As to how *I* knew about Aunt Sukie's place, that's simple: Cabe told me. My dearest husband admits to having been an assiduous client of the—well—service that evil old black witch purveys. In his younger days, before he married me, he swears. I suspect after, as well. Which is another of the many things I couldn't care less about. But if the subject interests either of you, I met Colin Claiborne quite by chance the other day when I was downtown shopping—or rather trying to, since there's practically nothing to be bought. And again, if the detail is of any concern to anybody besides me myself: Yes, I was glad to see him. Colin's a fine young man who's been punished quite enough for what's not exactly an unnatural sin. Incidentally, Ramb, I took advantage of the occasion to invite Colin to your wedding personally. I told him that you *wanted* him to attend . . ."

"As a matter of fact, I *don't*. But only because he's surely taken the invitation as a piece of pure meanness on my part—rubbing salt into his wounds, as it were. Well, it's done now, so let it stand. What about Cabe? Is he going to be able to get a leave? They're camped up around Fredericksburg, aren't they? That's not too far for him to get here . . ."

"Don't worry. My somewhat less than loving husband, who has always had polygamous ideas as far as you and I are concerned, Ramb, will be here with bells on. I honestly believe he would have deserted temporarily if General Jackson hadn't granted him leave for the occasion. Speaking of which, you're being highly honored, my dear! Cabe writes that when he asked for leave the general answered, 'Of course, Major. And if you haven't any objections, I'll come along with you. The Yankees are mighty quiet these days, and we owe that young lady an awful lot . . . ' "

"Ohhh, goodie!" Rose Ann squealed. "Old Jack Jackson in person! That means I've got *two* generals for the ceremony!"

"Two?" Mary Sue breathed. "Who's the other one? Not General —Lee?"

"Lord no, baby! I don't aim *that* high. Jeb, of course. He told Heros to ask me what I wanted for a wedding present from *him*, as long as it wasn't a button off his uniform, or a lock of his hair. Seems all the silly little dillies who're always pining for his love have cut so many buttons off his uniforms, and snippets off his cloak, they've left him practically in rags. And if he gives away another lock o' hair to all the lovelorn maidens who're always begging him for one as a keepsake, he's going to be as bald as an ostrich egg. So, after thinking the matter over, I told Jeb I wanted old Abe Lincoln's *whiskers*. Jeb swears he's going to get 'em for me, and bring me the Princess Salm-Salm in chains to be my personal maid from now on, into the bargain . . ."

"And who, may I ask, is the Princess Salm-Salm?" Gwen demanded.

"Honest Abe's fun filly. She's some kind of a dark-skinned foreigner who tells fortunes and suchlike, I'm told. Anyhow, she keeps poor fat little Mary Todd in a perpetual state of the howling jealous meanies by always kissing old long-tall and ugly right out in public when the damnyankees' First Lady is not around. Say, that's real crazy, isn't it? Mary Todd's as Southern as all get-out, and from a slaveholding family at that, and yet she's the First Lady of Yankeedom! But it appears to me she shouldn't take on over friend hubby's having himself a spot of innocent fun. I'm sure there's nothing to it. The Princess only kisses Abe 'cause he's President of these Disunited States. Can you imagine anybody's kissing that gawky, apish-looking creature for real? 'Cause she *wanted* to, I mean?"

"Yes," Gwen said soberly, "I can, quite easily. Ugliness doesn't rob a man of charm, Rose Ann. And I've been told by women who've met him that President Lincoln is terribly attractive. They say he has a wonderful sense of humor, and puts people immediately at their ease in his company. Which is something that can't be said for *our* President, y'know . . ."

"You can say that again. Old Jeff is as stiff as a board. And Varina Howell is just plain flighty. But what else did Cabe say? Is he bringing all those good-looking colonels and majors on old Jackson's staff with him too?"

"If so, he didn't mention it," Gwen said. "The rest of his letter was rather gloomy. He wrote several things that lend considerable weight to your complaints about the Conscription Laws. He feels that they've damaged the Army's morale to a disturbing degree. The chief offender being the clause in the exemption provisions that, come to think of it, would have been still another reason that Colin wouldn't have had to go back to war, even if he weren't wounded and hadn't started that arms factory. The Claibornes own fifty-five or fifty-six Negroes, as I recall . . ."

"The twenty-nigger law? That wasn't smart *at all.* It's got all the poor folks up in arms. Heck of a note for a man with forty acres and a mule to have to march off to face the Yankees and leave his wife and children to just plain starve, 'cause what eighteen dollars a month in Jeff Davis's shin plasters will buy at any grocery store or butcher's shop you could take home in a thimble, while rich nabobs, with hundreds of niggers at their beck and call, don't ever have to hear the whine of a minié ball. I don't blame the poor people for getting mad . . ."

"Nor do I," Gwen sighed. "The reasoning behind that clause was impeccable: that a large plantation owner could do the Confederacy much more good by staying home and growing foodstuffs for our armies than he ever could as an individual soldier. But it wasn't explained to the people beforehand, and now it's plain too late. Caleb writes that desertions are increasing every day. And not the cowards, the bounty jumpers, and the substitutes, whom everyone was glad to be rid of—General Jackson flatly refused to accept substitutes in his command, you know—but good, brave boys who've fought like tigers up 'til now. They're getting letters that read: 'Effen you doan come home, swear to God us is all going to die, Rufe boy!' "

"That's real *sad,*" Mary Sue sighed. "Gwen, I hate to mention it, but I'm as hungry as a bear. Now don't you stand on ceremony, you hear? If y'all are short t'day, just say so, and I'll head for home. Nowadays, *every*body runs short of grub at times, no matter how rich they used to be . . ."

"Well, we McKenzies have never been really rich," Gwen said with a smile, "but we've always been able to eat. And we'll go on being able to, as long as the government doesn't impress the Negroes into labor battalions as rumor says it's threatening to. We can offer you cornmeal ashcake, cooked in the embers of the fireplace on the blade of a shovel, which Aunt Cindy says is the quickest way to do it. Some ham, some sweet potatoes, all the buttermilk you can drink, butter for the ashcake and the potatoes, but all of it rather tasteless, because we haven't any salt . . ."

"Who does?" Rose Ann said gloomily. "Heros say he saw Jeb's troopers gorging themselves on salt by the handfuls when they captured a Yankee wagon train some time back, and so far as I know, there's only one salt mine in the whole blamed Confederacy. Of course, that *is* right here in Virginia, at Saltville, in the south-western part of the state. But even so, that's pretty far, and we have to share the production with all the other states. I keep telling Gwen we ought to send Cassius or Brutus down to the seashore to make us a little salina, by pouring seawater in a hollow and evapo-rating it in the sun, which will leave a thin crust of salt behind. But she's afraid that the Negroes have got a mite too skittish and just might run away. Or some farmer, needing a likely hand he hasn't the money to buy, will steal ours. Oh, Lord! Everything is wrong these days! Mary Sue, please do stay and break bread with us. I *need* company, y'know."

It was then that they heard the first rippling, rattling strum of banjo chords. A moment later, a baritone voice of true operatic quality soared effortlessly in a song whose words were totally in-comprehensible—more, even unrecognizable—to them. They wouldn't really have understood a French *chanson d'amour*, but they would have known the language was French. What this one was, they didn't know, except that it wasn't German, for Heros von Borcke had educated their ears sufficiently with his rollicking *Trinklieder* and romantic *Liebeslieder* for them to have also recog-nized German.

Mary Sue's eyes became twin blue saucers in her tiny face.

"*Him?*" she whispered.

"Yes," Rose Ann said sadly. "The one who's singing, anyhow. The banjo player is Sweeny, one of Jeb's troopers. His job is to ride beside Jeb picking that damn banjo with the bullets whistling and the bombs bursting all around 'em, 'cause that idiot of a Jeb thinks of himself as gallant troubadour singing love songs in the very heat of battle. Going to get himself killed like that, sure as hell, one of these days, and poor Sweeny with him, likely!"

"But now he's accompanying Count Radetzy—?"

" 'Cause Jeb loaned him to Kurt. Kurt always overdoes every-thing. These here damned serenades started when Heros told him: 'She's a most romantic little maiden. So if you really mean to wed her, you'd better pay attention to your wooing!' That song is prob-ably Hungarian, 'cause Kurt knows more songs in that language than in any other except German and French. He can talk seven or eight languages and sing songs in ten or twelve. Fat lot of good that does me, when I don't even know *English* worth a damn when you get right down to it . . ."

"You don't seem very happy about these gallant attentions," Gwen said harshly.

"I'm not. If he'd thought of them himself, I would be, but he had to be told, or at least reminded. He hasn't a romantic bone in his body. He's—a machine. I don't hate him, I reckon, or how could I be so powerfully attracted to him? But I just don't *like* the kind of man he is. I only hope I can change him a little after we're wed—"

"In that case, Ramb," Gwen said grimly, *"don't* marry him. The only way any woman in history has ever changed a man is with an ax. I'll admit that Cabe *has* changed, and for the better, but the war did that, not I. So don't be a fool, sister mine. Oh, I grant you he's the handsomest male human I've ever seen, but beauty is as beauty does, so—"

"Gwen, did you ever know one of those crazy people who smoke opium—or drink laudanum?" Rose whispered. "Well, that's *me*. About *him*. Don't ask me why. I *can't* tell you. I don't know the words. And anyhow, it—the reason I feel the way I do toward him —is just too awful . . ."

Gwen stared at her sister speculatively.

"Ramb," she said slowly, softly, "you—you haven't gone and let him—"

"No. Mainly because he's never tried. The whole question of— well—intimacies seems to rather bore him. He has never got the slightest bit out of line with me. A kiss or two—a gentle caress, that's all. I doubt I interest him enough to bother. Except as—an instrument to be used, a pawn in the only game that excites him— his wild, crazy scheme for dominating the whole damn world. And if he ever gets even close to doing that, he'll drop me like a hot brick. So I'm lost. Help me put something on. I'd better go talk to him a little or he'll keep on caterwauling 'til night . . ."

It was very quiet in the bedroom after she had gone. So quiet they could make out the rustle of the whispers from the garden outside the window. The two young women faced each other, their eyes appalled.

"God, in His infinite mercy, help her!" Gwendolyn McKenzie Henry said.

Chapter Seven

On the Wednesday before the Sunday on which her wedding was to take place, Rose Ann sat with Kurt in the bright yellow rattan trap he'd rented, admiring the skillful way he handled the much too spirited bay gelding he'd hired along with the little vehicle.

He does everything well, she thought, and that's another thing about him that's kind of scary. He can outride even Jeb's wild troopers. And I saw him hit three out of four bottles thrown into the air at the same time before they got back to the ground again, in that revolver-shooting contest all the officers stationed in Richmond held a couple of weeks ago. Besides, he's really trying to be nicer—gentle and attentive and—and tender! Maybe I got him wrong before. Maybe all that wild talk of his was only that—talk. These rides, now. Just because Dr. Hendricks said that I needed fresh air more'n anything else to awaken my appetite so I could put on a little weight, and thereby avoid going straight into a decline when the rains really set in, Kurt has been taking me for a spin *every* afternoon. In a trap that's got a folding top to it, in case a sprinkle comes up. And with his Negro manservant sitting on the little rumble seat behind us, so that not even the evilest old witch in town can say we've ever been anywhere alone, and besmirch my *spotless* reputation. That's a laugh. Me. A one-night bride. A divorcée—no, an annullee, if there's any such word. A—widow. Poor Joe-Joe. Poor sweet little boy baby doll. Rest in peace, sugar pie. And forgive me, will you, huh? Where was I? Oh, yes. My reputation. I've been Colin's—whore. No, that's wrong too. Whores get *paid.* Say, his fun filly. His play-time, good-time girl. Lord Jesus! S'pose Kurt expects me to be—untouched? A man with all the experience I'm certain sure he's had will know at once that—that some other fellow has been cherry picking, or rather cherry *busting,* out of season! Oh, Lord, oh, Jesus, I—

"Kurt," she said in a low and troubled voice, "I—I've got to tell you something—"

"What, my love?" Radetzy said, and flashed her a brilliant smile.

"Oh, Lord!" she moaned. "I just don't know how to—"

"Confess your sins?" he said, that ice-bright smile unwavering. "Tell me you've been passed through the entire regiment?"

Rose stared at him.

"Well, I'll be damned!" she exploded.

"Well, haven't you?" Radetzy chuckled. "I expected that much at the very least. Redheads are usually rather lewd little creatures. Something about the coloring, I suppose. The flames on their darling little heads being a rather accurate indication of their internal temperature . . ."

"And you wouldn't *care*," she breathed. "So—good. Fine. You're right. That's where I got my Yankee accent from. I learned it underneath the whole blamed Union Army!"

He threw back his head and laughed. Freely. Gaily.

"I suspected as much!" he said cheerfully. "Oh, all right! I'll come off it. I was only teasing you, my dear. Come now, what was it—this terrible thing you want to tell me?"

"That I've been—married before," Rose Ann whispered. "I eloped with a very nice boy I was truly in love with. Only he'd lied to me about his age. He was two years younger than I and a legal minor. So his father had it annulled. And anyhow, the poor boy was killed at Seven Pines—"

"Then I fail to see the problem," Kurt said gently. "Why were you so badly troubled over such an unimportant matter, my sweet?"

"I—I didn't want you to think that I'd been—bad. Fast. Loose. Immoral . . ."

"But why on earth would I think a thing like that?" he asked with genuine astonishment. Then he got it. "Oh!" he laughed. "You're referring to your—physical state. How quaint! Rose Ann, my love, most men demand virginity in their brides because they're so terribly unsure of themselves, and even more so of their abilities as lovers, that they quite rightly fear what will happen if the dear little girls have any basis for comparison. But since I once took the very queen of *les poules de luxe* out of the most expensive *maison close* on the Left Bank, and had her following me all over Paris in abject adoration for weeks until I tired of the creature and bade her be off, whereupon she drowned herself in the Seine that very night, whether you've had a lover or two before I came upon the scene is a matter for yawning over, if that. If you'd had too many, I should care, of course, but only because no connoisseur finds worn-out garbage appetizing. However, your youth, your freshness, your innocent candor all assure me that has not been your case. I shall, I know, have the supremely exquisite pleasure of awakening you to the delights of love, teaching that slender and angelic form the very meaning of ecstasy. Hence I see no reason for worrying about your schoolgirl's past of fumbling attempts and sad disappointments . . ."

"What makes you so certain sure I've been disappointed," she asked a little sullenly, thinking: He knows entirely too blamed much! Or he can read my face like a book, or—

"You live in a country where the males are predominantly Anglo-Saxons. And their ancestral prudery makes them the most abysmal of lovers. Which is why English and American girl tourists have been the delight of us wicked old Europeans for generations, my sweet!"

"Only my—husband—wasn't Anglo-Saxon. He was—Latin. Italian . . ."

"Even worse!" Kurt laughed. "When they go upstairs with some fair, frail daughter of commercial joy, they don't even tie their horses to the hitching rings. No need. They *know* they'll be back down again in one and one half minutes flat . . ."

"You're—too smug. I hate you. You're a horrible, beastly man, Kurt Radetzy!"

"Hmmmnnn," he murmured. "That's an interesting development. Let's see how much you hate me, Rambling Rose . . ."

"Don't call me that! And don't kiss me! I don't want you to kiss me, so don't don't don't— Mnnnnnnnnnnnnnnnnnnn— Mnnnnnnnnnnn— Oh. Ohhhhhhhhh. Ah. Ah. Ahhhhhhh— God!"

She sat there beside him, clinging to his arm and still shuddering. Quivering. Every nerve in her slender body a violin string, its anchoring peg too tightened, vibrating just below the breaking point, making in the darkness of her mind, her heart, one high, white, blinding, murderously sweet, despairing cry: Again! It's getting worse. He barely has to touch me now. So—Sunday night, I'm going to die. To shatter all to pieces like crystal and lie there glittering on the rug. And I hope I'll cut his damn feet all to hell when he tries to walk across me.

She murmured, "I love you, Kurt. I don't think you realize how much, how awf'ly, dreadfully much I love you. It's—killing me— by inches."

"Hmmm—another interesting development. So now you love me? Prove it!"

She straightened up. Stared at him. Whispered, "Prove it—how, Kurt?"

He pointed with his whip toward where one of the Union Army's two observation balloons was rising like a baleful dark moon against the limpid autumn sky. It was a long distance away. Across the Chickahominy, she judged. Of course, if they got high enough, they could see Richmond clearly. And the three camps around it General Lee had his army in. Jackson's—she thought—was still somewhere up near Fredericksburg, which meant that McClellan's Bluebellies, who'd crossed the Potomac again last week, on October 26, were between General Jackson's forces and Richmond, so maybe her sweet old crazy brother-in-law Cabe Henry might not get to her wedding at all.

Kurt's voice, speaking harshly, cut her off. "Go find out what makes that ruddy thing go up. You can do it, with that lovely smile and cultivated New England accent of yours, my dear. I'll put you across the Chickahominy before dawn tomorrow. After that it'll be up to you . . ."

"Find out—what makes it go up?" she whispered. "A gas, isn't it, dearest?"

"Of course. But what kind? Your stupid War Department has asked me to obtain precise information about that very question. Of course, they won't be able to do a bloody thing with the information once I—we—get it for them, but I rather think a friend of mine will. For the benefit of the Greater Pan-Germanic Reich, of course. Brilliant chap, Ferdie. Absolutely gone on the subject of flying machines. So if those Yanks have discovered a simpler way of manufacturing one of the lighter gases, helium, or hydrogen, say, he'll be delighted. He has half a dozen engineers at work now, trying to design a steam engine light enough to be lifted by a balloon. He does that, and we—you and I, darling—get him the formula for whatever gas yon Yanks are using, old Ferdie will produce an airship capable of pushing itself through the air at high speeds with huge screw propellers of the Ericsson type, and England's vaunted invulnerability will be done!"

"Ferdie—who?" Rose whispered, even more faintly.

"Von Zeppelin. *Graf*—Count—Ferdinand von Zeppelin. Prince of a chappie, Ferdie. He's trying like blazes to get himself sent as military attaché to the Prussian Embassy in Washington. He'll do it too. When Ferdie puts his mind to a thing, he always succeeds . . ."

"But why—Washington?" Rose Ann said a little angrily. "Why not—Richmond?"

"Because," Kurt said, "you Southerners have nothing to offer scientifically. The North is a hundred years ahead of you. They're even ahead of Europe in some ways. We'll probably see Ferdie in Washington when we come back from our European honeymoon . . ."

"We—we're going to *Europe*, Kurt?" Rose Ann gasped.

"Rather. Quite. Didn't I mention it before? No? Sorry, my dear. You see, I have to go to London, because there're two or three high lordly muck-a-mucks over there who were deuced interested in our cause before but who seem to have slackened off quite a bit here of late. I mean to put a bee in their bonnets, or a flea in their powdered perukes, as it were . . ."

"Oh, I see," Rose Ann said brightly. "You're going to tell them that if they don't grant us recognition right away, and later on send the British Navy to chase the Yankee blockaders out of our harbors, we'll *never* let them have any more cotton!"

Radetzy laughed at that one. Freely, gaily.

"My little First Secretary for Foreign Affairs," he chuckled. "Twitch the Home Office's bright red noses, eh, love? Rose Ann, darling, that wild idea you Southerners have about cotton's being king is utter rot. The British—conniving blackguards that they are!—stored up enough of your bales before this war, which any fool could see was coming, to last their textile mills at least three years. Seven hundred thousand bales of the bloody stuff, to be exact, my sweet. And they had in their warehouses, ready to be shipped for sale, some three hundred million pounds of already manufactured cotton goods. You and the Yanks, between you, saved their ruddy scheming arses for them. They'd overproduced so greatly that the bottom had dropped out of the market; the truth is, love, that the prices for British-made fabrics had actually fallen so low by '61 that the blighters were being forced to sell below cost. Their entire textile industry faced sheer ruin. So the Yankee blockade, which throughout '61 and well into this year was the biggest joke in history, since the Federals had approximately one seaworthy cruiser for every thousand miles of Southern coastline, was a godsend to them, because it gave that race of grubby tradesmen and shopkeepers the perfect argument to convince their customers that a shortage, instead of a crashing, thunderous surplus, existed, so they could sell off their shoddy, job-lot-manufactured rags at perfectly outrageous prices. Then, to make the situation even more hilarious, your noble Southern statesmen not only pretended that the Union blockade was effective but ordered your planters to cut back on the production of cotton, all on the basis that neither France nor England could do without your matchless staple—"

"Well, can they?" Rose Ann demanded. "I've always heard that the European textile industry *runs* on our cotton!"

"Ran. Past tense. Thanks to this charming Civil War of yours. Nothing, my sweet, stirs the dull brains of the mercantile classes into a reasonable facsimile of thought as rapidly as a threat to their purses. So now the John Bulls and the Emile Du Ponts have discovered, or had pointed out to them, the economic folly of depending upon a single, monopolistic source of supply. Result: The mills of Scotland are running wide out, producing excellent woolen goods; ditto those of Ireland, with linen from their native flax. Same story for Normandy and Brittany, as far as La Belle France is concerned. And to make the Confederacy's future even more dismal than it already is, the British are actively encouraging the Brazilians, the Egyptians, and the Hindus to plant cotton up to the very steps of their filthy hovels. When this cruel war is over, you won't have any markets. For one thing, Egyptian cotton is immensely superior to yours in quality. For another, even if you manage to hang on to slavery, which I doubt, you'll never be able to compete with the sort of *Lumpenproletariate* your British cousins have encouraged to enter the fray as far as the production of raw cotton is concerned. What *one* of your stout niggers eats in a day would feed two families of those miserable starvelings for a week . . ."

Rose Ann stared at her fiancé.

"Kurt," she asked him quietly, "why'd you ever come over here to help us out, when you—despise us so?"

"By Jove, that's a thought! Why did I really? Item one, my dearest Rose: I *don't* despise you. Backward as you indisputably are, you're all my idiotic cousins, say, since both the Angles and the Saxons came from Germany in the first place, y'know. In the second, as I told you before, only you Sothorons, after us Germans, of course, have a solid, if instinctive grasp upon the idea of the importance of race. And last of all, we'll educate you both thoroughly and quickly once you've come under our control . . ."

"Oh, Lord!" Rose Ann said. "Heros told me that you actually rode with Jeb's troopers during part of the second Manassas campaign. Didn't that give you any idea of what we do to folks who try to control us?"

"Of course. Bloodthirsty tribe of howling savages, aren't you? But, my dearest dear, we Germans have no intention of making war on you, since we'll be able to convince you of the wisdom of joining us by subtler means. Incidentally, you're going to have to free your blacks, y'know. At this juncture, they're the greatest handicap you have . . ."

"Whaaaat!" Rose Ann gasped.

"Precisely that. You see, my love, it is very easy to arouse noble sentiments in the breasts of people against an institution that they secretly fear is going to adversely affect their own scant and precarious economic well-being. Therefore the hearts of the wage slaves of Europe bleed for the poor damned *Neger*, who, in the majority of cases, is rather a bit better off than they are. No one throws old and useless blacks out to starve, a thing that happens to continental workers every day. So, today, no European government would dare declare itself openly on the side of the South. Which is why that rustic Machiavelli, Lincoln, achieved—on the level of propaganda only—*un coup de tonnerre* with that ruddy Emancipation Proclamation of his . . ."

"Don't know what good his fine proclamation did old Darwin's proof positive," Rose Ann sniffed, "since there's no way on earth he can enforce it!"

"Darwin's proof—? Oh, I say, that's jolly good! The missing link Du Chaillu was looking for along the Congo? Honest Abe does have a remarkably simian aspect, come to think of it, but believe me, *Liebchen*, he has a first-class mind. He doesn't *need* to enforce his scrap of paper; all he has to do with that meaningless scribble, and by its agency, he's already done: prevented the one nation who could have and was disposed—its upper classes, anyhow—to come to your aid from doing so. Just a little while ago, that swinish Jew radical Karl Marx addressed a meeting of English workers in London and won from them by acclamation the avowed statement that the success of free institutions in America was of great importance to them. So neither England nor France will lift a finger to help you. Louis Napoleon is too much involved in his wild dream of making Mexico a French protectorate, and Her Majesty's government fears its working classes. The British have long memories, and the upheavals on the Continent in 1848, especially those at Paris and Vienna, are too fresh in their benighted minds . . ."

Rose Ann peered at her decidedly exotic lover. At that moment, in that afternoon slant of light, the Oriental cast of his countenance was extremely noticeable. He didn't, she was again aware, seem at all to be a member of the white race whose supremacy he was constantly proclaiming. For all his obvious cultivation, and glib intellectuality, he appeared a wild barbarian from the steppes of Asia, albeit a remarkably handsome one. If his eyes weren't so light-colored, he'd look almost like a Chinaman, she thought.

"Kurt, tell me something," she said. "You're a Hungarian, at

least by half, and yet I've never even heard you mention Hungary.
And when I was small, back in the fifties, everybody was going
wild over Louis Kossuth. People—my family among 'em, 'cause
Papa took us all to Washington to hear him speak—traveled for
hundreds of miles to listen to his appeals for help to free Hungary.
And since I've known you, I've yet to hear you say the name of
your country's greatest patriot . . ."

He turned to her, frowning fiercely. It was very clear that her
reproach had touched a raw nerve.

"Rose Ann," he said harshly, "let's see if we can't straighten out
a few confusions in your weird little mind. I am *not* a Hungarian
by nationality, but only—and that only halfway—by race. As I told
you, I was born in Prague, the capital of Bohemia. I was a grown
man before I ever saw either Buda or Pest. I even speak Hungarian
badly; it is, I suspect, perhaps the poorest of my languages. Wait
now; don't interrupt! I have never denied nor am I ashamed of my
Magyar blood. It is chiefly that I don't *feel* Hungarian, because I
wasn't brought up as one. You see, my father, Count Ludwig—or
rather Louis—Radetzy was murdered in Prague, where he'd been
sent by the Austro-Hungarian government with a detachment of
Hungarian troops to keep an eye on the Bohemians in those unsettled times. Since it soon became apparent that his stay was going to
be a long one, he sent for my mother, who was in Pest, and in-
stalled her in Bohemia with him. They'd been there two years
before I was born. My father was assassinated three weeks after I
arrived upon the scene, so, as you can see, I never knew him. His
murderer was neither a Czech nor a Slovak, as you'd expect, but a
Croat, who traveled all the way to Prague in order to kill him. Or
rather was sent, by one of the underground terrorist organizations
that flourished in Croatia—then under Hungarian domination—in
those days. The year of my birth, 1830, rather marked me, because
I was to hear about it all my life. In that year, the people of Paris
rose against Charles X, the Belgians against the Dutch, and the
Poles against the Russians. There was even a revolution of a group
called the Carbonari against the Papal States. Now, my mother,
who was an Austrian baroness and brought up with very definite
ideas as to what the place of the lower orders was, took me back to
Wien—Vienna to you, love. There she married again—one Otto
von Schwarzenberg, a cousin of the Count Felix von Schwarzenberg who brought Franz Josef to the throne and smashed the revolt
of the Hungarians against the Empire, with, of course, Russian
troops, sent by the Tsar . . ."

"Kurt honey," Rose sighed, "you lost me—quite a ways back . . ."

"I know. The point is, my sweet, that I was brought up in an aristocratic Austrian family, with all the rather rigid concepts that entails. My childhood was desperately unhappy: I adored my step-father and he rather despised me—"

"Lord God, Kurt, why?"

"My looks. He referred to me always to my mother as the little Mongol. Or your little Tartar. It took me until a little after my eighteenth birthday to win him over. When he discovered the part I'd played as a voluntary spy for the Secret Police in smashing the revolt of the liberals in Vienna during that other terrible year of revolutions, 1848, and reporting their names to Prince Windisch-grätz, who hanged them out of hand—"

"Kurt," Rose Ann said in troubled tone of voice, "why'd you do a thing like that?"

"Because democracy is always and everywhere a mistake!" Radetzy thundered. "Along with the inferior races, the lower or-ders must be kept firmly in hand! A workable democratic system, my dear, would require that the swarming, ever-spawning scum and scourings of the cities and your mindless, brutal peasants in the country possess what none of them have—intelligence. Suc-cessful government, my dearest, is always the work of an elite, composed of the superior minds of a superior race!"

"Like you Chinamen?" Rose needled him.

"Chinamen!" he bellowed. "Why—"

Then, instantly, icily, he regained control.

"If you like," he said with a mirthless smile. "For we wild Mongols from the barren steppes of Asia have always been *ein Herrenvolk*, never slaves. And well we know how to deal with our inferiors. If you don't believe me, ask the Croats. Or the Rumani-ans. But it seems to me I've rather overstuffed your sweet little head with ideas of import for one session! So I'd better take you back home again. Best that you get to bed early, because I'm going to get you up deuced early tomorrow morning so that you can set about charming the Yanks into telling you what they put in their balloons."

"Ohhhh, Lord!" Rose Ann wailed. "I thought I'd sidetracked you on that one, Kurtie love! Got you so busy polishing up my poor little lame brains that you'd forgot all about that damn bal-loon . . ."

"Well, I haven't. I *never* forget anything, sweet maid. So now we'll just turn Rosinante around and—"

"Kurt, no! I'm—scared! I'm not brave anymore. Having a hole punched all the way through my middle taught me that all my so-called bravery before that happened was just plain ignorance. And stupidity too, I reckon. Kurt sugar, darling, I don't want people shooting at me anymore!"

"They won't shoot at you, my sweet. Why should they? You'll be just a simple girl to them, asking silly questions out of sheer feminine curiosity. And when you start turning on the charm . . ."

She peered at him darkly, her green eyes forty fathoms deep with beginning anger, with slowly, clearly dawning—hurt.

"Kurt," she whispered, "s'pose one of those damnyankees—well —sort of, kind of—figured that it just isn't smart to give away information gratis. S'pose one of the higher officers demanded payment in kind—not in specie, if you get what I mean . . ."

"In such a case, you pretend to acquiesce long enough to get the information out of him, and then, by hook or crook, you get out of there!"

"But—s'pose I *can't* get out of there. S'pose there's no way to—"

"Thus providing you with an excuse *a priori* to indulge your redhead's lascivious instincts?" he chuckled. "Then—enjoy yourself, my darling! After all, soldiers give their lives for the cause. So what's a casual donation of a small portion of your dainty anatomy in comparison?"

Thirty seconds after he'd delivered himself of that gem, she was tearing at her ring finger, trying to get the magnificent solitaire he'd given her off it; her eyes gone flooded, blind.

"May I ask just what you're doing?" he asked her coolly.

"T-t-trying t-t-to g-g-get this d-d-damn r-r-ring off!" she sobbed. "T-t-to g-g-give it b-b-back to y-y-you! 'Cause you d-d-don't l-l-love me, K-k-kurt! N-n-no m-m-man who l-l-loves a w-w-woman w-w-would s-s-sell her as a whore!"

"True," he sighed. "I'd forgotten how primitive your concepts are. I do love you, Rose Ann. It's just that I believe that nothing, especially not such retrograde emotions as human jealousy, should stand in the way of our noble cause. But opinions differ, I suppose. All right, you needn't get the information at all, if it comes to that . . ."

"I'll get it all right!" she stormed. "I—I'll sleep with—the whole damn Yankee Army!"

"And the Navy, if they're available, I suppose," he laughed.

"Come now, Rose Ann, I've changed my mind. You mustn't make those Bluebellies any offers. Not even the smallest hint. They're not fools, y'know. Should you make yourself too readily available, they'll realize at once that you're a spy. Then they just might shoot you—after passing you through the regiment, of course. Besides, who knows?, I just might adopt the posture of one of your jealous Southern troglodytes and hang you from the transom by your wrists, and stripe your little bottom with a riding whip." Then he bent and kissed her. A long, slow time. Left her gut-crippled again. Sobbing, breath-gone, blind.

"Kurt," she grated hoarsely. "Take me somewhere. Not—home. And make love to me—all night long. Then I'll get you your damn-yankee balloon. I'll bring it home to you—hidden under my crino-line!"

He laughed merrily at that.

"Oh, come now, my sweet!" he chuckled. "Our wedding's only three days off. Surely you can wait *that* long. Be a pity to spoil the occasion, don't you think?"

"No. I don't think. I only feel. And you've spoiled it already, kissing me like that. You've—debauched me. Made me find out I'm not decent. That I'm depraved. And I wasn't, before I met you. At least I don't *think* I was—"

He stared at her curiously.

"Don't you *know?*" he asked her. "You said that you've—"

"Been married. But he was—innocent. A child. It was just like you said. Bumbling. A disappointment. And now—"

"And now I'm going to take you home," he said gravely, "and let you get some much-needed rest . . ."

"No," she said again, but quietly this time. "Don't take me home. If you do, there'll be no way I can slip out of the house at five o'clock in the morning. Take me to—a boardinghouse, a hotel. Leave me there. Then ride past home and tell Gwen that we had a terrible fight. That I jumped out of your buggy and ran off through the crowds, and that you haven't been able to find me. She'll be-lieve that. Anybody who knows me would. I've got red hair, an awful temper, and the worst, bitchy-mean disposition in the state of Virginia. So we'd better kill time 'til it gets dark enough to make that barefaced lie believable. Tell you what—take me to the gun factory Colin Claiborne has started. I'd like to see it, and I want to ask Colin what we can steal for him from the Yankees while we're up North . . ."

"I've heard you were—engaged to him once," Kurt said drily.

"I was. Only he played the coward on the field, so I threw him over. I've apologized to him for that since. I wasn't fair. A man is brave, or he isn't. And after lying flat on my back for a month dripping stinking pus from a bullet hole clear through my guts, I know cowardice shouldn't be held against anybody . . ."

"And yet, it seems you didn't take him back . . ."

"I also found out I didn't love him. I'd never marry a man I didn't love. Except you. 'Cause I don't, y'know. I hate your perverse, dominating, cruel guts. Only I want you so bad I hurt. And that'll make up for the lack of love, I reckon. Anyhow, it'll have to. So turn this nag around. Drive back through Richmond. Colin's little gun factory is out on Sixth Street, near the canal about a hundred yards before you get to the Tredegar ironworks . . ."

"All right," Kurt said, and did so.

"You'll pardon me for not offering you my hand, Count Radetzy?" Colin said soberly. "But, as you can see, mine are absolutely filthy . . ."

He had on, Rose saw, a worker's blue jumper, jeans, a sweater. A heavy leather apron, a grimy cap. All of which, including his face, his hands, even his mustache and his hair, were plastered thick with grease and oil. Beyond the plain, barren office they were in, they could hear the whine and thumping of the machines in his factory.

"Of course," Kurt said easily. "The future Countess Radetzy and I have come to offer you our services. On our way home from our proposed honeymoon on the Continent and in England, we plan to disembark in Yankee Land. So if there are any items in your line we can procure for your inspection . . ."

"God, yes!" Colin grated. "One of Christian Sharps's breechblocks. The Army captured one or two Sharps breechloaders at Harpers Ferry, but they've turned them over to their own engineers to try to make copies here at the arsenal. They won't even let us poor civilians have a peek at them . . ."

"If those back-end-loading guns are so good, why doesn't every Yankee soldier have one?" Rose Ann demanded. "Cabe says Sharps invented that newfangled gun way back in 1848, and that means they've had time enough and to spare to turn out a million of 'em!"

"D'you know," Colin said soberly, "that very point has always puzzled me. John Brown's raiders carried Sharps breechloaders when they made their attack on Harpers Ferry, and yet I've never even heard of a Yankee company equipped with them. A blessing

147

from on high, of course. Because with a rifle that can be reloaded as fast and as safely as the Sharps carbine can, they'd have wiped us off the face of the earth by now. Why they haven't reequipped all their forces with them, I can't imagine . . ."

"I can," Kurt said gravely, "because I've had all too many experiences in my native land with the abysmal depths that human stubbornness and stupidity can plumb. Prussia developed the Dreyse needle gun as far back as 1841, and all the attempts of progressive military men to get our Austrian Chiefs of Staff to copy it, or produce another breechloader like it, have been laughed or damned out of court. The trouble is, we're going to have to fight the Prussians soon, and when we do, we're going to be slaughtered. Muzzleloaders simply can't stand up to breechloaders, but try to tell an Austrian squarehead that! As for the Federals, Lincoln had the misfortune to inherit as his Chief of Ordnance one James W. Ripley, in comparison to whom a jackass is a marvel of brilliance and a mule an example of sweet tractability. Ripley has simply defied the President's orders that the Union troops be equipped with breechloaders and, what's even worse—or better, from our point of view! —repeaters, of which the Yankees, Mr. Claiborne, have at least two decidedly workable models. Ripley has been known to tear up written orders directing him to supply the Yankee infantry with modern arms. He instinctively, I believe, loathes *anything* that's new . . ."

Kurt turned to Rose Ann then and flashed her his ice-bright smile.

"Which is why, my sweet," he chuckled, "you and I are going to call on General Ripley as soon as we arrive in Washington! I'm going to tell him how wonderfully right he is to resist all the foolish modern trends in armament, and swear to him that the Prussian needle gun has been a disaster—"

"It *has* been pretty bad, Count," Colin said. "That needle mechanism is too delicate. I had a few examples shipped to me from abroad, and while it might work for trained Prussian infantrymen, one of our hayfoot-strawfoot swamp rats or hillbillies would ruin it forever the first day . . ."

"That's true," Radetzy said, "but the Prussians are working on improvements. In the meantime, we'd better encourage the Ripleys in the Yankee ranks! You, Rose Ann, will praise the gentleman's intelligence—and his looks, and plant a kiss or two on his bewhiskered cheeks when I'm not looking!"

"Sure you don't want me to crawl into the hay with him, Kurtie darling?" Rose said darkly.

"Oh, I hardly think such drastic measures will be necessary," Kurt said gaily. "By the way, Mr. Claiborne—"

"Call me Colin," Colin said sadly. "Rose Ann's husband *has* to be a friend of mine . . ."

"Done!" Radetzy laughed. "I say, Colin old boy, wouldn't you like us to steal you one of the Spencer repeaters, or the even more advanced Henry?"

Colin shook his head, even more sadly.

"No," he said.

Rose Ann stared at him.

"Why not, Colin honey?" she said.

"Because I couldn't produce the ammunition for them," Colin said. "Nor could any other arms manufacturer in the length and breadth of the South. I suppose I could get the shells made in France. The Le Faucheaux people could do it, probably. But do you know what it would mean to try to get the tens of millions of pieces of small-arms ammunition that we'd need shipped to us through the Yankee blockade from abroad? This is a Le Faucheaux—"

He opened a wall cabinet and took out a heavy revolver, handed it to Count Radetzy.

"Unload it, and you'll see what's wrong with it," Colin said.

Kurt studied the heavy sidearm for a few seconds. Then deftly he drew the cartridges out of the back of the revolving cylinder. To Rose Ann's astonishment, they were made of brightly shining brass, except the conical bullet, jammed into the front end of the shell, which was of ordinary lead.

"Aren't they pretty!" she cried.

"A woman's reaction, truly!" Kurt laughed. "These, I take it, are the famous Le Faucheaux pinfire shells?"

"Yes. Would you like to have to load this revolver under fire?" Colin asked.

"God, no! The French are the world's worst engineers. It would take a calm man half an hour, sitting at a table at home, to slip the horizontally mounted firing pins into the slots in the sides of the cylinder correctly. It's a variation of the Prussians' needle gun, isn't it? Only, instead of making the needle a part of the gun, as the Prussians did, they've made it part of the cartridge. How French! I suppose this system is workable enough, but it obviously makes reloading the revolver almost as much of a bloody nuisance as the present method of loose powder plus a separate ball plus still an-other separate percussion-cap primer already is. This design is much too fancy. But then, that nation of bowing and scraping dress and perfume makers never does anything properly . . ."

"They invented the minié ball, didn't they?" Rose Ann said tartly. "And my brother-in-law says that that kind of a bullet in-creased the distance a gun can shoot twice over, and makes it at least five times as likely you'll hit what you've aimed at!"

She said that more than a little testily, because Kurt's chauvin-ism toward any nation or people who weren't, or didn't speak, German was beginning to irk her. She was not yet sufficiently subtle to realize that Heros von Borcke had it right: her fiancé's trouble was precisely the fact that he *wasn't* German, and wanted to be, a condition that has always afflicted both mongrels and sub-ject peoples throughout history. The realization that practically everything you've got—your language, religion, science, general culture, ethics, even, at times, more than half your blood—has been inflicted upon you by a dominant race, can become—a trifle annoy-ing, say. *Sic semper die Untermenschen* of this world!

Again Radetzy turned his icy smile upon her.

"The trouble with that statement, my love," he purred, "is that while the technical aspects of it are quite true, the historical ones aren't. The so-called minié ball is neither a ball nor Captain Mi-nié's invention. It's a conical bullet, and it was invented by Captain Nelson, of Her Imperial Majesty's 34th Regiment, in 1823. Captain C. E. Minié happened to get his well-manicured hands on an exam-ple or two—God knows how—and promoted it so enthusiastically that the French Army adopted it. To give Minié due credit, how-ever, he never claimed to have invented it. Other people did that for him. He simply didn't deny the error very loudly . . ."

"You know, I didn't know that either," Colin said humbly.

Which made Rose Ann even angrier. She didn't want Colin to be humble toward Kurt. She suspected that, coward though he was, Colin Claiborne was a far better human being than Kurt Radetzy. Later, when age and stability gave her time to think things through, she'd realize that courage is an irrelevancy, that whatever quality it has is lent by the circumstances surrounding it: its value —or total lack of it!—depends upon what you're being brave for, or about.

"Why can't you make pretty cartridges—bullets—whatever they are—like these, Colin love?" she demanded crossly.

"Like these, exactly like these, I don't even *want* to," Colin said.

"A firearm chambered to use pinfire cartridges would be even harder—and, what's worse, *slower*—to recharge for firing than the rifles we have now are. And God knows reloading an Enfield under fire is about as close to suicide as anything ever invented ever was . . ."

"I quite agree," Kurt said gravely, the note of slightly exaggerated pity in his tone obviously designed to let Rose Ann know that he knew the truth about Colin's wound, "but our Austrian system is even worse. Our troops are supplied with oversized balls, steel ramrods, and a wooden mallet. And there they are, standing there, hammering away, trying to force those oversized balls down the barrels of their rifles with those ramrods, while the enemy coolly and carefully picks them off, one by one. I sometimes think that when it comes to sheer stupidity, our Austrian General Staff have the original patent!"

"And yet," Colin said, holding Rose Ann with his eyes, his voice, the tone of it, the slightly bent, almost cringing posture of his long, thin body a naked plea, "the very ease with which a minié ball can be rammed home is not always an advantage. At Malvern Hill—" He paused while his dark gaze beseeched her visibly, heliographing the agonized prayer: *Listen to me, Rambling Rose! Hear and forgive me, please!* "I was leading a charge"—the words coming out too loudly, defiantly, challenging her doubt—"when the infantryman at my side opened fire. He was—a boy. One of those country kids who wrote the word 'eighteen' on a piece of paper and stuck it inside their shoes so they wouldn't be lying altogether when they swore to the receiving sergeant for volunteers that they were 'over eighteen . . .' Anyhow, he'd loaded his rifle, and forgot to fire it, and loaded it again, and forgot to fire it, or maybe his finger merely froze on the trigger at the thought of killing other boys exactly like himself. Anyhow, he'd loaded that Enfield sixteen times at the very least without ever having fired it once. But this time—mainly because I'd roared at him: 'Shoot, you damn fool!'—he did fire. His weapon—exploded. It peeled back like the rings of an onion—and then he hadn't any face. Just two astonishingly blue eyes peering wildly out of—bloody hash. No lower jaw. He didn't fall. He just stood there, petrified with astonishment. Then I—"

Swiftly Rose Ann crossed to him. Went up on tiptoe. Flattened the hateful, hurtful, self-lacerating words he'd been about to say against his speaking mouth.

Drew back again, her eyes twin tropic seas, luminous with tears. "It's all right, Colin love," she said. "It's perfectly all right!"

151

Kurt broke the painful silence then. And he broke it rather gracefully.

"I say, old boy," he said with a rueful laugh, "is it absolutely *de rigueur* that I challenge you to a duel? I'd rather not, y'know!"

"Don't be silly, Kurt," Rose snapped. "I only kissed Colin because I just didn't want him demeaning himself in front of a pig-dog like you. Aside from the fact that I love him very dearly, of course. Colin, you were saying that you didn't want to make pretty brass what-do-you-call-'ems like these. Mind telling me—us—why?"

"I'd much rather make—these, if I could," Colin said, and turned back to his wall cabinet. Out of it he took another revolver. It was very small. And quite beautiful in a sinister sort of way. He handed it to Kurt, butt first.

Kurt took it, studied it half a minute, less. Saw at once how it worked. He touched the catch just in front of and below the cylinder. The short barrel, three inches long, flew upward. Kurt eased the compact seven-shot cylinder forward, took all seven of the tiny .22 caliber brass-cased shells out of it. He examined them carefully.

"I confess I'm baffled," he said pleasantly. "Where on earth is the percussion cap, old boy? The primer—the fulminate, or whatever the devil they use to set these things off?"

"Inside that protruding rim they've got all around the back end of the casing. The hammer's designed to strike the top back rim of these little beauties. They're called rimfire cartridges—or shells. They and this dainty little piece of bloody murder—notice how light it is? Weighs only eight ounces—are made by the Smith & Wesson people of Hartford, Connecticut. They're not government issue. The Yankee officers buy them on their own. But that little gem, and its slightly bigger sister, a thirty-two, with a six-inch barrel, are the best damned sidearms made on the face of the globe today. The boys keep bringing 'em to me, taken off the bodies of dead Union officers, and begging me to duplicate 'em, but I can't. That's the hell of it, Kurt—I mean Count—"

"Kurt's perfectly all right, Colin," Kurt said gravely. "You were saying?"

"That I can't duplicate this advanced ammunition. I've neither the materials nor the machinery. Oh, I could make a few by hand. Or Lindsholm could. He's one of those Swedish mechanical geniuses who can make anything. But we'd need millions of them. And machinery that could turn out ten thousand of these brass casings in an hour. So I'm going to try to make a decent single-shot

breechloader that will use paper cartridges and percussion caps
like the Sharps. Anything more is beyond us. Oh, God, and to
think I used to sneer at mechanics, like every idiotic young would-
be cavalier of my class! We're so damn backward down here, Kurt.
Which is why we haven't chance one of winning this war in the
end . . ."

"I'll admit your chances are rather remote," Kurt said with genuine sadness. "But there is *one* good chance—and you, *mein Freund,*
have given that chance to me . . ."

Colin stared at him.

"I?" he whispered. "How, Kurt?"

"By making me see that my whole approach to our trip through
the Northern states was wrong. I'd intended to concentrate on
military intelligence, on pilfering whatever advanced designs for
small arms that race of mechanics the Yankees are has developed.
But you couldn't really use them, could you? So now—"

"Now what, Kurt?" Rose Ann said.

"We're going to specialize in psychological warfare instead, my
sweet! There's a great deal of disaffection, dissatisfaction in Yankee
Land, y'know. So we'll do everything conceivable to encourage a
dunderhead like Ripley in his mule-stubborn efforts to keep the
Spencer and the Henry repeating carbines out of the hands of the
Yankee troops—on the score—would you believe it?—that they
waste ammunition. And we're going to make the most fervent dec-
larations of tender love and abiding affection to that tribe of Copperheads in New York City and in the Midwest! We're going to
float them in champagne and fatten them on caviar!"

"Where are we going to get the money to do all that, Kurtie
pie?" Rose Ann demanded.

"From the Lord High-Muck-a-Mucks of Merrie Olde England,
Süsskins! 'Twill be easy to convince the blighters of the advantage to
their mercantile empire and political power that having two weak,
eternally quarreling petty nations instead of one gigantic, immensely strong one in America will be. Then off to Paris, where
I'll point out to Looie Nappy and Moth-eaten Leon just how long
his new French empire in Mexico will last if he lets the Yanks do
you poor bloody sods in, thus giving them a chance to turn to
helping Juárez, that ugly black monkey of an Indian, roast poor
Maximilian over a slow fire. Louis Napoleon will cough up the
coin of the realm when I tell him that; you can wager any odds you
want to! Out of which, I'll deduct sufficient commissions to drape

you in diamonds and sable and Paris gowns! So give friend Colin another kiss, for he's just given me the idea of the year!"

"No," Rose Ann said solemnly. "I won't give him another kiss, not for nothing anyhow. He'll have to pay me for it . . ."

"Pay you?" Colin said wonderingly.

"Yes, kind sir," Rose Ann went on the same tone of exaggerated solemnity. "You'll have to give me that little pistol, and three of the cartridges—bullets—whatever-you-call-'ems—it shoots. I only need three. That's fair enough, isn't it?"

"No," Colin said. "I'd have to know what you wanted it for, Rambling Rose . . ."

"To kill Kurt with, if he ever looks at another woman," Rose said slowly, quietly. "To kill the other woman, for poaching. And to kill *me*, so as to cheat a hell of a lot of folks out of the fun they'd get out of seeing me kicking and choking and turning blue on the end of a rope. Now, d'you want your kiss?"

Colin shook his head.

"On that basis, no," he said.

"Oh, give her that pretty toy!" Kurt laughed. "If she ever catches me out, I'd *deserve* shooting. That degree of stupidity has always been a capital crime, it seems to me. Oh, I say! We're being deuced presumptuous, come to think of it. I'll gladly pay you whatever you think that dainty little weapon's worth . . ."

"No," Colin said quietly. "I'll make Rose a present of it. But I definitely don't want a kiss in return . . ."

"Why not, old boy? I have no objections," Kurt said.

"That you don't is part of the reason, but a better one is that I've learned never to take anything Rose says lightly. And I don't want to be an accessory before the fact to murder—or suicide. However I'm paid for it," Colin said.

"Kurt," Rose Ann said plaintively, "couldn't you just forget that damn balloon?"

"No. I promised your High Command I'd get that information, and we'd better comply, or they just might look askance on this long honeymoon of ours. Well, here we are . . ."

"But—but—" Rose quavered. "What place is this?"

"My diggings. I'll sneak you up the back stairs so no one will see you. And you mustn't stir 'til I get back from weeping on dear Gwen's shoulder, pouring out my heartbreak over our terrible quarrel, and your cruel desertion of me. So just you wait, my dear!"

"Kurt," Rose Ann said dolefully, "I don't want to stay at *your* place—"

"You have to, my darling. There's nowhere else. All the lodging houses are jam-packed with refugees and camp followers. Besides, too many people know you in Richmond. How the devil d'you think you could get away with checking into a hostelry without luggage and staying there all night?"

"A heck of a lot better than I could having somebody's finding out that I stayed all night in *your* place, Kurtie pie!"

"But they won't find it out. No one ever finds out anything about my doings that I don't want them to. Come along, will you?"

"Kurt—" she wailed. "You—you'll come back. And—and make love to me. And I—I don't want you to! I don't want to spoil our wedding, Kurtie love!"

"Then don't," he said with that maddening indifference of his. "I won't make love to you. Word of honor, sweetkins. I'll sleep over there in my big armchair and—"

"Kurt," she said bitterly, "d'you also swear to—to fight *me* off? To tear loose a table leg and hit me over the head with it? You'll have to, y'know. Or else I'll let loose a fiendish, famished howl and—"

"Good!" he chuckled. "That should be most interesting, come to think of it. Now *will* you come along? Time's a-wasting, *Liebchen mein!*"

Ten o'clock that next morning, Rose Ann walked out of that grove of scrub oaks and dwarf pines straight into the camp where the Balloon Corps's one and only company was. She walked very slowly and sadly with her head bent, staring only at the ground.

She thought: I'll *tell* them I'm a spy. Then they'll hold a court-martial and condemn me to be shot. Or hanged. But anyhow, I'll be dead and at peace. Because dead people can't think, can they? Or —remember. And I don't want to do either anymore. Or else I— I'll go crazy. I knew I was sort of wild and giddy and foolish and even—even—tell the truth, Rose Ann!—a good bit more warm-hearted and—God forgive me!—hot-natured than it's comfortable —or safe!—for a girl in my circumstances to be. But I could always fool myself into thinking I was mostly decent, even after that— ugh!—afternoon at A'nt Sukie's with Colin. Told myself I was only treating the man I was going to marry to—to a little happiness, to one first-class tender memory, in case he marched off to war and got himself killed, poor, brave hero of mine!

What about *this* occasion? Worse. Far worse. Just terrible. But in a different—in the *opposite* way. Poor Colin didn't know *anything* about how a woman works—about how *I* work, anyhow—and Kurt knows *everything*—has forgotten more than all the rest of the he-male critters under heaven ever knew. The ice-cold swine sitting there letting me forcing me to make all the advances smiling with his mouth only, but with those swamp-mist foggy-bottom dirty-dishwater eyes just plain—what? Con-con-contemptuous, that's the word—mocking me while I went crazy wild disgraced myself acted like a whorebitchslut loose immoral bad— Ohhhh, Lord!

It had started out of so many little things that didn't matter—at least she'd thought they didn't until they began to add up and pile up until they'd got to be too much for her. In the first place, she'd been so tired. She was practically always tired now since Lieutenant Froggie had shot her. And she reckoned she was going to go on being tired for a good many years, if not for the rest of her life, because a .44 caliber pistol ball straight through your guts wasn't a thing that even a McKenzie recovered from easily.

So she hadn't seen any harm in lying down on Kurt's bed while she waited for him to come back. But even though the steel hoops of her *cage américaine* were collapsible in an up-and-down direction, as they had to be or else there'd be no way a body could ever sit down while wearing a hoop skirt, they weren't sidewise, so that if she dozed off, as she was pretty sure she was going to, and started to turn over, she'd bend them out of shape, and hurt her poor much too skinny self into the bargain. So she decided to take off all that scaffolding that gave a hooped skirt its pleasant bell shape. But when she did so, she saw that the only petticoat she had on was very old and, what was even worse, had two or three big patches in it. Which was almost the usual state of affairs for even women of considerable wealth in the Confederacy by late 1862, as their clothes began to wear out and the Yankee blockade kept them from being able to buy any more—that is, when they even managed to hang on to enough gold coins to buy anything with, since nobody —especially not the blockade runners—would condescend to take Confederate shin plasters anymore.

So now she was confronted with a cruel dilemma: She either had to put her dress back on or take her petticoat off. But if she lay down in one of the few good dresses she had left, she'd get it all wrinkled, and if she took her lone petticoat off, she'd be reduced to a degree of undress that simply wasn't permissible before a man

she wasn't—yet—married to. That a bodice, a whalebone corset—
which she still wore out of sheer habit though she had no conceivable need for it as terribly thin as she now was—and a pair of
ankle-length, plentifully ruffled pantalets really weren't all that im-
modest was an idea that neither she nor any woman of her times
would ever grasp. Besides, all sexual reactions are basically conditioned reflexes, and in an age when men went hog wild at the sight
of a dainty feminine ankle, her conviction that, down to bodice and
rather thin muslin drawers, however voluminous, she was both a
fetching and a provocative sight, was by no means off the mark.

Still, she was so blamed weary, and if Kurt came back and saw
her in her underclothes—after all, how much difference could that
make when in three more days he was going to be granted, if not
the privilege—she ruefully suspected it wasn't one any longer,
slab-side skinny as she now was—at least the right, to see her in the
altogether anytime he wanted to? So she took off the faded and
patched petticoat as well, and hid it under her dress, draping both
garments carefully across the back of a chair. Then she climbed
into Kurt's bed, drew the covers over her—and dropped straight
through the bottom of the world.

What woke her up, she didn't know. But from the completely
relaxed and rested way she felt, she realized she must have slept
three quarters of the night. The big clock on the mantel above the
fireplace confirmed her thought. It was almost four o'clock in the
morning. But it wasn't until five, or maybe even ten minutes later,
that it came to her that she shouldn't have been able to *see* that
clock, that at four in the morning in Virginia around the beginning of November, it was generally too dark to see your own hand
held six inches before your nose. She was quite sure that Kurt
hadn't lit one of the patented "coal oil" lamps because when he'd
left to go tell Gwen that barefaced lie she'd suggested as believable,
although dusk had been setting in, there'd been still too much light
left in the room for him to even think of it. And even if he had
thought of it, she would have told him not to, because coal oil was
another item that was getting mighty scarce nowadays.

But now at least one of the lamps was definitely lit, which
meant—

She flopped over in the bed. And there he was, sprawled out
with boneless grace in the big chair, just as he'd promised to. He'd
taken off his coat, waistcoat, cravat, and, she now saw, his boots.
Relaxed by sleep, his face became the face of another man altogether. The face of the man he very likely would have been if

idiotic, racist philosophers hadn't got hold of his mind. Or if he had not fallen victim to his own tortured feelings of inferiority over such quite unimportant, even meaningless physical character- istics as a skin that was golden-yellow, and eyes with the mongol- oid slant of his Magyar ancestors, who'd come from the steppes of far-eastern Asia in the first place. Or, most of all, if those feelings hadn't been deepened, made more anguished by a series of acci- dents of history that had set him down, forced him to live among a tribe of northern barbarians who were not only incapable of dis- cerning that the biological fortuity of race was unimportant, an irrelevancy, but who have persisted throughout their history in believing that their own peculiarities of feature, coloration, stat- ure, were not only beauty per se but the mark of what they fondly held to be their indisputable superiority over every other race and tribe upon the face of earth.

Seeing him sleeping there, carefully respecting the honor she no longer possessed, a great wave of almost maternal tenderness stole over Rose Ann. That feeling had not one iota of concupiscence in it. She felt warm and good, exalted by the discovery that Kurt repected her, which proved the high and holy quality of his love. That his choosing to sleep in the big armchair might equally have meant that he was utterly incapable of feeling love, except for some fanatical cause, and afterward for himself, that—beyond their utility as creatures for him to exercise his ice-cold lust for domi- nance, to torment, degrade, and ultimately break—women in gen- eral, and she in particular, interested him so little that sleeping in that chair had actually seemed preferable to crawling into bed be- side her and having to go through with the messy, smelly, monu- mentally boring act of sex, were ideas her still-healthy ego didn't, at that stage, permit her to even contemplate.

So far everything was just fine. And if she hadn't been one of the most impulsive poor sweet creatures under indifferent, uncaring, and tenantless—another idea she couldn't then conceive of— heaven, that blissful state of ignorance being infinitely preferable in her romantic case to the abysmal folly that the knowledge of some of life's bleaker realities always is, matters would have re- mained upon that level of rosy sublimation, which permitted her at least some measure of self-control.

But aswoon with that pure, completely non-carnal tenderness, she popped out of bed, flew to his side. Which was, of course, the very lower depths of idiocy. The biochemistry of physical attrac- tion is actually inexplicable. Why are we attracted to some people

—generally those we should flee the very sight of!—and indifferent to others—generally those who'd make us at least acceptable mates? Why was the lure that Kurt Radetzy exercised over Rose Ann McKenzie's senses so dreadfully, ungovernably strong?

None of the voodoo witch doctors who would come upon the scene—chiefly in Vienna and during her own long lifetime—would ever really explain it. To say she was highly sexed is to talk nonsense; toward other men, as attractive as, or much more so than, Sisimond, *Graf* Radetzy, she was as cold as ice. Besides, he who has not yet discovered that one man's close-to-nymphomaniacal mistress is another man's frigid wife knows nothing about women anyhow.

In any case, Rose kissed her gentle, respectful lover, her darling Kurtie pie, and immediately all the old, remembered stimuli were loosed, exploding depth charges in her blood. Her nerves coiled and uncoiled like a nest of frenzied vipers, turned—mixed-metaphorically!—into whiplashes driving her inexorably headlong into what she thought of even at that moment as utter shame.

Yet she couldn't draw back. She couldn't. And her very despair only made her reactions more frenzied. She ground her mouth into his, twisting, moaning, almost breaking his lips against his teeth.

Kurt opened one fog-gray eye.

"*Was ist los?*" he mumbled sleepily; then, his voice filled with purest contempt, he added in the purring, slightly slurred accents of Austrian German: "*Ach, Gott,* how sick unto death you overheated, man-crazy women make me! What d'you want from me, my slatternly little slut? That I tickle your — for you?" The word he used has no English equivalent. The German is *Schamberg,* "mount of shame."

"Oh, Kurt, Kurt," she wept.

"Or would you like to pull on my third leg?" he went on, cruelly teasing her, knowing she couldn't understand a single word of the absolutely abominable things he was saying to her in German, until she flared: "Speak English, damnit!"

"*Ach, so*—all right. D'you want me to make love to you, doll?"

"Yes! God, yes! But no! No! No, no, no, please don't! Don't don't don't don't—"

"—Only a little. So that you can sleep peacefully, my little love. Let me see—"

"Oh, no, Kurt, no!" she shrilled, seeing what he was about to do, but he paid her less than halfhearted protest absolutely no attention at all. Coolly and carefully he pulled her ruffled pantalets down about her knees. Then he lifted her into his lap. Once he had her there, he gently fished both her firm, beautifully formed breasts out of her bodice. After that he played with her small slight body with a skill as absolute as it was contemptuous. She didn't realize that, of course. She was too busy fainting and dying and coming alive again and setting off torpedoes and canisters and grapeshot and all other known types of high explosives on her own insides almost independently of what his tongue tip and lips and practiced fingers' slow, endless, maddening caresses were doing to her. She reached orgasm—or, as she put it, "got there," for, apart from a few exceedingly learned medical men, no one in her times had even so much as heard of that harsh and ugly word for a beautiful sensation—at least a dozen times. But when he growled, finally, "That's quite enough, my little dear," she knew that it hadn't been enough, or even exactly right, that lovely as it had been, it wasn't what she'd expected or wanted, and what she wanted was the real thing, the authentic one, carried to its final extreme, its ultimate consequences.

So she said, whispering the words, "No. Make love to me, Kurt. Really—make love. Go—all the way."

He shrugged. Picked her up. Tossed her unceremoniously across the hooked rag rug on the floor.

"No, Kurt! Not like this! Not—here—"

The sardonic quality of his smile cut off her words, her breath.

"My bed's too good for panting bitches," Count Sisimond Kurt Radetzy said.

So when all fifty of the NCOs and privates of the Union Army's new and experimental Balloon Corps surrounded her, whooping and hollering and laughing and saying things like: "Hallo, Josephine Reb! Whatcha doing on our side of the lines, pray tell? Lord Jesus, but you're pretty! How's about a sweet li'l Rebel-style kiss? Gimme one and I'll call this damn war off, so help me!"—she said in the drippingest Southern drawl she could manage, "Ah'm a spy, honey boy. They sont me over heah to find out how y'all manage to make them gret big bal-loons go up 'stid o' fallin' down lak it 'pears t'me they oughta . . ."

They all set up a roar of laughter, and two or three of them sang out: "The cap'n! Go call the cap'n. And the prof. So they can explain it to 'er!"

The captain of the Balloon Corps was a very handsome blond, which made Rose Ann feel considerably better, in spite of the fact that she was worn to a frazzle, ached all over, and had to walk with her thighs apart she was so sore. He introduced her to Professor Lewis, the Federal forces' Chief Aeronaut, and the two of them took her on a tour of inspection. They showed her the various carts, all of them drawn by four huge Percheron horses, except the acid cart, which needed only two. There was a cart for each of the two balloons that constituted the United States' entire air force. Which made it the biggest air force in the whole world in November 1862. In fact, it wasn't going to be equaled again until the Franco-Prussian War of 1870–71.

After that, they blithely demonstrated to Rose Ann the two big generators in which they made hydrogen gas by pouring sulfuric acid over scrap iron, of which they had a plentiful supply, gathered from the battlefields which lay all around them. That done, they proposed to take her up in one of the balloons, an idea that although it scared her half out of her wits to even think of, she decided it was her duty as a spy to accept.

But before they could get the big gasbag filled, Rose Ann discovered she was starving. And no wonder, after all that goddamn exercise last night—or rather this morning, she thought bitterly. So she said, "Befo' y'all teks me up in that theah bal-looon, would y'all mind wrastlin' me up a li'l grub? Ah'm so hongry my backbone's axin' mah stummick effen mah throat ain't been cut!"

Whereupon they proceeded to whip her up a virtual feast—more and better food than she'd seen since this cruel war got started. She ate so much that Professor Lewis swore that the balloon wasn't going to be able to lift her with all the ballast she was packing aboard.

But it did lift her. Just before she and the professor soared aloft, she told them again, plaintively, "Ah ain't bein' fair to you nice, sweet Yankee boys. Ah really am a spy, y'know. Best thing y'all could do would be to shoot me, or hang me, mebbe."

"Honey," the professor laughed, "we only shoot ugly old witches. And we finished off all the ugly old witches at Salem back in 1600. So c'mon, honey—you'll enjoy this . . ."

She did. But she saw at once that balloon observation from that distance wasn't effective. They could see Richmond and the camps, but General Lee's whole army could have marched to attack under the thick screen of brush and trees and the aeronauts wouldn't have been able to see them until they were within actual gunshot range.

When she pointed that out to Professor Lewis, he said, "Which is why we're suspending operations, Miss McKenzie. To be accurate, we need to be within a mile of our objectives. And what the smallest fieldpiece firing red-hot shot could do to a balloon filled with anything as inflammable as hydrogen is from less than a mile away is something I don't even like to think about. Balloon observation will never be practical until we learn to produce helium, which won't burn. In the meantime, it's back to cavalry scouts, I suppose . . . Besides, you don't think we'd have let you see all this if it would have done you Rebs any good, do you?"

So she came back to Kurt with complete and detailed information about the Union Army's Balloon Corps, including the fact that the Yankees were calling the whole thing off. But when he gaily started to kiss her, she turned aside her face, and said, "No. Don't kiss me. Not ever again. I'm not going to marry you, Kurt. You—you treated me like—a whore. You called me dirty names in German. And you didn't—make love to me—all sweet and slow and tender. You—you did it to me—like I was an—animal."

"Well, aren't you?" he drawled. "Ruddy fine one it appears to me. Nice lines, nice gait. And jolly quick response when one applies the whip and spur."

Blind with rage, she brought her right hand around, whistling in a slap calculated to break his jaw. But he ducked, caught her wrist in midair, twisted it cruelly, threw her down on the bed, held her there effortlessly with one hand, while he pushed up her skirt, petticoat, and steel hoops with the other. Then he ripped her pantalets off her and made love to her for so long that finally he had to stuff part of the pillow into her mouth to stop her from screaming the house down and alarming all his neighbors because of how awful terrible bad wonderful exquisite marvelous hurtful murderous goood—oh, God—good it felt.

When he got through with her she knew three things: One, she was going to marry him after all. Two, she was going to arrive at her own wedding looking like worn-out hell, instead of like a bride. And three, she had become the very worst thing that any human being can ever get to be: a slave.

A more hopeless, helpless one than any poor nigger wench chopping back weeds in between the rows of tobacco in the fields.

Chapter Eight

The wedding ceremony was performed at Saint Paul's Episcopal Church, on the corner of Ninth and Grace Streets in Richmond. That it took place in so imposing a setting—St. Paul's was called "the Church of the Confederacy," since so many of the South's leaders attended services there—was due to the fact that, years before, after the Clan had already allied itself through marriage with a goodly number of the FFVs, it had seemed wise to some ancestor of theirs to consolidate their new position by abandoning their dour Scotch-Presbyterian faith and joining the church of the elite. Even under the straitened conditions prevailing in November 1862, the wedding was a brilliant one. The FFVs turned out in droves. And they probably would have, anyhow, even if Gwen's little masterpiece of diplomacy, published in all the newspapers, hadn't given them *carte blanche* to attend, because *nobody* could remember a Virginia girl's having married a foreign nobleman before, not to mention one so mysterious, handsome, and rich as Count Radetzy was said to be. Those few ladies who had actually seen him, usually driving Rose Ann about upon a sunny afternoon, went into sheer ecstasies over his looks. The most extravagant similes were called up to describe them, "like a Greek god!" being among the most frequent. And since modern Greeks bear only a trace of the blood of their classical ancestors, for the Turks and Slavs, plus a wild Tartar or two, have imposed their physical characteristics upon the speakers of demotic Greek through centuries of rape, maybe the description wasn't so far off the mark after all.

As all the newspapers duly reported, the ushers actually had trouble keeping the center aisle clear for the wedding procession, so jam-packed was the church with self-appointed friends of Clan McKenzie. President and Mrs. Davis appeared, to be greeted with a splatter of handclapping and a feeble cheer or two. The First Family weren't popular, old Jeff because he had the supreme misfortune of being forced to try to impose order and sense upon a race of individualists who believed every man was as good as the next and just weren't going to take no damn orders from *nobody*, by cracky!—which was the rock upon which the Confederacy ultimately split and floundered—while Varina Howell Davis was too good-looking, too fashionable, too disposed toward light social amusements to please her critics, not all of whom were numbered among her own sex. On the other hand, everybody approved of

Mrs. Lee, yet, when she stole timidly through the church doors on the arm of her youngest child, a daughter, she was greeted by neither handclapping nor cheers. Those few—*very* few—who recognized her knew she wouldn't like it, and refrained out of respect for her. But the majority of the people at Rose Ann's wedding simply had never seen Mary Ann Randolph Custis Lee before, at least not to recognize her as the wife of the South's greatest general. The reasons for this were various. Mrs. Lee was a timid soul, conservative by nature, and was thought and spoken of as an "aged invalid." The invalid part was probably true; like all too many women of her times, Mary Ann Lee was simply worn out by too frequent childbearing, the daughter who accompanied her that Sunday morning being number seven of her brood. But even in 1862, a woman in her early fifties, as Mrs. Lee was, wasn't considered to be really aged. She seldom went anywhere, except now and again to church. Then, as always, she was very plainly dressed, a capital crime in fashionable Richmond. In any event, for all these reasons, and perhaps even a few more, her entry attracted scant attention except among the McKenzies themselves, to whom it was a motive for self-congratulation.

But when Stonewall Jackson walked through the church door with Major Caleb Henry, brother-in-law of the bride, the cheers became thunder, the handclaps a crash of musket fire. Yet popular as General Jackson was, the greeting he was awarded by the spectators at Rambling Rose McKenzie's wedding couldn't even be compared with the outburst that shook the rafters upon the arrival of Jeb Stuart. As that laughing jim-dandy of a cavalry leader clanked, booted and spurred, plumed hat in hand, scarlet sash around his middle, fox-fire beard blazing in the morning sun, down the aisle to his seat, the soprano shrieks of purest joy threatened to shatter the church's stained-glass windows. Every generation produces its quota of hysterical young females; the pity is, that beyond borrowing such Victorian anglicisms as "giddy minxes," their Civil War contemporaries seem not to have invented any special term for them. But Jeb Stuart's "groupies," given arms, could easily have taken Washington and ended the war by sheer force of numbers.

But even so, on that Sunday, for once, Jeb found himself outdone. For when the bridegroom at last stood in the doorway, even though he was towered over by his best man, that rollicking Pomeranian giant Heros von Borcke, the impact he made upon every feminine eye, heart, and even breath was overwhelming. For, with masterly showmanship, Kurt Radetzy had chosen not to wear his

Confederate uniform; instead, *shako* in hand, he walked quietly through the church door, clad in the parade dress of a captain of the Hungarian *huszár*. Now, the Hungarians invented the cavalry corps known as hussars, though, largely due to the almost unbelievable splendor of their uniforms, imitations of that corps, and especially of said uniforms, had appeared by then in every European army. Kurt's was a veritable marvel: of green and gold, blazing with decorations the size of saucers affixed to a sash swept diagonally over one shoulder and down his powerful chest, across his gold-frogged waistcoat, above pants that fitted him like a second skin, and arrogantly put his well-endowed masculinity—or at least the visible contours thereof—on full display. He made, as one much too audible female whisper put it, "every other man here look just plain *sick!*" Most striking of all was the second cape, coat, what have you, that dangled off one shoulder as though it had been carelessly thrown there at the last moment but was actually *sewn* to the rest of the parade dress at just the right angle, calculated to the millimeter to leave one empty sleeve trailing with breathtaking (female breath, anyhow!) *insouciance.* His cavalry boots were blinding. His saber hilt was, it was easy to see, of solid, massive gold. Its scabbard was of silver, inlaid with gold and precious stones. Even his spurs seemed to be golden.

This absolutely studied, coldly calculated *mise-en-scène* of his provoked a dead-stopped, crushing weight of total silence. Then the racking sobs of several hundred female breaths being drawn in at one and the same time, more nearly ingurgitated than inhaled, and after that, like a rising wind, the whispers:

"Better-lookin' than Jeb 'n' Heros put together, and that took some doing, I can tell you . . ."

"Will somebody pu-leeeze tell me how that li'l ol' *tacky* 'n' *vulgar* Rambling Rose McKenzie ever managed to get her she-cat's claws into that'un?"

"You just said it, honey chile. Tha's how. Grabbed herself two heapin' handfuls o' that there splendiferous he-male hide, after rippin' them scandalous skintight pants clean off o' him, 'bout two A.M. one mawin' at A'nt Sukie's, sho' as hell's afiah!"

"Sssssssssssh, girls! Sssssssssh! You're in a *church*, remember!"

But when, at long, long last, Rose Ann drifted, in a cloud of white brocaded satin turned eggshell, cream-colored by the years, through the church door, on Dave McKenzie's arm, her forest-fire hair, misted about with tulle veiling and white roses, her lily stalk of an upper trunk, unbelievably slender, small, and slight, above the immense, creamy bell goblet of her hooped skirt, a bouquet of still more roses, almost bigger than she was, in arms become willow wands by then, her face turned floorward, until she lifted it, and they saw how her sea-green eyes, owl-like and huge in a countenance that had practically wasted away, like most of the rest of her, were performing the curious alchemy, witchery, magic of distilling jewels—emeralds at first, then as they brimmed, spilled over her lashes, and hung there trembling, resisting the whole awful downpull of the world, diamonds, light-blazed and brilliant, slowly flashing white fire as they broke free, to convert themselves at last into pearls gone molten, star-tracking cheeks as white as death— the impact was even greater than the one Kurt had made. In two seconds flat, there wasn't a dry female eye in St. Paul's, including, be it said, those of Rose Ann's worst enemies, and every pair of male eyes except three were suspiciously misty. Those three exceptions were obviously, openly blind, scalded, and brimming. They belonged to Dave McKenzie, who was practically bawling like a yearling calf; Cabe Henry, who was perfectly conscious that he was making a spectacle of himself but simply didn't give a damn; and Colin Claiborne, who was totally unaware of the tears of anguished heartbreak, bitter loss that were pouring down his dark, aristocratic face.

But aside from needing flood control, the ceremony went off swimmingly. There was only one *contretemps*, and it was accidental. Its timing, however, was very nearly disastrous: for just as the Right Reverend Jonathan Erwell, Rector of St. Paul's, was saying, "Dearly Beloved, if any one of you here present knows of any impediment to the union in holy wedlock of this young couple, let him speak now, or else hereafter forever hold his peace!" Mary Sue Hunter, Rose Ann's bridesmaid, who for some unknown reason had been twisting her neck nervously to peer down the aisle and out the church door the whole time, let out a squeal like a stuck pig, and whirling in a cloud of organdy, dashed down the aisle and out into the street.

Amid the stunned silence, the rector said to one of the two altar boys, "Tim, go see what the devil's got into that young woman. We'll hold up the ceremony 'til you come back . . ."

Tim flapped away in scarlet robes that would have graced a Prince of the Mother Church, flapped back again, his freckled face split in a grin.

"Sir," he said, "it's Miss Hunter's promised, and the bride's brother, Lieutenant Jeff McKenzie of the Navy . . ."

"Ohhhhh, Lord!" Rose Ann moaned.

"Sez he got here so late that he didn't want t'come bargin' in and bustin' up the ceremony, so—"

"You go tell the lieutenant," Father Erwell said happily, "that by virtue of my appointment as chaplain to the naval forces in this district, my rating's equivalent to that of a full captain of a ship, and therefore I outrank him. Tell him I *order* him to haul his red-headed freckled-faced McKenzie self in here!"

"Father, Cap'n, sir"—Tim grinned back at the rector—"don't reckon you outrank Gen'l *Lee*, d'you, sir? 'Cause he's out there too!"

"You'll excuse me a moment, won't you, young people?" Father Erwell said. "I'll be back in a minute to finish tying the knot. But since General Lee is here, we can't leave him out there in front of the church, can we?"

"Oh, no!" Rose Ann breathed. "Please do bring him in, Father! Tell him we'd be so honored if he'd come in and sign the marriage certificate as a witness, wouldn't we, Kurt honey?"

"Absolutely!" Kurt said.

Father Erwell went to the door. Three minutes later he was back with Jeff, and a bundle of organdy and tulle that was wrapped all around the young naval lieutenant, and shuddering, sobbing, and babbling: "JeffohJeffmyJeffohmy darlingJeffie love!" Behind them came the stately figure of General Robert E. Lee, who, for all his immense and genuine humanity, always reminded Rose Ann of a marble statue walking. But, creature of impulse, as always, she left her bridegroom standing by the altar, dashed up the aisle, and caught the Commander in Chief of the Confederacy's armies by the arm.

"Oh, sir!" she breathed, blinking back a fresh flood brought on by this new excitement. "Would you come—and stand with us? Be our chief witness? We'd be so honored if you would!"

"The honor is mine, child," General Lee said gravely. "I owe you that much, and more, for—Malvern Hill. As well as my apologies for not getting there in time to take it for you . . ."

"Oh, no, sir!" Rose said. "Reckon I was the slow one. But I was having so damn much trouble staying on my horse . . . Oh, Lord! There I go! Saying a bad word before *you*, sir—and *in church!* I beg your pardon mighty humbly, sir!"

"It's all right, child," the general said. "I won't wash your mouth out with soap, *this* time. Lead on, will you?"

But by the time they got back to the altar, Rose Ann noticed the way Mary Sue was carrying on over Jeff, and that gave her an exceedingly sensible idea.

If Jeffie love doesn't beat her off with a table leg tonight, that there li'l girl is long gone! she thought; then she said, "Father Erwell—marry them too. Along with us. Make this a double wedding. You can fix up the certificate later, can't you? Long as they say their honest and solemn vows before you and in the presence of witnesses, it's already legal, isn't it?"

"Yes," the rector said, "but I must say this is highly irregular and—"

Rose Ann leaned swiftly close.

"Father, from where I sit," she whispered, her clear voice, in spite of her intention to keep the whole matter between her and the rector only, carrying at least five pews back, "*preventing* carnal sin is a sight more effective than forgiving it. And if you don't have any real *serious* objections, I'd just as soon keep my nephew or my niece off the county—uh—foundling rolls!" She'd been about to say "bastardy rolls" and had caught herself just in time, but the rector knew exactly what she meant.

"Why, Rose Ann, you—you're per-fect-ly horrid!" Mary Sue Hunter squealed. "Don't you trust *any*body?"

"Honey," Rose Ann sighed, "I trust practically everybody. It's human nature I don't trust. Father, you said you outrank Jeffie. So order him to marry Mary Sue, so I can quit arguing . . ."

"Ohhhhhh, Lord!" Mary Sue moaned. "Anybody would think—"

"Don't think, I *know*," Rose Ann said flatly. "Got any idea what size moon there's going to be tonight, snippie pie? Bigger than a pumpkin and twice as yellow. It'll go straight to your head and—uh—your other side of the coin too. Jeffie love, what d'you say?"

"I'm all for it!" Jeff beamed. "So get out that snow-white shotgun and force her to make an honest poor little old sailor boy of me!"

"You're horrid too, Jeff McKenzie!" Mary Sue cried. "You're insufferable and just plain *mean* and—" She halted, hung there. A great light broke just behind her eyes. She whirled toward where her mother sat, some five pews up the aisle.

"Mama!" she squealed. "Gimme your wedding ring! I'm going to need it—right now!"

And that, as the saying goes, was that. The rapidly expanded wedding was quickly completed. But as Count Radetzy bent to kiss his bride, Rose Ann hung back, searching his face, his eyes.

"Kurt," she whispered, "please don't break my heart. I ask you— no, I beg you—not to. It's the only heart I've got. And it's all yours. Forever. So—just don't break it—please!"

Kurt smiled at her with an expression of tenderness as totally convincing as only such pathological and conscienceless black- guards as he seem to be able to manage. Which is why their success with women is, in the overwhelming majority of cases, assured.

"I hardly think you need worry about that, my little love," he said.

She and Kurt, and Jeff and Mary Sue, spent the first night of their honeymoons at the Exchange Hotel. When, with malice aforethought, the desk clerk tried to give them adjacent rooms, Mary Sue put her foot down.

"When poor little old Jeffie starts hollering for help, I just don't want you busting in on us, Rose Ann!" she said.

"More likely I'll be the one trying to run down the fire escape," Rose Ann said, only half in jest, if that much. Kurt looked at her, studying her out of the corner of those eyes of a sleepy tiger. He had long since decided that as raw material she was first-rate, and he was certain that, buffed and polished a bit, she would become extremely useful for his own peculiar purposes, with which, for the moment, those of the Confederacy happened to coincide.

So now, studying her face with the acute, perceptive intelligence that megalomaniacal paranoiacs such as he are perfectly capable of —since the root of their disorder lies in a hopelessly awry appre- hension of the basic premises of the grandiose schemes they em- bark upon, never in their impeccably logical development of the steps leading from said premises—he instantly made up his mind to forgo threats, force, and fear—for the present anyhow—as his means for controlling her; it seemed to him much simpler to domi- nate his bride through her senses. He had already decided that she was *eine mannstolles Weib*, which is High German for a nymphoma- niac, said decision only proving once again that the final result of any tactics, however excellent in themselves, can never be disasso- ciated from the accuracy of the premise upon which they are based. That wrongheaded misapprehension on his part doomed, of course, his mission to failure from the outset. Which didn't matter: the missions of megalomaniacs always fail. The tragedy lies in what happens to other, comparatively normal people caught in their path: Sisimond Kurt Radetzy came close to wrecking Rose Ann's life, to destroying her as a person. And seventy-seven years later, his spiritual and intellectual descendants were going to institute their own *Götterdämmerung* and drench three quarters of the earth in blood.

But be it admitted that on that first night of their honeymoon, and for many nights thereafter, his tactics worked, for he decided to be very sweet and gentle with his bride. Rose Ann and he joined Jeff and Mary Sue, as had been agreed among the young couples beforehand, for a late, late breakfast. But the new Radetzys were much, much later than the new McKenzies in arriving at the hotel's breakfast room. So late were they that Jeff was beginning to fidget and to fret to an extent that caused Mary Sue to reach out and take his hand.

"He's a foreigner, remember," she whispered with a happy giggle, "so I reckon he knows a dirty trick or two that y'all nice, sweet, clean-living American boys haven't heard of yet. I suspect me 'n' the Rambling Rose had better have ourselves a sisterly heart-to-heart talk, reeel soon. And anything she can teach me, I'll be mighty happy to pass along to you, husband dear!"

Jeff stared at his bride, and his eyes were appalled.

"Mary Sue," he croaked. "You mean you—you aren't—happy? That I didn't—uh—satisfy you?"

Mary Sue was, of course, an utter neophyte in that branch of applied science, which should be—but generally isn't!—of prime importance to wives: masculine psychology. Therefore she was totally unaware how extremely fragile the male ego is. So blithely she violated that immortal canon laid down by the great Mark Twain: "The truth is such a precious commodity that it should be employed as sparingly as possible!" and plowed along like a crack racing Mississippi River boat, full steam ahead, thereby wounding poor Jeff McKenzie almost to death.

"Well," she sighed, "I could have done with a sight less repetition, and a heck of a lot more—duration, if you get what I mean, Jeffie love. Jackrabbits are dry-land critters, aren't they? Never expected to find one in the *Navy* . . . ."

"Mary Sue!" Jeff thundered, or gasped, or both, but at that moment he saw his sister coming through the double doors with her husband behind her. As was the case with ninety percent of all upper-class Southerners, Jeff's literary culture rested upon three rather shaky pillars: Walter Scott, the Holy Bible, and Shakespeare.

But at the moment it sufficed. In fact, Shakespeare alone served him admirably. When he saw his sister's eyes, and perceived the glow that shimmered in their emerald depths, the words from the balcony scene rose like music into his mind:

> Two of the fairest stars in all the heaven,
> Having some business, do entreat her eyes . . .

My God, but she's radiant! he thought. Shows you never can tell. Here I was, building up a head o' steam over her going and getting hitched to *another* damn furriner, and now . . .

But Mary Sue too was staring at Rose Ann, studying, with sure female instinct, her face, her eyes. It took the new Mrs. Geoffrey McKenzie thirty seconds to reach absolute certainty. With a squeal of purest delight, she bounced out of her chair, flew to Rose Ann, and clasped her sister-in-law as of one night lovingly in her arms. The two of them kissed each other two dozen times, burst into a perfect gale storm of tears, shot through with rippling, sunny breezes of immensely-pleased-with-themselves-and-with-the-world feminine laughter.

Wonderingly, Jeff stood up and put out his hand to Kurt.

"Women!" he said despairingly. "Can you understand 'em, Count?"

"No, brother-in-law mine, I can't. And I'd prefer not to. Their very incomprehensibility adds to their charm, it seems to me. Well, Geoffrey old boy, I hope you're happy? I must admit I am; divinely so, in fact . . ."

"Well—yes. I guess I am, come to think of it, Count," Jeff said with a manifest lack of conviction.

"Problems?" Kurt said with very nearly genuine kindness; then: "By the way, Jeff, I'd suggest that you drop that Count business, forever. I don't know whether Rose Ann has told you, but the fact is I've become a naturalized citizen of the Confederacy. It's extremely unlikely that I shall ever return to Central Europe again; there are various—well—political reasons that make an attempt on my part to reclaim my title, and my patrimony—which, incidentally, lies in Hungary, a country I'm not even a citizen of—extremely inadvisable. So call me Kurt, will you? That's all I am, plain Kurt Radetzy—a citizen of the CSA . . ."

"And a colonel in her armies," Jeff said. "Well—Kurt, I'll admit I'm kind of relieved that you're planning to stay. I was afraid you were going to drag my crazy little wildcat of a sister off so far I'd never see her again. And I'm mighty fond of her. All us McKenzies are, I reckon . . ."

"And all the rest of the people of Richmond and *environs,* it appears to me," Kurt said. "Let's sit, shall we? Those two seem to be indulging in feminine confidences of a rather personal nature, so who knows when they'll recall that a spot of nourishment's in order? Look, they've even drawn up a couple of chairs to that unoccupied table! And I could do with a cup or two of coffee. The pity is that it won't be real . . ."

"Thought of that," Jeff said happily, and dragged a carefully wrapped and tied package from his pocket. "One full pound of the best Brazilian! A friend of mine on the *Alabama* brought it to me. Let's call the waiter, and send it out to the kitchen to be brewed for this happy occasion . . ."

"With the stipulation," Kurt said solemnly, as the waiter came into earshot, "that I can distinguish the taste of parched peanuts even when the real article has been cut with them in as small a proportion as ten to one. So if one of the fat and saucy nigger waiters—or the cook—in this establishment thinks to procure himself a supply by the usual process of petty thievery, I personally will take the hide off him in stripes . . ."

"And I'll hold him for you to beat on," Jeff said cheerfully. "Here, Rodney—take this out back to the kitchen and have it brewed for us, hot and strong. And *all* of it, mind you!"

"Yassuh, Marse Jeff," the waiter said mournfully. "I won't even smell hit too damn hard. Y'all kin bet yo' bottom dollar on that!"

Jeff looked worriedly at his wife and his sister, whose native Virginian drawl didn't seem to be slowing down the speed of their mutual and apparently burningly interesting communication to any perceptible degree.

"I wonder what the devil they're talking about," he said.

"Us," Kurt chuckled complacently. "We're being consigned to the nether regions as animalistic brutes, or I miss my guess!"

"No," Jeff said sadly. "Not me, anyhow. Reckon I was a mite nervous, and a sight too careful, if anything, so my darling wifey candidly accuses me of being a cross between a jackrabbit and a milksop this morning. Hell of a way to begin your married life, appears to me . . ."

"Matters easily remedied," Kurt said smoothly, manfully trying to keep the derision out of his voice.

"How?" Jeff said hoarsely. "For the love of God, Kurt, tell me that!"

Whereupon, Kurt did, carefully describing to Jeff the age-old techniques that, because of a lack of vocabulary, because of prudery and shame, each generation has largely had to invent all over again, the mechanism for the transmission of folk wisdom having in this one special case broken down completely.

So, in a way, Jeff McKenzie was lucky: he obtained that late morning in November information that was full, accurate, and about seventy-five percent complete, delivered to him by an expert. The other twenty-five percent Kurt didn't dare give him, for fear of shocking him beyond the then permissible limits. It consisted of nothing unusual, being merely those heterosexual techniques that the conservative middle-class mind has always regarded as near or actual perversions, and that nearly every nation on earth accuses its next-door neighbor either of having invented or of the assiduous, constant, and sinfully unnatural practice of. Which was, Kurt mockingly conceded, as fine a proof of their universality as one could ask for.

This exchange of confidences among the newlyweds was interrupted by the reappearance of the waiter with the coffee, whose wondrous aroma brought tears to the eyes of all those within smelling distance. Rose Ann, generous to a fault, would have offered a cup to all those in the breakfast room, but both her husband and her brother forbade her that degree of folly, since it clearly meant they would have been left without any coffee for themselves. Still, as it turned out, they did have to share their scant supply, because, well before they had finished it, Gwen and Cabe came dashing through the door in some haste to join them.

"Forgot to ask you what time you'd be leaving for Wilmington," Gwen explained. "So I got this lazybones up—fairly had to kick him out of bed to do it—and came rushing into town for fear we'd miss you altogether . . ."

"A yen to stay in a nice warm bed, 'longside o' my—once in a great while, anyhow—nice warm wife," Cabe chuckled, "is no indication of sloth. The other way round, if anything. 'Twuz left with me, I'd of kept busy 'til past Christmastime . . ."

"Oh, you!" Gwen said disgustedly. "Must you always be so—vulgar, Cabe?"

"Yes'm," Cabe quipped, "I sho' Lawd must. A li'l vulgarity never hurt nobody none a-tall, 'pears to me. Been able to exercise mine a mite more frequent like, I'd of had four, five young'uns to leave the ol' homestead to by now. Ramb sugar—you happy?"

"And if I—weren't?" Rose Ann whispered.

"Make a widder woman outa you so damn fast it'll make your head swim," Cabe said in his truth-spoken-in-jest tone of voice.

"Mary Sue honey," he went on, "did this here long tall drink o' salt seawater make you happy last night?"

"No!" Mary Sue said mischievously—though that mischief also had its leavening of bitter truth, for listening to Rose Ann's paeans of joyous praise to Kurt's abilities in a department in which her Jeffie love had clearly turned out to be a short-fused dud hadn't inclined her heart toward wifely charity. "He didn't! Fact is, he treated me something *aw*ful!"

"Now looka here, Jeff," Cabe said mournfully, "fellow what don't know how t'take care of a toothsome li'l bundle o' honey-cured 'n' tender—uh—pigmeat like this'un plumb oughta be put outa his misery, by my lights . . ."

"Cabe," Gwen said frostily, "your vocabulary's—offensive. And so are you, as a matter of fact."

"Yes'm. I offend you all the damn time. Only every other eight-day week 'n' twice a double month o' Sundays 'pears to me you like it. Count, I sure Lord hope you're planning to treat this here poor stupid child—who just wasn't smart enough to grab ahold on to me when she had the chance to—right . . ."

"Of course, Major," Kurt said pleasantly, but his voice had a steely ring to it somehow. He'd put Caleb down as one of those bumptious and brainless Southerners whom it was difficult to suffer gladly for as long as five minutes flat. About the bumptiousness, he had—arguably—a point. About the brainlessness, he was dead, damned wrong. So now he added, languidly, in that nearly perfect British accent acquired from the English nanny his mother had imported for precisely that purpose, and which, by its very nature, seems deliberately designed to drive any red-blooded American straight up the nearest wall, "That is, of course, Major—eh—Henry, I believe?"

"Caleb Henry at your service, suh," Cabe supplied with what every living soul there, except Count Radetzy himself, realized was dangerous quiet. "You were saying, Count?"

"That I mean to treat the new Countess Radetzy very well indeed—so long as she knows her place and her station, and carefully observes all the rules . . ."

"I'd sure Lord admire to hear what them there rules be, Count," Cabe drawled.

"They're very simple, really," Kurt said, "since they're all derived from the motto of my family, which is *Quieta non movere*. In a phrase or two: she must realize that my word is law, my lightest whim her solemn duty, and that her stock reply to *anything* I say must be 'Yes, dear!' spoken in a soft and dulcet murmur . . ."

"And if she just don't see her way clear to obey them there mighty peculiar rules, Count?" Cabe all but whispered.

"Then I'll stripe her delectable little seat for her," Kurt said with a pleasant smile. Then he added, letting the word fall like a stone into the hurricane's eye of that vast and echoing silence: "Bloody!"

"Then," Cabe said with what sounded exactly like prayerful sorrow, "reckon I'd better sorta annul this here wedding of Rose Ann's—and by the most expeditious method possible. You got anybody you can call on to stand as your second, Count?"

Kurt Radetzy stared at Caleb Henry with icy calm, mingled with what was clearly incredulity.

"Oh, come now, my dear fellow," he said with a purring, absolutely mirthless chuckle, "you don't really imagine I'd condescend to fight a duel with a person so far below my station, d'you? That's jolly well impossible . . ."

Blind with rage, Caleb reached across the table and grabbed the Count by the ruffled shirtfront of the smart civilian outfit he had donned that morning for the train trip to Wilmington, North Carolina.

"Why, you—" he grated, but Kurt's voice cut him off. It wasn't even loud. But its icy, sibilant whisper was a blade, and flashed like one across the cool, rainy morning air.

"Take your filthy paws off me, you lowbred Southern cur," Count Sisimond Kurt Radetzy said.

Caleb, who was in full uniform, took said paws off; then, because a holstered Confederate sidearm was worn, butt forward, on the opposite side of the belt from the hand most people use to shoot with, he slanted his right arm diagonally across his own chest, clawing at the buttoned flap of the holster for several seconds before he could drag out his .36 caliber Navy Colt. The reason that he, like many Army officers, North and South, preferred the Navy model to the Army's official issue was that it was at least a pound lighter than the Army's .44, so, theoretically, could be drawn faster. Theoretically. Cabe had been staring into the twin owl eyes of Kurt's Remington over-and-under double-barreled .41 caliber derringer for several seconds before he even got his Navy Colt clear of that thrice-befouled and utterly unmentionable holster.

"I shouldn't do that if I were you, my dear fellow," Kurt said.

But the Count reckoned without the matter of temperament. *Southern* temperament. Cabe was perfectly aware that Kurt could easily kill him with that handsomely engraved toy at that point-blank range. But he didn't give a damn. He'd die forty times over before he'd let any greasy, mother-gripping furriner make him, a Southern *white* man—by God!—take low. In his calmer moments, Caleb Henry was capable of denying—intellectually, anyhow—even to himself, the Anglo-Saxon's most profoundly rooted conviction: that all other breeds that walk this earth are not merely lesser, and without the law, but sheer vermin in comparison to his own knightly, lordly splendor. Yet now, the pure unmitigated gall of this gawddamned foreigner's *daring* to confront *him*, a man from *God's own country*, the U.S. and/or CSA, drowned his thinking mind in the wild bull bellows of his rage, tore his supremely arrogant guts into bloody shreds. That he was facing a member of—at least in part—his own ancestral genetic heritage, who felt exactly the same way about the lesser breeds as he did and, what was even worse, included him, Caleb Henry, among them, was beyond his comprehension. More, it was beyond his apprehension as well.

So he dragged that Navy Colt all the way out and pointed it coolly and carefully at Count Radetzy's aristocratic breast.

"Now," he drawled, "let's see if all that there noble, reeel deep-purple blood you've done gone and got from all your 'ristocratic ancestors can make you aim any straighter o' shoot any faster than this heah mangy ol' Southern hound dawg can. 'Pears to me you's counted plumb out, Count No-Count . . ."

"Jeff!" Mary Sue shrilled. "Stop 'em! Ohhhhhhh, Lord! This is just plain *awful* and—"

But by then Rambling Rose McKenzie had already taken action: swooping down and forward, as gracefully as the legendary Swan Princess she had come to resemble, she inclined her upper trunk between those monstrous implements of male unreason so swiftly, and so deftly, that the muzzles of both weapons prodded against her on either side, with only her desperately quivering flesh, her fast-beating heart, her freely offered life, between them.

"Now," she said in the quiet, slow, much too calm accents of pure despair, "shoot. Either one of you. Or both. Makes no difference. 'Cause if one of you kills the other one, I couldn't live anyhow. So shoot and get it over with. Save me the trouble of having to do it myself . . ."

All the unbelievably harsh training of his youth, which had made him a linguist, an expert horseman, a swordsman skillful enough to have been declared champion of all *die fechtkunste Vereine* at his university, a crack shot, a marvelous ballroom dancer, a singer of almost operatic quality, an improviser of facile verse— everything, in fact, except a human being—constrained Kurt Radetzy to make that gesture first. He drew the muzzle of his derringer away from Rose Ann's side, slipped it deftly into his armpit holster, and with that matchless, apparent sincerity that was so convincing that it cost most people who knew him years before they finally stopped believing it, and him, said quietly, "No. Not even honor's to be bought at such a price, I think. Besides, I've behaved badly. So, Major Henry, since you are, after all, an officer of the Army of the Confederate States of America, and therefore, by that very commission, a gentleman, I offer you my most humble apologies . . ."

"Cabe!" Gwen seethed. "You apologize too! And right *now*. Or by heavens, I'll—"

"You'll what, Gwen o' my heart?" Caleb drawled, dropping completely the ungrammatical, swamp-rat and/or hillbilly dialect that was the most cherished of his affectations. "What can you do to me that you have not already done? So threats are bootless, my dear. A man who's seen his tenderest words of love despised, his very person made mock of, soon grows an armored hide. I'm not a noble nobleman, so I won't promise to get myself killed in the very next battle, leaving you free to marry your pretty little coward—"

"Oh, God!" Gwen got out. "Cabe, you're drunk! Or mad, or both!"

"Both. Upon the bitter wine of undeserved sorrows. Maddened by a madness without method. I can't even promise not to die. But if I do, I vow to come back and haunt you. And him. Until his liver's whiteness surpasses that of the drifting snows. Count Radetzy, no apologies! A truce, which I hereby take my most sacred oath never to break, until the hour I hear that in any way, either by word or by deed, you've made unhappy this sweet, wild Rambler, who's made a trellis of my heart, bled out my life through a million thorns embedded too deep to ever be torn free— save by Lord Death himself, whom sometimes I'd welcome. Then I'll find you, even if I have to wade through molten brimstone in hell's deepest pit to get there. And on that day or night, God in His infinite mercy pity you, my foppish little friend!"

He turned then, and pausing only long enough to slip his revolver back into its holster, started for the door.

"Gwen," Rose Ann said, "go after him. He's still your husband in the sight of God and man. And you heard what he said? Well, hear this on top of it: If ever *I* find out that what he thinks is true, I'll slosh through hell up to my armpits with the flesh dropping right off my bones to make you pay for it. And don't you ever forget it either!"

"I," Jeff sighed, "could do with another cup of coffee. And some sweet, blissful peace and quiet. We McKenzies are a mite too intense, too blood-and-thunder. And Cabe's acquired the habit. Count, forgive us our manners—or our lack of 'em. Rose Ann, sit down! You look like a seven-car train wreck on its way to happen. And as for this wife of my bosom, maybe you'd better give me a few lessons in seat striping, Count . . ."

"Well, I never!" Mary Sue McKenzie, née Hunter, said.

Chapter Nine

The Count and Countess Radetzy took the noonday train for Wilmington, North Carolina. From that town on the shores of the Atlantic, by then the Confederacy's chief port of embarkation for Europe, they sailed, or rather steamed, for France, because Kurt had decided that, since his whole effort in that country centered on the Emperor Louis Napoleon III, it could be easily and quickly disposed of, thus leaving him with what he hoped would be sufficient time to undertake the much more complicated and delicate negotiations he'd be confronted with in England. His high hopes for the French venture were based upon the well-known fact that Louis Napoleon was openly and outspokenly pro-Southern; a year ago, in November 1861, when the Confederacy's commissioners, James M. Mason of Virginia and John Slidell of Louisiana, the former being sent to London and the latter to Paris, were taken off the British steamship *Trent* in the middle of the Bahama Passage at gunpoint by Captain Charles Wilkes of the U.S. cruiser *San Jacinto*, the Emperor of the French had gone so far as to send the Union government an ultimatum, thinking, of course, that the British already had, or were soon going to back him up.

"Which only proves," Kurt explained to his bride as they walked the decks of the blockade runner *Cynthia*, the morning of the tenth day of their voyage to the Continent, in an effort to relieve one of the splitting headaches Rose Ann always complained of after another of his endless—and endlessly futile!—attempts to hammer so much as ten words of French into her sublimely stubborn little cranium, "that he didn't know the British, who are as slippery as eels. What's worse, he didn't, as he jolly well should have in his position, even know how much less actual power the English nobility and the aristocratic upper classes have than they seem to. Of course, Lord Russell and the Country Party were all for declaring War on the U.S.A., but the Prime Minister, Lord Palmerston, damned well wasn't. Besides, all those Lord High-Muck-a-Mucks had forgotten they had their own middle and lower classes to deal with, said classes being, sweet housewife mine, against our noble Southern Confederacy to the man . . . ."

"Why?" Rose Ann demanded.

"Your 'peculiar institution.' Or rather, your stubborn refusal to have enough respect for civilized public opinion in this day and age to be hypocritical about it. Nobody minds your *having* slaves, my dear; what both the English and the continentals resent is your *calling* them slaves, and not making the simple gesture of paying them a pittance, which you could easily cheat them back out of, as stupid as niggers are . . ."

"Kurt," Rose Ann said dolefully, "sometimes I think you're perfectly *awful!*"

"I am awful," he said cheerfully. "In fact, I'm bloody 'orrible, as the cockneys say. Which is why you love me, my sweet! Nearly all women admire and respect a good man, but no woman ever loved one. Runs dead against old Charlie Darwin's theory of the survival of the fittest. Women soon observed that the really nice chappies got themselves quickly devoured by saber-toothed tigers and what have you, leaving them and their apish little brats either to starve or to serve said tigers as dessert. While rum blokes like me picked up large and heavy stones and bashed those ruddy felines' heads in for them. Over the centuries that instinct for estimating exactly which chaps could both provide adequately for them and—well, attend to their more basic—and baser!—needs to their divinely lecherous hearts' content, became fixed in the human female. Which reminds me, let's go down to our cozy cabin and finish this conversation there . . ."

"No," she said.

"Why not, sweetheart?" he said with genuine surprise.

"Because we won't finish it. And I want to. I'm so awf'ly ignorant, Kurtie pie. For instance, you were saying—or implying—that the English actually do have slaves but they call them something else? Like—what?"

"The honeymoon's definitely over, isn't it, my sweet? When you prefer conversation to—"

"Making love? I don't. We can skip coming down for dinner tonight, and—well—make up for the time you've spent educating me. C'mon, tell me: What do they call 'em?"

"Factory workers. You've read Dickens, haven't you?"

"Yes. *David Copperfield* and *Oliver Twist* and *The Old Curiosity Shop* and—"

"Those will do. Dickens understated the case. The misery among the British working classes is unbelievable. And continental workers, except, of course, in Germany, aren't much better off. A Negro slave, any Negro slave, except, of course, one who has fallen into the hands of one of your not infrequent devotees of the Marquis de Sade, is far better off. The point is, *mein* Rose, *all* the modern industrial nations hold slaves, and they hold them much more profitably and with less nonsensical sentimentality than you do your blacks. But they're clever enough to pay the tribute of hypocrisy that La Rochefoucauld swore vice owes virtue. So they don't even admit to having slaves, and, better still, their slaves don't even know that they *are* slaves, which is just as well for the personal security of that elite whose maintainance, support, and even a deuced respectful pampering is, or ought to be, society's highest goal . . ."

"Hmmm," Rose Ann purred, "and chief among those being pampered being a little old Chinese-looking Hungarian *ex*-count or, as Heros says, a no-count, eh, Kurtie pie?"

Kurt looked at her and his pale gray eyes blazed almost white with sudden anger. But, as usual, his self-control was superb.

"The female instinct for clawing the scabs off a man's deepest wounds, my sweet?" he said quietly. "You're right; I've often had occasion to regret my looks, though if my father had been allowed to remain in Magyarország, I don't suppose I would have . . ."

"Magyah—whaat?" Rose said.

"Magyarország. The name of Hungary in the Hungarian or rather in the original Magyar language. Which I wish I knew better then I do. Perhaps one day I shall have the opportunity to spend a year or two in my father's country and learn it really well. But, as usual, you mistake my meaning, Rose Ann: I don't insist that the elite be entirely either Teutons or Nordics; I only ask that they be a master race, and that we Magyars indisputably were, and are. Even the name of our country and our people is a historical error: we are not Huns, but of Finno-Ugric stock; yet that our ancestors were a Mongol people, who came riding into Europe, bows in hand, on their shaggy little Mongolian ponies, is certain. But it is no less certain that they were conquerors, and that no one, either German or Turk, has ever succeeded in vanquishing us for long. And we've held all the people round about us in our thrall. Croatian, Slovak, Czech, Slovene, Serb, Slav, have all been our vassals. So in my veins flows the blood of not one but two master races, Magyar and German. And my spirit has been torn asunder by the fact that each of them despises the other. But enough of my petty personal problems! The goal is far too vast. We must establish the domination of the entire globe by a Pan-Germanic master race —for my father's people, the Magyars, retain too much of the Oriental in their outlook to ever be able to manage it. We'll allow your Picts, Scots, Celts, Jutes, Saxon mixtures—for your ancestors, my sweet, were all of these—to control some outlying areas: the British Isles, Canada, even Australia perhaps, but central North America is too important to be left to a people who have the sheer wrongheadedness and mysticism that always accompanies too great a proportion of Celtic blood. Whichever of your foolishly feuding Anglo-Saxon tribes wins this insane war, we Germans must ultimately take over for the good of humanity!"

"Including the niggers, the dagos, and the Eye-talians?" Rose Ann teased him solemnly.

"Including all the savage, backward, largely imbecilic races, like the blacks, who are fit only to be slaves. And the hopelessly inferior white—or near-white—races, the Latins, who have the advantage of being lighthearted, quite talented artistically, and not even too stupid, really. Their problem is that they lack energy, patience, and perseverance, on top of being the most astoundingly inefficient peoples who ever drew breath. But our domination will benefit all the inferior races, including a people as abysmally brutish as the Slavs. With us to guide them, set right the awful muck-up they always make of everything, apply a leaded lash to their tails when need be to get them hopping, they'll surely benefit. What a world we'll have then, my dear!"

"I'll bet. And all those poor, poor backward and stupid folks are just going to stand back and *let* all you tall, blond, blue-eyed Aryan Nordic Germans"—she put up a playful hand and ruffled his inky hair as she spoke, let her fingers stray down the Mongolian slant of his cheekbones—"do all that to 'em?"

He glared at her out of those fog-mist eyes. Then, very slowly, he smiled.

"Yes, quite. Just as you lie back, or gleefully bend forward, and allow me to do all *that* to you," he chuckled.

She stared at him.

"You know, I hate you, Kurt. I really do," she said.

"Good. Let's go downstairs to our cabin, so you can prove how much you hate me," he said cheerfully.

"No. Absolutely not. I don't mean to let you touch me for the rest of this voyage. And after we go ashore in France, it'll all depend—on how you treat me, I mean, and—"

He shrugged his massive shoulders with icy calm, said, with absolute indifference, "All right. As you like, my dear . . ."

The trouble with his indifference was that it was neither false nor feigned, and therefore struck fatally to the very heart of her femininity. Throughout history women have effortlessly controlled men because of the greater impetuosity of male desire. Rose

Ann was far too intelligent to believe that either of the two sexes was more ardent than the other. What women were was—slower. It took her sex far longer to kindle, to smolder, to blaze, to reach incandescence. But once *there*, she thought miserably, we stay there. All night. A week. Two weeks. A month, until a real pig-dog swine like this one comes along and cools us off mighty nicely, thank you! And just like he says, it's always a mean, cruel, heartless blackguard like him, like my Kurtie pie, who knows exactly how to manage us. Nice boys, like my poor little boy baby doll Joe-Joe, or Colin, or, from what Mary Sue says, my brother Jeff, just don't seem to have the knack. Most men blaze right up, and burn right out. But this ice-cold, uncaring, slow, so sllllloh ohohow, working into you working into you not ever pounding you to pieces in half a minute just working slowwwwly slowwwwllly oh so slowwwly until your—or anyhow, *my* insides turn to cream taper wax melting melting and all of me collapsing all over him crying weeping saying his name praying to him like to sweet baby Jesus nottostopit not to stop it not ever to stop it justkeepitup keepitup keepitup tear me in half up the middle killmedead ohhhhh Gawdddd!

She said, "All right. Let's go downstairs."

He laughed, yawned, not faking that either, said, "No. I've changed my mind. Much rather not, my sweet. Besides, we really had better do something about your nonexistent French, y'know."

"Why?" she snapped. "Let *them* learn English. They practically *live* off us tourists, don't they? Anyhow, I *can't* learn French. I can't learn *any* language. I've been working on English my whole life and I still mess up my grammar."

"English hasn't any grammar. It's not even a language, but rather a bit of a muck-up in itself. But French is not at all difficult, and yet you claim you can't remember how to say anything in it. Come on, try. Say something to me in French."

She said solemnly, *"Voulez-vous se coucher avec moi?"*

He laughed, said, *"Peut-être.* But only if you say that sentence properly."

"But, Kurt," she wailed, "that's right! I looked it up in the dictionary and the grammar book, just in case I met a nice handsome Frenchman one night when you're not around."

"He'd laugh at you if you asked him that," Kurt said cheerfully. "Or he'd think you were crazy. Oh, you've got the grammar right enough. Only, no one who speaks French would say it that way."

"Then what would she say? Tell me! How will I ever be able to cheat on you in Paris if I don't know? And that's what people go to Paris *for*, isn't it? To cheat on their ever-loving lawfuls, right?"

"Oh, yes. Quite. Look, my sweet, you'd never say *vous* to a person you wanted to climb into that old four-poster with. You'd say *tu*, which means 'thou' in English. So if you really wanted your nice little plum pudding gently poked, you'd say, '*Tu veux te coucher avec moi, mon petit chou?*' Not even that. You just close one of those great big green eyes slowly, lift one fox-fire eyebrow, and nod in the direction of the *boudoir* door. And twenty lecherous Frenchmen will get killed in the rush. Or they would if you looked a bit less like a clothes rack. You really must put on a bit of flesh, you know . . ."

"Ohhh, Lord!" she wept. "Remind me to kill you sometime soon. In a reeel bad, cruel way. Before you drive me all the way out of my mind. Now c'mon!"

"Come on where?" he drawled, tormenting, more than teasing her.

"Downstairs. To our cabin. To make love to me. All night long. Forty-seven different ways. All the feeelthy, feeelthy tricks! You heard me, Kurt! C'mon!"

He elaborately stifled still another yawn with the back of his hand.

"Very well, my darling, if you insist," he said.

Rose Ann didn't enjoy Paris at *all*. In the first place, she was infuriated by the unbelievable stubbornness with which the French persisted in speaking *French*. For, while she didn't share the number one Anglo-Saxon conviction that all other races and tribes were so much vermin to be squashed beneath her queenly little foot, as she'd proved by marrying two foreigners in a row, she did hold with unshakable firmness the second: that all the world damned well *ought* to speak English for her ease, comfort, and convenience, a conviction so stoutly held by all her racial brothers and sisters that well within her long lifetime they would have inflicted English upon three quarters of the inhabitants of the globe by the simple expedient of shouting it ever louder at the poor defenseless aborigines.

"After all," she fumed to Kurt, "we *are* the tourists. We come here and spend our money in their hotels and buy their perfumes and clothes and jewelry. And not only do they cheat our back eyeteeth out, but they don't even bother to learn how to talk so a body can understand them!"

"They," Kurt said, "are laboring under the misapprehension that this is their country, my sweet, in which their own language ought to be spoken. But give them time, they'll learn. They really are a clever people, y'know. Come on now; you're due at Mme Peluche's for a fitting. We're dining *chez les* Slidells this Friday, and you really must look your best. I've the strongest feeling that *Son Majesté* just might pop in unexpectedly. I've got him eating out of my carefully manicured hands, my dearest—and if he does appear at the Slidells' I'm sure I'll be able to wind matters up so that we can depart for England this very next week . . ."

"Oh, Lord, I hope so!" Rose Ann moaned. "For at least I'll be able to understand the people when they talk to me . . ."

"But you won't be able to eat the food, which is utterly abominable. They boil everything for thirty-six hours before serving it, and they have no idea of flavors and seasonings. Much do I fear you'll lose that charming pound or two you've put on since we've been in Paris . . ."

"Kurt," she said worriedly, "we're spending an awful lot of money . . . Where are you getting it from?"

"From the Royal Exchequer, of course. I've quite convinced Louis Napoleon that I, and only I, can keep the damnyankees off his portly backside long enough for him to consolidate his puppet empire in *Le Mexique.* He got quite a shock last year, y'know. He'd written Palmerston a friendly note offering France's support of England in any punitive action Her Majesty's government wanted to take against the North for their boorishness in having dared to actually fire shots across the bows of a steamship under British registry and pluck Slidell and Mason off of it. So old Palmerston fired back a most charming missive that could be interpreted any of three dozen ways. So Louis, who really isn't right bright, took it to be a go-ahead and sent an ultimatum to Washington. Whereupon, Palmerston took dear Louis's second note, and a copy of his ultimatum to the White House, to Prince Consort Albert, who immediately saw the political effects of having it seem to the world that Her Majesty's government was being dragged into a stupid war that it probably couldn't win on the tail of the Napoleonic kite. So like the good *German* he was, and in spite of the fact that he was dying—he left good Queen Victoria a widow three days later, y'know—Prince Albert reduced the furious note the Country Party had drafted to blast at Washington to something that sounded like an invitation to a Sunday afternoon's high tea at the vicarage. Result: Honest Abe released Slidell and Mason to Her

Majesty's Royal Navy, and told poor old Louis Napoleon to commit an unnatural act upon himself in any of a variety of contorted and painful positions. Scared him spitless, the poor old chappie!"

"Bet you could give him a pointer, eh, Kurtie?" Rose Ann sighed. "On the subject of unnatural acts in freakish positions, anyhow. But tell me, what's all this high politics got to do with *us?*"

"It's our key to fortune, doll. I was able to point out to Third Napoleon, *Son Majesté* Louis, that the longer I could prolong the American Civil War for him, the better would be Maximilian's chances in Mexico, that either a victorious and friendly South or a North too exhausted by an utterly Pyrrhic victory to lift a trembling finger would serve almost equally well toward the consolidation of his French protectorate south of the Rio Grande. And that while I couldn't deliver both of those *coups de tonnerre*, I could deliver *one* of them . . ."

"How?" Rose Ann demanded.

"By acting as *Son Majesté's agent provocateur* and *laissance* man to the dissenting Copperhead movement in the North, paying those traitorous swine off with Louis's good *louis d'or*. A good many of which will stick to *our* greedy little fingers—of that you may rest assured. Now, come along. I've made Mme Peluche a few suggestions about your *robe pour cette soirée*. It should be absolutely stunning, for, as you know, Mme Peluche admires my taste. The other day she suggested archly, in a jest that had much truth in it, that you and I should stay in Paris, so that I could become her chief designer. She swears that if she and I formed a partnership we could easily dethrone the current *roi de la haute couture*, Monsieur Charles Frederick Worth. Odd, isn't it? An English lad from Lincolnshire the ruler of Parisian fashions! Clever bloke, little Charlie. He's reconciled all the husbands of *les grande dames du haut monde et bon ton* to paying his outrageous prices by showing off his rags on *living* models. Quite a *coup*, that! While the *dames* are looking at his rags, their husbands are looking at the models. Result: Everyone's happy, including little Charlie's banker . . ."

"You should try it," Rose said somberly. "I don't believe you're sissified enough, though. But then, who knows? A lot of the things you do, and make me do for you—seem—downright unnatural to me . . ."

"*Ach, so?* Again Victorian prudery raises her deuced unlovely head? My dear, I really don't recall ever having forced you to do *anything*. Quite the contrary. I've been thinking of keeping a limber gutta-percha cane in our boudoir to keep you at bay so I can get some rest . . ."

She bowed her head, stared at the toes of her slippers, looked up again, her eyes liquefied emeralds, ablaze and brimming.

"You're—right," she whispered. "I'm plain awful, aren't I? One of those female maniacs you're always talking about . . ."

"A nymphomaniac? No, my sweet, absolutely not. What you are is perfectly normal in a world where women aren't allowed to be. A bit of a primitive, perhaps, but nothing more. I must say I'm sorry, though. Believe me, I was unaware that my—infinitely corrupt—European refinements and variations upon the basic theme were distressing you. Tell you what, any practice you really don't like, just speak right up and say so. I'll immediately remove it from our tender *repertoire* . . ."

"Then you'll have to remove them all," she said quietly. "Except —one. Except plain, ordinary lovemaking. 'Cause all those variations, as you call 'em, make me feel—disgusted with myself afterward, instead of warm and good and worn-out and happy. I don't want to feel that way, Kurt, all twisted and queer and—and—unnatural. I just want to love you the way a woman should love her husband and give you lots and lots of babies!"

"Heaven forbid!" he said fervently. "I'm not keen on brats, y'know. Oh, later, perhaps, when I've made our fortune and we can afford to settle down. But tell me, so that I can begin to conform to the Anglo-Saxon Protestant and Puritanical norms—just *how* should a good wife make love to her husband? Inside of a thick flannel nightgown, with all the lights out, after piously having read a verse or two from the Holy Writ?"

That made her laugh, which immediately cheered her up.

"Well, I could do with a lot less light, and a sight fewer mirrors," she giggled. "Always makes me think I'm leading a parade—specially when I'm on top! D'you know, I didn't even know it could be done that way? Me on top riding up and down on— Oh, Lllllord! C'mon, let's get out of here!"

Whom the gods would destroy, they first make mad. And there is no easier method for disturbing the mental equilibrium of a member of the human species than to grant him a series of easy successes until his own self-satisfied complacency blinds him to the pitfalls lying in his path.

That Friday night at the residence of the Confederacy's unofficial Ambassador to France—unofficial only because Louis Napoleon III was cautiously waiting for England to recognize the Confederacy *first,* which since Lincoln's issue of the Emancipation Proclamation on September 22 of that now fast-fading year of 1862, Her Majesty's government hadn't the faintest intention to ever do —went off swimmingly. A number of the French ladies present actually spoke English, after a fashion, and were delighted to try their *bons mots* in Shakespeare's tongue on Rose Ann. Which gave the poor dear a frightful headache, because, as she discovered to her chagrin, what *she* spoke wasn't English at all, but Virginia American, vilely corrupted by several regional dialects, among which the thick gumbo soup that the black slaves she came into daily contact with reduced English to predominated. But she plucked up courage and made a desperate effort to understand what these gaudy birds of paradise were saying—for their soup-strainer, locked-teeth British accent, overlayered with the absolute mayhem that a French intonation and tune commits upon English anyhow (and vice versa, of course!), had her on the verge of open tears until it finally occurred to her that her painfully acquired New England accent was far closer to what these dear ladies were trying to speak—and honestly thought they *were* speaking—than her corn-pone-and-molasses Virginia drawl could ever be. So she switched over to it, and matters immediately improved. Before long she became the star of the ball, as she playfully told those *grandes dames françaises* plain lies, barefaced lies, damned lies, and finally goddamned lies to their astonishment and delight. In fact, she was just finishing up her *chef d'oeuvre,* an elaborate fantasy about how she'd been kidnapped by a rebellious, gigantic, jet-black, ferocious, and lustful slave, from whom her father and her brother had saved her at the exact last hairsbreadth instant before she'd been about to suffer the fate worse than death—this last murmured in a tone of such ambiguous sorrow that half the dear ladies went home with the impression that her rescuers hadn't really got there in time after all, and the other half with the ironclad conviction that she, Rose Ann, was jolly well sorry they hadn't minded their ruddy business and postponed rescuing her at least until the following morning, when she noticed how the wife of the Austrian Ambassador was staring at her with grim disapproval and—what was even worse, she realized now—at her Kurtie pie with what was unmistakably absolutely murderous, ice-cold hatred.

The shock almost spoiled her story. She halted in midflight, to be assaulted with a chorus of "Do go on! *Continuez, s'il vous plaît!*" until she rallied and ended her tale with a gruesome description of how, after flaying all the black hide off him with leaded whips, her menfolks had boiled that nigger alive in a vat of peanut oil, until they could hear him screaming halfway 'cross North Carolina before he finally paid for his outrage by giving up the ghost . . .

But before she could ask her husband why the wife of his country's ambassador was looking at him like that, as well as why, as she now also perceived, the Ambassador himself was replying to Kurt's gay and incessant chatter in *Hochdeutsch* with frosty monosyllables, *Son Majesté* Louis Napoleon dropped in, accompanied by only two rather sinister-looking *Zouaves* who looked like North African brigands in their fezzes, burnooses, and baggy pants, but who actually were Corsicans, for the Emperor spoke to them—briefly—in effortless and fluent Italian, which contrasted strongly with a French that Rose, who spoke not one word of anybody's language save her own, didn't realize was God-awful. But when Kurt blithely presented her to the Emperor, Louis Napoleon complimented her beauty in quite adequate *American* English. To Rose Ann's breathless "Why, Your Majesty, you talk just like *we* do! I mean—not like English people! Like us Americans . . ." the Emperor smilingly replied, "Of course, my dear. I was a refugee in your country for several years. Besides, my father was Dutch, my mother Creole. And American English is remarkably easy to learn for one who speaks *Plattdeutsch*, or what your charming husband sneeringly calls *Low* German. And that was the language of my childhood, along with my mother's *patois*, which was more like the French of your New Orleans than the French of France. Kurt, I felicitate you! You've plucked yourself the fairest of roses, haven't you, my boy?"

Seeing the Emperor's marked display of favor, the Austrian Ambassador unbent, became almost fawningly affable toward Kurt, but when he tried to chat with Rose Ann, he found to his dismay that in an age when everyone with any pretense to culture spoke at least passable French, this American wildflower couldn't even say *"Bon soir!"* And since learning all the languages an Austrian civil servant had to learn merely to talk to the representatives of the racially diverse and polyglot peoples who inhabited the Austro-Hungarian Empire had given him no time to learn the speech of a country with which Austria had as little to do in those days as it did with England, he was forced to call upon his wife to translate his complimentary remarks to Rose Ann.

This she did, in a clipped, perfect British English that couldn't quite conceal the shake of utter fury that being forced by protocol to talk—even as a disinterested interpreter—to a person she obviously despised had put into her voice. Rose Ann reached out and laid an impulsive hand on her dark, burnt-coppery arm.

"Why do you—hate us, *Frau* von Zorndorf?" she said in her plaintive schoolgirl's voice. "Look, if I've done anything to offend you—it was unintentionally, I assure you. And I apologize for it, whatever it was . . ."

"May God punish you, Gerta!" the Baron *von* Zorndorf thundered in *Hochdeutsch*. "You cannot at all to this maid any blame give! Because—"

"I don't speak German either," Rose Ann sighed. "Reckon you all must think Kurt was crazy, marrying a poor, ignorant girl like me . . ."

"No, my dear," the Baroness von Zorndorf said. "We—I—don't think that. One sees that you are innocent—a child. So why should I distress you with my opinion of your husband? You'll discover exactly what he is soon enough . . . As my husband, the Baron, was saying just now, you really aren't to be blamed for your husband's crimes, nor even for his sins, of which, I see now, you are but one more victim . . ."

"Crimes? Sins?" Rose Ann whispered. "Ohhh, Lord—Heros said—"

"Heros?" the Ambassador said.

"Von Borcke," Rose supplied. "He's in my country, fighting on our side as a volunteer. And all the girls are in love with him!"

"Small wonder," the Baroness said with a wintry smile. "Heros von Borcke is a remarkably handsome man, and a jolly nice one as well. He's the one Prussian I know who is not a boor . . ."

"Not true, even so," her husband grunted. "Von Borcke is Pomeranian, not Prussian . . ."

"Small difference!" the Baroness snapped. "When they're from that far east, they're all Cossacks, as far as I'm concerned. Besides, racially, the Pomeranians and the Prussians are practically the same people. And you know what Goethe said about the Prussians—"

"What did he say?" Rose Ann asked. She was smart enough not to ask who Goethe was, although she didn't know that either.

"That they're savages," the Baroness said drily. "He was right: they are."

Rose Ann stared at her. The Baroness von Zorndorf was a striking woman, in her late forties or early fifties, she guessed. Strangely enough, the Ambassador's wife was quite dark; more so, in fact, than Austrians, who can be swarthy, generally are. And she looked—Oriental. Like—a Hindu, Rose thought; then, seeing the frown that seemed a permanent feature of the Baroness's face, added: Wonder why she's mad at the world. She said, impulsively, "You don't like people very much, d'you, Baroness?"

The Baroness sighed, relaxed. The frown went away. Without it, Rose Ann immediately discerned that she must have been an extremely beautiful woman in her early youth. In fact, she still was, though in a quiet, matronly sort of way.

"On the contrary, I generally like people very much," she said in that voice of hers that was as dark, and rich, as her skin. "With, of course, two qualifications . . ."

"And they are?" Rose Ann whispered.

"That the people in question are as simple, and as decent, as you appear to be, my child. But the second qualification's more difficult: when the people—even possessing those virtues of simplicity and decency—permit themselves to be liked . . ."

"But why shouldn't they?" Rose Ann said in utter astonishment. "*Every*body wants to be liked, it seems to me!"

"True," the Baroness said, "but not *by* everyone else."

"Now you've really lost me," Rose Ann said dolefully. "You'll have to explain that to me, Baroness—using simple words. I'm really not very bright . . ."

"Allow me to disagree," Gerta von Zorndorf said with a smile. "Your performance just now with the ladies of the Court was masterly. You're a fantastic spinner of fantastic yarns, aren't you, my child? You told that bunch of overdecorated and brainless dolls exactly what they wanted to hear, and made them believe it, too . . ."

"Attention, Gerta!" von Zorndorf growled. "They can hear you, you know!"

Seeing the look of utter blankness on Rose Ann's face—combined now with an expression of distress, even shame; for as bright as she indisputably was, the new Countess Radetzy already had begun to understand how great a mental and social cripple a monolingual person is in a polyglot world, and all the more so when that world was the one that one's spouse inhabited as easily as a fish does water, by natural right—the Baroness answered her husband in English, which, apparently, he understood well enough, though speaking it escaped him: "Of course they can hear me, Karl, but they can't understand me. You see, my love, I *speak* English, and they don't. Not even the ones who think they do."

She turned back to Rose Ann. "Let's see if I can't explain what I meant. D'you particularly care whether your blacks like you or not?"

"I'd *die* if they didn't!" Rose Ann cried. "Ohhh, Lord, you've been reading that horrible old lying book that vinegary damnyankee woman wrote. Look, Baroness, our colored people *love* us! They really do! And we love them. We *don't* beat 'em bloody with whips. Not—ever! Oh, well, almost never, 'cept when one of 'em does something really *aw*ful, as, being human, they occasionally do. But don't you realize what living on a plantation surrounded by people who *hated* you would be like? I'd go crazy. Take our cook, old A'nt Cindy. Let me come home from a party or a dance ten minutes late, and there she is, her hands on her hips, glaring at me and yelling, 'Now looka heah, Miss Rose Ann, I ain't gonna have you goin 'n' disgracin' me, y'hear! Next time you comes home this late, I'm gonna take my husband's belt to yo' li'l swishy tail, 'n' Marse Dave'll back me up, believe you me!' And Papa *would*, that's the bad part about it. And afterward, he'd probably add a few more welts to my poor little sit-down on his own . . ."

"Then the example I was going to use won't serve me," the Baroness said. "So I'll have to simply state the case, and rather crudely at that. In my native Austria, child, there are any number of good, simple, decent people who would never do me any harm, or even speak an unkind word to me, but who simply go to incredible lengths to avoid me. Unlike your monster of—eh—a husband, they don't want me dead, or even my husband dismissed from the Foreign Service for having married me. When they find out I'm out of town, they shower invitations on Karl here. But when I'm in Vienna, we dine alone—or with a circle of couples who're in the same predicament that we are, for having made mixed marriages, that number one social error wherever German is spoken . . ."

"That is not fully true," the Ambassador said sadly, "but—"

"It *is* entirely true, Karl," the Baroness said, "and you know it!"

Rose Ann stared at the two of them with breath-gone amazement. In her native Virginia, when a body said "a mixed couple, by God!" they meant that a white man was living with a colored woman—generally a quadroon or an octoroon, almost never a Negress—in open and defiant sin. Which was the only way they *could* live together, since the law wouldn't let them get married. In the old days, her pa swore, there'd even been couples the other way around, where the *man* was mulatto or quadroon or occasionally even black, and the woman white, usually of the indentured-ser-

vant class. But that had been a long time ago, before the Slavery
Question had heated things up more than somewhat. Today, such a
combination simply wasn't possible: The nigger would find himself the guest of honor at a lynching, and the woman would be
whipped bloody, the first night they tried it . . .

She peered at the Baroness's dark skin wonderingly. But it
couldn't be that! While dark, the Baroness simply didn't look nig-
gerish; she looked—again that thought came—like a Hindu. Rose
had seen Hindus, for a few of them had drifted down from the
North before the war to peddle rugs and real pretty things made
out of ivory and brass and suchlike. So now, she blurted out, "Are
you from—India, Baroness?"

"Good heavens, no!" the Baroness laughed. "Though Karl has
often accused me of being the daughter of a snake charmer. I am—
Jewish, child. And I sincerely hope that fact won't bother you, for
I'd like to keep your friendship, if possible . . ."

"Bother me?" Rose Ann's astonishment was obviously un-
feigned. "Why on earth should it, Baroness?"

Gerta von Zorndorf glanced quickly to the farthest corner of the
salon, where Kurt had the Emperor of the French surrounded. It
didn't seem possible that one lone man could surround another
man almost as big as he, but Kurt was managing the trick mighty
nicely. He was talking a mile a minute, not letting His Poor Old
Majesty get a word in edgewise. Straining her ears, Rose Ann
caught a word or two. The language was Italian. Oh, Lord! she
thought despairingly. I'll bet he even speaks Chinese and Malay!

"Your husband—just might object," the Baroness said bitterly.

"Let him!" Rose Ann hooted. "I'll tell him to go fly a kite!"
Impulsive as always, she bounced up from her chair and, leaning
forward, planted a fervent kiss on the Baroness's coppery cheek.

"There!" she gurgled. "We *are* friends, and a fat lot Kurtie can do
about it. We don't have those silly ideas down in Virginia where I
come from. Why, the Secretary of State of the Confederacy is Jewish, in case you didn't know. He came to our wedding reception,
though not to the wedding itself. I s'pose he didn't want to enter a
church, but, d'you know what? He and Kurt are real good friends!"

"Then he's a fool!" Gerta said darkly. "Look, Rose Ann, there's
more to this than the mere fact of my being Jewish. My maiden
name was Steinermann. Does that mean anything to you?"

Rose Ann thought about that. The name was familiar. She was
sure she'd heard it before, but—

Abruptly it came back to her. More. It smashed a fist made of

granite and ice, straight into her bullet-torn gut. She didn't so
much sit back down as collapse into her chair. She sat there staring
at her newly made friend, her small face utterly woebegone.

"That man Kurt k-k-killed," she stammered, "Your y-y-your father?"

"My uncle. But he reared me, and I loved him as much as if he
had been. So, as you can see, Rose Ann—"

But the new Countess Radetzy was out of her chair again and,
with total disregard for Mme Peluche's expensive creation, kneeling before Gerta von Zorndorf.

"I'm so sorry!" she wailed. "Ohhh, Lord! How could Kurt be so
mean!"

"Easily enough," Gerta began, but her husband cut her off with
several words in German, delivered in a jovial tone of voice.

The Baroness smiled at that.

"My husband says you're—angelic," she said. "But I think he's
wrong. Am I right?"

"Oh, Lord, yes!" Rose Ann said. "I'm positively—*awful*, but I
didn't know it showed . . ."

Gerta von Zorndorf extended a richly bejeweled hand and caressed Rose Ann's bright hair.

"It doesn't, because you're not," she said. "What you are is—
féerique, even elfin. With a great capacity for—joy in you. Of a
rather mischievous sort, I'd think. Or you would be if it weren't
for this deep and terrible sadness I sense in you." She nodded
brusquely toward where Kurt, oblivious to everything except his
own intent—To sell the Emperor a carload lot of wooden nutmegs,
plugged nickels, busted carriage springs, plus the keys to City Hall,
Rose Ann thought bitterly—was talking away. "Is *he* the cause of
it, this sadness of yours?"

"Yes'm," Rose Ann said with scarcely any hesitation at all.
"Sometimes I think—I—I hate him, Baroness. He's so—strange. I
don't know the word for what he is . . ."

"Get up from there," the Baroness said quietly. "The position's
uncomfortable, and it's beginning to attract more attention than
either you or I need. There. That's better. Tell me this, child: if
you already know enough about Kurt Radetzy to have your doubts
about him, why don't you just leave him? From a quite disinterested standpoint, entirely apart from all the excellent reasons I
have to loathe him, that's exactly what I should advise you to do
. . ."

"Can't," Rose Ann sighed. " 'Cause I reckon that I—love him—

more than I hate him. Only, that's wrong too. I *don't* love him. And I don't think I ever did. It's just that I can't do without him. To me he's like a poison, or a drug."

"*Why* can't you do without him, Rose Ann?" Gerta von Zorndorf demanded.

Rose Ann looked down, stared at the tips of her dainty slippers, looked up again.

"I can't tell you that, Baroness," she said simply. "And not because I don't want to, but because I don't even know the words to say it with. It's too awful. Reckon that if I did know 'em, I still couldn't, 'cause I'd be too ashamed. It's the kind of thing that decent women don't *ever* talk about. More than that, we don't even let ourselves *think* about it, most of the time. For, if we did, we'd have to admit to ourselves that we aren't really decent, after all, that we're no better than those painted hussies you see strolling up and down on the sidewalks, *trottoirs*, of the boulevards at night. No. We're worse. Because they do what they do for money, to make a living, not because they've been made over into slaves like we have."

The Baron and the Baroness von Zorndorf exchanged a long, significant glance.

"Quite the same that the poor little Ilse of him ever has said," the Baron muttered.

"Please!" Rose Ann moaned. "Let's change this subject! It's not fit to talk about anyhow and—"

"Later!" Gerta said sharply. Then, turning to the Baron, she said in High German, angrily, the intensity of her emotion making that language sound even harsher than it usually does, "Karl, I'm going to tell her! I will not be a silent partner to a deception as unspeakable as this one is! Nothing, not even your concepts of diplomatic discretion, justifies our sitting idly by and allowing this monster to destroy still another life. The life of a child like this, as angelic, as sweet—"

"Gerta, no!" Karl von Zorndorf thundered. "It isn't any of our business! Besides, how do you know in what manner this poor little creature will react to such dreadful news? Why, she might even—"

"Kill herself? Nonsense! She isn't the type. What's more, she doesn't love him. She is basically sound in the moral sense. And she will be much better off without him, as any normal woman would."

She turned back to Rose Ann, who had been listening to this

195

somewhat heated exchange more than a little sadly, thinking all the time: My goodness, how smart these foreign people are! Jumping back and forth between two or three languages while I can't talk all that well in the one I was born to. Reckon I was hiding under the porch steps when the Good Lord was handing out brains.

"Rose Ann," the Baroness said quietly, "you simply cannot remain with this scoundrel any longer. You must leave him at once. Wait! I *know* what the difficulties are. You are alone in a foreign country whose language you do not speak. And it goes without saying that he controls what money you have between you. No matter! Come to our embassy, and my husband will grant you a refugee's status, under whatever pretext he can dream up, legal or not, or else I'll break off diplomatic relations with him!"

"Good God!" the Baron groaned.

"And don't worry your pretty red head about your lack of money. Since my uncle Josef, whom this monster of yours murdered, could not dissuade me from the folly of marrying a Gentile, he consented to my wedding Karl only under the provision of our law known as *separation of means*, so the estate he left me when your darling shot him remains my own to employ as I jolly well please. Believe me, it will be a pleasure to spend whatever may be necessary to get you out of the clutches of the consummate blackguard that Sisimond Kurt Radetzy is. I'll cheerfully make you an outright gift of the funds to return to your country, take care of all the travelling arrangements, accompany you personally to Le Havre to take the steamer, the two of us escorted in our turn by a pair of rather villainous Austrian squareheads from the embassy staff whose primary mission it is to keep Karl and—somewhat reluctantly in my case, of course!—me, alive, anyhow. And, since xenophobia is an inborn characteristic of the Nordic races, the very thought that they might be able to dismember a Hungarian will make their handlebar mustaches stand up and bristle with delight. Come, what d'you say? I assure you that remaining with this scoundrel means the sure ruin of your reputation, the loss of your good name, the destruction, finally, of your youth, your beauty, even—much do I fear it!—your life."

"But—but," Rose Ann stammered, "why *should* you do all *that?*"

"Call it a burnt offering upon the tomb of my Uncle Josef," Gerta von Zorndorf said grimly. "That's motive enough, my dear! But another's a true woman's revulsion at seeing a member of my sex betrayed. And, last of all, there's the enormous liking, even fondness, I seem to have conceived for you, charming little primitive that you are."

"You said 'betrayed,'" Rose Ann whispered. "What did you mean by that, Frau von Zorndorf?"

"This," the Baroness said harshly. "Ask Kurt Radetzy who the woman—no! Who the other poor abused girl-child called Ilse is. And the identity of the man—the male creature, anyhow—who fathered her three children. And what the canons of the Roman Catholic Church, to which faith both he and Ilse von Hohlenrühe were born, have to say about divorce. And—"

"Gerta!" the Baron roared. "Hold thy mouth, woman! Even to implement your vengeance, you have no right to break this gentle little heart!"

Without another word, Rose Ann got up then. Turned. Walked out onto the balcony overlooking the Seine. Stood there, staring out into a night whose blackness was infinite. And it came to her that what she felt was—nothing. Absolutely nothing at all.

Behind her in the salon, the Baroness von Zorndorf was restraining her husband, almost by main force, from rushing out onto the balcony to make what amends he could.

"No," she said firmly. "She will get over even this. She has pride, Karl. Intelligence, will. Besides, *how* can you console her when you two have no tongue in common? Sweep her into your manly arms? Cover her face with kisses?"

"The suggestion's not to be despised, Gerta," the Baron growled. "Would God that I could!"

When Rose Ann came back into the salon finally, she saw the Baroness gazing at her worriedly, with compassion in her eyes, with sorrow, regret, perhaps even a little fear. Immediately she crossed back to her new friend's side.

"You aren't ill, are you, child?" the Baroness asked with genuine concern. "I know I must have upset you dreadfully, but it seemed to me necessary. To keep silent was to become an accomplice by default to this piece of unmitigated dastardy. You must forgive me, and try to understand—"

"I do," Rose Ann sighed. "It's not that. Reckon I always knew that he was tricking me, playing fast and loose with a poor little stupid Southern girl. I'm not mad at you for telling me that, Baroness. Sure as shooting when I get over the shock, I know I'm going to be mighty grateful to you for setting me straight. The main trouble with me right now is that I'm so blamed tired. Just

can't seem to get my strength back since that damnyankee shot me
. . ."

Gerta peered at her a little mockingly, started to loose a sardonic
chuckle, then saw, without room for any doubt, that Rose Ann was
telling her the simple truth.

"Tell us about it," she said, "but not too rapidly, so my husband,
the Baron, can understand . . ."

Rose Ann began, slowly and sadly, her bitterly remembered tale.
She told it well, thinking all the time, If it hadn't been for that
little, fat, pimply-faced and ugly Yankee Lieutenant Froggie Boy, I
never would have met Kurt, and then—But suddenly, abruptly,
Gerta stopped her.

"Wait, Rose Ann!" she said. Then, lifting her golden sun-dark-
ened voice, she called out, *"Venez ici, tout le monde! Écoutez l'histoire de
cette trop brave fille! Croyez-moi, c'est absolument formidable!"*

So once again Rose Ann became the star of the party, all the
more so because Gerta translated her halting phrases line by line
into impeccable French. That Victorian epoch was one of the most
sentimental, even the most lachrymose periods in recent history;
and besides, her tale was truly moving. All the court ladies were
weeping before she'd done, and every one of them hugged and
kissed her. So did the Emperor of the French, who was visibly
shaken by her story. Only Kurt, for reasons of his own, had to go
and almost spoil it.

"Je me suis souvent demandé," he purred, *"pourquoi ce type, lui, n'a pu
être mieux tireur . . ."*

For once, nobody had to translate for Rose Ann. By the very
expressions on their faces, she guessed what Kurt had meant: "I've
often asked myself why that beggar couldn't have been a better
shot!"

She walked quietly up to him and took his arm.

"Take me back to the hotel, Kurt. Then, once we're there, push
me off the balcony of our room. It's high enough, isn't it? I'll leave
a note saying I did it myself. Then we'll both be at peace, maybe.
Now, c'mon," she said.

Kurt stared at her. Frowned fiercely. Then he relaxed. Sighed.
She'd demonstrated to him once again that evening just how valuable she was. Once she'd ceased to be so, ridding himself of her
would be easy enough, he thought. But later on, not now.

"I was only joking, my dearest," he said, and bent and kissed her.
"Your Majesty, a thousand thanks for the favor you have granted
me! Ladies, gentlemen, most excellent host, your servant!"

He said all that, of course, in French, so Rose Ann got nothing out of it but the beginning of the splitting headache that the very sound of a foreign tongue, *any* foreign tongue, always gave her.

Then he took her arm and led her out of there.

Once they were back in their rather splendid hotel room, Kurt didn't push her off the balcony. Instead, he made love to her, very slowly and carefully, until the sunlight came stealing palely through their windows, and she could hear the clip-clopping of hooves and the whirring of carriage wheels on the boulevard far below.

So a little later, three quarters dead, as usual, from a night-long series of unending internal detonations having all the force and speed of the by then already invented Gatling gun, she judged that since they'd finished (she hoped!) their lovemaking, the time was perhaps ripe to get him to either confirm or deny what the Baroness Gerta von Zorndorf had told her. Blowing the wet red strands of her own hair out of her bitten-blue and swollen mouth, she whispered:

"Kurtie, love, who is—Eeel-say?"

"Who is what?" he grunted. "Oh, you mean *Ilse*. It's a woman's name. German. I-l-s-e. Eliza in English, I suppose. Common enough. I've known two dozen wenches who were called that . . ."

She raked her sweat-soaked mane out of her face, stared back at him over one glistening bare shoulder, noting as she did so that the room was redolent with the insistent musk of achieved passion, sated lust, satisfied desire. (Smells just like A'nt Sukie's on the morning after a busy night, she thought bitterly.)

"Not two dozen, Kurt," she said, too quietly. "Just one. A real special one. *Yours*. The mother of your children. Are you going to deny that?"

"Of course not," he said cheerfully. "I've got bastard brats all over. It's even possible that some of them are by a wench or two named Ilse. How would I know? I've never led a monkish existence, and Ilse is an awf'ly common name. If you were to shout it aloud on a crowded street in any large German city, at least forty women would sing out, *'Ja?'* Oh, I say! Who told you that?"

"The Baroness von Zorndorf," Rose Ann said.

"That goddamned Jewess," he said in a tone of icy calm. "I saw how she was buttering you up, my dear. Karl's a bit of all right, but of course he's ruined himself marrying that Yid bitch. We'll give him a chance to put her by, once we come to power. And if he refuses, he can accompany her to hell. What the devil else did she tell you?"

"Nothing. Only to ask you who this Ilse was. And who the father of her children is. Tell me—are you a Roman Catholic, Kurt?"

"I *was*," he said. "Before I abandoned ancient Hebraic superstitions. Why?"

"Kurt," she moaned, "don't tell me that you—"

"That I *what?*" he said contemptuously.

"That you have a wife. Children. That I'm nothing but your kept woman. Your concubine. Your whore . . ."

He smiled at her.

"Charming thought, that last," he drawled. "By the way, how much do I owe you for last night?"

She said, "Kill me. Right now. I'll go get that little pistol Colin gave me for a present—"

"Revolver," he corrected her. "Pistols are flat, like my derringer . . ."

"Ohhhhh, Lord!" she wept. "I'll go get it—whatever you call it. 'Cause I can't live, hurting like this! I can't stand this much shame!"

He said, pleasantly, "Why don't you throw yourself from the balcony, just as you are? You'll be famous. It's the sort of thing the French love. I can see the headlines now: *Morte d'Amour! Fille Nue se Jete du Balcon de l'Huitième Étage!*"

She stared at him. Then she whirled, already running. He bounced out of bed, caught up with her just as she burst out on that eighth-floor balcony. Grasped her by her flag-banner mane of flaming hair, yanked her flat on her dainty posterior by it, dragged her back into the bedroom. Picked her up, tossed her across the bed. Slammed his lean, muscular form down upon her, forcing her into bifurcation by sheer impact, burying his erection in her taut stretched fork upon the spur of that same instant, and she, already gone, turning her face sidewise and screaming into the pillow, choking, sobbing, gasping, while he pounded away, trying with insane fury to get there, to get there, to get there, but failing, failing, failing, yet trying still, while she outdid Dr. Gatling's murderous invention in lethality as well as speed, dying in gut-ripping bursts in volleys going straight down to anguished, hateful, hurtful hell, then up up up up sunward-soaring, wax of Icarus' wings melting against heaven's highest pinnacles, then, again, down down down trailing the scattered plumes of her own destruction, ice crystals, micro-meteorites, beams of sunlight, jets of flame, into the warmsweetsoft dark, into the womb of time, where nothing was, not even bleak despair.

When she came back, he was sitting on the edge of the bed, looking at her, and smiling his icy, perfectly maniacal smile.

"The subject's—closed, isn't it, my sweet?" he said. "We aren't going to have any more tiresome histrionics, melodrama, or folly, are we?"

She bowed her head, looked up again, dry-eyed, for by then she'd gone far beyond even the surcease of tears. She said, "No. You've got what that damnyankee General Grant asked for at Fort Donelson: unconditional surrender. I'm not—a human being anymore, but a slave. A thing. So I don't need to have pride anymore, do I? And how can I—how could anybody—respect what I am now? Your—fun filly. Your play toy. *Not*—your whore, 'cause whores get paid, don't they? Your little bitch, groveling belly-down to lick your boots, hoping you'll be kind enough not to kick her. Only—"

"Only what?" he said.

"Couldn't you—wouldn't you—be sufficiently considerate to—to deny it? To have the—the decency—to lie? To say, 'I don't know this Ilse. I'm not married to her. The children are not mine.' Couldn't you, Kurt?"

He went on smiling that ice-bright smile; said, "I don't know this Ilse. I'm not married to her. The children are not mine. Satisfied?"

She moaned, "Oh, God!"

"Look, my dear," he said calmly, in that pleasant tone of voice she was beginning to realize was one of the most terrible things about him, or a symptom of it, anyhow. "I am a member of the super-race, an elite even among *das Herrenvolk*, so the ordinary concepts of morality do not apply to me. I command. Other people obey. Especially women. Now go to sleep, will you? I must go bathe; this aroma of used slut you've left all over me offends my nostrils. We Germans are a cleanly folk, y'know . . ."

The stubborn embers of a McKenzie's will flared briefly in her eyes.

"S'pose while you're gone, I were to—" She left the rest of her threat unsaid, hanging ominously upon the gray morning air of that grayest of cities, Paris.

He shrugged with an unconcern that was neither assumed, feigned, nor exaggerated, even slightly.

"That's up to you, my sweet," he said, and walked out of there.

And one thing more: That night he announced to her calmly: "I'm going out. Don't wait up for me, my dear; I shall probably be very late . . ."

She stared at him.

"You—you're going to see—*her!*" she whispered. "To visit—your —your *wife*, and your children . . ."

He said calmly, coolly, with no apparent anger, "Let's get one thing straight, Rose Ann, now, henceforth, and forevermore: You don't question my comings or my goings. Not ever. And I'm not in the habit of offering explanations. Weakness and inferiority explain. *Macht und Recht*—might and right—don't. I'd suggest that you begin to gather up your belongings. We'll be leaving for London day after tomorrow . . ."

But when he left their little suite that night, she was sitting in the big chair glancing from the pages of the French novel she couldn't read to those of the dictionary whose words she couldn't even see. She was clad in her quilted *robe de chambre*, from under which trailed the lace hem of her nightgown. But what her tender and loving husband didn't know was that under the nightgown she was fully clothed, except for the one item that would have betrayed her: she had left her *cage américaine* off, because nobody wore the steel hoops that supported a hooped skirt to bed.

Seeing her apparent industry, he bent and kissed her.

"Capital!" he said. "Keep that up, and you'll probably learn something. You've a first-rate ear, and your pronunciation's jolly good. A dint of practice, even at reading such bloody rot as this, should work wonders . . . Good night, my sweet. Don't stay up too late. No, remain just as you are: snug, cozy, and—dutiful! I can let myself out quite nicely . . ."

Scant minutes after he'd reached the street, she was there behind him. She was more than a little breathless from having run down eight flights of stairs, for although in New York several hotels had lifts by 1862, which were steam-powered and called "vertical railways," that innovation hadn't caught on in Europe, and wouldn't until the arrival of electricity made it truly practical.

She saw the hotel's majestic doorman stop a cab for Kurt, bow respectfully over the handsome tip, and straighten up, smiling. But she didn't want the doorman to call her a cab, because she didn't even want him to see her, much less have to tell him where she was going. So head down, face turned to the street side of the *trottoir* so he wouldn't recognize her, she rushed on past him to the next corner. She was lucky. There was a cab waiting there.

Then her luck ran out on her. All of it.

She pointed at the rapidly retreating back of the cab Kurt was in, and hissed in truly melodramatic style: "Follow that cab!"

But before she could jerk down the handle of the door to get in, she saw the cabdriver was staring at her in baffled amazement, his little blue eyes, above the great mustache of a Napoleonic field marshal, opened very wide.

"*Qu'est-ce que vous m'avez dit, mamzelle?*" he said.

"Ohhhh, Lord!" Rose Ann moaned; then she screamed at him: "I said: Follow that cab!"

But inflicting a language upon the poor, benighted aborigines by shouting it at them ever louder takes generations. And Rose Ann hadn't even minutes to spare. By then she was hopping up and down in her sheer and towering rage at the French for their mule-stubbornness in insisting upon speaking only French.

"I said," she shrieked, "follow—" Then she saw what the cab-driver was doing. He had raised his index finger to his own forehead and was making a little circle there, an age-old symbol that even Rose Ann recognized. The French, having had, throughout their history, all too many uninvited guests—especially the English and the Germans—are the most xenophobic people in Europe. And from time immemorial Parisian cabdrivers had regarded —with good reason!—tourists as a very low order of life. This one made still another eloquent circle just above his temple.

"*Vous êtes folle, vous,*" he said succinctly, and flapping the reins across the back of his ancient nag, he drove away, leaving Rose Ann there, wringing her hands and crying.

Ignorance is usually the most expensive of all luxuries. But in Rose Ann's case, who knows? Since she really wasn't either ready or prepared to give her Kurtie pie up just then, the tap the Fool-Killer gave her with his mace that night was gentle enough, it may be said.

Chapter Ten

Rose Ann looked across the dinner table in the immense dining room of the extremely luxurious and, to a mind that retained much of the instinctive frugality of her canny Scotch ancestors, outrageously expensive apartment that Kurt had rented in Washington, District of Columbia, capital of the nation, the two men she loved best in all this world—her brother, Jeff, and her brother-in-law ("my *sister's* husband," she immediately reminded herself, as she always did whenever his name or his lean, sardonic image flickered across her mind), Caleb Henry, were fighting against in defense of all that they, and she, held dear.

"You seem—troubled, *Gräfin,*" her dinner partner, Count Ferdinand von Zeppelin said.

"I *am* troubled," Rose Ann sighed. "You're—aware of my sentiments, though this is hardly the place to discuss them. Put it this way, Count—"

"Ferdi, please!" Count von Zeppelin said.

"All right, then, Ferdi," Rose said, "but only if you will call me Rose. Agreed?"

"Agreed!" von Zeppelin said. "Do go on, my dear Rose; you were about to tell me your troubles. Believe me, I am all ears!"

"They're not easy to tell," Rose said. She liked Count von Zeppelin, the new military attaché to the Prussian Embassy, very much. He was a big man, courtly, extremely handsome, and, best of all, he reminded her of her good friend Heros von Borcke, whom, in fact, he strongly resembled. Which brought back to her mind the Baroness von Zorndorf's assertion that the Pomeranians and the Prussians were essentially the same people. "Because they're all a matter of mood, really," she added sadly. "I was educated in the North, so I always knew me—our side—couldn't win. But I consoled myself with the thought that we were—well, the better people. Nobler. More intelligent. With the higher civilization . . ."

Ferdinand von Zeppelin shook his massive head.

"I'm sorry, my dear Rose," he said gruffly, "but it would be awf'ly hard to prove that a people who whip black slaves to work in their fields have a higher civilization than those who don't . . ."

"You're right," she sighed. "I could give you all the old arguments about the miserable condition of the factory workers—sheer wage slaves—of the North. But does it really bleach the complexion of the pot to call the kettle black? Besides, being free, factory workers in the North can organize and gradually improve their condition. While our 'peculiar institution' is going to drag us down with it—"

"It's a thing the world has grown beyond," von Zeppelin said. "Your Confederacy is an anachronism—*per se.* Just as are the Austro-Hungarian Empire and all the petty principalities of Germany, before you remind me! However, we Prussians are going to do something about that. But, speaking of workers organizing, isn't that an idea your darling husband's a trifle opposed to, my dear? Our Secret Service, which is rather a bit better than the Austrian one, is sure that he was behind that recent incident in London at Christmastime . . ."

Rose glanced across the room—crowded with guests, as usual, for already invitations to the soirées given by the Count and Countess Radetzy were the most sought after social prizes in Washington—to where Kurt stood, laughing and bantering away with a little group of people who surrounded—That perfect example of military imbecility! her mind flared—Brigadier General James W. Ripley, Lincoln's Chief of Ordnance.

"He *was,*" she said with icy fury. "He sent that hired assassin to that meeting hall to kill Karl Marx. I don't agree with Professor Marx's ideas either, but I don't believe in murdering people because their opinions and mine don't coincide, or because the length and shape of their noses offend my aesthetic sense! It's a pity that those workers gave that pistoleer such a terrible beating that he died of it without ever regaining consciousness, or else—"

"Or else your husband would have been apprehended, tried, and, the laws of England being what they are, wouldn't see daylight uncrossed by iron bars for many a long year," Ferdinand von Zeppelin said gravely. "Which brings me to a point that's been puzzling me, dear Rose, ever since we met—"

"At that demonstration balloon ascension on the White House lawn," Rose said mischievously. "Did you obtain all the secrets Kurt swears the Prussian High Command sent you over here to steal, Ferdi dear?"

"Of course not—more's the pity!" von Zeppelin laughed. "Balloons are useless in warfare, especially since we still have to use inflammable gases to make them rise. My dream is to invent a system to move them under their own power, and a method of steering them that will be as effective as a ship's is. It's already been done, of course, though in a limited, primitive way. A

Frenchman named Henri Giffard piloted a sausage-shaped balloon, propelled by a three-horsepower steam engine, from Paris to Trappes, as long ago as 1851. His ideas were more or less correct, but the materials he had on hand with which to implement them were appalling. A steam engine's too heavy, and likely to set your fine airship afire. Its fuel also weighs too much, so you're left with no appreciable margin to carry anything else—"

"Such as—bombs," Rose Ann said bitterly.

"Well—yes," *der Graf* von Zeppelin admitted grudgingly, "but also, in peacetime, my dear Rose, people, mail, and goods. That sausage—or rather cigar—shape was jolly good. Neat penetration of the air there. But it needs to be made more rigid—some internal framework, say. But made of—what? And the engines? They'd have to develop several hundred horsepower each, while tipping the scales themselves at no more than five pounds per horse! Three would be much better, two ideal—and one my impossible dream! But then, as science and our general knowledge stand, the whole idea remains beyond human capacity, I'm afraid. But why am I boring a deuced pretty woman like you, *Gräfin*, with these heavy technical matters?"

"You don't bore me. I find them fascinating. And you'll do it, Ferdi. One day the skies will be crisscrossed with the airships you've made. I'm very sure of that!"

She didn't mean what she said; she was only paying the big, handsome Prussian Junker a compliment in an archly flirtatious sort of way. She had no idea that, almost half a century later, the man to whom she'd said those words was going to make them, quite literally, come true.

"At any rate, let's change the subject," the Count said quietly. "Your diversionary tactics are superb, Rose, but I simply won't be turned aside. You can, of course, tell me it's none of my ruddy business and flatly refuse to answer. There, you're well within your rights. And I apologize from the outset for asking. But how under heaven did a girl as beautiful and as intelligent as you ever come to marry a madman like Zizi—or rather Kurt—Radetzy?"

She said solemnly, "He asked me to. And since I was getting along in years, and nobody else had, and I had this horrible fear of winding up an old maid—"

"I apologize, Rose. Most sincerely," Ferdinand von Zeppelin said.

"No, *I* do," she sighed. "I married him because he was absolutely the handsomest male creature I'd ever seen and—"

"You were, or thought you were, in love with him?" the Count supplied.

"No," she said flatly. "I didn't think that. I was never deluded. The snake—just charmed, hypnotized the bird, that's all. Only that too is an oversimplification. Let's say, God makes 'em, but they find each other. Strange that you should say that, though. I've been laboring under the misapprehension that you were a friend of his . . ."

"I *was*," von Zeppelin said stiffly. "But you should be aware that while your—eh—husband—has immense charm, and makes friends with dazzling ease, he doesn't keep them. Not after they get to know him at all well . . ."

"You put that with compassionate mildness, Ferdi," Rose said. "But your statement—your chivalrous *under*statement—of the facts simply doesn't apply to—his women, dear friend. Your concern for me is—touching. But wasted. One needn't be so careful of the feelings of a—poor bedraggled concubine, *Graf* von Zeppelin! You know—Ilse, don't you? And the children? Tell me about her, about them. How many are there? What are they like? Do they—pull the wings off—living birds? Blind kittens with red-hot pokers?"

He whispered, "*Ach, gott!*" Stared at her in baffled astonishment. The collar of his magnificent uniform seemed to be choking him. Then he saw how star-blazed her eyes were, how blind, so he leaned forward and caressed her cheek with one of his huge pink-and-white hands.

"So—he tricked you, didn't he?" he said. "Entered into a marriage with you that was—"

"Both false and bigamous," Rose said crisply, shaking the tears out of her eyes. "And I thank you for the gentlemanly instincts that make you realize that it had to be that way. I don't think I need even say that I had—if not the essential decency I'd smugly given myself credit for—at least enough pride to have refused to agree to any such cozy little arrangement. So now I ask of you one —perfectly enormous favor, Ferdi: Don't ask me why, since he hasn't, and has never had, the slightest legal hold on me, I haven't left him. I—I *can't* tell you that . . ."

"Why not?" the Count said. "You'll find me a most understanding sort of a chap . . ."

"Because I'm a coward," she said flatly. "I'm simply not brave enough to face the logical consequences of my sins. Knowing that I deserve the worst—all the scorn, all the contempt that decent people could fling into my face, the most terrible punishment that

Almighty God could hand down against me, I'm still weak enough, hypocritical enough, to try to conceal what I'm really like from the eyes of the world. I'm perfectly aware I won't be able to get away with it for long. And on the day I am found out, I'll have to make up my mind about only one thing—"

"Which is?" the Count whispered.

"How to die. Oh, no. Not the simplest, the quickest, and the easiest way. The—slowest. The one that hurts the most. Let me find enough of the dignity I used to have, in order to punish myself for being what I know I am. Or to start the punishment, anyhow. His Satanic Majesty and all those charming little fiends will take over from there, I'm sure . . ."

"*Grüss Gott!*" he said. "Rose, listen to me! What you've said is a terrible blasphemy! Only God can judge us; we have no right to judge ourselves. And He, in His infinite mercy, has time and time again forgiven far worse sins than any you can accuse yourself of. Besides, you have the remedy for all your problems already at hand. I refer, of course, to young Forrester. A fine and handsome enough lad to suit any young woman, it seems to me. And he obviously adores you. By the way, I don't see him here tonight. Didn't you invite him?"

"Greg? He'll be along presently. With a man I asked him to bring, in order to lend a little excitement to this gathering. Which is another demonstration of my perversity, I suppose. For when General Ripley sees Colonel Hiram Berdan walk through that door, he's going to have a stroke of apoplexy, the sight of which I plan to enjoy. As far as Greg Forrester's concerned, I'll freely and frankly admit I like him. I could fall in love with him with ease if I'd let myself do so. Only I'm not going to. And don't ask me why not. The answer to that is exactly the same as the one to the question I asked you not to ask me a little while ago. In other words, the reason I can't leave Kurt, and *won't* love Greg, is the same reason, and just as unmentionable—no, unspeakable—in either case . . ."

"You're—beyond understanding," Count von Zeppelin sighed.

"And redemption," she added bitterly. "We'd better go join the others before the she-cats with which this town abounds add *you* to the list of all the poor dear innocents I'm supposed to have seduced, Ferdi dear. But before we do, will you please tell me something? You *do* know Kurt's darling *Hausfrau*, Ilse, don't you? What's she like? The truth, now! Don't spare my feelings. Such—nicety of scruple's unnecessary: I haven't any tender spots left. Is—

she beautiful? Passionate? Intelligent? Rich? Aristocratic? Of the—nobility?"

"Turnabout's fair play," the Count said. "I'll tell you that if you'll tell me how Zizi—Kurt—managed to get so confounded rich all of a sudden. As long as I've known him, he's never had tuppence to rub together. And now, the way you two live, the blowouts you throw *every* weekend—"

"That's simple," she said. "By chicanery and fraud. He gulled Louis Napoleon into believing he could keep the Yankees off his puppet emperor's neck down there in Mexico long enough for the French protectorate in that country to be solidly established. Then, once we'd arrived in London, he went down to what's called the City and gambled on the stock market with poor Louis's money. Did he lose his shirt as any *normal* man would have, and as he, my darling Kurtie pie, richly deserved to do? Not on your life! He made a hundred thousand pounds' clear profit. Part of that he spent trying to get Professor Marx killed, because, one, Karl Marx is a Jew, and also because, two, the laboring classes ought to know their place and keep it, touch their forelocks, and humbly bow when my Kurtie passes by, ideas that *The Communist Manifesto* isn't very likely to instill in them. But that didn't cost him very much. Clumsy bumbling idiots like the murderous tool he hired come cheap. After that, he met a most noble lord who was perfectly willing to introduce Kurt into circles where one can make tremendous killings—at a price. The price being—me. That senile old fool undressed me with his eyes so often that I almost caught pneumonia without even knowing why. He put Kurt on to a real good thing: two ironclad rams being laid down by Laird's Shipyard for, supposedly, the Turkish government. Or for Denmark. Or for China. The lie changed daily. Actually, they were for our splendid Confederacy, and if they start roving the high seas like the *Alabama*, our share in their prize money should make us millionaires. Kurt got in on that one early, thanks to His Lordship's designs upon my sacred honor. Good thing. Because, before long, the news of that hideous slaughter at Fredericksburg reached the City, and every high-muck-a-muck with teeth like old Dobbin's, and every Her Ladyship with a chin down to her *knees*, wanted to take a flyer, which sent the price of those shares up like a rocket on the Fourth of July. So we ought be fixed for life . . . Now it's my turn. Tell me—"

"Not yet!" the Count said sternly. "That—price. Did you—pay it?"

Rose got up from where she sat and dropped him the prettiest and the most mocking curtsy imaginable.

"I am—a dutiful wife, Your Excellency!" she said.

"*Ach, Gott!*" von Zeppelin said. "All right, I prefer not to believe you, *mein* Rose! About Ilse. Yes, I know her. She is not—beautiful, but rather, I'd say—lovely. Soft, and sweet, and very gentle. The palest of blondes. Kurt married her, I'm certain, to make sure his children wouldn't resemble him. He's suffered no end because of his exotic appearance, y'know. Handsome as he is, your—lover— appears far more Asiatic than European, oh quite! Then, he had to flee the Empire because of—"

"His murder of the Jewish banker Steinermann," Rose said quietly.

"Yes, that. Ilse's parents, who'd had enough of Zizi's antics by then, tried to have their marriage annulled. Couldn't quite bring it off, for, as venial as the ecclesiastical authorities generally are, there were, after all, the children. Two girls and a boy. Beautiful little tots—"

"They'll be—monsters," Rose Ann said darkly. "The boy, anyhow . . ."

"Wouldn't doubt it. Anyhow, Ilse herself put up so stout a resistance to having her ties to her lord and master severed that her parents, *die Herzoge* von Hohlenrühe . . ."

"*Herzoge?*" she asked, getting the pronunciation exactly right.

"The dukes," the Count said drily.

Rose Ann threw up her hands in mock despair.

"I knew it!" she sighed. "The highest cotton possible. Tell me, weren't there any princesses available, Ferdi?"

"Of course. But they'd hardly be allowed to marry an adventurer like Zizi, whose title, while authentic enough, became unavailable to him once his mother had him naturalized as an Austrian as a child. You see, she'd developed a rather keen dislike for all things Hungarian from having been forced to live among those slant-eyed barbarians a bit too long. Anyhow, as I was saying, the Duke and Duchess had to give up on that business, especially after Ilse ran off to Paris, taking the tots with her, merely because she'd heard that Zizi—Kurt—was there. He wasn't, and she and her brood nearly starved. So now her parents send her an allowance, since she refuses to come back to Austria on the score that Radetzy's sure to appear in Paris one day . . ."

"He *did*," Rose Ann said drily. "So it'll probably be *four* kids pretty soon. Oh, good! Here's Greg with the colonel! Come on! Now the fun begins!"

She was right. When they reached the edge of the group, Brigadier General James Ripley was saying, "And there he was, our long, gangling ape of a President, down on his knees, aiming that little popgun of a carbine at the target. Then he started shooting: bang, bang, bang, bang—seven times. And how many holes appeared in that target? I assure you, ladies and gentlemen—not one! So I said to him, 'You see, Mr. President—that little toy is a sheer waster of ammunition! As long as I'm Chief of Ordnance, I *refuse* to throw away the taxpayers' money like that!"

"All that story proves," Colonel Berdan said icily, "is that the President is a poor marksman, not that the Spencer carbine is a bad gun. For example, *I* put all seven shots that little beauty of a repeater holds in its magazine not only into the bull's-eye but in a pattern you could cover with the palm of your hand. Some of my boys have done better. But, unfortunately, neither the Spencer nor the Henry is available in sufficient numbers to equip even a regiment, thanks largely to your interference, General. But the Sharps breechloader has reached full production. And even though my boys had to almost stage a mutiny to get 'em, we've got 'em, by God! I have a *presidential* order in my pocket right now, commanding you, sir, to issue them to us, General. And the President, in case you've forgot, is Commander in Chief of the Armed Forces of the Republic, so he outranks you by more than somewhat!"

"I'll refuse that order!" Ripley howled. "I simply will not issue repeaters and breechloaders to our troops and have them wasting ammunition all over the place!"

"Instead you'd waste lives," Colonel Hiram Berdan said flatly. "It's very clear you've never been a combat soldier, General. Oh, I grant you that the Springfield muzzleloader is a good enough weapon—behind breastworks. But there any reasonably accurate rifle is, right down to a pre-Revolutionary War Kentucky flintlock. You talk about wasting the taxpayers' money, but I'm absolutely sure that said taxpayers would rather you wasted their money than their sons. In every battle we've fought so far, the major part of our losses—and theirs—have been due to just one thing: that a soldier, charging across a battlefield under fire, can shoot just once, before he has to stop dead still to reload, a complicated process that takes a full three minutes, and which can only be done standing straight up, thus offering his whole body as a perfect target to every sharpshooter in the enemy ranks. After that, of course, he can open fire, but only one more pitiful time, before he has to begin the whole practically suicidal business—on any open battlefield, anyhow—of reloading anew. That is, if he's stayed alive long enough to even get another round out of his cartridge box. At Antietam and Fredericksburg, generally he didn't. Jesus Christ! Give me an infantry division equipped with Spencers or Henrys, and I'll drive the Rebs into the Gulf of Mexico inside a week!"

"More likely, those pretty toys will break down after the first round, or you'll shoot away all your ammunition within five minutes," General Ripley sneered, "leaving the Rebels free to march in and gather your troops up like cattle. I've told you, Colonel Berdan, that as long as I'm Chief of Ordnance, the troops are going to be issued battle-tested and reliable arms, not some crackpot inventor's crazy gadgets!"

Colonel Hiram Berdan turned to his friend Gregory Forrester.

"May God in His infinite mercy," he said prayerfully, "deliver me and the men under my command from the hands of idiots!"

But Greg didn't even hear him. Lost and bemused, he was staring at Rose Ann, sculpturing her face upon the perfume- and candle-wax-scented air with chisel strokes of purest light, an anguished longing in his deep blue eyes, a cry louder than any man's speaking voice. And Rose Ann stared back at him, thinking: Oh, God, if I'd only met him before, while I was still fit to be a decent man's wife . . . But now, it can't be, Greg, fine, upright, noble, good sweet boy, because—

Then she heard Kurt's voice cutting through the abrupt silence, sibilant as a whiplash, saying icily, "Colonel, you're in my house— and not even as an invited guest. I beg you, therefore, to show the general the respect due his rank, not to mention the fact that he's absolutely right about your war-of-the-future toys. And if you can't comport yourself as an officer and a gentleman should, I must ask you, most respectfully of course, to leave!"

"You don't have to ask me anything, Count," Hiram Berdan said, "because that's exactly what I mean to do. Didn't want to come to this nest of vipers—of the Copperhead variety—in the first place. But Greg told me the general would be here, and I was duty-bound to deliver the President's message to him at my earliest possible opportunity. The President's *two* messages, of which I've already delivered one. And since Abraham Lincoln is a kindly man, with a degree of patience that seems to me both incredible and even, at times, counterproductive to the success of our arms, he asked me to hold the other one in abeyance unless Brigadier General Ripley *forced* me to deliver it. The condition under which I was to read the President's second order, as Commander in Chief of the Armed Forces of the Republic, to his subordinate, General Ripley, has already been complied with. That condition was that the general, as he has on several occasions in the past, deliberately refused to obey a direct command from the President himself. But since I believe in always playing fair, I hereby take note of the fact that General Ripley's words were spoken in anger. I concede him the opportunity to withdraw them. Therefore, in the presence of these witnesses, I ask you, Brigadier General James W. Ripley, once more: Do you refuse, sir, to obey this presidential order, signed by Mr. Lincoln himself, instructing you without further delay to supply my regiment of specialist marksmen with the Sharps breech-loaders we have requested?"

He put his hand in his breast pocket, came out with the presidential order, unfolded it, held it out to General Ripley.

Wild with rage, the Chief of the Ordnance Department snatched it from him, crumpled it into a ball, and threw it on the floor.

"There's my answer, Colonel!" he snarled.

"Then, sir," Hiram Berdan said, "the President asks me to inform you that you are hereby dismissed from the post of Chief of Ordnance, and ordered into immediate retirement from the United States Army, at, of course, your present rank. Which proves that Abraham Lincoln is a saint. Because, considering all the lives your mule-stubbornness and asinine stupidity have cost us, were I in his place, I'd have broken you back to buck private in the rear ranks and assigned you, permanently, to the latrine detail. And that's putting the most charitable interpretation possible upon your actions, General. For, looking about me, and seeing the company you keep, the smell of sheer treason keeps rising to my nostrils, some of it, of course, most delicately perfumed. Which reminds me—"

He whirled on his heels, faced Kurt.

"You've already shown me your door, Count Radetzy," he said evenly, "but I may come back again, both uninvited and unannounced. Accompanied by some friends of mine in the Secret Service. The—eh—political affiliations of the people that you—and your charming lady!—invite to your house strike them as rather odd, shall we say? Every known Copperhead in town has been your guest at one time or another; most of the prominent Southerners of distinctly dubious loyalty as well. And high officers of—uncertain temper, towering ambitions, and empty heads,

whom we know all too well—those weak enough to be bought"—
he lifted one corner of his heavy, drooping walrus-style mustache
at Rose Ann in a smile that was more than half a leer—"or seduced,
seem favored beneficiaries of your hospitality. Were I blessed with
the exclusive possession of so young and beautiful a wife as yours,
sir, I'd keep her under lock and key. But you, it seems, think otherwise, which is, of course, your right. But as the self-appointed representative of several of the younger officers who don't take our
patriotism lightly, might I suggest to you, my lord Count, that
travel's broadening? You show me your door; I, you the nearest
pier. Though from what our very good friends at Scotland Yard
have told us, you may find that your welcome's more than a little
worn out in your native land. Oh, well, the world is wide, isn't it?
And crossing frontiers in somewhat undignified haste, one jump
ahead of the local hangman much of the time, seems to be quite a
custom of yours . . . A very good night to the assembled company, to your lovely lady, and to you, sir! And, oh, before I forget:
we don't need proved or even provable charges; such a label as
'undesirable alien' or, say, *'persona non grata,'* would be quite
enough . . ."

Rose Ann stared at the colonel. He was tall, thin, going bald. She
loosed a peal of absolutely delighted laughter.

"Bravo, Colonel Berdan!" she gurgled. "May I say you're quite a
boy?"

The colonel bowed with theatrical grace.

"Thank you, dear lady!" he chuckled. "And if you want to put
me on your list of Army officers to be unduly influenced, while
your most understanding husband looks the other way, I'll be delighted to cooperate. Up—or rather down—to a certain point
. . ."

"Which is?" Rose Ann purred.

"I suggest that we leave that for our next encounter, dear lady!"
the colonel said, and bowed again. He added, "Good night, all."
And then, "Coming, Lieutenant Forrester?"

"Sir—" Greg quavered. "I—"

"Oh, stay and enjoy yourself, Greg my boy!" Colonel Berdan
mocked. "Considering how little you know, and how handsome
you are, the interest may even be—non-professional . . ." He
bowed again, straightened up, marched out the door, trailing a
glissando of deep-toned laughter behind him like a banner . . .

"I'd better *do* something about that arrogant ass," Kurt muttered.

"Oh, don't be silly, Kurt," Rose Ann drawled. "That one's a man. He'd eat you alive and spit the bones out between his teeth."

She put out a playful hand and ruffled Greg's heavy mane of dark brown hair. As deep as its color was, it had strands of red and gold running all through it. Lieutenant Gregory Forrester of the U.S. Army was another boy baby doll, Rose Ann thought. And even prettier than my Joe-Joe was. As nice. 'Cause nobody could be nicer. And me—ruined. In a way that people can't even imagine when they talk about morality. You don't, Greg love, need a trained circus bitch who jumps through the goddamnedest kind of hoops even before her lord and master cracks the whip. So I've got to get rid of you. I've got to break your nice clean boyish heart real fast before I ruin you too. Rottenness is contagious, Greggie love! She said, "Don't I even get a kiss, Greg o' my heart?"

"No!" Greg howled, tears almost breaking through his voice. "That's just the trouble! Sir, couldn't you and I, and Rose Ann, sneak off somewhere? We're *really* in trouble. Oh, I don't think I'm in deep yet, because I'm too insignificant for them to figure out my real connection with the two of you. But just as Colonel Berdan said, they're truly suspicious of you and Rose Ann. So we'd better have a talk this very minute, because—"

"Calm down, old boy," Kurt said imperturbably. "We'll be able to talk soon enough. Our guests will all be leaving within half an an hour, I'll wager. Because your boorish colonel has scared them *scheissefrei* . . ."

"That," Rose Ann purred, "means—how can I put it nicely? Oh, well—that they won't have to visit those cute little houses out back with half-moons carved into their doors for a month of Sundays . . ."

"Oh, goddamn!" Greg got out. "What d'you always talk like that for, Rose Ann? So—so flippantly. You *are* an angel, so why're you always trying to sound like a—a loose woman?"

"But I *am* a loose woman," Rose Ann said. "Aren't I, Kurt?"

"Practically dismembered," Kurt yawned. "There! Didn't I tell you? Here they go . . ."

General Ripley led the rush. Head down, muttering incoherently, he was, Rose thought, a pitiful sight. She felt sorry for him, even though she knew he richly deserved his disgrace. But as all of Washington's conservative, secretly pro-Southern elite made their stammering excuses and beat distinctly undignified retreats, she became aware of one thing: She and Kurt were finished in Washington. Whatever effectiveness they may have had was gone. Allan

Pinkerton's Secret Service wasn't very effective, but people feared it. After all, the great detective had managed to jail a female spy or two and hanged a number of male ones in most exemplary fashion. So now, Rose Ann thought wearily, we'd better take Colonel Berdan's advice and get out of town. Where'll we go? New York, likely. 'Cause back in '61, just before the war, one of their mayors actually proposed that the Big Burg secede from the Union and set itself up as an independent city-state, with close ties—commercial and political—with the South. If that wasn't treason, let Honest Abe, to misquote Cabe's great-great-great-granduncle Pat, profit from the example!

"All right, Greg old boy," Kurt said after Count Ferdinand von Zeppelin, who was the last of the guests to leave, had gone, "fire away. But first let me pour you a snort of this most excellent Bourbon and branch water to calm your nerves a bit. There really is no reason for you to be quite this upset, y'know . . ."

"Oh, yes, there is!" Greg said. "And damnit, Kurt, it's mostly *your* fault!"

"My fault?" Kurt said with his infuriating calm. "How so, old chap?"

"The way you act. About Rose Ann, I mean. She's *the* most beautiful girl in the whole damned world, and the nicest, and the sweetest, and the best—and you let her go out with *any*body, and stay out as long as she likes—*all* night, I suspect, once in a while—"

"Frequently," Rose Ann drawled. "When the party I'm out with is sufficiently promising or sufficiently fun or both. What's wrong with that, Greg o' my heart?"

"Everything!" Greg thundered. "It's unnatural! If you were mine, I'd shoot every horny bastard who looked at you sidewise. I'd—"

"You'd need the Army to back you up," Kurt chuckled. "And the Navy. And the Marine Corps. Quite a proposition, old chap. Besides, it's ruddy uncivilized. I let her go out with you . . ."

"I know! And it's goddamned insulting, Kurt! It's as if you think so little of me as a man that you don't even need to worry about me! And—"

"And not," Rose Ann put in a little sadly, "that friend wife is a creature of such unassailable virtue that he *really* needn't worry, Greg? Not about you, or about anybody?"

"I reckon that's so," Greg said humbly, "but all the same, I—I might get you drunk, or put some knockout drops in your wine, or—"

"Hit me over the head with half a brick," Rose Ann chuckled. "That's the quickest method. Or quicker still, just ask me. I'll fall into the hay with most anybody. Won't I, Kurt?"

"Absolutely," Kurt said pleasantly. "Main reason I encouraged her to go out with you, Greg old boy. Besides the fact that you're on our side, you really are quite a handsome broth of a lad, y'know, so I was rather hoping you'd take her off my hands—"

"You were *hoping* I'd take Rose Ann off your hands?" Greg whispered.

"But of course. She's *such* a howling nymphomaniac, and deuced perverted on top of it. Gets to be a bit of a bore . . . ."

"Perverted?" Greg croaked. "A nymphomaniac?"

But, by then, it had come to Greg that the two of them were having him on, taking rather cruel advantage of his vast and youthful innocence.

"All right," he growled, "you win, both of you. You've made a jackass of me. But all the same, that was what made the Bluebellies get suspicious. No man in his right mind would put a wife who looks like Rose Ann out to pasture on such a loose tether. So they figured you two were only posing as man and wife in order to operate as corn-fed agents. If you'd challenged a couple of the horny swine who're always after her, folks would have found that normal, and they wouldn't have looked at you so hard, but now—"

"Yes," Kurt sighed, "I suppose that in this benighted country sheer insanity is generally considered normal, but don't you see, Greg, that attracting public attention to oneself by slaughtering lecherous swine just wasn't—and isn't—the way to conduct an operation of this nature? The outcry over a 'goldurned furriner's' killing true-blue Americans would have been vast. And I would have killed them; I'm a better shot than any man in Berdan's regiment of marksmen; I was the champion of all Germany in swordsmanship during my university years—"

"Germany? Not Austria?" Rose Ann said; not that she cared, she simply wanted to catch him out.

"I went to the university in Germany, my sweet. At both Leipzig in Saxony and Berlin in Prussia. Which was how I happened to meet Heros and Ferdi, as well as a number of other prominent Germans. But you're right: I should have known that Americans would find a man who trusts his wife odd, for God knows they don't, and *shouldn't*, trust theirs . . . ."

"I'm American," Rose Ann said solemnly.

"But *I'm* not," Kurt shot back at her. "I've always contended that

217

the reason American females are so insupportable is that the devil inflicted American *men* upon them . . ." He paused, grinned at Greg mockingly. "What can be expected of the poor dears when they must endure lovers and husbands who're incapable of either bedding or beating them? At least not very effectively, at any rate . . ."

"Well," Greg drawled, "never had any complaints in that first department. As for the second, beating on women is generally frowned on over here. But, for curiosity's sake, Kurt, how would you go about it?"

"You phrase your question badly: not how *would* I, but how *do* I, old boy," Kurt said with a pleased chuckle. "This lovely little witch requires frequent tenderizing. As for my methods, perhaps you'd better ask her. She can vouch for their effectiveness; of that you may rest assured . . ."

Greg turned to Rose Ann, his eyes widening from sheer perplexity. He was beginning to learn that he couldn't take anything this exceedingly odd pair said, or did, for granted: their tall tales turned out, quite often, to be understatements of the facts being recounted, their lies bitter truth, their truths— But do they ever tell the truth? he wondered with sudden insight into the sardonic sophistication of their habits of thought.

"Later," Rose Ann said. "There's no time to explore my multiple perversities, nor yours, Kurtie pie. Look, you may take the mess we're in as lightly as you want to, but, to tell the truth, I'm *scared.* I've seen the Old Capitol Prison, and I'd just as soon stay out of it. Besides, one day it's going to occur to the damnyankees that the only way to stop us Reb belles from spying would be to hang a couple of us as public examples. And with *my* luck, they just might start with me . . ."

"An excellent idea, with much to recommend it," Kurt quipped. "Now, calm down, both of you. No experienced agent undertakes a mission before having carefully planned how to abort it, if necessary, and what alternative or alternatives to immediately embark upon. I agree we'd better leave Washington. I'll go to New York tomorrow, while the two of you must take the first train you can get for the Midwest. You'll pose as brother and sister; you resemble each other sufficiently to get away with that with the greatest of ease. And it has its advantages: It will enable you, Greg, to exercise your jealous instincts to the extent of affording Rose Ann some protection against the lechers her red hair and sylphlike form goad into foaming madness and despair, while not overly discouraging the hopes of certain gentlemen we may need to influence, some of whose intentions may even be honorable, who knows? You're to go to Ohio—Dayton, in fact—"

By then Gregory Forrester had had more than enough.

"Now see here, Kurt!" he exploded. "Who's going to protect her from *me?* The very sight of her drives me wild, and you know it! You're her husband before God and man, and that's a condition I'm doing my damnedest to respect, in part because I like you, but even more so because I want all the other poor hungry male critters a-howling in the underbrush to leave my woman the hell alone once I'm finally wed. You can trust my admiration for the two of you, and my honest to God honorable intentions, but you sure Lord can't trust my willpower, 'cause I don't. Not around Rose Ann. She'll have me baying at the moon and chasing my own tail before that locomotive gives out with its first toot a-going round the bend!"

"Nevertheless, I'm sure I can trust you, Greg. Your very candor makes cadhood an uncomfortable base from which to operate. And I *know* I can trust Rose Ann. She's not a perfect angel, but then neither is she a fool. And she already knows the cost of displeasing me. She learned that in London, to her sorrow. Or her delight. For I'll be blessed if I don't believe she enjoys having her little seat bloodily striped . . ."

"Now you're contradicting yourself," Rose Ann pointed out with eerie calm. "If I enjoy it, why would I refrain from turning Greg every which way but loose? He really is a boy baby doll, y'know. Besides, what proof have I got that you'd give two hoots up a hollow stump about *anything* I do? After London, I doubt it . . ."

"Oh, for God's sake!" Greg got out. "Will you two please stop trying to drive me crazy? Kurt, you're forgetting something else, an item that's mighty important: When our Spy Service sent me up to Hartford, Connecticut, in the early spring of '61, they knew damned well that a big, healthy hunk o' beef like me would attract a mighty heap too much attention walking round in civilian clothes, and that posing as a Yankee yellowbelly who'd gone and bought himself a poor bastard of a bounty boy to absorb Reb lead in his place would ensure that I'd never get within twenty miles of any useful information. So you're looking at an honest to God Yankee Doodle Dandy all dolled up in patriotic blue in the service of Yankeedom and Honest Abe. And who the hell ever told you that any sojer boy, North or South, can just take it into his addled

head to grab himself a train ride and enjoy the passing scenery, not
to mention that li'l—"

"Walking invitation to carnal sin at his side," Rose Ann supplied.
"That's what my brother-in-law always calls me . . ."

"Then I reckon your sister had sure Lord better *watch* that husband of hers," Greg said mournfully.

"And *me*," Rose Ann sighed. "If I could have figured out how to
get away with it, I'd have scooped me up two heaping armfuls of
Cabe right after First Manassas and headed for tall timber. But
poor Gwen *is* my sister, so . . ."

"Why after First Manassas?" Kurt asked her with unstudied
calm. "You've known Major Henry since childhood, I've been told
. . ."

"Yep. But First Manassas made me *see* him. Cabe's nothing much
for looks. Fact is, he's as ugly as a piney-woods shoat caught in a
picket fence and squealing. And like all real young female critters
with nothing between their ears but spiderwebs and moonlight, I
was always falling over my two left feet for real pretty boys like
Greg o' my heart here. Went to the hospital to visit Cabe—"

"Where that dainty coward you were so in love with had put
him in his haste to flee the field," Kurt mocked.

"True. Colin damn near whacked poor Cabe's arm off at the
shoulder. For which both Cabe and I have forgiven him. A person,
man or woman, is brave or he isn't. Doesn't count. Bravery, by
itself, doesn't matter. You're brave. And a lot of people, including
me, would be a damned sight better off if you weren't. But I went
to the hospital, and for the first time in my life, I *saw* Caleb
Henry—"

"Saw him how?" Greg whispered.

"Crying. He was crying because his poor old helpless grandaunt
Mrs. Judith Henry had been killed by the fire from both sides,
since her house was slapdab in the middle of the battlefield. But the
man who was crying had stopped the troops of his company from
running like rats—all except Colin, anyhow—rallied 'em and put
up such a fight that Stonewall Jackson himself gave him a personal
citation for valor on the field. Now he's a member of General
Jackson's staff, and has been in every major battle in the East. Won
so many medals he has to pin some of 'em to the seat of his pants.
Brave—a quality I said doesn't count. But it does—when it doesn't
exclude tenderness. When the man who's brave cares about people.
Loves them like Cabe does—"

220

"He's in love with you," Kurt said calmly. "That was pretty obvious . . ."

"And you?" Greg croaked.

"No. My love's been all used up. Tortured to death. Perverted into something—ugly. Slut like me's not fit to kiss the soles of Cabe's muddy boots. All I'm fit for is Kurtie-poo here. But let's quit this, shall we? How are you going to solve this problem, Kurt? Greg's right, you know. They'd pin a desertion charge on him so fast it would make your head swim. Haul him up before a drumhead court. And pump a couple of pounds of minié balls through him first thing in the morning . . ."

"Simple," Kurt drawled. "Greg, you pay a call on Colonel Mitchell, your commanding officer, early tomorrow morning. Tell him *I* said your presence is urgently required in Dayton, Ohio, to make sure that nothing—unpleasant happens to ex-Congressman Clement L. Vallandigham, who is currently running for the governorship of his native state. To the South, a resounding political victory on the part of Vallandigham and his cohorts would be worth any number of battles. They plan, you see, to form a Northwestern Confederacy, composed of Ohio, Indiana, Wisconsin, Minnesota, and Michigan, secede from the Union, and join forces with us. Colonel Mitchell will let you have written orders to go West on a 'Detached Service, Confidential Mission.' Especially when you show him—this."

He put his hand in his pocket and came out with a tiny object, held it out to Greg.

Greg took it, studied it a moment, saw what it was. Whispered, "Jesus God! The Colonel too?"

"Of course," Kurt said. "There's one thing that can be said for stupid, treacherous, cowardly swine: their numbers are usually overwhelming."

"Let me see that, Greg love," Rose Ann said.

Greg gave it to her. It was a Liberty's head, carefully cut, or filed, out from a copper penny. Rose knew what it meant; she had seen it before, quite often. It adorned the buttonholes of any number of prominent Washingtonians, proudly proclaiming that the wearer was a "Copperhead," as the proslavery, pro-Southern Northerners were called. She turned to Kurt.

"But why are they called that, Kurt?" she asked. "Copperheads, I mean?"

"Because some fiery editorialist labeled them snakes in the grass, and compared them with copperhead moccasins, a most deadly variety of the reptilian species," Kurt drawled. "He was right to call them reptiles, but 'Copperheads' is a compliment. They're far more like the common bull snake, which has no poison sacs at all, burrows in the earth, and feeds on rodents . . ."

"Kurt," Rose Ann asked him wonderingly, "you've spent money enough on the Copperheads here in Washington to have outfitted me in sables and diamonds. You've always maintained—and from what I've heard them say, quite rightly—that they're on our side. And now you profess to despise them. Mind telling me why?"

"I do despise them," Kurt said grimly. "They're as worthless as allies as they are as human beings. Look, my sweet, when I was a secret agent attached to the Death's-Head Squad of the Austrian police, I learned one thing forever: It doesn't matter what a man believes, as long as he believes it wholeheartedly. I've seen men die like heroes, undergo the most fiendish tortures that we could apply to them, without ever betraying their comrades or their cause, for ideas that were utter rubbish, intellectually speaking. And I've seen the holders of beliefs that were close to the sublime grovel on their bellies like mongrel dogs at the mere sight of the whip. A man without loyalties, who values his miserable hide or his poltroon's life above his beliefs or his friends, is a danger to both said friends and his cause. Give me a stout and defiant enemy every time. All right, I support the Copperheads; I have fueled their efforts with cash, and will go on doing so—as long as they maintain a certain nuisance value. Which won't be long, for mark my words, given half a chance, that rustic Machiavelli, Lincoln, will find a way to counter them. Because the *only* chance our beloved Southland has at all is for us to drag matters out so long, cost them so unbearably much in treasure and in blood, that the Northerners will get tired and discouraged enough to call it quits and, as one fainthearted writer put it, 'let the erring sisters go.' "

"Anybody who thinks that just doesn't know the Yanks," Greg sighed. "I went to school in a little town in Vermont, because my pa, who had taking ways, took one reach too many for a gal who belonged to a fellow who was a mighty fine shot, and left my mama a penniless widow. So she ups and married a Yankee drummer who was from that state. Which was how come I spent the years twixt five and fifteen there, 'til Mama persuaded my step-pa to move us back down South 'cause she just couldn't stand those awful cold winters anymore. Tha's how come I got roped into this miserable spying business: I can talk just like a damnyankee when pushed—"

"That makes two of us," Rose Ann sighed.

"Yep. Figgered it had to be that in your case too," Greg said. "But, like I was saying, anybody who's planning his future on the outside chance of the Yankees quitting ain't likely to have no future to speak of. 'Cause believe you me, Kurt, they just don't know the word. Rose Ann, you—you don't mind this business about us traveling together as brother and sister?"

"Of course not," Rose said mockingly, "because that's what we're going to not only act like but practically *be*. Kurt, what are you going to be doing in New York? You don't happen to have a wife and family there too, d'you?"

"Heaven forbid!" Kurt said. "A man must have sons to carry on his line. But once they are safely brought into this world, I'd much rather not have the noisy, messy little creatures underfoot. Nor their mother either. Maternity causes a woman to divide her time and her affections, both of which, I contend, should be devoted exclusively to my well-being."

"I know," Rose Ann said solemnly. "I've got calluses on both my knees from going down on 'em before my lord and master. C'mon, tell me: What d'you aim to do in New York?"

"See if I can't implement the plans of all the crackpots who seriously want the Empire City to secede from the Union. But I mean to go at it a bit more cautiously this time, so it may take me longer. First I'll call on two perfectly decent and eminently respectable men, who for humanitarian reasons are for 'peace at any price.' I refer to Samuel F. B. Morse, the inventor of the telegraph, and Samuel J. Tilden, the celebrated attorney. After that, I'll visit Governor Horatio Seymour and his brother Thomas, ex-governor of Connecticut. Then a certain Richard O. Gorham, Esquire, who's been a bit of a firebrand in his anti-Administration, anti-draft speeches. Last of all, and very quietly, I'm going to visit Fernando Wood and his brother Benjamin, and offer to buy stock in the latter's utterly despicable *Daily News,* thus making that precious pair of scoundrels an outright gift of ten thousand dollars . . ."

That struck Rose Ann's Scottish soul to its very core.

"But why?" she wailed. "Why should you go around giving *our* money to people you don't even know?"

"For the good of the cause, doll! We can easily spare that much; I made over a half million Yankee dollars at the current exchange rates in London, y'know. Besides, once those two ironclad rams come down the ways at Laird's, and start taking Yankee prizes all over the Seven Seas, we're going to be rolling in wealth, my sweet!

But I'm going to make my purchase of stock in their filthy rag conditional upon their reprinting that letter that Fernando Wood sent to the City Council back in January 1861. At the present juncture, it should be deuced effective. The elder Wood was mayor of New York City at the time, remember? What he said was roughly this: 'Disunion has become a fixed and certain fact. Therefore, considering where Our Fair City's primary commercial interests lie, I hereby propose that New York withdraw from the Union, and go it alone as a free city, with the whole and united support of the Southern states.' Then he added—a point that will hit the fat burghers of that greedy cesspool right down where they live: 'With but a nominal duty on imports, her local government could be supported without taxation upon her people. Thus we could live free from taxes, and have cheap goods nearly duty-free . . .' "

"Pipe dream!" Greg snorted.

"Of course. But a most appealing one! I don't see how I *can* fail in New York. At the very worst, I can quietly spend a little money among the leaders of the stinking brutal Irish riffraff and among soldiers on leave who're already grumbling: 'I joined up to save the Union, not to free a bunch o' burr-headed, liver-lipped black buck niggers!' A nice bloody riot could propel the wealthiest and most powerful city out of the Union, and if you two do your part in the Midwest, the establishment of the Northwestern Confederacy will make the North's position politically hopeless. She'll have to sue for peace then, despite the fact that her armies are making gains, especially in the West. By the way, Greg, your first act upon reaching Ohio should be to join the Knights of the Golden Circle. You know what it is, don't you?"

"Of course. That crackpot organization founded by Dr. Bickley back in '54. In '61, another crazy doc—one Bowles—sort of introduced it into the Northern states. Governor Morgan of Indiana found out they had a roll of fifteen thousand members in that state. Spring of '62, they tried to seize the state arsenal, but the governor was there before them with the militia. Result: 'the Battle of Pogue's Run.' Casualties: two dozen—all bloody noses. Much ado about nothing, say I . . ."

"And in Honest Abe's own Illinois? The Knights went into politics there, and actually got a resolution to recognize the Confederacy through the lower house. That was to be the start of the Northwestern Confederacy. Of course, they've mismanaged it, being fools. But a shrewd, smart lad like you, with your good looks and forceful personality, could easily worm himself to the top, and perhaps gain control of the organization. Just think of it, Greg! If I take out New York, and you and Rose Ann the Midwest, we'll have won the war for the Confederacy, accomplished more than even General Lee with his indisputable military genius has been able to do so far . . ."

"And me? What am I supposed to do?" Rose Ann asked.

"Make yourself available to Copperhead stalwarts who could do with being influenced a bit. Not *too* available, of course. Just—tantalizingly—promising, that's all. They'll go so wild with bestial and uncouth lust that Greg should be able to hoodwink them with ease. And if they crowd you too close, you can call upon your dear big brother to defend your maidenly honor. I'm sure Greg will fly to the rescue—won't you, old boy?"

"Damned right I will!" Lieutenant Gregory Forrester—of the USA and/or the CSA Secret Service—said.

Chapter Eleven

Rose Ann stared at Greg Forrester. He was looking out of the train window at the landscape slowly rolling backward past his bemused gaze, his young face set in lines of unaccustomed sternness, frowning and remote. She thought: I'm so blamed—lonely. And sad and blue—and—and just plain whipped. Reckon I'm the *first* McKenzie woman in all of history who's ever had to admit that . . . And now, to top it all off, the devil has to go and offer me this much temptation. On a silver platter. Without one damn thing to stop me from reaching out and—

She looked at Greg again, studying his face with care.

Grabbing him, she went on with her thought, except that I don't love him. I don't love anybody. I *can't* love anybody anymore. Except, maybe, Cabe. Oh, Jesus, there I go! Always reaching for what's off limits. And that's *why* I keep thinking about Cabe so much these days. What I can't have, I want. And what I can—like say this 'un— Just perfect. Like a hero out of Shakespeare. "Hyperion's curls, the front of Jove himself, an eye like Mars to threaten and command—" I could get lost with Greggie pie from Saturday night through Monday morning reeel easy. Say I don't want him on a permanent basis. But to sort of misplace the tail end of a week with, he'd do mighty fine!

And as—a husband? On the outside chance I *could* bust loose from old Schweinie-poo? No. Absolutely not. But why? Name of God, why?

She thought about that. About the kind of female critter, woman, person, she was. About the kind of splendid male animal, man, human being, Greg was. That they might meet, strike sparks, set a weekend afire. But beyond that—

He's so—good. So genuinely good. Wholesome. Rock solid. All the masculine virtues. And I'd cheat on him three weeks after our wedding day. Almost any woman would, come to think of it. The only reason why most of 'em don't, after boys like Greg o' my heart have bored 'em plank stiff, is that they haven't got the nerve. Only, I do have the nerve. And—the inclinations. Let's face it: I'm just plain wicked, and that's a natural fact. So here's my perfect opportunity to escape from Kurt gone a-glimmering. Apart from the moral side of the question, that it would be a sin and a shame to wish something like me off on a boy baby doll as sweet as Greg is, it wouldn't even work. Because I can stand *anything*—and Lord

226

knows I've proved that with my Kurtie pie!—better than I can being bored. Kurt—never bores me. He—torments me. Humiliates me worse than any real, honest to God woman with a drop of pride left would put up with. Never even tries to hide the fact that all he feels for me is—contempt. And I—poor bedraggled bitch!—come crawling on my belly to lick his muddy boots . . .

Greg turned away from the train window, faced her, said, his voice hoarse with suppressed fury, "What are you lookin' at me that way for, Rose Ann?"

"You're a treat for female eyes, Greg o' my heart," she purred. "Ever since we became brother 'n' sister this morning early, I've been wondering if—incest—really is all that terrible a sin . . ."

Greg's face went beyond beet red, into mauve, then into a regal purple.

"You stop that!" he snarled. "Stop it right now!"

"Stop what, Greggie love?" she said in her best schoolgirl's voice of sweet innocence.

"Talking that way. Trying to make yourself sound like—like a street woman!"

"The word's whore, Greggie lamb. Y'know—w-h-o-r-e. Or harlot, if you prefer."

"Jeeesus God!" Greg all but wept. "Rose Ann, why d'you—torment me this way? Are you trying to put me off so I won't be driven so far beyond my strength, by all the wonderful things any fool can see you are, that I'll forget you're another man's wife? I won't, I promise you. So be yourself. You—a little red-headed angel with a spray o' freckles across your nose and cheeks, and eyes like seawater, and a mouth—a mouth— Oh, Jeee—"

That was as far as he got. She leaned swiftly forward and kissed him, slowly, lingeringly, with considerable art, all through the rising whispers of "Wal, I'll be gawddamned!" from the male passengers and the "Well, didja ever!" and the "Brazen hussy!" from the few women in the train car. Then she drew back, smiling at him with delighted mischief.

"Would you still put money on that 'angel' business, honey boy?" she said. "By the way, I've been told I've the most kissable lips on two continents. D'you agree, Greg o' my heart?"

"Five," he groaned, "and all the islands of the Seven Seas. For God's sake, Rose Ann, why'd you have to go and do a thing like that?"

"An irresistible impulse. Combined with overwhelming temptation. I always surrender to temptation right away. Saves time. And gives me ever so much more leisure to repent in."

"Rose honey," he said from the depths of purest anguish, "don't do anything like that anymore, will you, please? I'm honestly trying to respect your marriage, even though it seems like a mighty strange one to me most of the time. The way you two bicker, and make real *mean* jokes about each other, I just don't see—"

"How we ever came to wed?" she said bitterly. "The answer is, we didn't. I'm not Kurt Radetzy's wife. I'm his—fun filly. His private—whore . . ."

He was, she immediately saw, on the verge of a stroke of apoplexy. She leaned forward and gently caressed his cheek.

"Don't—please don't—take it so hard, Greg," she said softly. "You had to find out sometime. It seemed, well, more honest of me to tell you . . ."

"He—he tricked you!" Greg said furiously. "You're a *Southern* girl. From a good family. And no Southern girl—"

"From a good family ever took off her lacy pantalets, lay down, and spread wide for some horny boar hog without prior authorization from church and state? You know better than that, Greg. Nobody's got around to declaring an Emancipation Proclamation from human nature, so far. And I wouldn't have heard 'em if they did, what with being half strangled from trying to bust loose from the chain that held me to my kennel and more'n a mite deaf from listening to my own self howlin' . . ."

He said, "Oh, Jesus!" Then: "I'll *make* him do right by you! I'll shove the muzzle of my forty-four down his throat and—"

"Apart from the fact you'd wind up dead as a mackerel if you tried it, 'cause Kurt would put six shots through your long-tall handsome hide while you were still trying to get your sidearm out, he can't. His wife, his three children, and the Roman Catholic Church just might object. Don't believe in bills o' divorcement and suchlike, y'know . . ."

"I'll kill him!" Greg grated. "I don't care how fast he is on the draw or how good a shot, I'll—"

"You'll leave that there fine, manly carcass o' yourn looking kind of moth-eaten from having so many holes punched through it," she drawled. "And, believe me, Greg love, that would get me mighty upset for real. Wouldn't like that at *all*. On top of which, even if you could do the blighter in, as they say in London, why should you? Apart from giving you a first-class opportunity to entertain the assembled company with your version of the Highland fling. On the end of a rope, that is . . ."

He stared at her. His blue eyes widened, filled with light.

"That's right!" he whispered. "You—you're not married to him! You don't even need to go through that ugly and messy business of petitioning the state legislature for a bill of divorcement! You can just leave him and—"

"Light out for parts unknown with you, Greg o' my heart? No, I can't. And I'd deeply appreciate your being enough of a Southern gentleman not to make me explain why . . ."

He peered at her aghast.

"You—you're not—in the family way, are you, Rose?" he croaked.

"No. As a matter of fact, I don't think I can have children. Took a Yankee bullet through the wrong part of my insides just before Malvern Hill and—"

"My God!" he said. "I read about that! It was in all the papers. You saved Gen'l Lee's whole army and—"

"Didn't. Tried. And messed up, as usual. Let's not talk about that, huh, please?"

"And to think I never even tumbled to the fact that you were *that* Rose Ann! The greatest heroine in the history of the South, who—"

"Is now the biggest slut in the South's whole history too. Keep that there ugly little old fact in mind, will you? Don't get things all —mixed up, sugar plum. Keeping 'em straight is no guaranteed road to happiness, but it sure Lord saves a body a bushel and a peck o' trouble . . ."

"Rose Ann—leave him. Run off with me. I'll make you happy! I'll—"

"Make an honest woman out of me?" she asked him drily.

"Of course! We'll find a preacher or a justice of the peace just as soon as we get to Dayton and—"

"No. Thank you mighty kindly. I'm honored and I'm touched, the far from maiden cried, but no, Greg honey. And please don't ask me why . . ."

"I do ask you," he said sternly, his face taking on that aspect of a minor, younger, beardless, but exceedingly wrathful Old Testament prophet that she found so deliciously funny. "In fact, I *demand* that you tell me!"

She bowed her head. Looked up again.

"I can't leave him," she said. "It's just not possible for me to. If I tried it, I'd go crazy. Stark raving. Will you—accept my unsubstantiated word on that particular point, Greg o' my heart?"

"You mean—" he whispered, "that you—you *love* him so much that you—"

"No. I don't love him. I hate his bloody, cruel, twisted guts. But —I can't leave him. I haven't—the willpower to. You see, nice, sweet, innocent American boy, I'm not just his concubine, I'm his —slave . . ."

"Jesus!" he got out. "Rose Ann, you're—white. Even if there was maybe a drop o' two of—of colored blood in your family a long time back, he couldn't—"

She threw back her head and laughed aloud.

"Planning to take yourself on one of those 'beautiful octoroons' like in the storybooks, Greg love? Come off of that one, will you? You just can't be this dumb. Nope. Nary a drop o' Cuffy in me anywhere, so far as I know, which is all a descendant of any old family can say, and means about as much. Luck was changed right pert frequent back in the old days, y'know. But that wasn't what I meant. My slavery has nothing to do with race or color . . ."

"Then what has it to do with?" he asked.

"With me. The way I'm made. The rottenness way deep down inside of me that I didn't even know was there—until he dug into me and brought it out for me to see . . ."

"Rottenness?" he snorted. "You're an angel, Rose Ann!"

"Mighty putrid one, then. Look, baby boy, I was never deceived by Kurt; I knew from the first exactly what he was like. Put it this way: All the ways he's vile appeal irresistibly to everything in *me* that's—weak, contemptible, and—most of all—depraved . . ."

"I don't believe you!" he said again, but there was a quaver of uncertainty in his voice.

She shrugged.

"Don't," she said. "That doesn't matter. But please *do* believe this: I'll never leave him. Not any more than a real drunkard will ever leave the bottle. He's my—ultimate degradation, and I love it. The degradation, I mean, not him. I can't do without him. I'd go mad if I tried it. I—need him too bad. My—body—needs his. Is that—disgustingly clear enough to suit you, Greg?"

"Wal, now," he drawled, beginning to recover a bit by then, and thinking himself on familiar ground, being one of those randy Southerners who boasted they'd hump a snake if somebody'd hold his head still. "Couple o' fillies a while back kindly allowed that this here honey-cured hunk o' ham hock wasn't all that bad . . ."

"You're a child," she sighed. "A boy. A nice little old Southern boy with his ears washed clean on his way to Sunday school. I'd— wreck you, Greg. Destroy you. And you—deserve better. So forget me will you, huh, please?"

"Never!" he said, total conviction once more back in his voice. "I'm going to forget you, sweet Rose, the day they lay the pennies on my eyes to keep 'em shut."

She bowed her head, whispered, "Oh, God!" Looked up again. Said, "Do I have to fall into the hay with you the *first* night we get to Dayton? In order to convince you what I'm like, I mean? I'd rather not. Nicer to save that tender occasion for the last—the one before we leave, going our separate ways. Smarter that way. You could get to be—a habit, boy baby. And I don't need any more bad habits."

He shook his head; said, his voice vibrant with emotion, "No. Not either one. Neither the first nor the last. I want—all your nights, Rose Ann honey. And all your days. I won't settle for a one-night stand from you. I want you at my side forever, as my wife, the mother of my kids. So, all right, you said you can't have 'em, maybe. Then we'll adopt half a dozen, after giving the matter a whale of a try, of course . . ."

She stared at him, her green eyes ninety fathoms deep with pity. But with a glow in them too, misty, troubling, unsettled.

"Greg love, you're a fool," she sighed. "I'm afraid I'm going to have to do something about you, after all. To have hung on to as much pure innocence as you have is dangerous. Specially in this filthy business we've both been dragged into. So I'd better teach you your sums—in French arithmetic, boy baby. And which end is up, which can be contrary to all natural law. Long and short division: what goes into what and vice versa. Lots of both. Vice, I mean, and versa. And some Shakespeare: 'There are more things in heaven and earth, dear Gregory, than are dreamt of in your philosophy!' Worse things, Greg love. Now, let's not talk anymore. Not about *this*, anyhow . . ."

"Then what'll we talk about? It's a helluva ways to Ohio still, you know . . ."

"Our 'mission.' But with a straight face and laughing now and then so none of these busybodies I've shocked spitless will be tempted to eavesdrop. Greg, you'll be careful, won't you? 'Cause this isn't going to work out. It can't. None of these outsized schemes of Kurt's ever do. The smaller ones, yes. He's a great hand at mercantile fraud, manipulating the stock market, and so forth.

But pipe dreams like New York City's seceding from the Union, and this Northwestern Confederacy his Copperhead friends have cooked up, are a sight too big for anybody who's not really gifted to handle them. And all he's got to count on is—pygmies. Dwarfs. Sort of like sending General Tom Thumb to wrestle against Barnum's Jumbo. The best two out of three tumbles, winner takes all. Only this time I'm betting on the elephant . . ."

"Me too," Greg said morosely. "Rose Ann, ever since you 'n' Kurt sort of treated me to a steady parade o' our Nawthern friends, I been wondering whether we—our side, I mean—just might not be—well—wrong. Bluebottle flies always do go swarmin' over a dead body, y'know. And the worse it stinks, the more—"

"They swarm. We *are* wrong, honey boy. My grandpa, who taught the classics at West Point—only McKenzie since the beginning of time who ever had any brains in his head—used to tell anybody who'd listen, which damn nigh limited his audience to me, and I was nine years old when he died, that the South's 'peculiar institute' has no moral justification whatsoever. He was right. But he missed the point, just like you're missing it now . . ."

"Am I? Sugar, I'm purely craving enlightenment, specially from them sweet 'n' kissable lips o' yourn . . ."

"What's wrong with slavery is that it's not even profitable. We've just gone and got ourselves treed, worse than a coon with twenty hound dogs barking round that dead trunk he's crawled up, by our pride. 'Cause the morality of an institution hasn't got much to do with anything; it's how workable it is that counts. For instance, no country on earth has ever been able to outlaw whoring. And nobody—not even a first-class member of the profession like me—"

"Jesus!" Greg gasped. "Rose Ann, will you please—"

"Quit it? I mean to, but not at the expense of a sweet innocent like you, Greg o' my heart. As I was saying, not even I can defend the morality of going back on one's not so dainty little seat for pay. But is it ever profitable! The trouble with that crowd of 'not worth the powder 'n' ball it would take to kill 'ems' we had parading through our salon in Washington wasn't that they were polecats, which they were, but that they were stupid. The first is a mere misdemeanor, but the latter is a capital offense. A body can get away with absolutely everything in this world o' sin, Greg sugar, except two things—weakness and stupidity. And the trouble with our nest of Copperheads is that their poison wouldn't kill a baby lamb, and they hiss too goddamn loud. So you're right in your contention that any nation what attracts people like them as friends is done for from the outset. Which leaves our Confederacy with the unsolved problem—among others—of our strong tendency to attract lamebrained skunks as friends, because *smart* skunks are too busy making millions in war profiteering and speculation to bother with us, while only an idiot would leap to the defense of anything as tail-end-forwards as slavery is anyhow. But my grandpa said another thing that worries me—"

"What did the ol' cuss say?" Greg asked her solemnly.

"That a serious people will always beat a frivolous one. And a scientific, industrial civilization will eat alive one of hayseeds—even when a few—a mighty, mighty few—of said hayseeds have got niggers to do their plowing and cotton picking for 'em. And he was right. Tell me: d'you know the words to 'Dixie'?"

"Lord, Rose Ann honey—of course! All us Sothorons know that there song!"

"D'you know *all* the words to it, Greggie lamb?"

"Wal now, that much I wouldn't swear to, but, anyhow—"

"Listen!" she whispered sharply, and leaned forward until her lips were inches from his ear. Then she sang, very softly, so that only he could hear her:

> "Ol' Missus marry Will-de-Weaber,
> Now dat Will he wuz a gay deceber,
> Look away, look away, Dixie Land!
> 'N' when he put he arm around 'er,
> He grin jes' as fierce as a forty-pounder,
> Look away, Dixie Land!
>
> He face wuz sharp as a butcher's cleaber,
> But dat 'ere didn't seem to grief 'er,
> Look away, look away, Dixie Land!
> Ol' Missus her act de foolish part
> 'N' died fur a man whut broke her heart,
> Look away, look away, Dixie Land!"

"Well, what's wrong with that?" Greg demanded. "Sounds mighty good to me."

"And to me. But then I've got a corn-pone-'n'-lasses type o' mind too. But listen to this one." She leaned even closer, so that her lips were almost brushing his ear, and began singing in a dead-slow, funeral-dirge marching beat:

"Mine eyes have seen the glory of the coming of the Lord;
  He is trampling out the vintage where the grapes of wrath
      are stored;
  He hath loosed the fateful lightning of His terrible, swift
      sword;
                His truth is marching on.

  He has sounded forth the trumpet that shall never call re-
      treat;
  He is sifting out the hearts of men before His judgment seat;
  Oh, be swift, my soul, to answer Him! be jubilant, my feet!
              Our God is marching on."

"Well," Greg said uncertainly, "that ain't nothing but 'John Brown's Body' with some new words put to it . . ."

"Yes. But what words! Listen!" Again she sang:

"In the beauty of the lilies Christ was born across the sea,
  With a glory in His bosom that transfigures you and me;
  As He died to make men holy, let us die to make men free,
              While God is marching on."

"Mighty—solemn words," Greg said. "And—and kind of grand too. Got to admit that . . ."

"Yes. And d'you know what, lambie pie? A woman wrote that. A red-haired woman just like me. But that's not the point. The real point is—'scuse me, honey, but I got to use some of my fifty-dollar Back Bay Boston vocabulary on you now—the reeel point is that a people who've got the intellectual capacity to write something like that just ain't a-gonna be stopped by folks whose so-called and alleged minds work like this—" Again she sang into his ear:

"Just before the battle the Gen'l hears a row.
  Sez he, 'The Yanks're coming, I kin hear their rifles now.'
  He whirls to git things started, 'n' what d'yuh think he sees?
  Why, jist the Georgia militia eating goober peas!"

"Oh, Gawd!" Greg groaned. "Honey, you're saying we're a bunch o'—clowns?"

"No, 'cause we're not. Just—backward, that's all. Now hand me my carpetbag. Good . . ." She took the bag, opened it, and, without closing it, put it down beside his feet.

"Now," she said with a mocking grin, "you feel down amongst all my frillies and pretties until you find a package wrapped in oilskin. Don't you take that package out of my bag. Just lay it on top of my things, and open it reeel careful-like. As you'll be able to see, I couldn't take them there play toys of mine out in this train car without starting a panic. Found it? Go on, open it. None of these Nosy Parkers can see you without looking over the back of the seat, and they've had too much Yankee-style home-training to do that . . ."

Greg opened the oilskin-wrapped package. Stared up at Rose Ann in utter astonishment.

"Honey," he breathed, "you aimin' to *kill* somebody?"

"Yep. You. But not with them there. Druther just *wear* you out, bear-wrestling style. Those cute li'l play toys, Greg o' my heart, are proof positive of why we just can't win this here gentlemanly disagreement nohows. The little one was given to me by a friend of mine who has a gun manufactory down home. He swears it's the best sidearm, small as it is, on the face of the earth. Only not he nor anybody else on our side can make the ammunition for it, for the very simple reason that the machinery for punching those pretty little cartridges out of sheet brass is kind of in short supply in our brave Southland. By which I mean there aren't any. Not one. So, while my friend could make a cute li'l toy like that'un with the greatest of ease, he couldn't make what you need to shoot in it. So he gave it to me—as a 'virgin's pistol,' natch . . ."

"But this here other piece o' artillery," Greg said solemnly. "Don't tell me you've got the gun carriage 'n' the hosses to pull it hid in your bag too?"

"And a couple of handsome gunners to keep me company nights," she quipped. "That, lambie, is a Sharps cavalryman's carbine, with the stock and most of the barrel sawed off of it, to make it small enough for me hang around my waist under my crinoline when I head down home again. Promised to bring my gunsmithing friend one to copy. You see, it's a breechloader, another item us brave and gallant Southern chevaliers ain't got none of neither. But since it uses paper or linen cartridges just like our muzzleloaders do, and ordinary percussion caps to set 'em off, he can make the ammunition for it. You don't need a technical explanation of the advantages of a breechloader, d'you, sugar?"

"Nope. Colonel Berdan's explained that to me fifty dozen times. Hmmmn—so when you pull down on the trigger *guard*, the breechblock plumb slides up outa your way as easy as you please.

So's all you got to do is to throw a paper cartridge, minié ball and all, into the chamber, push up on the trigger guard, 'n' the whole works closes up sweet and smooth. Lord Jesus! If the Bluebellies was equipped with these, the war would of been over last Christmas! Why ain't they, Rose? With a li'l practice a man could get off a shot every half a minute, lying nice 'n' cozy on his belly whilst he was doing it. No wonder the colonel's sharpshooters threatened to mutiny if they weren't given little beauties like this'un! The Yankees must be crazy not to have issued every footslogger in the ranks one of these!"

"Not crazy. Just oversupplied with idiots with stars on their collars, like every army everywhere, hon. Soldiering isn't a career that smart fellows take to kindly. As Cabe says, a man smart enough to make a good soldier is too smart to make any kind of soldier. And that's so too. Now wrap it back up, will you? I've got to keep it safe 'til I can get it to my gun-making friend . . ."

Greg's Old Testament prophet's frown knitted his brow into incipient thunder.

"Rose honey," he growled, "I'll admit the Bluebellies haven't hanged one of our female spies yet, but if you get caught with an advanced arm like this'un, they just might change their minds . . ."

"Won't get caught. And 'tain't advanced. You ought to see a Spencer or a Henry. I had the fellow I paid to get me this one—a fine Copperhead who *works* in one of the factories up there in Connecticut—steal me one of each. But when I saw they used brass-cased cartridges too, I gave up on them . . ."

"Rose, I'll take it through for you. You just tell me the name and the address o' the old duffer who gonna make these glory-hal-lelujahs for our boys and—"

"Greg, they *would* hang you. While I can always talk 'em out of it. If worse come to the worst, I can always horse-trade. Offer 'em a fine substitute for my neck . . ."

"A substitute?" he growled. "Like *what?*"

"I'm sitting on it," she said sweetly. "Wrap my play toy up, Greggie pie. I'll get it to Colin personally. By the way, he's *not* an old duffer. Reckon he *is* a year or two older than you are, lambie, but no more. Mighty pretty boy too. I was engaged to him once . . ."

"Oh, Lord! Here we go again! Tell me something, Rose: why didn't you marry him, then?"

"Fell out of love with him. Then Kurt appeared on the scene, so—"

"And you preferred," he grated, "to be the—the—mistress of that creepy-acting furriner than to be a decent Southern fella's *wife?*"

"Well—yes," she drawled. "Something like that, anyhow. You see, Greggie-poo, y'all nice, sweet, clean-living Southern boys just don't know any vile, unnatural practices to speak of, not to mention any reeel low-down feelthy tricks . . ."

"And *he* does?" Greg croaked.

"Every one in the books, plus a few he invented himself," Rose Ann said solemnly. "Sure knows how to make life interesting, that boy . . ."

"Rose Ann, for God's love! You've got to leave him! Run off with me and—"

"Lambie, aside from the fact that I'd wreck you inside of a week, you aren't even next in line. The only man I know I'd most likely leave Kurtie for would be my sister's husband . . ."

"Jeeee-sus!" Greg got out. "Haven't you got a whit o' respect for anybody or anything, Rose Ann?"

"Not much. Messy world we live in, lambie. You see, Cabe married my sister Gwen 'cause I went up North to Boston and stayed too blamed long. And she married him 'cause she couldn't get Colin, whom she's in love with, 'cause he was engaged to me at the time. Cabe's worth twenty of Colin, and Gwen knows it. But since what a woman knows hasn't one clinking ding-danged thing to do with what she feels, we have a witch's stew, everybody married to the wrong party, or *with* the wrong party, or in love with the wrong party, or to get right down to grit and gravel, with a big fat healthy yen for the wrong party, which is what the whole business amounts to anyhow, were we to be honest enough to tell the truth about things . . ."

"And in the case o' your brother-in-law, which is it?" he said darkly. "You're in love with him or—?"

"Or," she said mockingly. "Always was an exciting kind of a cuss, that Cabe. He's little. Skinny. Only half a head taller than I am, and that's short for a man. And all my life I've been slapping him off and telling him that not even a mother could love a phiz like his'n. But he's got the sweetest, saddest, funniest, crookedest, sidewise grin that gives him a look like vinegar mixed with honey. Talks real wild too. And half an hour after he's got through saying one o' the craziest tomfool things you ever heard in all your born days, it'll come sneaking back into your head edgewise, and you realize you've never heard more truth spoken than that, put with half that much elegance and wit. So, all right, I've got all kinds o' feelings about and for Cabe, mostly of the unconfessable variety. The sort that nice, sweet, magnolia-scented Southern girls ain't s'posed to have about nobody, nohows, 'cause they just ain't decent. But when you've had it demonstrated to you every which aways but Sunday that decent is the one thing you sure Lord can't lay claim to being, you can just relax and entertain all such feelings royally. I'd climb into the hay with Cabe in a minute if he weren't Gwen's husband. But, in spite of the fact that she really doesn't love him, she *is* fond of him. Besides, Gwen is as straitlaced as all get-out, so she'd be shocked and horrified if I relieved her of him. Mainly, though she's incapable of realizing it, because then I would have put her down, low-rated her as a woman. And I wouldn't want to do that . . ."

"Mighty glad to hear there's *something* you wouldn't want to do," Greg said bitterly. "But for curiosity's sake, considering what you *are* doing, why wouldn't you?"

"She's an angel. She saved my life. She went without sleep for weeks, nursing me day and night, after I'd got my fool self shot. And I've made enough of a mess of things already, wouldn't you think? When this fuss is over, I'm going to leave Virginia forever. Go West. Set myself up as a parlor-house madam, likely. *After* I've made enough money flat on my own skinny back to afford it . . ."

"Jesus!" Greg whispered. "All right, you've got me off my feed, for tonight anyhow, if that's what you were trying to do . . ."

"Say, it *is* getting dark, isn't it? Greg sugar, what day is this?"

"Saturday," Greg said sourly.

"And the date?"

"May second. And the year is 1863, if you want to know that too." He was thoroughly out of sorts. He had convinced himself that he loved this small, slight, red-haired creature beyond all bearing. That he couldn't live without her.

"Thank you," Rose Ann said sweetly. "Now be quiet a couple of minutes, will you? I've got to say a prayer . . ."

"*You*, praying?" Greg said sarcastically.

"Yep. For my brother, Jeff. And for Cabe. Jeff's in Alabama, according to the last letter I had from Gwen, just before we left London. To do some real, deep scientific work at Mobile. So I reckon he's safe enough. But I don't know where Cabe is. And they say that the prayers of the righteous availeth much, don't they? So, here goes: 'Dear Lord, keep Jeff safe. I mean, go on keeping him safe, just the way You have so far. And—Cabe. Make him stop being so confounded brave, so he won't get his fool self killed. Gwen—needs him, even if she is too stupid to realize that. And I—need him too, Lord—sinful as the thought may be. But You always understood female sinners, didn't you? So, keep him safe. Wherever he may be. Amen . . .' "

Lieutenant Colonel Caleb Henry, at that very moment, was riding at the point of a little vee of horsemen into the gathering darkness toward the Union lines, beyond the little plateau that historians were going to call forever after Chancellorsville, following the local custom that had named it that, just as if it were a village or a town. It was, actually, the junction of two roads and a big white building called the Chancellor House, with its barns, stables, and slave quarters, nothing more.

Nice-lookin' place, Cabe thought, but that don't make it appetizing none at all to die at, Lord. I want to get back home in one piece, Lord Jesus. Make it up with Gwen, if she ain't departed for parts unknown with her pretty, crippled coward. And if she has, I won't, I promise You, follow 'em, or shoot him, or whup on her li'l tender pink tail. I'll let 'em go, with Your blessin', 'n' mine. But You'll just have to excuse me whilst I do a little shootin' and carvin' and whittlin' on that there furrin snake in the grass who's stole my Rose Ann. Know them sentiments ain't Christian, but You'll grant me a small-sized furlough from Your teachings to do what's sensible 'n' necessary, won't You, huh, Lord, please? But for the moment, make them Dutchmen miss me, tha's all I ask right now . . .

The Dutchmen he referred to were Major General Oliver O. Howard's Eleventh Union Army Corps, who were grouped around Dowdall's Tavern, which, with that sublime Southern irrelevance about names, wasn't a tavern, any more than Chancellorsville was a ville. Dowdall's Tavern was the home of a good man of God named Reverend Melzi Chancellor. And Cabe wasn't prepared to bet that the Bible-pounder's name had anything to do with the place either. The South was like that. But with the possible exception of Deven's division, the Dutchmen damned well *were* Dutchmen—that is, Germans, or anyhow German-Americans—though some of 'em weren't even hyphenated yet. Apart from Deven and MacLean, the names of their commanding officers were: von Glisa, Carl Schurz (who afterward became famous as a liberal politician), Schimmelfennig, Krzyzanowski, von Steinwehr,

Buschbeck, and Schirmer. And they were all as good soldiers as Germans always seem to be, so Cabe knew that they couldn't be counted on to panic and run like ordinary Yankee counterjumpers.

He turned in the saddle and looked behind him. After him came Captain James Power Smith, and at the captain's side, old Jack Jackson himself, wearing his ancient, beat-up flat-topped cap and mounted on Old Sorrel, that big, awkward-looking, ugly horse that could outrun a steam locomotive when he had to. Old Jack was slumped over in the saddle. He looked tired, Cabe judged, and old. And yet, he ain't even forty yet, Lieutenant Colonel Henry realized. This here damn war is plumb using all of us up too fast . . .

That was all he had time to think, because a squad of "them damn Dutchmen" rose up in the dark and split the night with tongues of flame. Cabe heard his mount scream like a woman in childbirth, plunge, start to go down. He tried to fling himself from the saddle so he wouldn't be crushed if his fatally hit mount rolled and thrashed the way gut-shot horses always do. He almost made it, but not quite. His left foot caught in the stirrup, and as the dying horse reared, plunged, crawfished, pump-handled, bucking his way into a good steed's Valhalla, Caleb Henry was finally flung free, but with his left ankle broken straight across and very cleanly.

He bunched all his body against the impact, and rolled. But when he tried to get up to scurry toward the Confederate lines, knowing that it was at least possible to make them in the gathering dark, that pain bit into him with fangs of utter agony. So whispering prayerfully, "Jesus!" he lay still, and watched Old Jack Stonewall Jackson pounding away to safety with his whole staff grouped around him, riding like centaurs, going on.

Bless 'em! Cabe thought. Looks like I'm the only Judas goat. Better that way. They're all good men and true, while I—

Then he saw those shadowy figures rise from the Confederate lines. They were the 33rd North Carolina, under General Pender. But Cabe didn't know that. When he and the rest of Stonewall's staff had ridden out with Old Jack, there hadn't been anybody there. Nor, in their defense, did the 33rd know that there were Southern horsemen between them and the Bluebellies. Anything living coming from that direction was, had to be, a foeman. They whitened the night with a solid sheet of flame. Two of the staff officers went down, forever. On the north side of the road another squad of Carolinians stood up and wrapped Old Jack in white fire that silhouetted him and Old Sorrel against the night, against time and eternity. Old Sorrel bolted. Thomas Jonathan Jackson—or rather the shot-hashed apparatus of bone, blood, and flesh that housed his soon-to-depart-him warrior's soul—was thrown clear.

"Oh, Jesus!" Cabe wept aloud. "Why'd it have to be *him?* His missus and his young'un was here day before yestiddy to see him. He had that—a lovin' woman and a child to raise and the respect of everybody that knew him. A great man. A real great man and You take him, and leave me, who ain't got nobody, not even a home to go back to, really. 'Cause a home's got to have *love* in it, and mine—"

Then he looked up into the sheen of bayonets reaching for his eyes.

"Do you give up yourself, Yankee?" they asked him.

Slowly Caleb Henry raised his hands. He was out of that war that was going to last two whole years more and cost at least another million lives.

"The prayers of the righteous availeth much," Rose Ann Mc-Kenzie had said.

Chapter Twelve

Greg stared intently at the float that was parked next to the speaker's stand. On that float there had gathered most of the thirty-four buxom Ohio girls in cheesecloth who had represented the thirty-four states of the Union in the parade. The girls were shivering. The evening was cool, the cheesecloth, thin. To his unbounded delight, Greg had discovered that he could make out enough of the salient geographical features of those particular states through the billowing draperies to decide just where he should go about establishing squatter sovereignty, in utter disregard of states' rights. Along the middle border, he thought happily, in the bushes 'neath th' fork, where the b'iling springs meet the great divide!

But Rose Ann's voice cut through his reverie.

"Tell me," she said, "did you join up?"

"Sure did," Greg snorted disgustedly. "Worse tomfool ceremony you ever did see. Just like one of them silly college secret societies. Plumb infantile, if you ask me."

"So now you're a Knight of the Golden Circle, are you?" Rose Ann said.

"And a Tyler of the Lesser Council, City of Cleveland, Ohio," Greg said solemnly. "Whatever the hell *that* is. Look, honey, after having met and got to know the members of this here terrible conspiracy to take the Northwestern states outa the Union, I figgered I'd better sorta arrange for the two of us to get out of here when the whole thing falls down on these here idjuts' heads. As it's going to. You read Gen'l Burnside's General Order Number Thirty-eight? 'Twas in all the papers this morning . . ."

" 'The habit of declaring sympathies for the enemy will not be allowed,' " Rose quoted. "Don't see how he's going to stop it. Free speech is backed by the law in Yankee Land. Of course, he just might tell his arresting squads to be a mite careless with their muskets and shoot some of you Golden Knights a wee bit dead, but aside from a little old dirty trick like that there . . ."

"Anyhow, we're getting out. I got new orders from the nice sweet Yankee colonel whose regiment I was assigned to by Colonel Mitchell—on detached service, natcherly—sending me down to Nashville. This colonel here, name of Reynolds, carries a butternut in his left pocket and a copper penny in his right, just like Mitchell did. Anyhow, in good ol' Nashville, I'm to walk around real carefree-like, memorize the fortifications 'n' sichlike, 'n' when I can, skip south, j'ining Gen'l Bragg's forces down around Chattanooga. Be good to put a gray uniform back on ag'in. Anyhow, I'm taking you with me, sugar plum . . ."

"How? Hitting me over the head with something heavy, Greg?"

"If necessary," Greg said grimly. "After what you told me he done to you in London, I ain't even starting to let you go back to that dirty-minded, evil, twisted-up furrin son o' his two bits a tumble li'l ol' mama nohows!"

"But I *like* being treated like that," Rose Ann said solemnly. "I've got to go back to him, Greg. I can't live without his—well—delicate attentions . . ."

"Why, goddamn!" Greg howled. "Rose Ann, you're talking about the man who beat you damn nigh t'death 'cause you wouldn't—wouldn't—"

"Prostitute myself—why, do tell! That's really a delicate way o' putting the matter, isn't it, lambie?—with the old fool he was trying to get something out of. I'm sorry I told you that. Just like my sister Gwen says, I suffer from hoof-and-mouth disease, an ailment common to jennies. Besides, in a way it isn't entirely true. I hadn't the slightest objection to engaging in the world's oldest—and noblest—profession. It was just that Kurtie failed to tell me what was going on, or warn me beforehand. So when this skinny old scarecrow—clad in a striped nightshirt, grinning at me through damned nigh toothless gums, with his breath having the delightful aroma of an outside pit privy—appeared in my bedroom in the middle of the night—after, of course, my darling Kurt had conveniently been called away to London—I reacted like a true-blue, magnolia-scented Southern gal: I parted his wig for him—he hadn't a hair of his own left to his name, natch—with a bullet . . ."

"For which your so-called ever-lovin' husband stripped you mother naked, hung you from the transom by your wrists, and—"

"Striped my little hindquarters for me real *good*," Rose Ann drawled. She flashed a sublimely wicked grin at Greg. "Enjoyin' the mental picture, Greggie love?" she purred.

Greg turned beet red. He had been. But being forced to admit it, even to himself, made him uncomfortable. Very.

"Now, see here, Rose Ann!" he blustered.

"See here, nothing. Y'know, I really don't believe my contretemps with His Lordship had anything much to do with that. Except to give Kurtie-poo a perfect excuse to carry out a scientific experiment he'd been longing to . . ."

"A—scientific experiment?" Greg said.

"Yes. To determine whether the temporary possession of a sore and tender tail doesn't give a filly a better gait." She paused, long and thoughtfully. Then she added with absolute calm, with no discernible expression at all, "It does."

"Oh, Jeeee-su—" Greg began, but Rose Ann caught his arm.

"Here's his nibs himself, at long, long last!" she said.

Congressman Clement L. Vallandigham strode to the rostrum. On that May afternoon in 1863, the congressman was running for the governorship of the state of Ohio. He was, Rose Ann saw, a very handsome man, sporting a fringe of whiskers, but with his upper lip clean-shaven, much in the same style as President Lincoln wore his whiskers, except that Congressman Vallandigham's were sparser. The congressman was soon off, and in full cry, soaring above the unceasing bull bellows of his numerous supporters. The cheesecloth-clad states caught the wild enthusiasm of the moment, and stood up to clap and cheer, affording Greg a better view than ever of their hills, dales, promontories, and even the shadows of their deeper valleys. Through the roars and the soprano shrieks of his followers, Rose Ann caught the words: "The dead, the dead, the numerous dead! Think of Fredericksburg, let us make peace!"

She poked Greg in the side, hard, and nodded toward the cheering group of men at the very foot of the rostrum. Two of them, she'd already seen, were neither clapping nor cheering. They were much too busy. Notebooks in hand, they were taking down, with the skill of police court reporters, every word that Clement L. Vallandingham was saying.

"Saw 'em some time ago," Greg whispered. "Them there butternuts in their lapels don't mean a damn thing. They're Army Intelligence officers sure as shootin', 'n' old Muttonchop sent 'em . . ."

General Ambrose Burnside, Rose realized with wry amusement, had achieved the minor miracle of—in that day when every conceivable form of hirsute facial adornment graced the majority of male countenances—creating an entirely new style of whiskers. His consisted of an enormously bushy mustache that looped southward past the corners of his mouth to join the huge, fluffy muttonchops that foamed down from his temples, but with his massive chin shaved absolutely clean. It was almost exactly the reverse of the style of whiskers that many men, including President Lincoln and ranting rabble-rouser Vallandigham, wore, and it caught the public's fancy so greatly that they identified such whiskers as "Burnsides" at first, then later on as "sideburns." So the ambitious Union general was going to be granted the accidental mercy of having his tragically inept military strategies and his tyrannical civil administration forgotten and himself remembered only for his whiskers. Many another blue-clad duffer might well have envied him his fate, Rose Ann conceded, even then.

"Well," she whispered back, "doesn't seem to me he's said anything they could arrest him for so far . . ."

"Don't worry, he will," Greg said evenly. "Heard him before. In love with the sound of his own voice, that Vallandigham . . ."

Which the congressman immediately proceeded to prove: "The war for the Union," he bellowed, "is in your hands—a most bloody and costly failure! There is mourning in every home! Make an armistice! Call a constitutional convention! The Union will reestablish itself!"

"He's getting there, isn't he?" she said to Greg. In a way, she actually *wanted* Congressman Vallandigham to get himself jailed by uttering a clearly treasonable pronouncement. It would end the strain she was under. With the congressman in jail, the Copperheads would be finished as a political power, since he was their heart and soul and, more importantly, their brains. Without Clement Vallandigham, they'd collapse like a house of cards. Then her mission—and Greg's—would be over. Greg could head south then, to the comparative safety of the Confederate lines. And if, after reaching them, he got killed after all, his death would be—honorable. A soldier's death—in battle. She didn't know why the way a man died should make any difference, but it did. There was something—repugnant about being hanged like a thief or a murderer. She didn't want him to get killed at all, of course. She wanted him to live, marry some nice sweet girl, get old enough to see his own great-grandchildren. But mostly she wanted him the hell away from where she was, miles beyond the reach of her yearning arms. Because not only was she not fit for, and didn't deserve, a good sweet wholesome boy like Greg; she'd wreck him, make him terribly unhappy. Him, and herself.

I have, she thought bitterly, been corrupted far beyond the curative powers even of his purity. So—back to Kurt. Back to—evil. Back to all the unnatural practices I've learned to—enjoy. And to despise myself for enjoying. I'll be free of Kurt the day I die, or the day he leaves me. Same thing. I'll die that day, by my own hand. And not out of grief because he's cast me off. I don't care about *him.* I'll be glad to be rid of him. No, I'll cut my throat to make goddamned sure I won't start looking for another two-legged lump of clotted filth, to—wallow with. To service all my—acquired peculiarities . . .

She was thinking all those bleak and ugly things when she heard Clement Vallandigham cry out: "I have the most supreme contempt for General Order Number Thirty-eight! I have the most supreme contempt for King Lincoln! Come up, united, and hurl the tyrant from his throne! The men in power in this country are attempting to establish a despotism more cruel and oppressive than any that ever existed! Do you know that a proposition has been made for the reestablishment of the Union, and the refusal, in Lincoln's handwriting, is still in existence? He does not wish to end this war! He'll continue it as long as there are any contractors or officers to enrich!"

The congressman paused, the perpetual sneer he seemed to have been born with twisting his florid, handsome face.

"So I say to you," he concluded, "let us end this wicked, cruel, and unnecessary war—for the freedom of the blacks—and the enslavement of the whites!"

Pandemonium broke loose. But neither Rose nor Greg was paying any attention to that mob of shrieking, roaring madmen and madwomen. They were watching the two officers in civilian dress who stood quietly amid the screaming rabble before the rostrum. The two men nodded to each other, snapped their notebooks shut.

"That's it," Greg said quietly. "He'll dine on bully beef and beans in a jail cell before night tomorrow . . . ."

Greg was right, Rose Ann realized a dozen times during that terrible week that followed. But the quick solution she'd thought that Vallandigham's arrest would bring to the thorny problem of galloping treason in the Northwestern states, and thereby to the torture of Tantalus that Greg's clean, young, manly presence inflicted constantly upon a heart she'd thought far beyond both dreams and yearning, turned out to be no solution at all. Vallandigham was arrested, of course; jailed. Tried before a military court. "Speech of the defendant," the Court handed down, "was both in fact and in intent seditious. Accused is guilty as charged, and hereby sentenced to perpetual imprisonment. Approved, Ambrose E. Burnside, Major General, Commanding, Department of the Ohio."

But instead of ending the matter, that sentence only made things worse. Every newspaper in the land, North and South, took up cudgels for, or against, Clement Vallandigham. The Northwestern states were on the very verge of civil war, within and among themselves.

Rose Ann and Greg received a telegram from Kurt: "Congratulations!" it read. "You've done nobly! Keep up the good work!"

"And we've done nothing!" Rose Ann wailed.

"We don't have to tell him that," Greg snorted. "In fact, we don't have to tell that silly bastid anything but goodbye. And that's just what we're going to!"

"Oh, Lord!" Rose Ann moaned. "I was so hoping that when they threw this windy polecat into the cooler and sort of lost the key, this whole business would be over, and we—"

"Could head for parts unknown," Greg said fervently. "Oregon, maybe. Or California. Ain't no war out there on the Pacific coast worth a damn to speak of, and we could settle down and start working on our li'l family . . ."

"Greg," she said quietly, "we aren't going to have any family, you and I. Get that through your divinely thick head, will you? When this is over, I'm going back to my unlawful husband. He's a swine, and therefore all I'm fit for. It's not only that I'd ruin you, wreck you beyond repair, if I tried to use your sturdy backbone as a ladder to climb up out of the mire I've fallen into; it wouldn't work anyhow. I'd fall right back in with a thick, slimy splash and, what's worse, drag you down to perdition with me—"

"If perdition's where you're going, Rose Ann, then that's purely my destination," he declared stoutly. "Quit argufyin', will you? You're an angel, and you're *mine*. Leastwise you're gonna be . . ."

"That's what *you* think," she said darkly. "Oh, Lord, if somebody would just go and shoot that polecat Vallandigham!"

"Wouldn't work neither," Greg pointed out. "Make a martyr out of him that way, and things would be in a bigger stew than ever . . ."

Which was a point of view fully shared by the Honorable Abraham Lincoln, President of these United States. Even as it was, keeping the congressman in jail was doing precisely that, along with making the shallow scoundrel deliriously happy over the priceless publicity he was getting. So Honest Abe paced the floor of the Oval Room, back and forth and back again, thinking: Elections are coming up next year. And this son of a dastard will be a thorn in my side, as if I didn't have thorns enough already. Burnside's inflated him twenty times his size by being fool enough to arrest him in the first place. But I can't turn him loose. That would be to give carte blanche to every traitorous scoundrel in the land, and Lord knows we've our share and more of the varmints!

He kept on pacing, his long, lank figure that was the delight of every cartoonist in the nation stooped under the burden of this new worry.

Suddenly he stopped. A slow smile stole across that craggy, wonderfully, beautifully, ugly face. He strode to his desk, sat down. Dragged out a steel-tipped pen, affixed his half-moon spectacles to his big, warty nose. Then the man who was, among other things, the greatest *writer* the United States of North America ever produced, scribbled happily:

"The sentence of Clement L. Vallandigham to perpetual imprisonment, recently handed down by the military court of the Department of the Ohio, is hereby commuted to banishment to the Confederacy, where this Noble Tribune of the People will presumably be able to enjoy the liberty he has praised so highly. Signed, A. Lincoln . . ."

Then the President leaned back in his chair, his long frame loose with purest contentment. He had reason to be contented. For once again Abraham Lincoln had proved that, in comparison to him, Niccolò Machiavelli was the rankest of amateurs.

Which, of course, only precipitated the crisis between Rose Ann and her would-be lover. The day after Clement L. Vallandigham had been marched, with all his belongings packed with exquisite courtesy and care into the black trunk that accompanied him, under a flag of truce, to the sound of a trumpet, into Confederate General Braxton Bragg's lines, where he pompously declared to the first Reb he met, "I surrender myself to you as a prisoner of war!" whereupon the whole Copperhead and/or Butternut conspiracy simply blew away—in that part of the country anyhow—before the gales of laughter rising both North and South at the ridiculous figure its supreme leader had cut, Rose Ann found herself with the fight of her life on her hands.

A mule, she discovered, was a paragon of sweet reasonableness when compared to Gregory Forrester's utter determination to bear her away by main force, if need be, from her shameful life into the sweet and placid bonds of honorable matrimony. She made the monumental error of conceding that there were no legal reasons why she and Greg could not be wed. The moral and psychological ones turned out to be beyond her—for her times—really quite rich and cultivated vocabulary, since the habit she shared with Cabe, of talking like a black field hand or a swamp-bottom poor white much of the time, was one of the quirks of people of her high social position in that particular epoch. That these obscure but crushingly valid reasons were beyond Greg's capacity, and more especially his willingness, to understand was another factor that made her task difficult to the point of impossibility.

So finally she said, "All right. I'll go away with you, but on one condition, Greg—"

"And that is?" he growled, his voice torn between suspicion and delight.

"That you—demonstrate to me that you—can—are able to—to satisfy me. I really am a rough one in that department, honey lamb. A kind of she-fiend. Aside from Kurt, I've never met a man who could give me as much as I want, as long as I want it, as hot and heavy—and—and as many variations, call it. I get bored, real easy. So I like—changes of gait and pace. Of the ways we go about it. The—positions we can fit into. I know—twenty-seven, not that I really like 'em all. How many d'you know, Greggie pie?"

"Jesus!" Greg whispered.

"Tell you what: You go out and buy us a bottle of whiskey, since it isn't likely you can take me into a barroom in this straitlaced state. I want to get drunk—just a little, so I won't be nervous and spoil things. And it appears to me you could do with a snort or two to calm your nerves as well . . ."

"You're damned right I could!" Greg croaked.

She put out a playful hand and ruffled his hair.

"Go get us that bottle, lambie. And when you get back, come on in my room, 'stead of this cozy little sitting room. Don't knock. Just come right on in, boy baby . . ."

"I'll do that little old thing," Greg whispered.

He came back with the whiskey. Without knocking, he entered her hotel room, which was next to his, separated from it only by that cozy little sitting room in which up until now they had always met. He hung there with an expression on his face exactly like that of a poleaxed steer the moment before it falls.

"What's wrong, lover boy?" she purred. "Don't you like me?"

He didn't answer her. He couldn't. She wasn't naked. She had on a short white whalebone corset, decorated top and bottom with Breton lace. A pair of silvery white silk stockings, held up by huge, lacy garters. A pair of high-heeled dancing slippers. Period. That was it. That was all.

The corset pushed her firm young breasts up higher than they normally were. She had darkened their areolas and her nipples with a lip salve she had bought in Paris. The corset squeezed her waist in unmercifully, which made her slender hips look much wider than they were. Between the bottom of her corset a scant three inches below her navel and the tops of her stockings, there was, of course, only Rose Ann.

The effect, strangely enough, wasn't fetching. It was exactly what she'd intended it to be. Shocking. Even, a bit—obscene.

"You," he got out at last, "look just like a whore!"

"I *am* a whore," she said wearily. "Told you that two dozen times already. But don't worry. For you, lambie, the occasion's—free . . ."

He hung there, holding that bottle and staring at her. She crossed to him, went up on tiptoe, locked her hands behind his head, and kissed his mouth, grinding hers into his, forcing his lips, his teeth apart, then giving him her tongue like a professional, serpentine, busy, ardent expert.

She felt his mouth go cold and sick, and realized that she'd gone too far. She stepped back, said, "Did I frighten Mama's baby boy? Open that bottle, Greggie love. Then—drink up. Or else you're going to disappoint me, and I wouldn't like *that*, not none at *all* . . ."

He got the bottle open and began to drink, guzzling the whiskey, desperately, avidly, trying to blind his eyes, stun his thinking mind. He was a gentle soul, and the dreams of the gentle die hard. He hadn't been prepared to have the temple of his idolatry profaned by the very goddess he had raised it to, nor to see her leave her own high altars to descend to the courtyard, and there amid the teeming flies, the splattered, stinking camel dung, open her splendid robes, her thighs, her life, to grimy pilgrims upon the very stones in meaningless, ritual copulation for a dirham, an obol, or a dinar—or for nothing at all, if it were her whim, while every hope he'd ever had, self-mutilated, mad, lifted sunward its bloody severed parts and went gibbering and screeching out of life . . .

She waited patiently until his blue eyes glazed. Then she got up and took the bottle away from him.

"That's enough, lambie," she said sadly. "Too much and you'll disappoint me even worse . . ."

He stood up, began to tear at his clothing. She said, "Let me . . ." And began to undress him very slowly, her hands, her fingers, her lips, her tongue tip, diabolical upon his tormented flesh.

She pushed his trousers, his smallclothes down around his ankles, stood back contemplating his nakedness with the same mocking appreciation with which men generally regard the nude bodies of women.

"Hmmmmnnn," she said, "nice! A real big boy, aren't you, love? Well, Greggie-poo, shall we commence the—waltz?"

What transpired thereafter can only be described as a state of general hyperactivity, carried out by a pair of acrobatic contortionists. When the goal is not procreation, but the subtlest refinements of sensual pleasure, the genitalia may be dispensed with, or misused. The human body, male or female, has any number of erotic zones, even additional orifices supplied with the requisite properties of heat and moisture, which can be, and all too often are, substituted for the ones designed by nature for the purpose at hand. This, every reasonably sophisticated fool knows . . .

But what no fool at all, and few wisemen, know is that the major sexual organ in the human species is the mind. And if used well, with imagination, generosity, willingness to give, to share, it can achieve that rare miracle that men call love. But when used ill, with perversity, malice, cruelty, contempt, its destructive powers are unlimited. And she, with sad, sick self-loathing, was using hers to shock, profane, disgust, to drive away from her side this decent man she knew she had no right to, couldn't have . . .

In short—to murder love. To disembowel tenderness. To send poor dreamer hope, auto-castrated, self-blinded, howling away into the desert away from the sound of the wet slapping of bellies, goddess's and beggar's, from the stink of rut, to where the sirocco rises and only death is kind . . .

She succeeded only too well. He broke at long, long last the Gallic geometrical figure they'd spent a languid hour constructing, stared at her with eyes that had death's own sickness in them, and leaping to his feet, clawed clothing awkwardly, badly, mistakenly over his nakedness, howling: "Bitchbitchbitchfilthypervertedbitch —here! Take your pay! You've earned it!" Hurled a sheaf of greenbacks to the floor and stormed from that room, from the hotel, from her life—she thought—forever . . .

And she, lying there, staring at that clutch of crumpled bills, not even crying yet because she couldn't, thought suddenly about how it had felt when Lieutenant Froggie Boy's .44 caliber slug had gone smashing through her guts, the sear, the shock, the utter numbness, the sticky flooding before the pain had come.

It was the same now. And when the incurable hurt, the slow,
still ultimately fatal recognition of loss would hit her finally, she
wouldn't even scream. She was alone in the wilderness. Naked.
Semen-splattered. Sweat-glistened. Smelling—used. Violated, not
so much in her bruised and aching flesh as in her—identity. In her
perception, her recognition of what and *who* she was.

Some hours later, she got up from there. Went to the washstand,
cleansed her whole body, inside and out, with ritual care. Dressed
in the simplest, soberest clothes she had, she descended the stairs,
paid the bill. Took a cab to the railway station, a train to New
York. To—Kurt.

As a means of auto-immolation, she realized, that choice was as
good as any. Slower, perhaps, but just as sure.

Chapter Thirteen

Rose Ann put down the copy of the New York *Daily News* she had been reading and turned to Kurt.

"Looks like we've bet on the wrong horse as far as the Copperheads are concerned," she sighed. "Even the *Daily News* admits that Vallandigham has done nothing but make a damn fool of himself ever since old Abe shipped him South. Reckon that plumb sinks the Copperhead movement, doesn't it?"

"No, my dear, it doesn't," Kurt said. "The Northwestern states aren't the center of power in the Union, y'know. I'd say that the East Coast, especially including this charming city, actually is. And here we have such sinuous and reptilian stalwarts as the Woods, Fernando—"

"Who, when he was mayor, back in '61," Rose Ann said drily, "actually tried to get New York City to secede from the Union and go it alone, with, of course, close ties with 'our friends in the South.' And his brother Ben, who owns this rag"—she indicated the *Daily News* with a disdainful gesture of her hand—"sure Lord doesn't try to hide his sentiments, does he? If any newspaper in Richmond were to print editorials and news stories favoring the North as strong as the ones Ben Wood prints in his paper in defense of the South, cotton, and slavery, he'd have found himself roasting in the burning ruins of his establishment long before now!"

"Quite so," Kurt said calmly, "but then, my sweet, one of the major defects of democracy as a system is that it *must* permit public dissent, so windy thieves like the Woods can print anything they want to. Actually, that fine pair aren't important. Remember the sterling crew of dear friends of our beloved Southland present upon the stage of the Academy of Music on the Fourth of July?"

"Hmmmnn—" Rose Ann murmured, and consulted her notes. That was one of the things she did for Kurt now. She put her flying pencil and a self-invented private system of shorthand to the service of what he called "our noble cause" by taking down very nearly verbatim everything that was said at important public meetings. And three weeks ago, she had employed her really quite remarkable skill at drawing—she'd won first prize at that art as a student in Miss Bradstreet's school in Boston—on behalf of one of Kurt's mysterious "projects" by copying, in beautiful detail, a street map of the city. When she'd done with it, Kurt had made her letter in the exact location of the major police precincts and that of every district office of the Federal Enrollment and Conscription Act, the hated draft that the whole city was seething over, the position of the New York State Armory on Second Avenue at Twenty-first Street and of the Union Steam Works one block north of that. When she'd asked him why he wanted the steam works put in, he'd said drily, "It's been converted into an arms factory. They're making a new type of carbine there . . ."

So she'd shut up and hadn't asked him anything else, not even when he'd taken her beautiful map away from her and marched out of their lodgings in the still new Fifth Avenue Hotel on Madison Square with it in his hands. Some days—eight or ten, really— later a delivery cart had drawn up to the hotel and the hall porters and bellhops had brought huge bundles smelling of fresh ink up to their rooms. Rose Ann opened one; after all, Kurt hadn't told her not to. It was her map, duplicated by a first-class engraver and printed up in thousands of copies. She didn't ask Kurt why he'd had that done, not because he wouldn't have told her, but because she didn't want to know. She'd thought he'd wanted the map for Southern saboteurs, especially after he'd asked her to block in the stretch along the East River where Webb & Allen's shipyard was. Webb & Allen made ironclads for the U.S. Navy, so their dry docks, shipways, and other facilities would have been legitimate targets for Rebel agents or even Copperhead Southern sympathizers. But you didn't print maps intended for the use of the Confederate Secret Service by the thousands. One or two would have been plenty enough. No, these had a more sinister objective. And since her Kurtie pie's objectives could be sinister indeed, she recoiled from too precise a knowledge of what this one was.

Now, finding the notes she had made at the Academy of Music on Fourteenth Street during the Independence Day celebration, she read back the beginning of Democratic Governor Horatio Seymour's address: "I appeal to you, my Republican friends, if you yourselves in your serious moments believe that national unity is to be produced by seizing our persons, by infringing upon our rights, by insulting our homes, and by depriving us of those cherished privileges for which our fathers fought and to which we have always sworn allegiance . . ."

She looked up. "Kurt," she said dolefully, "let's pack up. Go home . . ."

"Why?" he said cheerfully. "This war is far from over yet . . ."

"Oh, yes, it is," she sighed. "And it's been over since the Fourth of July. I don't need to give you the reasons, 'cause you've read the papers. Gettysburg, Kurt. Vicksburg. Both in the same damn week. Don't they mean anything to you?"

He turned upon her his perfect megalomaniac's ice-bright smile.

"Temporary setbacks," he said. "Important ones, I'll grant you. But *I* shall reverse them."

"How?" Rose Ann snorted. "By calling for help from that bunch of pig-dogs on the rostrum of the Academy of Music on the Fourth? Or do you go along with this pipe dream that Richard O. Gorham, Esquire, the last speaker of the evening, spent two good hours on: that the state militia be armed to the teeth, under the command of Governor Horatio Seymour, so that New York could 'dispense with provost marshals'? In other words, resist the draft by force; start a small-sized civil war, the state and/or especially the city of New York against the Federal government! And the rest of the time he devoted to pointing out how uniquely equipped the city is to exist and prosper, were the Union dissolved, as a 'separate sovereignty.' Kurt, Kurt! We don't need friends like those! People that treacherous and that *stupid* would make us impossible neighbors even if we could get shut of the Yankees in general, which you know damn well we can't!"

"I quite agree that we can't beat the Yankees on the battlefield, because, as stubborn as they've proved themselves to be, to do that, we'd have to destroy them utterly—a feat which we lack both the resoures and the men to accomplish," Kurt said gravely. "But there are other methods available, my dear! We can infiltrate their home fronts, capitalize upon the discontent among their stinking, unwashed masses, cause them so ruddy much trouble *behind* their lines as to make the Unionists give up the struggle and 'let the erring sisters go,' as these Copperhead blighters are so fond of saying . . ."

"But how?" Rose Ann persisted. "Tell me *that*."

"Perhaps," Kurt said coolly, "by putting into action the final remarks Governor Seymour made to his vastly approving audience on the Fourth . . ."

Rose Ann flipped the pages of her notebook over, searching for those remarks. She found them, read: "Remember this: that the bloody, treasonable, and revolutionary doctrine of public necessity can be proclaimed by a *mob* as well as a government!"

She hung there, staring at her so-called husband.

"Oh, Kurt, no!" she breathed.

"Oh, Rose, yes!" he mocked. Then, "You've some way to amuse

yourself this evening, I trust? I'd suggest that you join some of the patriotic Yankee ladies in this hotel you've become so friendly with and visit one of the hospitals. They're filling up with the victors of Gettysburg, I hear. Bloody business, that. And as a proper Bostonian, my sweet, your abolitionist sentiments should be constantly on display, your patriotism most fierce!"

"All right," Rose Ann said tonelessly, "I'll go to the hospital. Even though I hate going. Those poor boys—are so much like ours. Makes the whole thing—this cruel and stupid war between people who should be friends, even brothers—"

"And often are," Kurt interrupted her.

"Yes. And often are. Lots of Southerners stood by the Union, y'know. Which makes this war even more—sickening. Kurt, you're coming home soon—tonight?"

"I doubt it," he said coldly. "In fact, I may not come home at all. My *dear* friend John Andrews of Virginia is going to show me the sights—and introduce me to several sturdy, but useful citizens. From Five Points, Paradise Square, the Bloody Auld Sixth, and suchlike. I'm taking along a camphor-soaked handkerchief to overcome my natural aversion to their stench—and his—"

"Why? He seems clean enough. He's a lawyer, isn't he?"

"So he claims. I doubt it. And he is clean, as people of his class go, but he's a practical amalgamationist—and that—ugh!—rancid stink of the darker sister doesn't scrub away easily, it seems to me . . ."

"You mean he—he goes around with *colored* women?" Rose Ann breathed.

"Amend that to 'sleeps with.' Or rather to 'stays busily awake with,' to be more accurate. One in particular. Josephine Wilson, an old professional who has risen to the madamship of a house on Green Street. But since he has strong feelings against the darker brother, for all that he sees no contradiction to those feelings in his practice of wallowing with black wenches, and is most patriotic toward the Old Dominion and her cause, in spite of his being a thief, a fence for stolen goods, a pimp, and what have you, he should be *very* useful, especially when the fact that he has a degree of formal studies of some sort, and is deuced fluent of speech, is taken into consideration. He'll enable me to keep completely out of sight while he—poor bloody sod!—does just what I tell—and pay—him to . . ."

"And you're going to stay out all night—drinking with awful people like those—again?"

"Yes. Rather. In pursuit of the goals of our noble cause. Any—objections?"

"Yes. I—don't like sleeping alone, and you know it. You're—neglecting me, Kurt. And if you don't quit it, I'll—"

"Find someone else. Do. 'Twould be a relief, I assure you. A thought on the subject of masculine psychology, my dear. Maidenly reluctance, even resistance, lends—savor to the play. While—eager bitchery destroys it . . ."

"I'll run away for good!" she stormed. "I'll join Greg in Nashville and—"

"Nashville? So that's where the useless beggar is? Poorest excuse for a Secret Service agent I've ever run across." He fished in his waistcoat pocket, glanced at his watch, drawled, "Oh, well, I can spare you a quarter of an hour, I suppose. All right. Go into the bedroom. Strip. I haven't time to waste, y'know. I'll be along in a moment. I'd better make a note of a certain detail to pass along to Andrews before I forget it . . ."

"No!" she stormed. "I won't! I'm—a human being, Kurt! A woman. I need—I want—"

"What?" he said in a tone of utter weariness, total boredom.

"Love," she whispered. "A word you don't even understand. It's not—*that*. Or it's not *just* that. All right, you can always—make me —respond. Bring me around."

"So?" he said.

"But I—I'm tired of—of feeling so—so sick, afterward. So—used. I want to feel warm—and tender—and loved. I want to feel happy, Kurt! Not worn out and tired and disgusted with myself for being so—so easy for you. So spraddle-legged loose and—and dirt cheap. Cheap? Huh! I'm yours for free. You don't even pay me with a smile, a caress, a little kindness—a honeyed word. No—it's always whip and spur, isn't it? You take advantage of an inborn defect in my nature: that I was built in a boiler works, and they forgot to put in a safety valve to cool me off when I build up a head o' steam and all my gauges spin around and around like crazy! My whole life long I've paid the price for being a red-haired McKenzie woman: that all men have ever wanted from me were my tits and my tail, never *me* a person, living, yearning, dreaming in this world. Even—thinking, once in a while. Having immortal longings in me. So now—go away. Find somebody else to—ride. To turn into a sweaty, drippy—mess in a mucked-up bed. Smelling like the morning after a busy night in a parlor house. Crying 'cause her own body has cheated on her again. Acted like the treacherous

bitch thing you've trained it into. When it ought to be—the temple
of the soul. The soul of—a good woman, Kurt. A wife. A mother.
So go—away. Get out of here, you hear me!"

He smiled, his gray eyes floe ice, stepped up to her, caught her
by the back of her neck as one catches a rebellious dog. Kissed her
cruelly, hurting her mouth, breaking her lips against her teeth,
until she opened them, shuddering convulsively against his own,
slackening, blooming, blood-gorged, sweet-sighing, lost. He went
on kissing her, caressing her, until he had the response he sought,
until he felt her flesh convulse into waves of shuddering, taper wax
melting, become an anguished scald, the beginning of a cry.

And then he stopped. On the intake of her first sobbing breath.
Straightened up. Stepped back.

"Oh, Kurt, Kurt—please!" she moaned.

"Your lesson for tonight," he said. "You'll always await my return, Rose Ann, however long I may choose to stay away. And by
the way, don't bedevil those poor wounded beggars in the hospital,
will you? I rather fancy they aren't up to it . . ."

Then, very calmly, he turned and walked out of there.

When, three days later, on Monday, July 13, 1863, there began
what was to be known to history as the New York Draft Riots,
practically everyone agreed that they had broken out almost by
spontaneous combustion, fueled by the poorer citizens' resentment
at the clause in the Enrollment and Conscription Act that allowed
a rich man to "bombproof" his cowardly hide by armor-plating it
with the shot-torn carcass of some starveling beggar he'd paid
three hundred dollars to take his place. But Rose Ann McKenzie,
who all her life had been either blessed with or cursed by the
possession of an independent mind, while freely conceding the
resentment, was far from convinced of the spontaneity.

For one thing, she had been present with Kurt at the Academy
of Music on Fourteenth Street when Independence Day had been
celebrated in what seemed to her a most peculiar fashion. She had
heard those speeches. They rang and resonated through her
weirdly bright little mind. How spontaneous is a fire when you
pour coal oil all over the place, and then throw in a lighted match?
she asked herself. And from last Monday, the one after the Fourth,
the papers have done nothing but pile fat resinous pine lightwood
onto the blaze! She picked up Benjamin Wood's New York *Daily
News* and read: "The manner in which the draft is being conducted
in New York is such an outrage upon all decency and fairness as

has no parallel and can find no apologists. The evident aim of those who have the Conscription Act in hand, in this state, is to lessen the number of Democratic votes at the next election . . ."

The Journal of Commerce cried: "Those in power in Washington are using the draft for their own ends. Some men say, 'Now that the war has commenced, it must not be stopped till slaveholding is abolished.' Then the *Journal* added, in italics: *"Such men are neither more nor less than murderers."*

The New York *World,* in a long, furious article, compared the Draft Act with the press gangs that the British Navy had used to kidnap poor Englishmen in former times, then sending them to their deaths at sea. "The only difference we can discern," thundered the *World,* "is that the draft is incomparably worse."

On the other side of the fence, Horace Greeley's New York *Tribune* printed a story meant to shock, under the bold headline: PRO-REBEL ATTEMPT AT REVOLUTION, but then, hedging its bets, buried the story on an inside page. Rose Ann read:

> That the more determined sympathizers in this vicinity with the Slaveholders' Rebellion have for months conspired and plotted to bring about a revolution in the North which should place the whole tier of Free States bordering on the Slave region in alliance with and practical subordination to the Rebel Confederacy, is just as certain as that we are involved in Civil War. Had Meade been defeated at Gettysburg —as the Copperheads had no doubt he would be—they would have been ready to raise the flag of rebellion and proclaim McClellan the head of a Provisional Government. Here follows one of their manifestos which was extensively circulated through our city on the night before the 4th . . .

But Rose Ann didn't read the copy of the manifesto that the *Tribune* had printed. She didn't need to: she had the original, or at least one of the originals. She had found it in Kurt's coat pocket on Sunday morning while her *soi-disant* husband was sleeping off the effects of the monumental drinking bout he had indulged in with the seedy John U. Andrews and his even seedier friends the whole of Saturday night. Beyond making him sleepy, liquor had no discernible effect on Kurt. She knew he rather disliked it, and seldom drank, since he held that a member of the master race must always be in perfect control of himself, but when he did drink—always for some conspiratorial purpose—he managed the "vile, abominable stuff," as he called it, very well indeed.

General McClellan? she thought now. What's he got to do with it? One of old Greeley's crackpot ideas, sure as shooting. This here gem of literachew is pure, unmitigated Kurt Radetzy! She read:

> The Federal government has become a filthy hybrid; a monster smeared with the bloody sacrifice of its own children; detestable compound of crimes and vices; a despotism which cannot fitly be described in decorous language . . .

Hmmmmmn, she thought. You should know about crimes and vices, Kurtie-poo, 'cause Lord knows, you're an expert at both . . . And even, come to think of it, at decorous language. You very seldom use a cuss word, d'you? . . . She went on reading:

> Should the Confederate Army capture Washington and exterminate the herd of thieves, Pharisees, and cutthroats who pasture there, defiling the temple of our liberty, we should regard it as a special interposition of Divine Providence in behalf of justice, judgment, and mercy.

Rose Ann looked up from her reading. Frowned thoughtfully. She had seen the error that literate people, especially when they were as intellectual as Kurt was, always commit: the illusion that the written word ever has, or even can have, any immediate effect upon what goes on in life. It doesn't. Doers are seldom influenced by the processes of cogitation or reflection. And thinkers don't *do*.

Besides, she saw at once, here the problem was even more basic: How the devil did Kurt ever hope to rouse to destructive fury through his much too ornate prose people who couldn't read their own names, and who used newspapers only for the essential purpose that—from the standpoint of poetic justice, anyhow!—they are perhaps best suited for?

Then it came to her: The illiterate can always be reached through the thunder, passion, magic, rhythm, mind-stunning mesmerism of the spoken word. Which meant—Andrews. John U. Andrews of Virginia, self-proclaimed attorney-at-law. Rose Ann had met him by then. He had called on Kurt several times during the week that followed the Fourth of July. He was tall, well favored, with blue eyes, light brown hair, and a sandy beard. He spoke well and fluently, in an almost cultivated Virginia drawl. And yet—

He belonged in the same category as Yankee Lieutenant Froggie Boy had: he was the kind of man that no woman in her right mind could ever love. And the fact that he wasn't at all bad-looking changed that dismal aspect of his personality not at all. John Andrews just didn't have that mysterious aura by which a man attracts a woman. Rose Ann and her generation called it "animal magnetism." Her descendants would call it "sex appeal."

But whatever it was, John U. Andrews didn't have it. He could only find a pitiful, badly faked counterfeit of love with a hired slut in a rented bed, and being not without sensitivity, he soon realized that the strumpets of his own race didn't trouble to hide the instinctive disdain that all women feel for a zero to the left of the decimal point like him with the degree of care that would have prevented his perceiving it. So he had turned to black whores in the idiotic presumption that the attentions of a lordly *white man*— by God!—like him would be flattering, and was accidentally rewarded: the poor bedraggled black bitches he consorted with were far better at dissimulation than their white sisters for hire, rent, or sale ever were. The abysmal conditions of their lives and the rock-bottom bigotry of their times forced them to be. The alternative was a relatively quick death by hunger instead of their habitual slow demise by drugs, disease, and the abuse inflicted upon them by their clients and their pimps.

Even so, John U. Andrews—of Virginia!—was left with a festering wound to the very core of his self-esteem that converted him into a two-legged bombshell waiting for the occasion to explode. On July 13, 1863, and the four days following it, duly primed by a megalomaniacal monster named Sisimond Kurt Radetzy, he found it. And from one end to the other, the island of Manhattan burst into flame.

The first three days the riots lasted, Rose Ann didn't go out at all. Most of the time, Kurt stayed with her in their suite at the Fifth Avenue Hotel, with only occasional forays into the streets "to check developments," as he put it. She guessed that he was taking unusual care, after the debacle of their efforts in Washington, to make sure that no one associated his name, face, or presence with the flare-up of the most absolutely destructive riots in the history of the United States.

But she soon noticed something: He quite often returned from his sightseeing expeditions in a decidedly amorous mood. Rose Ann, of course, didn't even bother to inquire into the reason for this state of things; after suffering weeks of almost complete neglect from this icy aberration she had married—the legality of the ceremony being quite beyond the point, in view of the total honesty of her intentions—she simply proceeded to have herself what she naïvely and candidly called "an ever-loving ball!"

Being, as she was, several quite contradictory people rolled up into one decidedly fetching package: a highborn Virginia belle, a proper Bostonian, and a true Victorian (this last most of all, since it meant she was a charter member of one of the most sexually bedeviled generations in modern history, the one whose heroic efforts to suppress, even eliminate their own almost volcanically ardent natures was to fasten more traumas, nervous breakdowns, quirks, aberrations, deviations, and crimes *contra naturam* upon them and their immediate descendants than any other since Messalina reigned in Rome), she had no idea what was responsible for that first marvelous—and marvelously busy!—session she had with her Kurtie pie. Nor did Kurt, at first. It was only much later, thinking back over events, that he remembered his earlier experience with the *Totenköpfer* squad of the Austrian Secret Police, and realized just what it was that had triggered him into desire.

That morning, dressed in workman's clothes, unshaven, with his face most artistically smudged and dirty, Kurt had watched the assault of the mob, led by "the Black Jokes," a volunteer fire company, so called because that was the name they'd given to their beloved hand-pumped engine, upon the Third Avenue Enrollment Office at number 677, near the corner of Forty-sixth Street. At the moment the building was blazing merrily. From the upper stories, the tenants—poor Irish families, exactly like the howling crowds below them—came tumbling out into the avenue. The mob beat some of them back; they wanted to see them burn. By then, they'd killed two half-crippled members of the Invalid Corps sent to put them down, one of whom was said to be a veteran of Fredericksburg, and, catching him alone, had beaten Police Superintendent John A. Kennedy not merely into insensibility but into total unrecognizability as well. Now other buildings on the block were catching fire. The mob milled about aimlessly, waving placards that proclaimed NO DRAFT! in still-wet red paint, the letters scrawled, badly formed.

Kurt saw a man, whom he perhaps alone of all those thousands recognized, climb upon the roof of the watchman's shanty on a construction site across the street from the burning buildings. For the first time John U. Andrews of Virginia had appeared upon the stage of history, from which he was, within another week or two, so totally and mysteriously to disappear.

He was, Kurt saw, nattily attired. He had on a blue coat, striped trousers. His short blond beard was freshly and neatly trimmed.

"You have done nobly!" he cried out. "But I tell you what I want and what you must do if you wish to be really successful! You must organize!"

"That's the talk!" the mob roared back. "You're the b'hoy, me chicken!"

"You must organize and keep together!" Andrews howled. "You must appoint leaders, and crush this damned abolition draft into the dust!"

"That's the ticket, me bully b'hoy!" the crowd bellowed. "Give the dommed naygur-lovers hell!"

"If you don't find anyone to lead you," Andrews cried, "by heaven, I'll do it myself!"

Kurt shook his head sadly, moved off. As he'd thought, the man was a fool. He'd instructed him to stir the mob up, but he'd warned him to take no prominent part in the action. Because if the coppers arrested John U. Andrews, they'd beat a confession out of him with their nightsticks inside of five minutes, and the jig would be up for one Kurt Radetzy as well. Of course, Andrews was expendable, but not on the *first* day of the rioting. To wreck New York City to the extent that would force even the present Republican administration under Mayor Opdyke to surrender to the strong Copperhead movement's demand that the metropolis secede from the Union and make a separate peace with the Confederacy would take, Kurt judged, at least five days. But as he moved away, he saw that Andrews had climbed down from his perch and was losing himself among the crowd.

Good! he thought. The vain ass is following instructions, after all. But he's mucked things, rather, dressing like a Beau Brummell. I told him he was not to make himself so bloody conspicuous . . .

As he wandered about the streets, Kurt saw things were going better. That spontaneous mob was spontaneously cutting all the telegraph wires, and even—spontaneously again, of course!—chopping down the telegraph poles with axes. In that day before the telephone, each of the thirty-two precincts in New York was connected with every other by Samuel Morse's invention; each had its trained, lightning-fast telegrapher. The Central was the Thirteenth Precinct on Mulberry Street. But now that spontaneous, disorganized mob was making coordination among the forces of law and order impossible.

A crew of winsome Irish lassies, any one of whom could have strangled a full-grown ox with her dainty hands, and the lightest of whom weighed fifteen stone, were blithely tearing up the tracks of the Fourth Avenue street railway with crowbars, so Kurt had to admit that disorganization and spontaneity were working jolly fine.

He decided not to attend the attack on the armory at Second Avenue and Twenty-first Street, or on the so-called steam works one block north. He didn't want to be seen at the pivotal point of the master scheme of that major and crucial battle of the Civil War, because he suspected that there were plainclothesmen mingling with the mob and that a countenance as unusual as his was, was sure to be remembered. Besides, he had come to the conclusion that an Irish bully b'hoy with liquor in his gut was one of the single most savage creatures on the face of the earth, so he judged it to be deuced unwise to be anywhere within range when they got their hands on the muskets, rifles, carbines, and other small arms in the armory. Even less did he want to be anywhere close to one of those lovely and gentle colleens, because he'd already seen them in action that morning. Anything their men were capable of the women could easily triple. Kurt had seen those Irish women whom on the morrow all the papers would label "Amazons" take bayonets from the Invalid Corps and stab those poor crippled devils with them, and with their kitchen knives reduce a fallen patrolman to bloody hash in something under two minutes flat.

So he joined the smaller mob that was surging up Fifth Avenue with the express intention of sacking the palatial home of Republican Mayor George Opdyke. By then looting had become general, and every store in the block between Twenty-fourth and Twenty-fifth streets on Broadway had already been stripped and set afire.

But the assault on Mayor Opdyke's home failed. A certain Colonel B. F. Manierre, who lived nearby, called out forty or fifty of the mayor's neighbors to stand guard, armed with revolvers, shotguns, and rifles, which, since most of them were wealthy sportsmen, they possessed in God's own plenty. These aristocrats cowed the mob quite easily. So far unarmed, and not yet as drunk as they'd be by night, the bully b'hoys hadn't the stomach for that kind of opposition . . .

So they drifted south down the avenue until they came to the Colored Orphan Asylum between Forty-third and Forty-fourth streets. And there they stopped. Kurt heart the mutters: "Dommed naygurs! Wasn't fur them they'd be no dommed war, and no double-goddommed draft! Kill the naygurs! 'N' after that kill iver livin' Black Republican naygur-worshipping sonuvabitch in town, 'n' burn their foine houses!"

Some more kindly soul among them said, "Hell, the li'l black bastids ain't nuthin' but kids. Leave 'em alone, sez I . . ."

"Hell, naw! They's naygurs, ain't they? 'N' they'll grow up to be black liver-lipped woolly-haid apes jist like the rest!"

Kurt stood there, smiling his ice-bright, maniacal smile. That he loathed, despised, and detested blacks was not, for his times, unusual. Nor, one suspects, for any times whatsoever. That feeling is instinctive, visceral, and incurable. It inhabits the psyches of one hundred percent of the Caucasian race. Whatever slight amelioration has been effected since that day has come about because a fairly sizable minority of whites have learned, or have been taught, to be ashamed of it.

Where Kurt differed from his fellows was not in his hatred of blacks—and, of course, of Jews—but in his calm conviction that genocide was not only possible but feasible. To him, the Latins and the Slavs would supply a sufficiency of slaves to humbly serve the needs—and the whims!—of his peerless race; therefore, such ugly, brutish subhumans as the blacks were expendable. That the Jews had also to be done away with was an idea that existed on another level altogether in his mind. He paid them the compliment of considering them not superfluous, but dangerous. In a way, he feared them. To him, the Jews were ethical cancer cells, undermining the pure, hardy, virile, cruel social fabric of the *Herrenvolk—ergo, Judea delenda est* as well.

So now he stood there, shivering with anticipatory joy at the thought of the pleasure that witnessing the massacre of two hundred black children, all of whom were under twelve years of age, was going to afford him.

But his pleasure was thwarted. William Davis, superintendent of the orphan asylum, accurately judged the temper of the mob. He had his assistants bolt the front door and pile furniture up behind it. Then they led the trembling, frightened children out the back door and across the grounds behind the orphanage to Madison Avenue. They were busily loading them aboard the omnibuses there when it occurred to Kurt that every little black and kinky head had disappeared from the windows of the upper story. He raced around through Forty-fourth to Madison and saw what was going on. Catching a huge and hugely drunken Irishman by the arm, he howled: "Run around front to Fifth Avenue! Tell your pals they're letting the little niggers get away!"

The big man stumbled off. But by the time he got to Fifth Avenue, he'd quite forgotten why he was even heading in that direction, not to mention that anyone had given him a message. He sat down on a curb and began to pull on his bottle.

After a while, Kurt realized that if the mob didn't arrive at Madison Avenue soon, Davis and his assistants were going to have all the little blacks aboard the omnibuses and on their way to the Twenty-second Precinct police station and safety before they got there. So he ran around to Fifth Avenue again to summon them. By then he was too late; the mob was inside the asylum. He stood there watching in cool disappointment the destruction being perpetrated upon the handsome building by the people who had been admitted to the United States of North America en masse in order to keep them from starving to death in their native land—those were the years of the potato famine, remember—to whom every facility had been extended, including twenty-four-hour naturalization papers from the stalwarts of Tammany Hall, and who were now repaying the generosity of an at times far too generous nation by rioting before they'd consent to serve in her armed forces and practically destroying her largest city.

Then a man appeared in one of the upper-story windows. He had a child in his arms—a black girl child nine years old. Somehow, she had been overlooked.

"Here!" the man called out. "Foine naygur meat!"

And hurled her down. Kurt was too far away to hear the sickening thud her small body made when it hit. But by then those blithe and winsome colleens from the Auld Sod were upon her. They moved in with crowbars, brickbats, their oh so dainty feet.

Kurt elbowed his way in close, stood there looking down at that. A smear of bright blood. A jumble of broken bones, piercing through purplish black and bluish red. A splatter of too white teeth. A red eyeball dangling on the grayish string of an optic nerve across what had been a cheek. A child. An orphan girl, nine years old. But the ethics of the matter escaped him. He had his people's berserker love for blood and death.

And it was then that that feeling hit him. He felt the searing stab of the purest, most bestial lust he'd ever experienced in all his thirty-three years of life. He whirled, already running. From where he was, the Fifth Avenue Hotel wasn't very far. He raced southward, toward Madison Square.

But in the following days, his plans, and those of the other conspirators that sheer logic indicates were—had to be—behind the wrecking of the Union's greatest city, went awry. Caleb Henry's paradox—that there can never be a brilliant soldier or an efficient slave, because the intelligence necessary for the successful performance of the tasks assigned to either would preclude a man's submitting to the dangers of the one or the ignominy of the other—here applied. The mob was, after all, a mob. It very likely *wanted* to follow instructions such as the ones that John U. Andrews—of Virginia!—poured into their ears. But being a mob, it couldn't.

Item: The attack upon the armory on Second Avenue at Twenty-first Street was carried out in fine style. But while the bolder and surely the more intelligent of that horde were upstairs inside the building, snatching up the old smoothbore muskets, the newer rifled Springfields, and, newer still, the Sharps breechloaders whose worth Colonel Berdan's specialist marksmen had proved for all time at Gettysburg, as well as—it is possible—even some of the eight-shot Spencer and fifteen-shot Henry repeaters that were going to be used at Chickamauga before September of that year was out, cramming their pockets with paper cartridges (with the leaden balls in one end of them tied away from the powder in the cartridge proper with a piece of string, and the whole thing closed by twisting the loose end into a rat's tail), grabbing bayonets, revolvers, everything in sight, and throwing them out of the windows of that third-floor drill hall to their jug buddies in the street, the police arrived.

The b'hoys and the colleens in the street had scant taste for the feel of a locustwood billy club against their craniums; they scattered to the four winds. Those inside on the ground floor made a break for it. The coppers made mush of their noggins; those still on their feet beat it back inside. Upstairs, on the third floor, the Amazons and their bully warriors barricaded themselves to resist attack.

And then, of course, someone with a can of turpentine, which that spontaneous mob, in their total and casual disorganization, always seemed to have with them, set the armory afire. It was a very old wooden building, tinder dry. It went up like a torch. Colleens and b'hoys tumbled out of every window. Those who carried no weapons, the coppers didn't touch. But they beat the brains out of everything in pants or skirts with a gun in its paws. On the third floor, in the drill hall, the raiders quickly learned the facts of modern warfare: that loading a smoothbore musket was one thing but ramming a ball home down a rifled barrel was another altogether—that is, if you'd even been lucky enough to pick up cartridges with the right-sized ball in 'em in the first place, and if you could see to load at all through the choking smoke. There was no time for men who'd never before had one in their hands to figure out how a breechloader worked, and the brass-cased cartridges of the repeaters baffled them utterly. Anyhow, by then the smoke was shot through with flame.

So they jumped from those third-floor windows and died on the stones below or, converted into quadruple paraplegics, lay there and screamed. At that, they were lucky. The majority of the b'hoys and colleens in the armory didn't get out at all.

Three weeks later, the garbage collectors carried away fifty barrels crammed with human bones to potter's field. And the next day, of course, the police backed up a line of wagons before the Union Steam Works and hauled those new carbines away.

Item: Of course, it occurred to that spontaneous, leaderless mob to attack Horace Greeley's *Tribune,* which had had the city's numerous Copperheads foaming through their fangs for years. Old White Coat, as the mobs called him, could be legitimately damned as a "naygur-lover," so the mob did attack the *Trib,* three times, and thrice were beaten off. But the defenders of the spontaneous-combustion, legitimate-public-ire theory of the Draft Riots' origin were hard put to explain the assault upon Webb & Allen's shipyard and the attempt to burn the ironclad ram *Dunderberg,* nearing completion for the U.S. Navy there. The mob did have its valid grievances; this *was,* all too often, "a rich man's war, but a poor man's fight!" Yet to destroy—or try to—a mighty weapon whose only use was against the Confederacy didn't fit the popular theory very well. In all New York, only the *Tribune* and the *Times* knew how to spell the word "treason" in those days.

From her suite in the Fifth Avenue Hotel, Rose Ann could hear the roar of cannon as the troops began to clear the streets with canister and grape. During the last three days, her Kurtie pie had sallied forth more often than ever. And always, when he returned, the results were the same. He'd pick her up, toss her into bed, and indulge in a magistral bout of concupiscence that left her sweat-soaked, mouth-bruised, hair wild-tangled, and the whole of her trembling with exhaustion.

What she didn't know was that Kurt had given up, conceded that his—and his Copperhead friends'—plan to force the city of New York to leave the Union was a failure. It could only have succeeded if their attacks on the armory and the steam works, incited by the cries of Andrews and other *agents provocateurs*—"Arm yourselves, boys! To the armory! To the armory!"—had actually resulted in the mob's being able to procure enough firearms and—what ultimately proved more important, for it is in the overlooking of such seemingly minor details that the grandiose schemes of megalomaniacs always fail—sufficient and *matching* ammunition to have stood off not only the police but the troops now pouring into the city. Many of those troops had fought at Gettysburg and were killing mad at what they rightly considered a betrayal of their fallen comrades by the unruly, largely Irish slum dwellers of the metropolis.

And there too lay another miscalculation on the part of Kurt and Reptilian Company. They simply hadn't believed that New York's eighty percent Irish police force would take the stern measures they did take with their compatriots. But New York's finest were solid citizens and believers in law and order. What's more, they were bitterly ashamed, even outraged by the behavior of people of their own race, and shocked to the core of their pious souls by the almost unbelievable ferocity the female members of the mob displayed. So they cracked thick Celtic craniums right lustily and, when they had to, opened fire. What's more—to give fairness her voice—not all the Irish poor joined in the revolt. In almost every neighborhood there was a family or two who refused to join in pillage and murder. Some of them graced their race and faith by taking in and hiding the blacks who rapidly became the chief victims of the mob's fury.

Besides, Kurt & Friends had simply forgotten New York's second-largest ethnic minority, the Germans. At times in their history, the Teutons' respect for authority and blind obedience to any order firmly given has been a vice, because it has enabled forceful madmen to lead them to disaster. But in New York City, in July 1863, it was the salvation of entire neighborhoods. The Germans did not join the mobs. They barred their doors, kept quiet, and waited for the *Sturm und Drang* to blow over.

So, on those final days, having acknowledged defeat, Count Sisimond Kurt Radetzy simply went out to enjoy the spectacle provided him by sheer bestiality unleashed. By then all political considerations had been forgotten; the mob was simply following its natural bent toward sheer wanton destructiveness, looting, and racial hatreds. For New York's numerous black population, the city had become a hideously dangerous inferno.

They caught black William Jones on the corner of Clarkson Street with the loaf of bread that was to have been his breakfast beneath his arm. They hanged him to a tree and loosed the women on him. After those shrieking harridans and harpies had ripped him to shreds, they built a fire beneath his feet. When the police cut him down, the loaf of bread was still beneath his arm, only now it was charred black. At Washington and Leroy streets, one block north of the place where Jones's unrecognizable corpse was swinging, they caught another black named Williams and repeated the performance. Peter Hueston wasn't even a black; he was a Mohawk Indian. Small difference: his complexion didn't appeal to the aesthetic sensibilities of the b'hoys and biddies. They surrounded him, kicking, left him for dead on the sidewalk. He wasn't. Not then. Four days later, from a bed in Bellevue, he went to join the Great Spirit of his ancestors.

Restaurants which had black waiters were wrecked, the tumbledown tenements housing them destroyed. In one such, in the section known as the New Bowery, the black tenement dwellers were unlucky. The mob chased them back into the building, barred the doors, doused the place with turpentine, and watched, howling with glee, as the blacks, driven to the roof by the flames, hung from the eaves until their fingers burned through. One by one they dropped to the street below. At once the mob was upon them, kicking and clubbing. And so they died.

So, granted his somewhat less than overwhelming fondness for the darker brother, Kurt was having himself the time of his icy murderer's life. And poor Rose Ann was paying the consequences of the arousal of instincts in him which seemingly couldn't be aroused in any other way. At that time Havelock Ellis was four years old; Sigmund Freud, seven. A pity. For Kurt Radetzy would have been wonderful material for their weighty tomes. It is curious how badly he chose his time to be born, for the quite remarkable aberration of his life escaped the attention not only of the scientists but of the literary men as well. You see, Donatien Alphonse François, *Comte* de Sade had been dead nearly fifty years by that late date, while Leopold von Sacher-Masoch, who was both Kurt's compatriot and contemporary, being six years his junior, wouldn't get around to publishing the series of novels that would accurately describe one of the—sternly repressed!—aspects of his personality until long after Sisimond Kurt Radetzy would have ceased to trouble the world of living men.

Yet now, having brought Rose Ann to the very edge of sheer damnation, Kurt proceeded, quite accidentally of course, to put her small and dainty feet firmly back on the road toward salvation.

How? To repeat, the major sexual organ in the human species is the mind. In physical love, subjectivity is everything. And one of the things that her instinctive subjectivity teaches the more highly evolved female mind is that neither she nor any other woman can live, breathe, have her being, and above all *love*—without tenderness.

And since this element is *normally* absent from the brute male's psyche, the result of this age-old dysfunction between the sexes inevitably is that when the male partner, transformed into the god Pan, satyr, goat, appears at all hours rearing for immediate action, snorting, foaming, tumescent, wild, the reaction of the female, more often than not, becomes sheer, sick, shuddering—disgust.

In short, Rose Ann now discovered that that imaginary creation of overheated male concupiscent dreams, a nymphomaniac, she wasn't, that she jolly well wanted to be let alone a goodly portion of the time, and that, above all, she wanted to be *loved*. What she meant by that, she wasn't entirely sure, but she knew that it didn't consist of being raped, violated, outraged, penetrated both fore and aft, simultaneously strangled and devoured, and finally bullbeast-stallion For-Unlawful-Carnal-Knowledged out of her ever-loving mind!

Her complaints that enough of a thing was enough served her for nothing, so finally it came to her what to do. It was a curious fact that money, as such, meant nothing to Kurt; he valued it only for the power it placed in his hands. Therefore he was generous to a fault; he had spent a sizable portion of the sums he had gained on the stock market in London's City and continued to gain on New York's Wall Street—where his uncanny flair for successful investment in high-risk stocks had gained him a following of hangers-on who begged him for "hot tips"—on a matched set of magnificent emeralds for Rose Ann, necklace, earrings, choker, tiara, rings, even a jeweled stomacher to be worn around her tiny waist, all because they matched her sea-green eyes, and attracted the attention and the envy of men and women alike whenever she wore them to the opera, the theater, or a ball.

So now she took the whole collection down to Tiffany's on

Union Square, determined to sell it to obtain the money to speed her flight. I'll go to—Nashville, she thought. Join—Greg there. That is, if he'll even have me now. If he won't, I don't know what I'll do. Kill myself, maybe. Better that way, 'cause then I won't ever get too tempted to relieve Gwen of—Cabe . . .

At New York's foremost jewelers, she was asked to leave her treasure, over a signed and itemized receipt of course, until a careful and, they assured her, fair assessment of their value could be made. But the last time—during one of Kurt's absences—she had made her way down there, in a cab whose driver constantly changed his route for fear of the mobs, they had been closed, for the same reason. So now she started out again, but before leaving the hotel, which had been barricaded and had a company of soldiers stationed in it for its protection, she remembered something: On her last trip downtown, a crowd of women had cut her hansom cab off. But when she'd poked her head out to ask them to stop chivying her driver, they'd seen her bright red hair under her saucy bonnet and her clear green eyes in her freckled face, so one of those monstrous Irish women, who weighed all of two hundred pounds or more, had sung out: "Be ye Irish, me pretty dear?"

To which Rose Ann, reflecting that a good many of her ancestors *had* been Irish and that there wasn't much difference between the Scots and the Irish anyhow, had answered, "Yes!"

"Pass on, dearie!" the huge woman had cried, and that had been that. So now Rose went back to their suite with the intelligent idea of transforming herself into an inconspicuous replica of a slum colleen. Actually, it proved simple: an old brown dress with no crinoline under it—slum women couldn't afford *cages américaines*—her glorious hair combed loose, a smudge of soot from the fireplace on her forehead, and she was sure she'd pass muster.

But before she could leave the suite, Kurt reappeared and sternly forbade her going out at all.

"As I suspected," he growled. "The Irish, as a race, are stark, raving mad. So you stay here, Rose Ann, until I return!" Then he pulled out a brace of revolvers and proceeded to reload them. Which took him quite a time, since the revolvers weren't Smith & Wessons—the *only* handgun in that epoch using the brass-cased combined cartridges and bullets that nowadays are called simply bullets—but very likely Colts. Which meant he had to load each chamber with loose powder from a small powder horn, tamp down each of the six round balls on top of the powder with the loading lever, which was nothing more than a miniature hinged ramrod,

272

and after that fit a copper percussion cap to the nipple on the back end of each of the six chambers. Watching him do all that, Rose Ann realized why the Union officers who had managed to find and purchase Smith & Wessons considered them jewels beyond all price. The tiny one Colin had given her could be loaded fully inside of a minute, and now it occurred to her she'd better lay in a supply of the brass-cased .22 caliber cartridges for it—if she could find any.

But she waited patiently until he'd finished repeating that tedious operation twelve times; then, after he had stormed out of there, she followed him. He headed east on Twenty-first Street, racing along so fast she was hard put to keep him in sight. When he got to Lexington Avenue, he turned north. Again she followed him. Afterward, she was sorry.

In those days, above Forty-second Street, Lexington Avenue had many vacant lots. In one of them, a group of Negroes had been cornered. They were evidently families, for there were men, women, and children among them. Some of the children were babies in their mothers' arms, the others from five to ten years old, but, all the same, a gang of bully b'hoys and a few colleens were beating their brains out with clubs or using them for target practice with the carbines and pistols they had stolen from a sporting-goods shop less than a block away that they'd broken into and wrecked.

Then, as she watched, her darling Kurtie pie opened fire, demonstrating his matchless marksmanship. His special delight seemed to be to shoot the babies out of their mothers' arms. He was surrounded by burly Irishmen who let out a lusty cheer each time he fired.

But he had exploded no more than three small black faces into blobs of crimson before Rose Ann was upon him, her hands curved into claws, her fingers raking for his eyes. He sidestepped deftly, shifted that heavy service sidearm to his left hand, and drawing back his right, slapped her so hard that she measured her full length on the ground. Instantly a crowd of elephantine biddies surged forward screaming: "Kill the naygur-lovin' bitch! Stomp 'er!"

But Kurt lifted a languid hand, said pleasantly, "Nay, lassies, let 'er be. The wench is me missus. But sure it is, I 'aven't trained 'er right, methinks. T'night, I'll stripe 'er wee bum fer 'er, fer fair!"

Rose Ann lay there, gathering her strength. She was sorry she hadn't brought her little pistol with her. At that moment, she would have killed Kurt, and gladly. She didn't ask herself why. She didn't need to. To her, any man who would deliberately murder a child, even if said child were black, deserved nothing short of death.

But she couldn't stay there. To witness that was more than she could bear. She told herself that she loved Negroes too much to see them killed. Which was quite true. That she also loved Prince Rupert, her horse, all the dogs on McKenzie's Hundred, the sheep, and the slaves in exactly the same fashion—except that the slaves occasionally exasperated her beyond all bearing by behaving in ways that shook her rock-bottom Southern conviction that they were at least one evolutionary step below true humanity—was equally true. If she had had to kill a chicken for dinner, she would have starved to death. She just wasn't prepared to see any of her pet animals killed, and whether they had two legs or four didn't especially matter.

So she got up from there, and ran off, moving southward. Kurt didn't try to stop her; he was having too much fun. By then, none of the horsecars of the street railways were running; neither were the omnibuses (which were also, of course, drawn by horses, but differed from the horsecars by looking more like elongated coaches than cars and more importantly by the fact that they didn't run on rails, as the horsecars did) or even the lighter, smaller, faster, yellow-painted coaches called "bobtailed stages." That mob, in its spontaneity and disorganization, had set out to bring New York City to a standstill and had very nearly done it.

But the hansom cabs and the hacks were running, because the mob, considering their drivers to be members of the proletariat, generally let hacks and cabs alone. But they weren't doing very much business; nobody in his right mind was wandering about the streets of a city in the hands of mobs so rabid and so dangerous that already on two widely separated sections of Thirty-second Street—yesterday at its intersection with Second Avenue and not an hour ago where it crossed Eighth Avenue—they had charged into the very mouths of cannon, light pieces, of course, only six-pounders, but loaded with canister and grapeshot. And on both occasions they had charged not once but *six* times, in spite of a carnage rivaling anything to be seen on such battlefields as Antietam and Fredericksburg. Thereafter, by the fluke that he had returned to his own home on Second Avenue to see how his wife and children fared, they caught Colonel H. J. O'Brien of the Eleventh New York Volunteers, who had *ordered* Lieutenant Eagelson to open fire with those six-pounders yesterday. He faced them saber and pistol in hand. But they knocked him down, beat him bloody, tied ropes to his feet, dragged him up and down the avenue. A priest passed by. They paused while the padre administered Extreme Unction to the dying man. Then the priest left, thinking, perhaps, that the author of yesterday's frightful bloodshed had it coming. After that they turned the colonel over to the women, who'd learned their trade by then. They dragged O'Brien into his own backyard and went to work on him with their knives with such commendable artistry that it took him all the rest of that long, hot afternoon to die.

By then close to one thousand people had died in the streets of New York City, so it occurred to Rose Ann that disposing of that many bodies with a riot still going on must have been more than a bit of a chore. So she pushed up the trapdoor in the roof of the hansom cab and asked the driver about that.

"They jist diappears, miss!" the driver said. "Them b'hoys come outa Five P'ints and the Auld Sixth 'n' carts 'em aw'y come dark. Them streets ain't paved, ye know, 'n' them tenements 'ave all got dirt floors. 'Tis sure I yam that they buries 'em all afore the break o' dawn . . . Well, here we be. Union Square, missy!"

Rose Ann got out of the cab, paid the driver, but before she could tell him to wait, as she fully intended to, a well-dressed man dashed up in great haste and commandeered the cab. Oh, well, she thought, I can always get another . . . She was dead, damned wrong. And that fact almost cost her her life.

Again Tiffany's was closed. The management weren't fools; by then they'd heard what had happened to Brooks Brothers' clothing store on Catherine Street. Jewelry is the perfect loot; it is small, light, easily carried away. And there were dozens, if not hundreds, of "fences" perfectly willing to take it off the looters' hands with no questions asked, at the tiniest fraction of its actual value. So they'd packed their geegaws and sparklers into their huge safe and prudently kept out of sight.

Despairingly, Rose Ann turned northward again, but walking now, for there wasn't a cab to be had in the neighborhood. A few blocks away from the Square, the mob caught her—and quite literally so. But they did her no harm. Her small elfin face had a definite Celtic cast; her eyes were green, her hair red as fox fire. And her slender, dainty form tickled the vagrant fancy of those big, beefy Irish women. They stopped the b'hoys from chivying her, took her by the arm. "Come along, me pretty lass!" they told her gaily. "We'll show ye a bit o' fun!"

Thereafter, half dead of weariness, Rose Ann found herself hustled from one side of the lower part of Manhattan to the other, and back again. To save her fair, sun-freckled hide, she engaged in looting, hurled brickbats at policemen. And hard as she tried to miss, she accidentally felled a stout copper, which endeared her to her captors all the more.

By then, she didn't even know where she was, though she had the general idea that she was considerably south of the district around Fourteenth Street she'd started homeward from. Then her luck ran out on her. And again the cause of her disaster was a child: a rather handsome, fairly light-complexioned mulatto boy. At the sight of him, her blithe and buxom companions from the Emerald Isle immediately began to screech, "Kill 'im! Stomp the little naygur!"

Rose Ann hung there a long moment. She just couldn't believe they really meant to do a horrible thing like that. But they did. And now they were starting to. Small and slight as she was, Rose Ann didn't even hesitate. She sailed into that herd of rogue cow-elephants like a tiny tigress. For a long moment their astonishment saved her, and thereafter another thing did: The little boy's mother appeared and joined the fray. Accept this as history: She was a white woman. Her name was Anne. The boy's father, a black sailor named Derrickson, was away at sea.

When Rose Ann regained consciousness again, she discovered that she was in a bed in Bellevue Hospital, it was Sunday, July 19, and the Draft Riots had been over nearly three full days. She lay there very quietly and stared at the ceiling through the narrow slits that were as far as she could open her eyes, both of which were decorated with two of the most artistic "shiners" ever seen in the whole of pugilistic history. Passing her tongue around the inside of her mouth, she found out that by a major miracle none of her teeth were missing. And aside from being covered with bruises from head to foot both fore and aft, and having only one, longitudinally fractured rib, she'd come through her battle with the Irish defenders of racial purity in fine shape.

So now she lay there and thought about what she'd better do. Number one was to prevent Kurt's finding out where she was. And since her head was the only thing about her that was in first-class working order, she immediately decided to pretend amnesia until she could get her bearings.

She could, she told the stiffly starched nurse who came to take down her personal data, remember being beaten up, but before that, nothing, not even her own name. The nurse believed her; she'd seen people whose memory hadn't come back for more than two years after a beating as bad as the one this poor slim girl had taken. And she cheerfully answered Rose Ann's questions; a young person so slender, soft-spoken, and obviously cultured as this battered little darling wasn't the kind of patient they generally had to deal with at Bellevue. Yes, the riots were over. Yes, she supposed that businesses would be opening again tomorrow morning. How many people had been killed? The papers estimated twelve hundred. She, from what she'd seen of the shot, slashed, crushed hulks brought in so far, thought that figure ought to be doubled, if not tripled. Rose Ann then asked whether she could talk to the poor woman who had been brought into the hospital the same time as she had . . . Of course—that is, if the poor thing ever regained consciousness. The doctors hoped to save her, but she, Nurse O'Mallory, doubted they'd be able to. The little boy? The little *colored* boy? Oh, he was taken to the city hospital on Blackwells Island; that's where they have all the colored children from the orphan asylum that was burned to the ground on Fifth Avenue. No, he wasn't hurt at all. Only—

Here Nurse O'Mallory stopped short. Her blue eyes opened very wide. She stared at Rose Ann in unrelieved horror.

"Miss," she whispered, "that child was—aw'fly light-colored. He isn't—isn't—"

"Mine?" Rose Ann said. She was too tired and depressed and sore all over to even feel offended. "No. He was—hers. The other woman's. That's what I want to ask her about. I just don't understand how she—a young, nice-looking *white* woman could—"

Nurse O'Mallory shook her head in aching wonder. In sorrow.

"Me neither," she said.

But ten days later, just before she left the hospital, and some weeks still before Anne Derrickson died from the effects of the beating those colleens had given her for her failure to uphold the purity and the dignity of the white race, Rose Ann did get to ask her that question. And got the answer she deserved, the one that was to trouble her mind life-long after that.

"I—love him. That's why I married him in the first place. What's —color—got to do with that? Or with—anything, really?" Anne Derrickson said.

It was all of ten days before the doctors would consent to let Rose Ann leave Bellevue. During the first five of them, she lay there shivering from her fear that any moment Kurt would appear at the hospital to claim her. But on the sixth or seventh day, it came to her that he probably didn't care enough about her to even bother, so she relaxed and concentrated upon hating him a little more than she already did. That feeling fueled her recovery. One bright morning she walked out of there, took a cab to Union Square. To Tiffany's.

She explained her shabby appearance on the truthful score that she'd been hospitalized as the result of mob violence. Her lodgings and her clothes, she lyingly declared, had both been burned. She needed money for new clothes, for the rental of a flat. Were they, she demanded, prepared to make a deal for her emeralds?

They offered her twenty-five thousand dollars for the lot, admitting from the outset that the emeralds were worth considerably more. But that was all they could afford to offer. If she wanted to try her luck with other jewelers, or even private purchasers, they could give her a list of names of both who conceivably might be interested, but even so, they doubted that they'd be able to sell them for very much more. There was a war on, the late—ah— disturbances had depressed prices, and—

Rose Ann accepted their offer. On their advice, since to carry that much cash around *was*, as they told her, dangerous, she took five thousand in cash and the rest in letters of credit, issued by the Morgan Trust Company, their bank. Any bank in the Union would honor them gladly, they assured her. Nashville? But of course, that fair Southern city had been in Union hands two years now. Life—and business—were entirely normal there . . .

Rose Ann spent the next three days shopping, staying the whole time at a modest rooming house. Then, splendidly attired all in black, she took a suite at the Metropolitan Hotel on Broadway at Prince Street, signing in as Rose Ann McKenzie and inscribing the word "widow" behind her name. That was entirely believable; widows, even stunning young widows, were in anything but short supply by August 1863. And as this one was obviously well supplied with cash, the hotel management, and the numerous sharpies hanging out in the lobby hoping for a "quick kill," found her charming. But she gave the sharpies no chance; she spent all her time in her "sky parlor," one of the Metropolitan's most noteworthy features, gazing down on Broadway far below.

The reason she didn't immediately leave for Nashville was simple. She had a burning desire to find out what had become of Kurt, and while she couldn't care less about her collection of Paris gowns still at the Fifth Avenue Hotel, she wanted that cut-down Sharps breechloader she'd also left there. From a wounded Yank among the many she'd visited at the hospital along with the delegations of wealthy ladies from the Fifth Avenue Hotel, whom she'd accompanied in order to establish her credentials as a "patriotic Bostonian," she'd heard in detail how fearsome the execution wrought by the new weapon in the hands of Colonel Berdan's "sharpshooters" had been at Gettysburg. She was endlessly stubborn: since she meant to be home to McKenzie's Hundred by Christmas, with, she rather hoped, Greg Forrester, but alone if need be, she was determined to put that breechloader in Colin's hands to be copied for her beloved Southern boys . . . But what if Kurt were still there, waiting for her? With that icy monster, one never knew . . .

Finally she hit upon the perfect strategy. She sent a note up to the management of the Fifth Avenue Hotel inquiring if Count and Countess Radetzy were numbered among their guests. She, her unsigned missive declared, had met them abroad and would like to renew the acquaintance if they were still in residence there . . .

Back came a reply posthaste: The Countess had disappeared during the late rioting; the Count, although grief-stricken—"I'll bet!" Rose Ann snorted aloud, reading that—had been called away from New York upon urgent business, but had left their suite paid for a full three months, as well as a missive and important sums for the Countess in the hotel's safe, should she finally appear. After so long a time, of course, the management feared the worst, but—

Rose Ann changed into white—also acceptable for widows—and took a cab uptown. The managers were delighted to see her. They had been terribly afraid that something dreadful had happened to her, for, after all, their fair city had passed through most troubled days . . .

Rose Ann was charmingly pathetic as she told them that something indeed had: Weeks in Bellevue Hospital, with her memory lost as the result of a rioter's blow. Only yesterday had it returned; she'd paused just long enough to purchase this simple frock, since the clothes she had been wearing were in rags.

"And my dearest darling husband?" she demanded.

The Count, they believed, was in Boston, Or, perhaps, in Philadelphia; they weren't sure. But the missive he had left her would certainly make known to her his whereabouts . . .

It did. She retired to her suite to read it. Kurt wrote:

Doll:

That perfect ass with the short blond beard—no names, understand?—has allowed himself to be captured. The police
took him at one of his usual haunts, abed, also as usual, with
his habitual side of smelly dark meat.

And since neither the gentleman's valor nor his resistance to
—well—pressure, call it, inspires much confidence in me, I
have skipped, while the skipping's good. Small dark rooms
with too well-protected windows and miserable views awake
unhappy feelings in my breast. And people who are careless
with firearms near stone walls, even more so.

So, join me in Chicago, where I go to make old Muttonchop
Whiskers uncomfortable. I shall be at the Hotel Clifton on the
North Side.

Strangely enough, I miss you. And if you've got that lovely
red head bashed in, believe me I shall shed a tear. No, I'll
concede you two.

Your Kurt

Rose Ann gave that tender missive the exact treatment she figured it deserved: She crumpled it into a tiny ball and threw it on
the floor. Thereafter, she spent the next three days packing. She
then had the bulk of her clothes shipped to her Aunt Cornelia's in
Boston, with a note explaining that she'd call for them after the
war was over. Betimes she had the management send her up all the
back issues of the more prominent newspapers they could find. She
had no trouble at all encountering the item that she sought: John
U. Andrews, of Virginia, had indeed been arrested. And—to the
outrage of all the reporters, who, while advocating freedom for
blacks, held to the man that sleeping with them was carrying
equality too far—while in bed with his dark mistress, Josephine
Wilson, whom they identified as the madam of a middling-fashion-
able "house of ill fame" on Green Street. His hideout had been at
10 Eleventh Street; the arresting Officers: Detectives Thomas Du-
senbury and John McCord, backed up by two others, Officers Rad-
ford and Farley, whose given names weren't listed. They had taken
him without a fight; by trickery, some of the papers hinted. En
route to the Mulberry Street police station, he'd declared that if
he'd known what they were up to, they would never have taken
him alive.

The *Tribune*'s reporter interviewed him in his jail cell, got nothing out of him but a pack of lies, which the paper went on to

contradict hotly. After that, in view of the fact that the Mulberry Street station was crowded with refugees, black and white, who had reason and to spare to speed Andrews of Virginia's departure from the land of the living, he'd been transferred "for safety's sake" to a cell in Fort Lafayette in New York Harbor.

After that, a few more stories, growing shorter and duller as the days went by.

Then, to Rose Ann's vast astonishment, John U. Andrews of Virginia, the man who at one point had been seen dashing about the city's streets, mounted on a splendid cavalry steed and waving a saber as he urged the mob on to greater fury, disappeared from history. He was never brought to trial. The papers of every political persuasion simply stopped mentioning his name. Not one editor ever published even a short article under the heading "Whatever Happened to Andrews?"—as, logically, someone should have done. Whether he died in prison at an advanced age or was quietly freed within a month or two, the fact is that he vanished. That bothered Rose Ann no end, outraged her sense of justice. Being a stubborn little female cuss, she went on inquiring into what had happened to John U. Andrews of Virginia for many years after the war. She never did find out. Nor did anyone else.

But at the moment, she had more immediate concerns. Her things packed and ready, she took a train for Nashville, Tennessee. Her objective was to launch an all-out assault on the fortress of Greg Forrester's heart, said fortification already three quarters ruined by her in the first place. So she didn't think that carrying it by storm was going to cost her too much trouble.

The trouble lay elsewhere. The salient she really wanted to take and keep forever was already occupied by her sister, Gwen.

So poor Greg would have to do. Trained right, he wouldn't make too bad a substitute at all. As for Sisimond Kurt, *Count* Radetzy, let him shed that tear!

Chapter Fourteen

Almost as soon as she got to Nashville, Rose was confronted with what seemed to her conclusive evidence that Kurt had been as busy as a bumblebee in the Midwest, and in the employment of his now classic tactic of stirring up public discontent. The papers were full of the story: Provoked beyond his strength by the slanting of the news, and the tone of the editorials appearing in it, General Burnside had sent a squad of soldiers to occupy the offices of the Chicago *Times* and others to surround the building in which that paper was edited and printed. Such disloyalty, the general huffed from beneath his sideburns, would be permitted no more. All Chicago exploded into a well-orchestrated rage, behind which Rose Ann perceived Kurt's fine Machiavellian hand: Twenty thousand people attended the Public Indignation Meeting in the windy city's Courthouse Square. The mayor, the governor of Illinois, and at least five local generals fired off telegrams to President Lincoln in Washington: This sort of high-handed military interference into what were, after all, civil affairs simply wouldn't do! Sighing, Honest Abe agreed; he had troubles enough without idiots in muttonchop whiskers adding to them by their failure to understand what democracy was all about; that it included the right to hold and express unpopular opinions, even when said opinions offered moral aid and comfort to the enemy. So the President canceled the suppression of the Chicago *Times* by executive order, told General Burnside to go comb out his fancy whiskers but to let the citizenry, including sinuous individuals of the Copperhead variety, write and say whatever they wanted to; treason consisted in *acts* not words. And to prove that freedom of speech existed in the Union, he ordered Secretary of State Stanton (whose whiskers were even funnier-looking than General Burnside's) to turn loose all the dissenters whom that bad-tempered official had already sent "where they won't even hear dogs bark!"

So Rose Ann reckoned that Kurt and friends had won themselves another victory in their low-down, crooked, dirty war, fought by treachery behind the lines. She wanted the South to win, the Confederacy to establish itself as an independent nation, but, as she bitterly put it, "if you pick up a stick that's been used for cleaning out what's generally found underneath an outhouse's seat, to beat your enemy over the head with, what happens to your hands?" Dirty fighting's no way to win an honorable cause, and besides—

Besides, she remembered the nice Yankee boys she'd danced and flirted with in Boston, and the nice Southern boys she'd done the same with in Richmond, and it came to her that what she really wanted now was for both sides to quit killing each other and shake hands and even give each other a brotherly hug and have a drink together and forget it. It was perfectly clear to her that keeping a passel of good-for-nothing niggers in slavery wasn't *worth* fighting over, that maybe the best thing to do would be to round 'em all up, pack 'em into steamboats, and ship 'em straight back to Africa, where they'd end the race problem forever by eating each other for supper every night 'til there weren't any of the useless critters left . . .

Which was, she realized, only an indication of how swamp-bottom low her spirits were. She didn't want the poor darkies exterminated; she wanted them to live and be as happy as they could. She suspected that, once freed, they were going to catch it, that very likely Southern white trash and Northern riffraff, whipped on by a few murderous madmen like her Kurtie pie, were going to get together in one great big nationwide lynching bee, so shipping the helpless, childish black folks back to Africa would likely be the best thing to do with them . . .

Which didn't help her indigo-colored mood at *all*. Nothing did. Not even the news in this morning's papers that Dr. George Bickley, Supreme Grand Imperial Potentate of the Knights of the Golden Circle, had been arrested at New Albany, Indiana, and the Second Grand Ruler, Dr. Bowles, had been caught at one of the "castles" of the Order, surrounded by prominent Indiana Copperheads, with the detailed plans for a pro-Southern uprising in the Northwestern states spread out on the table before him. The Nashville papers played the story up for all it was worth, since it was at the Union lines just before the Tennessee capital that the two agitators had appeared, dressed in Confederate uniforms, claiming to be surgeons from Ohio, held in the Rebel medical services against their will because the outbreak of the war had accidentally caught them in the South. They'd asked for passes to go home, which General Rosecrans, who commanded the Federal forces of the Cumberland, had given them without blinking an eye. But immediately thereafter he'd detailed two of the best sleuths in Military Intelligence, clad, of course, in civvies, to dog their trails. A telegram to Governor Morton's counterespionage headquarters had

sent posses scouring the entire state of Indiana—with most satisfy-
ing results: Not only were the two heads of the conspiratorial Copperhead order caught, but the membership rolls of the Knights
were taken with Bickley and with Bowles, sufficient ironclad proof
of plain treason to hang the Copperheads by carload lots.

Which meant that the pro-Southern movement was definitely
smashed at last. Rose Ann candidly admitted to herself that she
was glad of that, because these so-called friends of the South hadn't
done her country and its cause one clinking ding-dang bit of good,
and maybe had even hurt it, since when decent foreign nations saw
what kind of pig-dogs and snakes in the grass supported the seces-
sionists, they took a second look at the Confederacy's frantic pleas
for recognition. After all, a man is judged by the company he
keeps. And so is a nation, I reckon, Rose Ann thought.

But then it came to her that she'd probably got one good thing
out of the debacle of the Copperhead movement: Her darling Kurtie pie was sure as hell heading for Canada or even Europe by now.
Only—

Only what good did that do her, when every time she left her
lodgings to go for her evening's "constitutional," she ran slapdab
into Greg Forrester parading triumphantly by, with a long-tall,
skinny-shanked, slab-sided, Unionist hill-wilhelmina from East
Tennessee clinging lovingly to his manly arm?

Swear to God, Greg's got no taste at all! she fumed. All right I—
I treated him real *bad.* Shocked him spitless 'cause I thought I had
to get shut of him since there just wasn't any way I could bust
loose from—Kurt. Well, I'm loose from old Kurtie-poo now. He
signed my Emancipation Proclamation with bullets smashing into
poor little kinky heads . . . So there's only one question left:
Granted that I can take Greg back from that clay-eating hillbilly
female—that is, if she even *is* a female; got a jawbone Samson could
have used on the Philistines, and the only way to tell whether she's
coming or going is to look at her feet, 'cause damned if she ain't
table-flat before and with nothing much to speak of there behind—
should I? I mean, do I have any right to? I thought I wasn't fit to be
a decent man's wife back then. Well, am I any more fit—now?

She thought about that. She was an honest little soul, so she
didn't quite subscribe to the basic tenets of female morality: that
sin was what you'd got caught *in flagrante* doing, while virtue was
anything you could get away with while maintaining a lofty public
pose. She believed in sin, of the old-fashioned, Bible-pounding variety, in fire and brimstone, and in the wrath of God.

But weren't there such things as—repentance and redemption? Mercy and forgiveness? The tender loving-kindness of a stern but just God? Didn't He go after that one lost lamb? Pity the dying sparrow? More, hadn't He lifted up such almightily fallen critters as the woman at the well, Mary Magdalene, the sinful woman of the town who poured perfume all over His feet and wiped them with her hair? And what had He said to the woman taken in adultery, the one the mob had been about to do in by chunking rocks at her 'til she died? What were the words? Those soft, sweet, oh so beautiful words? "Neither do I condemn thee. Go and sin no more . . ."

She felt exalted, suddenly; cleansed, purified. With a breathed, whispered "Thank you, Lord!" she sprang from the bed she'd been lying in all afternoon—more from sad lassitude than from actual sloth—and—

Her gaze fell upon the topmost of the piled-up morning papers she'd bought when she'd sallied forth to do just that, and to have a cup of coffee at a little tearoom near the state capitol. "MASS ARREST OF COPPERHEADS PLANNED, FEDERAL AUTHORITIES VOW!"

She hung there, giddy and sick. Her bullet-torn gut ached suddenly, as it always did when she was cornered and afraid. Because she had just remembered something: Acting upon Kurt's as usual quite diabolical orders, poor Greg had *joined* the Knights of the Golden Circle. He had even been appointed to the post of some minor official capacity in the Copperheads' conspiratorial order. And he held a commission in the U.S. Army. That he also held one in the Army of the Confederate States of America was of lesser importance, because they wouldn't even find that out, maybe. But by now the Secret Service *already* knew that First Lieutenant Gregory Forrester was a—a what? Oh, yes! A Tyler of the Lesser Council, Knights of the Golden Circle, Cleveland, Ohio, Chapter! The civilians who'd joined the Order would be counting the bars on the windows of their cells for the next forty years. But an Army man?

She could hear that bugle cry out, sharp and clear, against the pearly edge of the first crack of a dawning sky. The rattle of a snare drum, slow-beating, funeral slow. The dirge march; a platoon before him, another behind. And all alone, head up and proud, his arms pinioned behind him—her Greg. Her honest to God good sweet boy baby doll with the face of a minor prophet. Marching—toward that wall. That awful wall. Would he refuse to let them bind those glorious smoky-blue eyes of his? Would he pronounce some ringing, inspiring last words? No, that was hack scribbler's novelizing. When you looked into the muzzles of twelve rifles three yards away, your throat choked up on you sure as all hell, and your mind was so damn busy trying to figure out how to keep yourself from dropping to your knees and begging and beseeching, or struggling to bust loose from there and running, or maybe disgracing yourself in other ways, like peeing your pants the way Kurt had told her some condemned men did, that them there noble last words just didn't seem to come . . .

And he, the sweet loving damn fool, had taken that ridgepole in skirts to church this morning. The Presbyterian one, natch—what other one would a broomstick jockey like that fugitive from the pine barrens belong to?

She was clawing her way into her clothes by then. Which didn't take her long; she hadn't taken them all off, just her dress, her petticoat, and her crinoline, so that she could lie down. In minutes she was outside and flying up the street in the direction of the rooming house where she'd already found out Greg lived.

His landlady was a big, beefy Irish woman, and aside from the fact that Rose Ann had had enough and to spare of big, beefy Irish women in New York, this one was obviously disposed to be contrary. She, Rose Ann shrewdly guessed, approved of the hill-wilhelmina. She took your ill-favored female's instant dislike for all such blessings upon male eyes as this flaming fox fire, and seawater pools of mischief and delight, golden-speckled snow, and sweetest wine before her. She didn't even stop long enough to be further offended by Rose Ann's smart clothes. To her, girls like Rose Ann were always flaunting their nakedness even when they were buried under forty ells of cloth.

"Git away from here, ye brazen hussy, a-comin' to me hame axin' after a man!" she howled. "O' ilse I'll tek me broomstick to ye!"

"Why don't you try straddling it and flying three times around the church steeple?" Rose Ann suggested sweetly. "Oh, for God's sakes, ma'am, go call Greg! I'm his sister, and I've just had a telegram from home and this is a matter of life and death!"

"Dun't believe ye!" the landlady snorted.

"You go in there and tell Greg that his sister Rose Ann is here. And that Mama just wired me that our uncle—Tyler Lesser Council—is dying back home in Cleveland, Ohio, and she wants us to come home right now!"

"Thot ye sounded like a dommyankee. All right, I'll call him. 'N' the two o' ye kin talk right where ye be—in the street. I runs a decent hame, 'n' I'll have no sinfulness in it! His sister—huh!"

Then with elephantine dignity, she turned and flounced off, which, Rose Ann conceded, was quite a trick for a woman her size. Within minutes, Greg was there, his blue eyes wide—and wild. Rose Ann had immediate proof of the fact that his landlady had delivered her message accurately, for while Greg wore the single-breasted coat reserved for lieutenants and captains (the higher ranks being favored with double-breasted ones), he had it buttoned wrong, with some buttons through the wrong buttonholes, and others left loose because, in his haste, he hadn't been able to find where they ought to have gone. He caught Rose Ann by her elbow in a grip that actually hurt her and propelled her down the street. He looked more like a stern Old Testament prophet than ever now. But—a lieutenant prophet, Rose Ann thought with wry amusement, not even a bird colonel one, not to mention a general . . . She said, "This is far enough. Stop and let Mama button you up right, boy baby. Else people are going to think we just got out of bed. And you wouldn't want li'l Miss Hill-wilhelmina to hear that kind of ugly talk, would you?"

"Hill-wilhelmina!" he howled. "Rose Ann, you're the limit!"

"Well, I can't call her a hillbilly, can I? She *is* female, ain't she? Though from the way she's built, I wouldn't lay money on it. A reeel fore-'n'-after, that one. You sure Lord can pick 'em, boy baby doll . . ."

But by then Greg had heard the authentic edge and bite of jealousy that had got into her voice, and it mollified him considerably.

"You should talk, you li'l witch," he said complacently. "I'll admit Milly's nothing much for looks, but she's a nice sweet girl and—"

"I'll bet," Rose Ann snorted. "Hold still, will you? I'm not surprised that she doesn't know how to fasten buttons, 'cause up thar in them thar hills whar she comes from, they don't have any. Pin their rags together with pine needles, for a fact. But I didn't drag you out of that Irish she-jumbo's den to talk about li'l Miss All's Clear. Greg, honey boy, love of the rest of my life—I hope!—you're in trouble. Baaaad trouble. Now come on!"

"Nary a step 'til you tell me a whole passel o' things, witch chile—"

Rose Ann stared at him solemnly.

"You reeel sure you're spelling that with a 'w'?" she drawled. "Oh, Lord, Greg, c'mon! We can argufy later!"

"No. First, why do you call Milly 'All's Clear'? That don't make no sense at all, 'pears to me . . ."

"Sentry talk," Rose Ann told him solemnly. "Means 'Nothing up front 'n' just a couple o' li'l old skinny skirmishers behind . . .' "

"Ohhh, Jesus!" Greg whispered prayerfully. "Rose Ann, how come you come over to my place talkin' so wild to Missus Murphy? She ain't dumb worth a damn, y'know. Took me a couple o' minutes to even catch on to what you were trying to get across. I'd plumb forgot 'bout that silly old Knights o' the Golden Circle business anyhow . . ."

"Well now, maybe you'd better call it back to mind," Rose Ann said drily. "Aside from getting you out of the clutches of Mildewed Milly from the Mountains o' Tennessee, I'd just as soon that the father of all my future children, including them as don't look like him none at *all*, didn't get his long-tall sweet li'l old hide punched full of holes by a damnyankee firing squad. A holey hide's drafty. You just might catch cold or something. Greggie pie, love of my life, they caught Dr. Bickley at a place called New Albany, Indiana, a couple of days ago. And among the things they took off him was the membership rolls of the Squires of the Tarnished Brass Ring, catch? Now, when I read that, I started in to think, and whut I'se done gone 'n' thunk is that *anybody* in a pretty dark blue uniform, even if he don't know how to button it up right, whose John Hancock is found on them thar rolls is *ipso facto, per se,* and *a priori* guilty of treason. And the damnyankees *shoot* traitors, y'know. That is, 'less you goes and 'fesses up that you're a nice innocent corn-fed sesesh spy. Whereupon they'll hang you instead. Six o' one hand and half a dozen o' the other, 'pears to me . . ."

"Holy Jesus!" Greg whispered.

"Now, there were more than fifteen thousand names on those rolls, so it ought to take the Yankees a while to catch 'em all. Only they just might skip the civilians as not being worth the bother. And if that list was in alphabetical order, as it likely was, they'll get down to 'F' as in Forrester a sight too fast, from where I sit, or rather stand. So skipping's in order, baby boy. Right now. Good thing it's Sunday. You can just take yourself a little ride out in the country—with me. After procuring yourself some travel orders to Chattanooga from that Copperhead colonel you reported to when you came out here. Got 'em all over, haven't they? What's his name?"

"Newton. Lieutenant Colonel William S. Newton. Tha's a damn good idea. But once I've got them orders, why don't we just run into each other kind of accidental-like on a train car? Staging a Sunday-evening horseback ride is a waste o' time. 'Sides, what'll we do with the nags? Just turn 'em loose someplace? Or bring 'em back to the livery stable here in town? That way we'll miss the train sure as shootin' . . . Or do you propose that we ride clean down to Murfreesboro and catch it there? Stupid arrangement, that horseback ride. Complicates things more than somewhat . . ."

"No, it doesn't," Rose Ann sighed. "You haven't been doing your homework, Greg o' my heart. Nat Forrest and his irregulars have busted up about forty-'leven miles of track right in the middle of nowhere twixt here and Chattanooga. Again. And as usual. So the only way for you to get down there and join General Rosecrans's blue-clad heroes is to ride a horse. Alone. 'Cause I'm not going with you. I'm just your cover for getting out of town without attracting anybody's attention except maybe Mildewed Milly's. And when you *do* get to that fair city, I'd suggest that you change into civilian clothes and keep right on riding—south. Across the Georgia line. So today's going to be goodbye between us, Greg. Goodbye—forever. Reckon that will be best for everybody, after all . . ."

"I'll be damned if it is!" Greg thundered. "I'm taking you with me, Rose Ann!"

"No, you're not. You just don't need a—let's see, what *were* all those nice, sweet, endearing terms you called me? Oh, yes. A filthy, perverted bitch. And—a whore. A cheap whore. Well, maybe not so cheap. You paid me the honor and the compliment of granting that I was worth all of twenty-five dollars. You know, I've got those particular bills pasted in my scrapbook. To show my grandchildren. 'Look, sugar plums,' I'm going to tell 'em, 'this here is the first honest money your poor old grandma ever made!' "

"Don't expect me to apologize for that," Greg said sternly. "You damn well had that much coming, Rose Ann. You set out to do a job on me—to convince me that you were the lowest-down, dirtiest female critter who ever walked the earth. I was getting to you, wasn't I? So you started in to throw me off my feet for a month o' Sundays. But dumb as I freely 'n' humbly admit I am, *that* dumb I ain't. The kind of tumble-ass, anything-goes, wrong-end-to kind of a critter what yells, 'C'mon, honey boy, knock out the lights with a whiskey bottle 'n' let pandemonium reign!' looks the part. Bedraggled, droopy mouth, crepey neck, dull eyes. A whore always looks like a whore, even the expensive, high-class ones. They look expensive and high-class, but whores just the same . . ."

"And I, what do I look like, Greg?" she whispered.

"An angel. Out of God's own glory. So pure 'n' good that not even that miserable scoundrel you went and got mixed up with—God knows why!—could do you any real harm—"

"Didn't get mixed up with him," Rose Ann said. "I married him—in the church. Thinking that I kind of, sort of loved him. Or anyhow, that I couldn't do without him. Only he's—taught me to, finally. I—I've left him, Greg."

"Thank God!" Greg breathed fervently. "But—but—what about this missus and three kids you told me about on the train on the way to Dayton? You said you *wasn't* married to him that time, and now—"

"I'm not. When he married me, he neglected to inform me that he had—well—prior commitments. I found it out in Paris—quite by accident—on our honeymoon. Reckon a little old trifle like bigamy didn't seem important to him, in comparison to all his other sins—and crimes. Anyhow, we've talked enough for now. You'd better head back home and get your things together. Don't take anything with you that you really don't need, Greggie pie. You've got to travel light. And for God's sake, don't take anything—incriminating along. Anything you have to report, do it verbally. They may not even be after you yet for that Copperhead Knights business. But if they stop you for any reason and find materials on you that'll make them suspect you've been spying, they'll hang you first and ask questions later . . ."

"Rose Ann, come with me! I'll put on civilian clothes and—"

"We'd stick out like a pair of sore thumbs. A young couple riding through Nat Forrest's stomping grounds? Nobody'll believe *that*, Greg. Runs against all the teachings of Southern chivalry, y'know. Now, tell me a couple of things, talking reeel fast, 'cause there's no time. If you and I were to get together after this outsized squabble is over, could you—*forget* what I've been? Even sort of wipe our little—Lord-awful!—one-night stand out of your sweet little mind?"

"No," he said sternly, "I couldn't."

"Then this evening will have to be goodbye, honey," she said quietly. "When I marry—if I ever do—I want to be treated as—a wife. Loved, honored, and cherished. Just as I aim to love, honor, and obey my husband, and be faithful to him 'til we both die. A real honest to God mother to his children, if I can even have any. I've been—a kept woman, Greg. A more or less pampered concubine. So I know what living with shame, daily, hourly, with every hurtful breath I draw, feels like. I'll never do that again. I'd die first. Or stay alone the rest of my life . . ."

"I don't want you that way, Rose Ann," he said gravely. "I want you for my wife, and the mother of my children. To—love, honor, and cherish, just like you said."

"Which, not being able to forget, you won't be able to do," she said sadly. "A marriage based on—suspicion, mistrust, jealousy— would be hell on earth. You know that, Greg. Let's not ask—impossibilities of human nature, huh, baby boy? Given my druthers, I'd rather lose you right now, quick and clean, than to have—our love bleed to death, a long, slow dying, drop by bitter drop. So—"

"So you're forgetting a few things, Rose Ann. Right now, you don't love me very much, if at all. But I aim to learn you to, by loving you the way no woman has ever been loved since God Almighty kicked Adam 'n' Eve outa the Garden of Eden and put that flaming sword before the door. I mean to—wrap you in love— putting my whole heart, body, mind, and soul into the job—'til you soak up so much of it that you'll glow in the dark! Ain't gonna be suspicious, jealous, o' what have you. Mean to trust you with the sacred honor of the home we're gonna make, with my worldly goods, the last breath I'll ever draw, with my very life. You said something about—impossibilities—a little while back. Well, now I offer you one more: That any woman who's loved the way I'm gonna love you *could* cheat. That the idea could even tiptoe 'cross her mind, let alone that she'd ever want to. Tha's how come I ain't gonna be jealous none at all. Jealous o' who? Of what? Our house shall be built upon a rock—the rock of God-fearing, Christian married love, and against that, Rose Ann, the host of hell shall not prevail, so help me God, amen!"

She put out her arms to him, her cheeks awash. He crushed her to him, kissed her mouth, mingling his own tears with hers. It was one of those incandescent moments that ought make up for a lifetime of sorrow. Only they don't. Sometimes, by sheer contrast, they make the sorrows worse.

She walked back with him to his boardinghouse. They talked very little. When they got there finally, he said awkwardly, "I hate to ask you to wait for me down here in the street, but I dasn't invite you up to help me pack. Ol' Missus Murphy's got a powerful evil mind. I could use some help, 'specially in hiding away a couple o' items I've just got to take back with me—incriminating though they be. Things I was sent here to get. And ain't no way I can convince my superiors in the Secret Service I couldn't get 'em. I've had time and to spare to get 'em 'n' fifty more . . ."

"What kinds of things?" Rose Ann asked him tonelessly.

"Maps. Of the fortifications of this here town. In case Gen'l Bragg ever gits up off his bragger 'n' attacks it, which 'pears to me he ain't got a mind to do. Like this 'un. Made it this morning before I took Milly to church. I mean, I made it ag'in. Can you make it out? I always was Lord-awful at drawing . . ."

"I should say you are!" she snapped. "In fact, you're worse than that. Nobody who's never been to Nashville could read this, Greg. How many have you made?"

"Just three. Ain't that many fortifications. But they're just as bad as this 'un, I hafta admit . . ."

"Go get 'em," Rose Ann said. "Bring them down here to me. While you're packing and going after the horses, I'll redraw them for you. I won first prize at drawing at school. As for hiding them, we'll wrap them in oilskin, put them under your saddle, next to your horse's hide. They'll search your saddlebags, and you—right down to the skin—but they won't think of looking there, it appears to me. Anything else you're planning to take through?"

"Yes'm. I mean, yes, honey—a rifle. A Henry repeater."

"Lord God, you idiot, why?" Rose Ann rasped. "I've told you and told you—"

"That it ain't no use stealin' Yankee repeaters 'cause we'uns just can't make the brass-cased cartridges for 'em. But I ain't all that sure about that particular drawback anymore, Rose honey. Fella I know in Mobile—Navy fella, H. L. Hunley—"

"Why, my brother Jeff works for him!" Rose Ann said.

"Works for the best, then. If there ever was an ever-lovin' genius it's old H.L. I figgered if I could get that sweet-shooting carbine to him, he'd come up with a machine that could turn out them cartridges on one side, while peeling spuds and tendin' the baby on the other. I was debating with myself twixt the Spencer and the Henry, but the Spencer can't shoot but eight times before you hafta reload, while a Henry holds fifteen of them pretty shells. I bought it off a fella in Wilder's brigade of the Indiana mounted infantry. He had two of 'em, and needed a grubstake. Them Indiana boys paid for them advanced firearms outa their own pockets, since Ordnance was a little leery about issuing repeaters . . ."

"I know. They're old mossy-backs in Ordnance, thank God! Which is why *some* of our boys are still alive. Now go get me those maps. As for your Henry—don't try to hide it. Stick it in your cavalry carbine boot. You'll be traveling through rough country; I don't think they'll even question a carbine. And when you and I go riding, you might explain what a mounted *infantryman* is. I thought that when you got up on a horse, unless you were a general or one of his aides, you automatically became a cavalry-man . . ."

"There's one basic difference," Greg said with a grin. "Instead o' whoopin' 'n' hollerin' and shootin' off revolvers and waving sabers around, the way them hoss troopers do, the mounted infantry rides to the battlefield, sends their nags to the rear by a couple o' corpo-rals, drags out them repeating carbines, then lays down on their bellies 'n' *fights*. Don't reckon nobody's ever seen a dead cavalry-man, and this here disagreement's nigh onto three years old . . ."

"That's unfair. I know Jeb Stuart well, and his boys fight."

"Don't see how they ever have the time, they's so busy riding herd on all the fillies," Greg said. "Oh, all right! Reckon I had better get on the budge, hadn't I?"

She drew those three maps, beautifully, perfectly. Kissed her now truly pledged and promised lover goodbye. She extracted from him three Bible oaths: that he wouldn't desert, that he'd get out of the Secret Service, for which he was almost comically un-suited, and that he would never, never, never volunteer for any mission whatsoever, unless it was driving a grub wagon for the Quartermaster Corps or leaning on a shovel with the latrine detail.

"Love of the *rest* of my life, I hope!" Rose Ann told him. "I want a home, with, if necessary, a *live* coward in it. Mighty cold comfort laying posies on a dead hero's grave. So every time you get an impulse to whip the whole blamed Bluebellied Army single-handed, just remember that it's the foxhole diggers and real fast retreaters who come home to—well—comfort all us left-lonesome girls. Tell you what, you get your fool self killed, I'll put on black and mourn you—two weeks. And nine months and five minutes after that, I'll name my first young'un after you, no matter who his pappy is . . ."

"Honey," Greg told her solemnly, "you've just painted a a streak up 'n' down my spine tha's so damn yellow that my belly button's getting the jaundice by contagion. Now pucker up and kiss me one more time, 'cause now I gotta ride . . ."

One hour after that, a cavalry screen that General Rosecrans had thrown out to apprehend all the blue-clad members of the Knights of the Golden Circle that he shrewdly suspected would be bustin' out all over, now that his own intuitive insight into their twisted souls had caused the two Supreme Potentates of the Order to be caught, apprehended Greg Forrester. His name was on the list of Copperhead traitors within the Union armed forces that the general had had compiled in a single night by putting twenty-five trained secretaries on the job simultaneously and dividing up the pages of the captured membership rolls of the Order among them. Fortunately or unfortunately, depending upon where your sympathies lie, Bickley had listed the military men among his followers by name, rank, and corps, which made weeding them out child's play for the Yankee Secret Service. Greg's name was on the written travel orders Lieutenant Colonel William S. Newton had given him; both his and Colonel Newton's name appeared on Dr. Bickley's membership rolls.

Greg debated for a long moment whether to run for it or try to stand them off with the Henry, but, like most cavalrymen these days, they were armed with Sharps breechloaders. And there were more than twenty of them in the patrol. The odds were too great even with that beautiful lever-action Henry. Maybe he could talk his way out of this mess, stay alive, and come home to Rose Ann.

Fat chance. First of all, there was that Henry. By then, the Spencer repeating breechloading carbine was being issued to the troops in driblets, but Henrys were never government issue at all. Several crack outfits, usually either cavalry or mounted infantry, simply dug down into the pockets of their uniform pants and bought them with their own money. With them, less than a month later, Wilder's Indiana brigade was going to hold up masses of Confederate troops twenty times their numbers long enough for General George Thomas, great Union leader despite his being as much a Virginian as Robert E. Lee, to get into place, hold that line, and add that "Rock of Chickamauga" to his name. So Greg's captors knew one thing for certain-sure: No Yankee lieutenant on detached service had any damned business having a Henry lever-action fifteen-shot carbine in his saddle boot. In the Army of the Cumberland, *only* Wilder's mounted infantry had Henrys. A Sharps he could have got away with, a Spencer with considerably more difficulty, but a blue-clad soldier from some other outfit besides Wilder's who rode with a Henry in his boot was in trouble, deep and bad.

Their search was thorough. As a spy, Kurt Radetzy had declared, Greg Forrester existed in a state of extreme urinal poverty. Caught, he kept glancing nervously at his horse. So they searched the horse too, and found those beautiful, beautiful maps Rose Ann had made.

They almost saved Greg's life. Brought to headquarters, they were shown to General Rosecrans's Chief of Cartographers, who whistled in amazement and delight at the sight of them.

"General," he told his commanding officer, "promise him *any-thing* to tell you who made these maps! A commuted sentence, a big feed, and a night in Nashville's best parlor house, before we ship him north to that Springfield prison camp—"

General Rosecrans frowned. He was a devout Catholic, and the parlor-house suggestion offended his moral concepts.

"And if he does tell us the name of this cartographer, what then, Major?" he said.

"I'll lead the raiding party personally to capture this fellow!" Major Lewis exulted. "Bring him here, install him in a red plush velvet tent with rugs on the floor, feed him daily rations of caviar and champagne. Until he draws me a map of every salient in this sector, General, sir! And with maps like these I'll flank the Rebs with a corporal's guard and chase 'em down past Atlanta!"

"True, half the time we don't even know where we are in these mountain gorges and river valleys," the general sighed. "All right, Major, you may bargain with the prisoner—a commuted sentence in exchange for this most skillful collaborationist's name and whereabouts . . ."

But Greg wasn't having any. In the Unionist papers in Nashville, in those in Ohio, he'd seen too many outraged demands that the Union courts-martial stop handling female spies so gently. "After all," one editorialist thundered, "these Rebel witches have cost thousands of our brave boys their lives! Time to put a halt to it, to throw the fear of God into these women, who, far from being Southern ladies, are generally members of the most ancient profession! Hang one or two of these fair and treacherous darlings, and see how fast the rest will scurry back to warmer climes!"

Rose Ann could get a body wild, set a man's teeth on edge without half trying. Greg knew that from sad experience. Of all the girls he'd ever met, he couldn't recall another who could make a man's noble and chivalrous instincts vanish quite so fast. She mocked all things, even herself. He could easily conceive of her getting a court so damned pissed off that they'd hang her out of hand, after—good Lord!—passing her through the entire regiment sure as hell!

So Greg held out four whole days, in spite of Major Lewis's endless pleading with him, wheedling, coaxing, cajoling. He was young, the major pointed out, handsome. He had his whole life before him. Why did he insist upon dying in this stupid fashion? The war was practically over and the South had already lost it. This Reb cartographer must be a very special friend of his. A relative? A—brother?

Seeing the very special glow of tenderness that appeared in Greg's eyes at this line of questioning, it came to Major Lewis quite suddenly what to do. And no sooner did that thought occur to him than he put it into action: He anticipated one of the twentieth century's favorite political devices. He deliberately "leaked" to the leading Nashville paper the story of the handsome young Rebel infiltrator and spy who was going to the gallows with his mouth tight shut, although offered his life for the name of his matchlessly skillful accomplice.

With that newspaper under her arm, Rose Ann went flying toward the livery stable. As she passed Capitol Hill, she looked up at the breastworks of cotton bales and the palisade of cedar posts that Military Governor Andrew Johnson had had thrown up around it for fear the devil's own twin brother, Nat Forrest, would suddenly appear and burn the Capitol building to ashes. She wished Nat Forrest would show up right now. She'd sell him a yarn that Greg was a distant relative of his: Forrest, Forrester—just two more letters—and she'd ride with him straight into General Rosecrans's headquarters and pull Greg out of there. Nathan Bedford Forrest was the greatest cavalry leader of the war. He wasn't as handsome as Jeb Stuart, but he was a far better fighter. He fought with cold ferocity, to win, while Jeb fought for fun, with Sweeny at his side plunking on that banjo. People told fearful lies about Nat, making up stories that he talked worse than a buck-nigger field hand. One citified reporter visited his camp and asked him how he won so much. Nat said, "I keep on the move. One man on the budge is worth three sittin' on a stump." The reporter reported that as: "Ah gits thar fustest wit' the mostest." Which made a better story, maybe.

Well, she was on the budge right now. She was going to go riding into the Yankee headquarters and offer her neck for Greg's. Maybe they'd hang her, after all. The papers said that was what they were going to do with the next female Reb spy they caught. So all right, what had her life been but a stupid, unholy mess, filled with sin and shame, accomplishing exactly nothing? If she couldn't stand up to the altar with a nice good honest sweet boy like Greg at her side to help her straighten out her damn-fool messy way of behaving forever, she'd stand up on the gallows and set him free to marry some sweet pure untouched girl just like he ought to in the first place. She was long gone, anyhow. Finished. In all her twenty years she'd never done anything even halfway right. She'd eloped with Joe-Joe, fallen into bed with Colin—in a creepy old smelly place dedicated to casual carnal sin—got mixed up with, committed adultery with, bigamy with, you name it with—Kurt. So now she was prepared to bust hell wide open and slosh fire and brimstone all over everything when white-bearded, stern God Almighty hurled her down to where she purely deserved to go to burn forever, as long as good sweet Greg, whom she was truly fond of and maybe even loved a little, went free. The newspapers had said that the Yankees wanted the man who'd drawn the most precise maps of military fortifications ever seen in this whole war. Well, that man was her: Rose Ann McKenzie of McKenzie's Hundred. Greg knew how much a man she was; he'd found it out the rough way that night she'd sent him out for a whiskey bottle up there in Ohio and turned him every which a way but loose. Ohhh, Lord! she moaned. I'm just too awful! Lord Jesus forgive me, cleanse my filthy soul, but let me get Greg out of the mess me 'n' Kurt got him into!

She was thinking all that when she felt that hand clamp down on her arm, heard that voice in her ear, sibilant, calm, slow-grating like cracked ice.

"Hire two nags, doll. One for each of us. The Pinkertons are just one jump behind me. And since 'tis my ambition to die in bed of extreme old age with all my sluts and brats weeping around me, we'd better get out of this charming city, fast!"

"No," Rose Ann said. "Let 'em catch you! Baby-murderer!"

"But what babies have I murdered?" he said with genuine puzzlement; then: "Oh dear God! Those little black chimpanzees! But, Rose Ann my sweet, blacks aren't human beings. They're slightly evolved—in the Darwinian sense—apes. Shooting them amused me, so why not? Go get those horses, will you? We really must make haste y'know."

"I hope they catch you. I hope they hang you. I hope they geld you like a hog. Let go of me!"

"Don't be silly, sweetkins. You need me. Get us those horses. I'll gladly help you get Forrester out that prison barracks and speed you two lovebirds on your way. Who knows? You may even deserve each other. Besides, your beloved Southland is finished. No matter how many more battles she wins, she cannot win this war. Only I could have won it for her, if I had had better materials to work with. But what did I have? Blockheads and asses! So now to take my talents elsewhere. It's back to tired old Europe for me, my sweet. To Prussia, likely. The Prussians are barbarians, but they have a keen respect for technical progress. One day they're going to dominate Europe, mark my words . . . Well, here we are, it seems! Go get us those horses, *ma chérie* . . ."

"Kurt," she whispered, "you will—you're really going to help me—get Greg out of there?"

"Of course," he said, smiling his ice-bright, maniacal smile. "Why should I play dog in the manger? You've been pleasant enough company, Rose Ann, but in Germany, in the spheres I shall move among, you'd be a disaster. I was never able to get five words of French through your little red *tête d'âne*, so how could I ever teach you German? Besides, while *les grandes dames françaises* found your *gaucheries* charming, they'd horrify a gracious, high-born *Frau* from Prussia. Still, you've served me well, so I shall reward you. I'll make it possible for you to settle down in a log cabin with your handsome oaf and produce little *Dümmlinge* by the dozens! *Die Pferde, bitte!* The horses, please!"

They rode out of Nashville to the north, away from the Union lines, after, of course, having stopped by the boardinghouse where Rose Ann had been staying, to get a few minimum essentials she thought she was going to need. And among those, although she didn't tell Kurt that, were the little .22 caliber Smith & Wesson revolver that Colin Claiborne had given her and—though she'd debated with herself whether it made any sense to bring it along at this stage of the game—the stockless, sawed-off Sharps breech-loader she had been hanging on to all these months in the forlorn hope that she could smuggle it safely through the lines for Colin to copy. Finally, she decided to bring it, on the outside chance that she and Kurt and Greg—she hoped!—might have to stand off a whole passel of Yankees in order to make good their escape. In fact, she even loaded it, in order to have it ready, just in case. And on that small detail, her and Kurt's and Greg's—and ultimately her father's fates were going to hinge.

She did that simple task dexterously enough. She was very far from being the total ignoramus about anything mechanical that women were supposed to be in her time. And anynow, loading a Sharps was simple; it was precisely in the ease and rapidity that this single-shot carbine could be loaded or, more importantly under combat conditions, reloaded that its value, especially as a stop-gap arm until enough of the new repeaters could be produced to replace it, lay. So Rose Ann did the job of loading it just right. She pulled down on the hinged trigger guard, which caused the heavy breechblock to slide upward until the empty firing chamber was clear. Then she laid a paper cartridge, complete with its .52 caliber ball, in the chamber, pushed up on the trigger guard until the breechblock slid down along its grooves and closed the whole works up again. After that, she eased back the side hammer, slipped a percussion cap onto the nipple of the firing chamber, and the Sharps was ready to fire. Too ready. For Rose Ann had made those paper cartridges herself.

Again she had done the job almost exactly right. She had seen the old men, cripples, and even women that Colin had hired making cartridges in his little arms manufactory the time she had visited it with Kurt. It wasn't hard to do. You laid the round or conical lead ball on the exact center of a sheet of heavy, rather stiff paper. Then you folded the paper up around it, and tied a piece of string, as tight as you could without breaking through, like a noose to separate that part of the paper holding the ball from the rest of the cartridge. After that, you rolled the free ends of the paper up around a smooth, cylindrical piece of wood until you'd made a tube of paper, just behind the tied-off ball, that looked just like a fat cigarette with no tobacco in it. Into that tube you poured the loose black gunpowder, after, of course, having carefully weighed it first, because each caliber of ball needed only a certain amount of gunpowder behind it and not even one grain more. Last of all, you twisted the surplus paper tube, above the correct amount of powder, into a sort of rat's tail, and that was it. Now, Rose Ann had seen Colin's cartridge makers weighing out the powder carefully before pouring it into the paper cartridges, but she didn't own a scale. She had bought the loose powder in a sporting-goods store, but they didn't have the kind of really exact and delicate scales she needed to do the job right, and anyhow she didn't think it made much difference as long as you got enough powder into the cartridge to make that ball really fly. And that was where she was wrong; since she was sure to err, it would have been better to put too little powder into her homemade paper cartridges than too much. As it was, she poured from twice to three times as much powder as a .52 caliber ball needed to propel it to maximum range.

Which meant, of course, that if she ever had to fire that sawed-off piece of hand artillery, one of several things was sure to happen: The excess charge of powder was going to blow the breechblock off the chamber, squirt live flame into her pretty face, leaving her hideously burned and probably stone blind for the rest of her life; or, if the chamber held, the Sharps was going to kick so hard it was sure to break her shooting arm; or the short barrel was going to peel back like the skin of a banana in star-shaped formation and mess her up right pert bad; and/or if she tried to shoot that overcharged monster from the saddle, she was going to be blown sure as hell out of it, and what happened to her would then depend upon how and where she hit the ground. And that, as every horseman knows, included consequences ranging from broken arms, legs, or ribs to the waist-down paralysis resulting from a broken back, the total paralysis from a broken neck, or death from a fractured skull.

It all turned upon whether the paper cartridge she'd loaded the cut-down Sharps with had, say, somewhat less than twice the gunpowder in it that it should have had, or more than three times as much. In the latter case, her chances of surviving shooting that hand cannon at somebody were exceedingly remote, to put it mildly.

When they had gone several miles east of Nashville, they veered due south. Rose Ann knew that General Rosecrans's headquarters was somewhere south of Nashville, but that was all she knew. Actually, it was far below Tullahoma at a tiny place called Stevenson, in Alabama, near the Georgia line. But they had to head south anyway because the Rebel forces under General Bragg, now being reinforced by General Buckner, were concentrated around Chattanooga, and with Greg or without him, they had to reach the Tennessee River to be safe. How far? Say one hundred to a hundred twenty miles, depending on the route they'd be forced to take. Four or five days, killing the horses. It took them far less, because between Wartrace and Tullahoma, they found a huge Yankee rearguard camp and supply depot, whose mission was to keep open that vital railroad running from Nashville all the way down to Rosencrans's headquarters in Stevenson, Alabama. The Union engineers had built the railroad back by then, and cavalry patrols from this rearguard camp and two more, one at Shelbyville and another at Manchester, were out round the clock to keep the devil's own twin brother, Nat Forrest, from wrecking forty miles or so of tracks again.

Hope told Rose Ann that the rearguard camp was Rosencrans's headquarters, lying in its pearly teeth as hope nearly always does. Long military experience, plus an icy intelligence unaffected by his paranoid megalomania (for paranoiacs are not only usually brilliant but supremely logical about everything except the premises they start out from), told Kurt that no two human beings were going to get a prisoner out of a camp like that one, and that if they entered it they were going to remain in it as prisoners themselves or be buried beneath it as corpses. But when he told Rose Ann that, she put out her hand to him and said flatly, quietly, "Goodbye, Kurt."

Which was where Kurt made his great mistake, which turned out to be his final one. He should have let her go. Nothing much would have happened to her. Not even rape, which during the American Civil War was a pastime of only bushwhackers and skulkers, since regulars on both sides knew they'd get hanged for it, pronto. But in spite of all his contemptuous disclaimers, Kurt was fond of Rose Ann, even loved her to the slight degree he was capable of loving anyone. So he said, "Don't be a fool, love. Why ask for trouble? Let us be on our way . . ."

She shook her bright head.

"No," she whispered. "I'm going in there. Give myself up, in exchange for—his life. Maybe they'll hang me. Maybe they won't. What difference does it make?"

Kurt stared at her.

"And if they've already strung the ruddy fool up, as they most probably have?" he drawled.

"I'll still give myself up. And *ask* them to hang me. Because you and I would be the cause of his dying that awful way, Kurt. And I wouldn't want to live . . ."

"Heaven deliver me from female melodramatics and folly!" Kurt grated, and reached out to take the bridle of her horse. While he was busy about that, Rose Ann clawed into the saddlebag behind her and came out with the little Smith & Wesson.

"Turn my horse loose, Kurt," she said.

Kurt was a superb horseman. He touched his mount with a spur, sawed at the bit, made that nervous gelding dance. It slammed into the flanks of Rose Ann's horse. Kurt lashed out with his crop, caught her across the back of her gloved right hand. The pain was blinding, despite the protective leather. Her fingers opened; the little revolver lay in the dust beneath her horse's hooves.

"Come along, doll," Kurt said gently. "Be a good girl now. Don't try my patience . . ."

Again Rose Ann clawed behind her into the saddlebag. This time she came out with that sawed-off Sharps.

"Ach, Gott!" Kurt laughed. "Where have you got the gun carriage and the horses?"

Furiously, Rose Ann jerked the trigger. The Sharps bellowed, spat out a yard-long tongue of flame. Earth and sky cartwheeled, changed places. Rose Ann flew skyward in a ballooning of skirt, crinoline, petticoats, a sprawl of nainsook, lace, and silk-clad legs, then downward again to crash into utter night.

Kurt kicked one booted foot free of the stirrup in order to dismount. Then he saw that vee of blue-clad horsemen pounding toward him in a glitter of uplifted naked sabers, so he jerked his gelding's head around, dug in the rowels of his spurs, and started away from there, riding like a centaur, at a sight-blurring gallop, leaning forward, going on. He heard a splatter of revolver shots behind him. Which troubled him not at all; the man who can hit anything with a revolver from the saddle while at a gallop has yet to be born. He was drawing ahead of them when his luck ran out. An infantry squad who knew just how to handle charging riders formed shoulder to shoulder in the road before him, and waited, the first row kneeling to let the back row fire over their heads. That double volley stopped horse and rider like an invisible wall. The gelding sunfished, snapping his own spine cleanly across before he even hit the ground. A steam trip-hammer broken loose from its moorings went to work on Kurt's chest, his guts. He felt his rib cage breaking up; hot, hard, intolerably heavy objects slamming into his upper trunk, his middle, making a shattering, a tearing. His lungs had no more room for breath; they had turned sponges, soaking up his flooding life; the suffocating red tide erupting up his throat, bursting from a mouth opened to scream, from nostrils flaring to drag in air, dyed all his chin, throat, breast with crimson viscosity. He suffered an awful moment's awareness of unbelievable, unthinkable, more than hellish pain, for nothing hurts worse than being shot. Fortunately, it didn't last long. He felt the spurting, the jetting, the terrible outflow, the invading all-pervading weakness. Then suddenly it was very dark, and after that it was very cold, and after that it was—still. So still. The roaring, crashing, thunderous stillness of—nothing. Nothing, nothing, nothing—nothing at all.

"Farewell, my little love!"—that gallant madman, Sisimond Kurt Radetzy, thought with the last flickering wave pattern of his once powerful if erratic brain. Then it was over. All over. He was spared even feeling the sodden impact his long, fine body made striking the dusty road. He was spared all else from that moment on. He was lucky. Far better men have had worse deaths.

Greg Forrester, for instance.

Chapter Fifteen

"I drew those maps," Rose Ann McKenzie said. "I was Lieutenant Forrester's direct contact. I passed along to him all the information our Secret Service needed. That was one of the things I did . . ."

"And the others?" the Yankee bird colonel in charge of her interrogation said.

"Agitation and propaganda. My husband was my superior officer in that—"

"Your *late* husband," the colonel said, a little grimly.

"Yes," Rose Ann said, and shed a tear of quite genuine sorrow. She had had very bad times with Kurt, but she'd also had some quite marvelously good ones. Now that he was dead, she preferred to remember the good times and forget the bad. She was an essentially decent soul with an immense capacity for forgiveness. She had forgiven Kurt Radetzy for all the pain, torment, contempt, wreckage of her psyche, her personality, her pride, even her identity, he had inflicted upon her. Besides, it didn't matter anymore. Nothing did. She was going to die.

"Look, my dear," the colonel said with real kindness. "Tell me the truth: Why were you and Count Radetzy snooping around our camp? And spare me a penny-dreadful romance about your activities as a Rebel spy. I happen to have personally interrogated two of the Confederacy's best female agents. I refer, of course, to Aurelia Burton and Rose O'Neal Greenhow. I haven't seen Belle Boyd, that saucy little Virginia minx who's become notorious for her rather amateurish efforts to hoodwink our Army's officers here of late, but I've had a very accurate description of her, by which I mean of what *kind* of person she is, her modes of behavior, more than her looks. So I say you're not a spy. You simply couldn't be. I'd stake my professional reputation on that."

Rose Ann looked through the flap of the tent she was in, at the limpid morning sunlight. Her left arm was in a splint, because it was broken in two places. Her whole upper trunk was swathed in bandages, drawn so tight she could hardly breathe. The bandages were to immobilize completely the three fractured ribs she also had as the result of having blown herself completely out of the saddle with a sawed-off carbine so overcharged with gunpowder that it had been found a measured fifty yards two feet nine inches from the spot she'd fired it off. The ball, the Ordnance people swore, was probably in the Atlantic Ocean. The Yankee medicos had set up that tent next to the camp's field hospital, and put her in it, because their mid-Victorian sense of morality wouldn't allow them to place a lone woman in a rough-and-ready military camp clinic full of sick and wounded men. Aside from the proprieties, one look at Rose Ann convinced them that she'd kill off all the casualties by sending their blood pressures up well past the danger point, and finish the massacre by giving the rest raging fevers. Not to mention distracting the surgeons and the medical orderlies to an extent that they'd exterminate even more poor blue-clad soldier boys than they normally did anyhow. So the chief reason that Colonel Stephanson had been sent to interrogate her was to find out where she was from so they could ship her back there pronto, before she drove a sizable portion of the Union Army out of their ever-loving minds.

"And what kind of a person is a female spy supposed to be?" she asked the colonel now.

"Nothing like you, my dear," Colonel Stephanson said with a chuckle. "Most of them are rather—brazen, to tell the truth about it. A bit on the—well—scarlet woman side, if you'll forgive me for putting the matter so crudely . . ."

"All right," Rose Ann said. "Then hear this, Colonel: I wasn't married to Count Radetzy. I've simply been living in sin with him for the past year. And Lieutenant Forrester was—my lover . . ."

The colonel stared at her. Rose Ann had been right about one thing: Poor Greg's court-martial had, in fact, been carried out in this very camp, simply because it was the nearest major one to the place where he had been caught. And they had hanged him outside of it, at the crack of dawn, two days ago. Colonel Stephanson, as the Chief Intelligence Officer, had been in charge of his interrogation too—with the cooperation of Major Lewis, General Rosecrans's Chief Cartographer. That a handsome lad like Gregory Forrester might have been this absolutely stunning little redhead's lover seemed to him well within the realm of possibility, and even probability. The colonel had conceived a real liking for Greg Forrester. In fact, he hadn't been able to get a solid meal down since witnessing the lamentable spectacle of the eight long, agonizing minutes it had taken the comdemned man to die, kicking and choking and slowly turning blue from strangulation because the squad detailed to carry out the hanging had botched the job from start to finish, being shaken and made clumsy by the same feelings of compassion, pity, even sheer unwillingness to kill a gallant foeman in that ugly fashion that had swept through the entire camp, he was sure. But that this delightful little captive, who was making all his years of practice at the mind-numbing drudgery of counterespionage suddenly worthwhile, was the person whom that poor, nice, stupid Rebel boy had been protecting over the question of those superb maps wasn't even conceivable, not to mention possible.

Colonel Stephanson lived in calm comfort upon the broad plain of a Victorian gentleman's absolute certainties. Among them was that women were generally charming little creatures, delightful to have around most of the time, but they really hadn't any brains. He was immensely kind to them, treated them with impeccable courtesy, since another of his certainties was that it was a gentleman's *duty* to be chivalrous toward, and to take exquisite care of, the poor, sweet, flighty, dim-witted little darlings. He even conceded that in their place, the home, obeying his orders without question, ministering to his comfort and his darker needs, providing him with splendid sons to carry on his line, they were indispensable. But when they started meddling in military affairs as spies and/or camp followers, they were a damned nuisance. And as for drawing maps like those—"Why, hell's bells, gentlemen! That's beyond the capacities of any woman whomsoever!"

So now he said, with benign calm, "You'll forgive me if I refuse to believe either statement, my dear? Oh, I can readily accept the idea that either or both of the—departed—were very likely in love with you; and in the case of young Forrester, that you may even have reciprocated, shall we say? But this auto-accusation of gross immorality on your part simply doesn't ring true. In any case, it's beside the point. The only thing that interests me is *why* you were here."

"I've told you. I was trying to get Greg out of your clutches. I was afraid you'd find those maps I drew for him under his saddle, and hang him for a spy. And you did. I messed up. Again. And as usual . . ."

But now Colonel Stephanson was peering at her narrowly. To his certain knowledge, nobody had discussed young Forrester's arrest and his subsequent court-martial with this highly unusual prisoner at all. So how had she known precisely *where* those maps had been found? He asked her that.

"Because I told him to hide 'em there," she said sadly. "I figured that stupid as men generally are, and those men being Yankees on top of that, you'd never find 'em. Reckon poor Greg must have given himself away somehow—now, didn't he?"

Colonel Stephanson stared at her, and now a bit of frost and flint got into his gaze. He wasn't used to having his male dignity handled with such a total lack of circumspection.

"You insist you drew those maps?" he growled.

"Colonel, send one of your nice Yankee soldier boys out to bring me a lead pencil and a few sheets of paper. Or a bottle of ink and a steel pen. And a board to draw on. I'm going to give you a demonstration . . ."

"But—but—how can you? Your arm's broken in two places, the surgeon tells me. And you're evidently a southpaw, because you fired that hand cannon with your *left* hand. Your arm was not only broken by the recoil, but your fingers and the back of your hand were burned by the blast. Don't tell me you're ambidextrous, my dear?"

"No, I'm right-handed," Rose Ann said. "Like most folks, Colonel. The trouble was I had that cut-down Sharps in my left saddlebag, so I grabbed it with the hand that was nearest to it. And I was scairt that Kurt would knock it out of my hand with his crop just like he did my little lady's pistol. So as soon as I got it around and level, I blasted. Reckoned that at that range I couldn't miss, even if I fired with my left hind foot. Kurt had made me so blamed mad that—"

"Yet, you did miss," the colonel pointed out drily.

"Yes. But only because I'd put too much powder in those cartridges. Made 'em myself, only I didn't have a balance to weigh the powder with. So I guessed at it. And I guessed wrong—as usual. None of us McKenzies has ever been right bright . . . So be a nice little old colonel birdie and send out for my drawing materials, will you? I want to get this over with . . ."

"Colonel birdie?" he said quizzically.

She pointed with her good hand at his shoulder straps. On each of them he had a little golden eagle, with wings and feet both spread wide. It looked more like a scrawny chicken than an eagle. And one fried without being plucked first, at that, Rose Ann thought. Which meant he was a full colonel. A lieutenant colonel would have had twin oak leaves on his shoulder straps instead of that silly-looking bird, she knew.

"I see," the colonel said. "All right, I'll send out for your paper, pencils, and pens. But before I do, even conceding the possibility that you can draw a fairish map—many women are quite good at drawing, come to think of it—why do you want to risk being sent away to the federal penitentiary in Washington for a good many years? Why don't we just ship you home and forget the whole unpleasant business? It's cost two men their lives so far, which is quite enough, it seems to me . . ."

"No. Not—enough. Too much," Rose Ann said. "I got both Kurt and Greg killed by being stupid. So I don't want to live anymore. All the papers said you Yanks were going to hang the next Reb female spy you caught. Well, I'm her—I mean, she. All I'm asking for is equal rights. You hung my Greg. So now hang me. I'd thank you mighty kindly for doing me that favor. What's my life to me that I'd want to go on living it? Waking up every morning with another whole day in front of me—to think in. To remember. Oh, no. Please, Colonel, send out for the paper and something to draw on it with. That's all I'm asking you right now . . ."

Colonel Roderick Stephanson took those three maps from her and stood there beside the little Army cot she was lying on, studying them. A little tremor, almost imperceptible at first, got into his hands. It grew until that good, stiff paper, of map maker's weight and quality, rattled. It takes considerable force to shake a man's world down in rubble around him. And Rose Ann had done that now with those maps. Those exquisitely drawn—or rather redrawn—plus-cum-perfecto maps of the fortifications around Nashville. She'd done them from memory, but she hadn't forgotten the tiniest detail. Every gun emplacement was there, every buttress, watch tower, breastwork, interconnecting line of interior trenches. She didn't realize that she had excavated the emotional foundations from beneath a male chauvinism so complacent and complete that it not only did not recognize its own nature but lacked even the vocabulary to describe it. A woman—a girl—a saucy little red-haired minx who looked like a fugitive from the seraglio of some opium-befuddled Bohemian painter's dreams had drawn freehand and from memory three of the most perfect examples of the map maker's craft, or art, that Colonel Stephanson had ever seen.

With a muffled, explosive, whispered "Well, I'll be goddamned!" he turned and marched out of there. He went straight to the crude, barrackslike structure beside the now double-tracked railroad that was providing General Rosecrans with all the logistic support he needed for his coming attack upon Chattanooga, and entered the office of the camp's telegrapher. Taking a sheet of paper from the telegrapher's desk and a lead pencil from the box beside it, he scrawled: "Major T. A. Lewis, Camp Stevenson. Have captured your Rebel cartographer. Imperative that you come at once. Signed, R. B. Stephanson, Col. Mil/In. Tullahoma."

With a hand that still trembled slightly, he thrust that paper almost into the telegrapher's face.

"Here, Sarge," he barked. "Send this!"

Twenty-five minutes later, Major Theodore Albert Lewis, Chief Cartographer to General Rosecrans's army, was on a northbound train.

"Sweet Baby Jesus and His Mother Mary!" Major Lewis said. "Colonel, you don't mean to stand there with your bare face hanging out and tell me that a *woman* drew these!"

"You heard me the first time, Ted," Colonel Stephanson said. "What's your verdict, as an expert?"

"That she's the damned best cartographer, bar none, in these United States of America," Major Lewis sighed. "From which it follows, as the night the day, that she's as guilty as all hell of spying for the Rebs."

"Concur," Colonel Stephanson said testily. "But the real question is: What do we do about it?"

"What *can* we do? You know what happens with female spies, Rod. They're sternly admonished, sent to jail for a few months, or even weeks, then quietly shipped South, to start all over again. That's been fixed official policy ever since I've been in this man's Army. What does this one look like?"

"A five-alarm fire on its way to burn down a city," Colonel Stephanson said.

"Ha! Your complete horizontalist, eh? The Rebs never learn. They always send us whores . . ."

"And we return the compliment. But this time, no. She looks like an angel. Oh, yes, that fire I mentioned is there, all right. But it's smoldering, banked, well hidden . . ."

"Then a stern admonishment and a suspended sentence. She'll be back in Dixie Land next *week*. May I see her?"

"Yes. But later. I want to work this out with you while you're functioning with some degree of rationality. After you've seen her, I couldn't be sure of that . . ."

"You've seen her and you—"

"I wouldn't bet a plugged lead nickel that *my* head's screwed down tight at the moment. Nor would I take my oath as to what might have happened if she'd asked me in that low, husky, sweet voice of hers—swear to God, it can melt *rocks*, Ted!—for the complete plans for old Rosie's coming attack on Chattanooga. I'm not sure I wouldn't have marched right out of there and brought 'em back to her—in exchange for a due portion of her dainty little anatomy, of course! But she didn't ask me for them; what's more, she's disposed to confess everything. For which you, my friend, are responsible . . ."

"*Me?* Name of God, how, Rod?" Major Lewis said.

"You, Major, in gross and flagrant disregard and disobedience of every military regulation I've ever heard of," the colonel said drily, "deliberately told one of those ink-stained, grubby scandalmongers of the public press the story of Gregory Forrester's noble refusal to name his sources and his accomplices. Now, having seen her, I understand *why* he refused. She says he was her lover. And damn me for a sinner if a roll in the hay with *that* isn't worth getting hanged for! But to get back to *you*, and your gross breach of Army discipline, my friend! The story that demon reporter friend of yours wrote—Gad, how I hate newspapermen!—was the reason that little Miss McKenzie, and her so-called husband—which it seems he *wasn't*, that relationship being irregular too—decided to invade our camp. To rescue Forrester, understand? So now, here's what I propose: That we shatter regulations a little more. Through your reporter friend, you *invite* the leading Nashville papers to send journalists to her trial. Think they'll do it?"

"Of course. Not one thing of interest to the general public has happened since the Battle of Gettysburg and the fall of Vicksburg. Except the New York Draft Riots, maybe . . ."

"Which she claims her departed paramour engineered. After having seen these maps, I'm disinclined to doubt anything she says. So I've asked for a complete dossier on friend husband's activities from Pinkerton's office in Washington. Tyler, who was attached to that department until the Copperheads heated up the Midwest, swears it's as thick as the Bible, and that they got most of it from London, through Scotland Yard. Appears Radetzy was a candidate for the noose in half of Europe. Which doesn't matter now, of course. What I mean to do, even before this trial opens, is to convince the Court of the supreme wisdom, and the timeliness, of handing down a death sentence upon a female spy for the first time in this country's history . . ."

Major Lewis stared at his good friend the colonel.

"Rod," he whispered, "I confess I'm—distressed. Hell, I'm shaken. I would never have believed this of *you*. I've always held you up as the very paragon of honor. And now, just because this cute little dilly turned you down, you—"

"Now just you hold on there, Ted! She *didn't* turn me down. And I doubt that she'd refuse anything in pants, as long as those pants were blue, and if their wearer had even the slightest access to the information she was after. The question of my bedding her didn't even come up. She's completely *hors de combat* with three fractured ribs and a left arm broken in two places . . ."

"And yet you want to *hang* her. Mind telling me why?"

"That's simple: I *don't*. I want her *condemned* to hang. Thereafter, I, personally, will ask the Court for a stay of execution, in view of her poor physical condition. During that stay, her sentence will, of course, be commuted to a stiff jail term, because *nobody* would dare hang a pretty woman in these United States, even if she's caught bending over her husband's dismembered corpse with a bloody meat cleaver in her hands. All I want from Governor Johnson, General Rosecrans, and even President Lincoln, is a promise not to commute her sentence, or pardon her, *publicly*. By the time what's really happened to her—which, as you know damned well, is going to be nothing, or very nearly!—is noised abroad, I want this war to be over. An ambition that will be greatly facilitated by the scurrying back home of all the little doxies the Rebs have loosed on us, once we've convinced the darlings that their dainty necks are in serious danger of being stretched. I want to get rid of all the Reb belles who're currently having a divine and delightful go at spying. They're truly dangerous. That first-class little information-gathering device and/or persuader nature equipped them with between their thighs makes 'em so!"

"Oh, Lord!" Major Lewis laughed. "How right you are! And, d'you know, your idea's not half bad, come to think of it. Its main weakness is going to be persuading the august gentlemen you mentioned not to bow to public pressure, which is going to be intense, you realize, and spoil things by making a grand and chivalrous gesture. How d'you mean to get around that problem, Rod?"

"When you get back down to Stevenson tonight, or tomorrow, you call upon the general and acquaint him with our plans. The fact that he's both a Roman Catholic and as straitlaced as all get-out on moral questions will incline him to go along with it, I'm sure. If necessary, you can—delicately—inform him of dear little Miss McKenzie's living arrangements, which were in the nature of what the French call a *ménage à trois*, or I miss my guess. That'll dampen the flames of chivalry in his breast more than somewhat, it appears to me. I, in my turn, will call on Governor Johnson personally in Nashville tomorrow. Thank God for the railroads! We can do in hours what would have cost our fathers weeks to do. Speaking of which, I'm firing off a wire to Allan Pinkerton tonight: 'Important female spy caught. Ask President not to interfere. Explanation on its way by courier.' How long d'you figure it'll take Tyler to get to Washington by train from Nashville?"

"Three days, at the worst."

"Then I'm going to have to stay up all night drafting my missive to the President. This is going to be the finest propaganda coup of the whole damned war, so we can't have Nice Nellies and Prissy-Britches Johns spoiling it . . . ."

The trial of Rose Ann McKenzie—a nineteenth-century anticipation of the "show trials" that were to disgrace the twentieth—quickly got out of hand, producing results and side effects that its authors had neither thought of nor imagined. In the first place, during the eight days—September 1 through September 8, 1863—that it lasted, for Stephanson and Lewis milked it for all it was worth, nothing of any importance happened on any of the far-flung battlefronts, since the evacuation of Fort Wagner in Charleston Harbor by the Confederates on September 6 wasn't the sort of thing to capture the popular imagination, while General Rosecrans obligingly didn't get around to occupying Chattanooga until the ninth, after the whole gaudy show was over. Long before then, Rose Ann had once more become an instant celebrity. By the third day of the trial, reporters were pouring into Nashville from as far away as Chicago, Pittsburgh, Baltimore, Philadelphia, New York City, and even Boston. The headlines, always containing the words "BEAUTIFUL REBEL SPY," got bigger and blacker with every passing day. For almost the first time in history, an enterprising local editor hired a female reporter of the sob-sister variety to interview Rose Ann. The dear girl was *good;* she had women readers spotting the page with tears and males burning with righteous indignation that "a poor little she critter could be treated that goldurned, low-down *rotten* by them billy-blue-damned sojers!" over the entire northern half of the now divided nation. But what caused the greatest howl of absolutely furious outrage since General "Silver Spoons" Ben Butler had ordered that New Orleans ladies who insulted Yankee occupation troops be treated as "women of the streets plying their avocation" was Rose Ann's reply, when asked—after she had been sentenced to be hanged by the neck until she was dead, dead, dead, with the accompanying pious request that the Almighty have mercy on her soul!—whether she had anything to say, any requests to make: "I am guilty. I want to die, because I caused the deaths of two men I—loved. So I thank the presiding officer and the Court for the death sentence, which I consider—a mercy. And my only request is that a cord be tied around my skirts below the knees, when I am hanged, to preserve my modesty . . ."

That last line caused screams of editorial anguish across the entire nation. And rioting in the streets of Nashville, which, fortunately, was put down without loss of life. Governor Andrew Johnson, in spite of his prior promise to Colonel Stephanson and Major Lewis not to do just that, had to be almost forcibly restrained by the two conspirators from freeing the prisoner outright. By then, General Rosecrans was too busy to interfere, and in Washington, Abraham Lincoln, among whose finer characteristics was a genuine love for women, as people, human beings, instead of pleasure objects, was studying with great care that dispatch that Captain Philip Tyler had brought him from Nashville by train, after the head of the Secret Service, the great detective Allan Pinkerton, had asked that he reserve judgment until it arrived. He'd just about decided that the propaganda value of this show trial as a deterrent to spying by Rebel women had been far outweighed by the disaffection it was causing in the Northern states, when his wife walked into the Oval Office to find out what was keeping him so long, and to complain that supper—as usual!—was getting cold while he sat there fiddling with papers.

So he asked her viewpoint on the matter—as a woman, as a representative of her sex. She snapped that she was of the convinced opinion that hanging was too good for forward little hussies like Rose Ann McKenzie, and the Princess Salm-Salm, and if she had *her* way, they'd be drawn and quartered and thereafter boiled in some nice hot oil!

Then, as always, long Abe quailed before his short little Mary, so the Tennessee show trial was allowed to run its course.

By that time, of course, the story had leaked through the porous borders separating the Confederacy from the Union. Only, because of the military situation, which was building up momentum toward the hideous butchery that was going to take place at Chickamauga Creek in northern Georgia on the nineteenth of that same month, it leaked south into Georgia along the telegraph lines beside the newly laid railroad tracks, rather than straight east into

North Carolina and Virginia, so that it reached Richmond only after considerable delay, having looped back up through Georgia and the Carolinas in a huge circle instead of traveling by the most direct route. And in the process, passing through the hands and keys of many telegraphers, some of them not as skillful as they should have been, it became hideously garbled. So it was that Caesar, the oldest of the McKenzies' slaves, slow-trotting through the streets of the Confederacy's capital with a bottle of rotgut cradled inside his shirt that his master, Dave McKenzie, had somehow managed to promote the money for and sent him after, heard the news vendor bellowing like a madman:

"Read all about it! Terrible atrocity! Unbelievable Yankee dastardy! Local girl hanged by Federals as a spy! Rose Ann McKenzie a martyr to the cause of the South! Read all about it!"

Caesar hung there, his black face turning ash-gray. He'd been feeling poorly ever since his son Brutus had run away to the Yankee lines and signed up as a sojer in a labor battalion. So he wasn't all that sartain-sho' he could stand this. Wuz hit—true? Lawd, yes! Anybody whut knowed Missy Rose Ann coulda figgered she wuz gwine to end up gittin' her damn-fool self shot o' hung. But wild as she allus wuz, now she done gone 'n' managed to do bof. Shot fust, then hung second. And all the wuk po' Miz Gwen 'n' that nice li'l ol' Missy Mary Sue Hunter, who'd done married up wit' Marse Jeff, had done gone and done to save her life when them damnyankees had done made her a extra belly button—'cordin' to Cindy 'n' Venus, anyhow—wit' a forty-fo'—had gone fur nothin'. Hung up by her po' sweet li'l neck like a shoat. 'N' her so good to us po' niggers, even wit' all her snappish ways . . .

He edged up to the news vendor, touched his sleeve.

"Please, suh," he got out. "I ain't got no mo' money, but I'se one o' the McKenzie niggers. I come back 'n' pay you tomorry, Cap'n Newspaperman, suh. I jes' gotta tek one o' these here papers home to my white folks. Missy Rose Ann they gal baby, suh!"

The news vendor whirled. Snarled: "Git away from me, nigger!" out of pure conditioned reflex. Then he saw the flood of tears that were pouring down poor Caesar's ashy cheeks.

"Reckon you *is* a McKenzie nigger, ain't you, uncle?" he said gruffly. "Awright then, take this paper. Present from me to yore master. Fine Christian gentlem'n, Dave McKenzie. Tell him that everybody in Richmond what knowed his daughter shares in his sorrow. Now doncha fergit, uncle; you tell him that . . ."

"Yessuh, I tells him sho'," Caesar said, and trotted away from

314

there. Behind him, people were pouring out of all the houses, surrounding the news vendor, snatching at his papers. The pile
melted like snow in a sudden spring sun. Now they were all gone
and the voices were rising, babbling, shouting:

"Damnyankees! Knowed they was capable of most anything, but
thought killing wimmen was beyond 'em!"

"Ain't no hope for it now, we've got to lick 'em, by cracky! With
what? Our bare hands if need be!"

"Poor li'l Rose Ann . . . Spunkiest female critter I ever laid
eyes on!"

"And the prettiest," another male voice added, sorrowing. "To
die like that—hung up like a thief—"

"Like the Good Thief, brethren, there beside Our Lord," Father
Erwell said gravely, but his florid face was awash. Then he gave a
great bound forward and caught Colin Claiborne, who was clearly
on the verge of fainting outright, by both arms. "Easy, son," he
said, his big, melodious voice dying into a husk scrape, a whisper
from pure compassion. "Come with me. To the rectory. To do
some mighty powerful prayin' in this our hour of need . . ."

Lurching like a spasmodic, trembling from head to foot, throwing his board-stiff, self-crippled leg out before him in one wide
desperate arc after another, Colin allowed the old priest to lead
him into the rectory. All the shouts and screams and babbled
curses died abruptly out of time and mind as the two of them
passed through that street. And the silence at their going was—
eternity's. Was doom. Heartbreak. A cry.

And one thing more. When Caesar came into the big house at
McKenzie's Hundred, Dave McKenzie roared at him: "Why,
gawddamn! How come you took so long, old nigger! If you've been
into my drinkin' whiskey, I'm gonna have your rusty black hide off
in strips!" Then he stopped, staring at Caesar, the seawater-green
eyes that all his children, except Gwen, had got from him widening in his boiled-lobster-colored face, which was already paling as
he whispered: "You're—crying. And that good-for-nothing runaway nigger boy o' yourn is perfectly safe up there in that damnyankee contraband camp. So—so—my boy Jeff! Oh, Jesus, Caesar,
you old fool bearer of ill tidings, don't tell me—"

"Nawsuh," Caesar croaked. "Marse Jeff he all right, him, so far
as I knows. Hits—hit's Missy Rose Ann, Marse Dave. Them damnyankees, they—" His voice choked up on him, he couldn't get it
out. Wordlessly he thrust the folded newspaper out toward the

man who owned him like a mule, but whom he—loved—in spite of that.

Dave took the paper, spread it wide. The headlines were black upon the page: YANKEE ATROCITY! LOCAL GIRL HANGED AS SPY! ROSE ANN McKENZIE, SOUTH'S FIRST FEMALE MARTYR!

His big, hairy, freckled and red-splotched hands gripped the paper. His grinding, convulsively tightening fingers tore it apart. His teeth ground together too, mad-dog snarling. Foam came from between them, wave-cap white at first, then scarlet-flecked, then entirely red. The blood from a heart broken, even physically now, came roaring up his throat in a thick, hot, choking tide. His eyes, red-streaked, bloodshot, wild, glared at those headlines. They went on glaring at them after they couldn't see them anymore. They glared up into Caesar's black face, after the owned thing, the two-legged beast of burden, had eased to the floor all that was mortal of the master who had owned his life, his labor, the get of his loins, even his immortal soul, perhaps. Caesar knelt there, through a measurable portion of the backing-up, ebbing, reverse flow of the wave form in nothing that men call time, crying very quietly. Then he put out the black, rusty, work-hardened paw of an owned thing, a mindless beast of burden, and gently, tenderly, closed those glaring eyes.

"Dear Lord tek he soul," he muttered. "He was a good ol' red-headed fella, by his lights. A mite stupid, but then all white folks is. Ain't never learnt the difference twixt a chile o' God 'n' a mule. But reckon us kin fergive 'em fur that, cain't we, Lord?"

He eased his aching-tired black body upright. And gazed straight into Gwendolyn McKenzie Henry's pale blue eyes.

She stared down at her father. At the author of her being.

"Is—he—?" she got out.

"Yes'm. Brung him that paper. 'N' he read 'bout how them evil Yankee white folks done hung po' li'l Missy Rose Ann. 'Twuz too much for him, I reckons. Drapped down daid, him, wit' the paper in he hands. I'd of knowed he wuz gwine to tek it so hard, wouldn't of brung him that paper. But then he would of found out anyhow, now wouldn't he, Miz Gwen?"

"The—Yankees—*hanged*—Rose Ann?" Gwen breath-etched the words, shaped them, a hairsbreadth beneath the felt vibrations the ears can capture, the mind define, as sound. Which was all she could manage then.

"Yes'm," Caesar said. "Hit's in this heah paper. Lemme see effen I kin git hit outa he hands . . ."

He bent and tore the sheets of ink-smeared newspaper deftly around those clutching hands, leaving a semicircle of it still clasped in stiffening fingers. He held it out to Gwen.

Her blue eyes flared, paler than an Arctic daybreak, reading those headlines. Then she whirled, already running.

And crashed headlong into Colin Claiborne as he lurched through the door.

He put his arms around her, drew her close. She nestled against him like a captive snowbird, trembling, trembling.

"I was trying to head this nigger off," Colin said harshly. "Knew he wouldn't have enough sense not to throw it right into your faces. Damned nigh killed my horses trying to get here first. Only—"

"Only what, Colin?" Gwen whispered, making of his name eiderdown, blue velvet, a felt caress.

"My guts had come apart and started screaming. Had to get 'em back together again," Colin said.

She stiffened in his embrace, made a motion as if she would break free. He tightened his clasp about her, whispered into her sunlight-on-snow hair: "That's—over with, Gwen. By the hand— of Almighty God. So maybe what is, was meant to be. Now you go upstairs and lie down. Caesar and I and your wenches will attend to your poor old man. I'll bring Father Erwell out here first thing in the morning. You want anybody else to attend the burying?"

Gwen shook her bright head.

"No, Colin," she whispered. "Nobody else—just you."

Chapter Sixteen

Rose Ann looked at the series of scratches she had made on the wall of her cell in the Old Capitol Prison in Washington. She had started those scratches the morning after she'd got to the Federal capital, to which she had been shipped—with two big, ugly-looking Secret Service men sitting on both sides of her on the train and iron handcuffs on her wrists—from Nashville, Tennessee. By plain accident she'd hit upon exactly the right place to put those scratches, because she'd waked up early enough to see which patch of moldy, crumbling wall the sunlight hit first when it came through the bars of her window in the morning. Each scratch represented a day. On the seventh day, she cut a long diagonal slash through the other six, thus marking off a week. So, as nearly as she could figure, it must be somewhere around the fifteenth or the sixteenth of February 1864, and she had been in jail, counting the fifty-odd days they'd kept her locked up in Nashville, for nearly five months.

Both Major Lewis and Colonel Stephanson had visited her while she was still in prison in Tennessee. They'd come to tell her not to worry, that she wasn't going to be hanged, after all. And when she'd declared she'd rather be hanged than spend the rest of her life in jail, they'd both promised her faithfully on their honor as officers and gentlemen that they'd see she was let out the minute the war was over.

But after the Battle of Chickamauga, they hadn't come back to see her anymore, and Rose Ann found out they'd both been killed. Which was just her luck, because neither of them had been front-line, fighting soldiers. Only, at two o'clock in the afternoon of the first day of one of the bloodiest battles of the whole war, General Hood punched right through the center of the Union line all the way back to General Rosecrans's headquarters, where the two of them were, so they'd had to fight just like everybody else. And had got killed just as dead. So now, her getting out of jail before she was ninety-seven years old depended on somebody who knew and loved her finding out she was there and making an awful fuss about it. But she'd been out of touch with *every*body since she'd left England last year, so she couldn't even depend on that. Still, she wasn't worried. She believed that Jesus Himself would set her free. And her reasons for believing that were a fine example of McKenzie-type logic:

If the good Lord wanted to call me home, or throw me headfirst and a-hollering to my just deserts down below, He's had all the chances He's needed to, long before now. And now I've been shut up in this pesthole where folks die of bad food, dampness, dirt, cinch bites, and every kind of sickness a body ever heard tell of.

She paused and added in her mind: But what they mostly die of, really, is giving up. And I haven't. Don't know why. Reckon in part it's because I think that after all I've been through and stayed alive—and even sort of clothed and framed in my right mind, though I wouldn't push that there contention any further than it goes, which is about two *inches*, maybe—the good Lord must be saving me for *something*. To do good in this world. To make some fine upstanding man—as much like Cabe as possible, Lord!— happy. Or failing that, to be a sweet old maiden—maiden, hell!— spinster aunt to the forty-eleven dozen nieces and nephews that Jeff and Mary Sue are sure to give me . . .

Speaking of which, dear Lord, take a letter. Sent up to you by through-train express. Subject: Cabe. Save him, Lord Jesus. Not for me. Maybe for Gwen if she ever opens up them—those—too pale eyes of hers and *sees* what she's got. A pint-sized masterpiece from Your hands, good Lord. Shaped out of mud and blood, but with *Your* breath in him, the breath of the spirit as sweet as wine You breathed into his nostrils one extra-special day when You were feeling right pert good about things, I reckon. With—lightning bugs and hoot owls and bats inside his head—and Your own blessed starlight in his eyes. Crazy? Yes, Lord! But, Lord Jesus, why didn't You go and make a few more crazy folks like him—*one* more, anyhow, just for me?—instead all those sane, wise, dignified people who start wars—wars, Lord Jesus!—over whether they've got the right to whip a pack o' liver-lipped, kinky-headed, blue-gummed, good-for-nothing niggers to work. That's a thing to *kill* people over, Jesus? People like Cabe, like my brother Jeff?

Part two. Him. Jeff. Mary Sue will go *crazy* without him, Lord. And Pa will drop down doornail *dead*, you hear me? And I, and I—

She couldn't even finish that prayer of hers. There in her filthy, ice-cold, stinking cell, she bent her head and wept.

About Caleb Henry, she needn't have worried. He was down to skin and bone by then, devoured by vermin from head to heel. But he had made up his mind to survive, there in that Union prisoner-of-war camp just outside of Jersey City, simply because he figured that after having had as much pure D miserable hell pinned on him as he'd had, he was sure to have some happiness coming. He didn't inquire into the nature of that happiness, because he knew damned well that the kind he wanted and the identity of the girl he wanted —hell, *meant*—to have it with were both skirting the outer edges of what good Christian folks generally called sin. So it wasn't a thing he could pray over, or even shape too clearly in his mind, because that much hoping, yearning, longing was a sight too close to prayer, anyhow, and he didn't want to crowd the good Lord too far . . .

So the only prayer he ever said aloud sometimes, and silently *every* night, while digging enough cinches out of his poor tormented hide to allow him to drop off into sleep, went like this:

"Lord, You're all-powerful, the preachers say. You can do anything You set Your almighty mind to. So, the first couple o' days I'm back in Ol' Virginny, Lord, just You will Yourself to be deaf, dumb, and blind while this here poor sinner goes about straightening things out a mite, by some kinda rough but expeditious ways, and after that You will Yourself into a state of forgetfulness while I tend to my woman, my lands, my crops, and bring up my young'uns, bastards or no—You ain't going to go and blame *them* for how they was got, are You, Lord?—to ride, shoot, respect good wimmen, pin merry hell on the other kind, stand up straight, speak the truth, fear You, and obey Your commandments. And, oh yes, hold their likker like Southern gentlemen, and a few other items I can't call to mind right now. After that, it's up to You, Lord Jesus. You want to roast me over a slow fire forever 'n' ever for a program as plumb downright *sensible* as that'un there, I reckon You're within Your rights . . ."

But her brother, Jeff McKenzie, was at that very moment standing in the need of prayer. He stood on the docks at Charleston, South Carolina, and regarded the peculiar object before him with intense and soul-deep loathing.

That peculiar object was a submarine. Even then, in that early afternoon of February 16, 1864, it wasn't the first submarine ever built. The first one that Jeff McKenzie knew about (though he was perfectly willing to concede that some damn fool among the Egyptians or the Babylonians or what have you had probably tried to construct one of these sneaky Pete instruments of murder a couple of thousand years before the birth of Christ) had been built at Saybrook, Connecticut, in 1775, by a man named David Bushnell. He had named it the *Turtle*, and in it, a triply distilled damned fool of a hero named Sergeant Ezra Lee of Lyme, Connecticut, had actually come pretty close to sinking the sixty-four-gun ship of the line *Eagle*, flagship of the British fleet, as she lay at anchor in Long Island Sound during the Revolutionary War. What's more, Sergeant Lee—in spite of the fact that the *Turtle* was made of wood, stout oak held together with iron hoops like a barrel, and the whole suicidal mess smeared over with tar—had lived to tell the tale and even survived the war.

Which is more than anybody'll be able to say of this sonuvabitch! Jeff thought grimly.

Even after that, Robert Fulton, the inventor of the steamboat, had tried it again. He'd built a submarine—powered, as Bushnell's had been, by human muscle pumping away, hands and feet, at pedals and a crank—that was a vast improvement over the Connecticut Yankee's. But he couldn't get the U.S. government to show the slightest interest in it, so Fulton had taken it to France and tried to sell it to Napoleon Bonaparte. But the Emperor of the French was a professional military man, and had about as much brains as professional military men always have, which was, Jeff had long since despairingly come to realize, none—including in this gloomy prognostication even Robert E. Lee, after having studied the battles of Malvern Hill and Gettysburg—so he had refused to buy the invention which would have made his invasion of England very nearly certain, by sinking the British fleet. After that, Fulton took his invention to the British, who *did* buy it, only to wreck it with sledgehammers, and keep the plans under lock and key to make mighty sure nobody would threaten their domination of the seas in such an underhanded, ungentlemanly, scarcely pip-pip-and-tallyho manner ever again. Those plans were, Jeff McKenzie, whitehaired and portly at seventy-four, supposed when he read about the German U-boat attacks in the papers in 1914, still locked up in some safe in the Admiralty in London.

And there matters had rested until Jeff's good friend H. L. Hunley had designed at New Orleans still another one, which had been built in the shops of James R. McClintock and Baxter Watson and launched at the government yard on New Basin in February 1862. This one was made of iron and called the *Pioneer*. On her trial run on Lake Pontchartrain she had blown a barge sky-high with her first torpedo, which, Jeff would have to explain to his grandchildren during the First World War, wasn't the seaborne, self-propelled, motorized missile they called a torpedo, but rather the motorless, floating bomb they called a mine. However, in April

1862, when the *Pioneer* had set out, running fully submerged to attack the Union fleet under Admiral Farragut, she had stuck her nose in the mud and drowned her crew.

Characteristic behavior for submarines, Jeff thought bitterly as he gazed at that ungainly object before him. He had worked on said object for more than a year, with undiminished fervor and devotion. Most of that year had been spent in a futile effort to build an electromagnetic engine to turn its screw propeller.

And when we failed to do that, we should have quit, Jeff mused sadly, because that's just where the catch to submerged operation lies—in the consumption of oxygen. I told H.L. that the reason that Bushnell's and Fulton's man-powered subs worked was because they had a crew of *one* man, period. So even with him pumping away at the pedals and the crank, the air inside the toy tub lasted him quite a while—specially if he let the fool apparatus drift with the currents most of the time. But H.L. designed this one for a crew of *nine*. A chief officer, a petty officer, and seven able-bodied seamen. So when they're engaging in the violent physical exercise it takes to propel her at any kind of speed, as in an evasive action, say, they use up all the air inside her pronto, so they either have to pop to the surface and surrender, or try to hold out long enough to get out of range. And they get dizzy. And somebody does something wrong. *Anything* wrong in this here tin coffin where the slightest mistake is fatal—and down she goes . . .

Poor old H.L. He was so proud of her he put his own name on her: the *Hunley*. Used to quote Shakespeare—no, that's wrong; it wasn't Shakespeare he quoted, but Ben Jonson—about this fine underwater torpedo boat of his. What was that line? Oh, yes: "A most brave device to murder their flat bottoms . . ." So now she's gone and murdered him . . .

And nobody *ever* called her the *Hunley;* even in Mobile, up to the time she drowned her first crew, anyhow, we called her the *Fish Boat*. And since we brought her here to Charleston on a flatcar from Alabama, she's drowned four more crews. Thirty-six good men and true. No, forty-five, counting that first crew lost off Mobile. So now the boys call her the *Peripatetic Coffin*. Apt. Fitting. Poor old H.L. had to demonstrate his faith in his—our, because, damnit, I contributed quite a bit too: the foot pumps to clear the water from the ballast tanks; the quick-release mechanism that drops the detachable cast-iron keel when you have to pop to the surface in a hurry; the—oh, hell, why list all my bright ideas that went into this monstrous man-killer? Where was I anyhow? Oh, yes; poor old H.L. had to demonstrate his faith in his invention, so last week she sailed—or rather *sank*—under his command. So now he's dead too. Along with the rest of crew number four . . .

And tomorrow, *I'm* going to take her out. On her first offensive mission. To attack one of those blockaders out there. I volunteered. Jesus God! As if I didn't know that the first rule for survival in this man's Navy is never to volunteer for *anything*, not even to take the admiral's pretty daughter to a ball! Only I was so goddamned sad over what happened to poor Ramb, and so mean-mad and mixed up and thirsting for revenge agin every Bluebellied bastid born— to hang a *woman*, by God! And her my baby sister!—that it didn't seem to matter. Dying didn't, I mean. But now—

He took that letter out of his pocket and unfolded it for the twentieth time since it had reached him yesterday. The words leaped up at him from the page like light, like fire, searing his heart, burning it to cinders with purest joy:

Oh, Jeffie love, darling, honey boy, sugar pie, my own! I am, I am, I am, I am, I am, I really and truly am! And I can guarantee that it's going to have red hair and green eyes and a freckled face and look just like its pappy! So you can put your dueling pistols away, Jeffie love, you old short-fused *dud* you! Looks like somebody's been giving you lessons in point blank small arms fire, and when I come to Charleston I'm going to kill her! Oh, I'm so happy! I wasn't going to tell you yet. I was sure the first month after you came home for Father Dave's funeral. That was *five* months ago, now, wasn't it? Poor man, he did love his dear, departed daughter, didn't he? When the Yankees killed his sweet, wild Rambling Rose, there was nothing left for him in this world. And d'you know what? I—I loved her, too; specially after she changed her mind and quit opposing our marriage and started being so nice to me. So now I'm as big as a house, and I've still got four more long months to go.

And before you even mention it, if our baby is a girl we're going to name her Rose Ann after the auntie she'll never even know. And I don't care a fig if she takes after your sister, and turns out to be wild and crazy and even downright *naughty*, the way Ramb *was*, y'know. But then, so am *I*, aren't I? Grabbing you like that with your poor old papa not even one whole night in his grave! But I didn't know when, if *ever*, I was going to be able to clasp you in my loving arms again, and in the worst of all cases I wanted something to remember you by: a little *you* all over again. Your image. Our love made flesh! Oh, drat it! Here I go again, spotting what ought to be a happy letter, with foolish tears!

Like I said, I wasn't going to tell you yet. I was going to wait 'til my little duplicate of you or maybe of poor Rambling Rose arrived and then break the news. But Gwen said the last letter she got from you was so sad that she thought I'd better tell you now because she's scared you just might commit what she calls, and I quote her, "a piece of pure McKenzie jackassery, such as volunteering for a suicide mission, say." Oh, Jeffie, you won't do anything real *foolish*, will you? Just you come home to me and our baby, and—

But Geoffrey McKenzie didn't read any more of his wife's letter. He rammed it back into the breast pocket of his uniform, without even bothering to fold it carefully. Then he whirled and ran straight down to South Battery, at the foot of Meeting Street, where Commodore Murray Wilkes, in command of the Port of Charleston, and thereby his commanding officer, had his office.

Be it said that standards in the Confederacy weren't all that strict. Much of the time, there was an easy camaraderie between officers and men. As a conscientious young officer, Lieutenant McKenzie stood high in his commanding officer's good graces, but Jeff wasn't counting on that now. What he meant to do from that moment on was to stay alive, and if he had to spend the rest of the war in a prison brig for disobedience of orders, he was prepared to accept that too. He'd even desert if he had to, but he preferred to try lesser methods first.

"Sir," he burst out, after saluting smartly, "what happens to an officer who asks to withdraw from, or be relieved of, a mission he's volunteered for?"

Commodore Wilkes eyed him sternly.

"You're referring to your submarine attack on the Yankee blockaders tomorrow, Lieutenant?" he said.

"Yes, sir! Commodore, sir!" Jeff said.

"State your reasons, Lieutenant," the commodore said.

"Cowardice, sir!" Jeff piped up. "Pure and simple! I'm so scared I'm *growing* white feathers behind my ears and my backbone's gone and caught itself the finest case of jaundice you ever did see, sir!"

Commodore Wilkes threw back his head and laughed aloud.

"Now that's what I call an honest answer," he chuckled. "Only,

Lieutenant, it so happens that I don't believe you. You took one of the Davids out, and rammed a spar torpedo straight into a Yankee frigate's side, not more than a week ago, as I recall . . ."

The Davids were another Confederate invention, and a rather good one, as such things went. They were steam-powered torpedo boats that ran so low in the water they were practically awash, so that the only visible parts of them most of the time were their smokestacks. In calm water they were great, but even a slightly choppy sea swamped them immediately, so that they'd killed more crews than poor Hunley's submarines had. But there was one important difference, Jeff thought; the Davids occasionally came back from a mission, while so far, not one of the three submarines that Hunley had built—the *Pioneer I*, the *Pioneer II*, which had floundered while under tow, without a crew aboard, thank God, and the *Hunley*—had ever managed to do that.

"The torpedo didn't go off, sir," Jeff said ruefully. "And the Yankees cut my smokestack in half with small-arms fire. Damned near choked to death from the smoke, coming back. And when we came ashore the sheriff was all set to grab us as runaway niggers. That's how black we all were from the soot, Commodore, sir!"

"Oh, come off it, Lieutenant!" Commodore Wilkes chuckled. "You took that David out. You rammed a Yankee frigate with her— or rather with a torpedo attached to a damned short spar, bow-sprit-rigged. That the torpedo didn't go off wasn't your fault, but rather BuOrd's. And you brought your craft and your crew safely home under pretty intense fire. That doesn't look like cowardice to me, Lieutenant . . ."

"You're right, sir," Jeff sighed. "That wasn't cowardice. That was craziness, Commodore. I was loonier than a snake-bit hound dog baying a moon what ain't even there. You see, I got to brooding over what happened to my poor little sister . . ."

"I heard about that," the Commodore said gravely. "My condolences, Lieutenant. She was a very gallant little lady indeed . . ."

"Well, sir, I don't know how much of a lady my sister was, but gallant, yes, sir. Every day in the week and twice on Sundays. So I had myself a mighty crazy mad on, topped off by a burning desire to kill myself some Yankees. But now my senses have come plumb back, sir. The only burning desire I've got left, Commodore, is to dandle my grandchildren on my knee . . ."

"A commendable ambition, of course. But would you mind telling me what caused this change?"

"This letter, sir," Jeff said, and dragged it out of his breast pocket. "Please read it, sir. It's private and personal, but it's the best way I know to convince you that you're looking at the worst, most lily-livered, arrantest sniveling coward in the South's whole history, sir, not to mention the Navy's. And since that cowardice is sure Lord going to be permanent, Commodore, sir, from here on in, I ask you mighty kindly to bust me back to able-bodied seaman, *third* class—y'know, diminished mental faculties—and give me the job of peeling spuds for the shore officers' mess for the duration . . ."

"I'll be damned if I will!" the Commodore snorted, and took that letter. Some minutes later, he looked up with a rueful smile.

"You win, Lieutenant," he sighed. "This is a mighty powerful argument, I have to admit. Especially in view of the fact that poor Hunley's underwater torpedo boat is practically a deathtrap. Tomorrow's mission is entirely voluntary. I am neither ordering nor forbidding it. If it works, maybe with improvements, the submarine could become a valuable weapon, especially in our country's circumstances."

"No, sir," Jeff said. "The only improvement that will make the undersea boat work is a motor that doesn't burn air to run, sir. And that means an electromagnetic motor powered from Leyden-jar-type-electrical storage batteries. We're a hundred years away from that, sir. Otherwise the design is sound. Only, those poor fellows use up all the air pedaling and cranking to make her move. Then—they suffocate, sir. Down there, the crews will have to exert as little bodily effort as possible, or else—"

"All right. But you're not getting off scot-free, Lieutenant. Due to your well-known abilities at scrounging around for materials and making something out of practically nothing, I'm giving you a new and mighty important commission. And also in honor of your departed sister, Miss Rose Ann. You're to proceed to London, England, by the fastest available transport, and serve as our liaison officer at a certain shipyard there. They're converting a fast steamer, formerly of their London–Bombay line, into a cruiser for us. You're to ride herd on the Limeys, see that they don't drag their feet, and to prevent, by any means, fair or foul, the Yankee Ambassador, Adams, from scaring or bluffing them out of complying with their contracts with us, as he did in the case of those two magnificent ironclad rams back in '62—"

"I heard about that," Jeff said. "Threatened the British with war, didn't he, sir?"

"'I am ignorant of the precise legal aspect of the question,'"

Commodore Wilkes quoted bitterly, " 'but if these vessels escape, it is superfluous to point out to Your Lordship that it is war!' The arrogant little popinjay! Pure bluff, but he pulled it off. We didn't get those rams. That mustn't happen this time, Lieutenant. You must see that Adams doesn't even find out what's being done to convert that liner into a commerce-raiding cruiser. And when she's finished, you're to ship out on her—as an ordinary merchant seaman—as far as Lisbon. There you'll pick up a Portuguese crew and sail her out to the island of Madeira. Captain Waddell will take her over from there, after she's armed and fueled. I rather think he'll offer you a berth aboard her, as chief gunnery officer, say. It's a great opportunity, McKenzie! Your name will go down in history, my boy . . ."

"Thank you, sir," Jeff said dolefully. "Don't reckon I can refuse this one too, can I? Oh, I know that commerce raiding is not dangerous hardly at all, but Lord God, sir, when will I *ever* see my wife and baby?"

"There's a war on, Lieutenant, in case you've forgot," the Commodore said drily. "But since the *Shenandoah* won't be ready for you to bring her into port at Madeira until mid-August, say, you may have ten days' leave before proceeding to Wilmington, North Carolina, and from there to England. Now get out of here, you impertinent young pup, before I change my mind!"

"Yes, sir!" Jeff beamed. "Thank you mighty kindly, sir! God bless you, sir! I'm on my way!"

On February 17, 1864, the night after Lieutenant Geoffrey McKenzie, C.S.N., had permanently resigned from both heroism and its exact synonym, sheer folly, the Confederate submarine *Hunley*, under the command of a volunteer who wasn't even a seaman, Lieutenant George E. Dixon, an artilleryman from the Alabama state troops, sank the U.S. frigate *Housatonic* as she lay at anchor five and one half miles off Fort Sumter in Charleston Harbor. The *Housatonic* went down with all hands. Caught in her eddy, so did the *Hunley*. There being no records demonstrating the contrary, that was the first time in history that a submarine sank a warship.

And the last, for the next fifty years.

Chapter Seventeen

On September 2, 1864, the day that Sherman telegraphed to President Lincoln: "Atlanta is ours, and fairly won!" Rose Ann McKenzie was released from the Old Capitol Prison in Washington. By then she had been in jail for almost a year, during which, for her, time and history had stood still, so that she emerged into the world as a living ghost, a creature out of a past that no longer existed, set free to face a future that, given her druthers, she'd much rather hadn't existed either.

Of her release, and the manner of it, what really can be said? Call it a fluke, a mocking sport of the indifferent, lecherous, and ribald old sots who rule a cut-rate cosmos where everything works by hazard, and nothing ever, even by accident, makes sense? Or was it engineered by the direct intervention of some particular one of them, a little more nectar-and-ambrosia-befuddled than usual, swung down by old Euripides, say, to this jerry-built stage of (limited) time and (temporary) being, upon a crazy device of ropes and pulleys, blocks and tackle, to straighten out the unholy messes the tired old playwright, his faculties failing him, had written his characters into? Perhaps something of each of these. Except that the plot, or the absence of one, was pure theater of the absurd, and the god, staggering out of the machine to take his pratfall before the jeering audience, surely not a creation of solemn Euripides, but, much more likely, of mocking Aristophanes.

Or—to rectify again!—the goddess. Her name—oh, well—her *nom de guerre*—was Sal. Saucy Sal. But in Washington, an essentially Southern city, that Saucy came out Sassy, and was generally shortened to Sass, with the Sal dropped altogether. She was big, beefy, blowsy, and blond *pro opera et gratia* of the frequent and fervent application of the then available chemicals, helped out with lemon juice. She much preferred the substitution of such perfumes as were within the reach of her limited purse, and the perceptions of her appalling taste, to the tiresome chore of even weekly ablutions, with the result that her presence was pre-announced, and discernible even to a blind man from a full five yards away. Which was all to the good; some of her clients *were* blind men. Well past forty, and running to fat, Sass couldn't afford to be choosy, and knew it.

On the day—August 25 or thereabouts—that she lent a quite accidental hand toward the alteration of Rose Ann McKenzie's fate, she was headed full steam ahead straight toward the Old Capitol Prison, with the declared purpose of visiting Rose Ann herself. The Old Capitol was practically a second home to Sal. Since the very existence of the sisterhood to which she belonged offended the pious Victorian dames of Washington—with Mary Todd Lincoln at their head!—to their straitlaced souls, she had been thrown into it so often on charges of "loitering and soliciting" that, as she cheerfully confided on one such occasion to Rose Ann, "Dommed if I dun't think sometimes I wuz *born* here, dearie!"

But just before she reached the sentry box—where she'd have to stop, give her name, the name of the prisoner she wanted to visit, and have any package she had with her looked into, though not her person searched, that outrage, in those times, being inflicted only upon women who crossed the frontier, bound for the South—a pleasant baritone voice hailed her: "Why, Sass, as I live and breathe!" the voice said mockingly. "What foul deeds, low skulduggery, and filthy tricks be you up to this fine day, my winsome lass?"

"Oh, 'tis ye, eh?" Sassy Sal said disgustedly, falling heavily out of the pose of arch—and elephantine—seductiveness she had automatically fallen into at the sound of a male voice. "Thunk the Rebels had mayhap done ye in by now, from all the lyin' 'n' braggin' they prints over yer John Hancock in that rag ye writes for, Ray me blinking b'hoy. 'N' what, may a body ask, be ye doin' in this neck o' the woods? Ye ain't a lowly police reporter fer a yaller sheet no more; nay 'tis a foine war correspondent from the far-flung battlefronts ye be now, according to yer paper. O' hev they got wise to ye 'n' busted ye back to chasing ambulances 'n' interviewing floozies, as of auld, Mr. Raymond Carr, gintlemun reporter?"

"Not a bit of it, Sassy, me luv," Raymond Carr chuckled. "Though you'd give your solid-brass eyeteeth to see me brought low, wouldn't you? Never thought that when I hung that nickname on you the day you cussed poor old Judge McGinnis out so bad that the air in the courtroom turned brimstone blue, it was going to stick. That wasn't smart, Sass me lass. Threw the book at you: another ninety days on top of the thirty he'd hung on you already, for trying to get a congressman, no less, to stray from the straight and narrow. So you ran up and down his family tree in hobnail boots. And I wrote that paean of praise to your matchless vocabulary. With the result that it's been Sassy Sal ever since, hasn't it?"

"Yis. 'N' the back of me hand to ye, ye blighter. Ain't nuthin' worse than noospapermen, not even snakes 'n' spiders!"

"Oh, come now, Sass," Carr laughed. "You know I'm the love of your life, the dream of your maidenly heart. Tell me, what have you got in that huge basket? Which reminds me; I'm deuced hungry . . ."

"Ye reach yer paw in the direction of it, 'n' ye'll draw back a bloody stump!" Sass said grimly. " 'Tis rations I've got in there. For a angel outa Gawd's own glory. Sweetest li'l missy ye iver did see, Ray me b'hoy. Saved the lives o' half the wimmen in this here jail, single-handed 'n' all by her lonesome . . ."

"If she's a friend of *yours*, Sass," Carr hooted, "the only thing she ever saved was a sawbuck or two made by going right back on her southernmost promontory!"

" 'Tis wrong ye be, me b'hoy," Sass said proudly. "Me fran' she be, but nanetheless she is a lyedy. Talks like a blooming duchess, that she does, fair-spoken 'n' foine, so thet a' times it costs me to unnerstan' 'er. 'N', fer yer information, Raymond Carr, she ain't no hoor. She wuz sent up fer reasons o' state no less. The gels in there swear 'twuz fer spyin' fer the blinking Rebels. Been in there nigh onto a whole year, 'n' the talk is thet auld Abe has took his Bible oath niver to let her out whilst there be breath still in 'er. Seems thet the information she passed alang to the Johnnies cost the Union ferces two whole divisions—or somethin' o' kind—at a place called Chickaloogah . . ."

"Chickamauga," Carr corrected her automatically. "I was there, you know, Sass. As correspondent for my paper, right in the thick of things. And afterward I was at Lookout Mountain and Missionary Ridge with Generals Grant and Thomas, when we licked the pants off Braxton Bragg and—" He stopped short, stared at Sassy Sal, his eyes widening, widening. "Holy cow!" he whispered. "Her name, Sass! Tell me her *name!*"

"Rose Ann McKenzie," Saucy Sal said.

"But she was hanged!" Carr howled. "It's true they caught her spying near the camp at Tullahoma, but they hanged that little girl, to throw the fear of God into the rest of those Rebel witches . . ."

"Thet's whut *ye* thinks!" Sass snorted. " 'N' if ye dun't believe me, why dun't ye come alang 'n' see?"

"Yes," Rose Ann said to the reporter as they sat in the visitors' hall, or rather cage, because that's what it looked like, with bars all over everything that could be barred, and a stout iron grille between the prisoner and the visitor, its interstices too small to pass even a knife or a file through, not to mention a pistol. "I was condemned to be hanged, but for some reason or other, my sentence was never carried out. I don't know why, except maybe the Army authorities thought that they could gain the same ends, or have much the same effect upon other female spies, by letting the world believe I actually had been executed, without having the burden of—a woman's death—upon their consciences. So they took the most extravagant and absurd precautions to bring me here from Nashville without any of you newspapermen finding out about it. I confess I don't follow their reasoning. Why should there be different penalties for the same crime when it's committed by a man than when a woman does it? A crime's a crime, it seems to me. Besides, they did me no favor. I should have—welcomed death at the time. In fact, I still would . . ."

Raymond Carr tore his utterly fascinated gaze away from her small face. By then it was all bones and hollows, eclipsed by her eyes. Those are twin emerald seas a man could drown in . . . he thought. He said, "Is that why you gave away all the good food Sal brought you to the others, without even tasting it?"

"No," she sighed. "It's just that I have no appetite. None at all. Maybe if I could get out of here, go back home, see how my family's faring, it would come back. To be assured that my brother is still alive, and my brother-in-law, for that matter; that my sister's all right, my father—would do wonders for me, likely . . ."

"There's no one else?" Carr asked her eagerly. At the moment, he'd forgotten his dull, complaining wife and the three howling brats who made the risks of front-line reporting, much of the time fully equal to those an ordinary soldier ran, preferable to enduring the unceasing slow, daily, hourly torment of a bad marriage.

"No," she whispered. "There's no one at all."

"Odd," he said gruffly, having remembered his own stifling legal state by then. "As beautiful as you are, one would think . . ."

"Don't think," she said gently. "I've found it serves for nothing, except to remind me of things I'd rather not remember . . ."

"By Jove, that's right!" he said. "There was some mention in the Western papers of a husband who—"

"Was killed at Tullahoma," she said, her voice flat, calm, expressionless.

"I'm sorry," Raymond Carr whispered.

"Don't be. I'm not. We—didn't get along. He was even—cruel to me at times. Physically cruel. But then, I've come to realize that he was more than a little—mad. So I've forgiven him. Besides, I wasn't referring to him. I'm thinking of the man I—I caused to be hanged, because he was convinced that if he confessed I had made those maps he was caught with, I'd be strung up in his stead. As it turned out, he was wrong, but that doesn't change the fact that— he died for me. Too heavy a burden for me to want to support for long . . ."

"Look!" he got out, his voice breath-torn and ragged. "You're not going to, you don't mean to—to—"

"Harm myself? No. That's—cowardly, and I've never been a coward. Besides, it's not even necessary. This place will finish me off soon enough, without my having to lift a finger . . ."

"I'm going to get you out of here!" he said fervently. "I don't know exactly how yet, but I've got an idea. The power of the press, y'know, Miss McKenzie. Suppose you tell me your story. All of it. Starting with whatever on earth it was that made a cultivated New Englander like you even want to benefit the slaveholding South in any way . . ."

"A cultivated New Englander?" she said wonderingly. Then suddenly she threw back her head and laughed aloud. "You mean the way I talk, don't you? That there's jest a pose, honey boy! I'm from Old Virginia, and about as Southern as they make 'em. Brung up on corn pone and 'lasses, and tha's an ever-lovin' fact . . ."

"But—but—" he said. "I don't understand! I would have sworn you were born on Beacon Hill!"

"Born there, no. Just spent a good many years there, going to a Yankee school my pa sent me to in the hope of keeping me outa trouble. Fat chance! Trouble's us McKenzies' middle name. Anyhow, all that's water under the bridge now. What d'you want me to tell you, Mr. Carr?"

"Anything useful in—well—awakening public sentiment in your behalf. Some meritorious action that—"

"Then I'm lost," she said with a sadly mocking grin. "The story of my life, printed in the public press, would make the Yankee government change its mind and decide to hang me, after all. My pa always did swear I was a natural candidate for the presidency of the A.B.&W. railroad line . . ."

Carr searched his memory. "Never heard of that line," he said at last.

"Ain't no sich," she quipped. "Pa made it up. Those letters stand for—well—Hindquarters Backwards and Wrong. Tha's poor little old me, all right . . ."

"Tell me your story anyhow," he said. "Let me be the judge of its value. Slanting a newsworthy item, without ever descending to outright lies, is one of the subtlest aspects of the reporter's art . . ."

"All right," she sighed, "but that there won't be a slant; it'll be the steepest ding-danged toboggan slide you ever laid eyes on!"

She was, he realized an hour later—for, due to his paper's political clout, no time limit had been placed upon his visit—very nearly right. Not even her genuinely regretful final statement—"I'm sorry I—we—did all that. It almost surely prolonged a war we can't possibly win. And every day longer it goes on only costs more brave boys, North and South, their lives . . ."—could do anything to reduce or ameliorate the stubborn fact that, from a strictly legal standpoint, she should have been hanged twenty times over. But he couldn't leave her here in this damp, cold, evil-smelling pesthouse to die. She was so thin, so fragile. And now and again she gave vent to a hollow, racking cough that had a most ominous sound to it. He conceded that he was being foolish, but by then he'd discovered, as many another man already had, and several more were going to, during her long life, that good and bad, right and wrong, even the law and the prophets became curiously irrelevant when you were dealing with Rose Ann. Cudgel his brains as he would, Raymond Carr could think of no way at all to—

Then all of a sudden, a great and blinding light burst just behind his eyes. What was it that Sassy Sal had said? Something about—saving lives . . . Slowly it came back to him: "Sweetest li'l missy ye iver did see, Ray me b'hoy. Saved the lives o' half the wimmen in this here jail, single-handed 'n' all by her lonesome . . ."

He leaned forward, eagerly, said, "But what about the lives of all the women prisoners in this jail you saved? According to old Sal, you—"

She shrugged.

"Much ado about nothing," she said tiredly. "Virginia is one of the most fever-ridden states in the South. We all catch everything imaginable when we're young. And then, we either die—or survive. Under those conditions, if we live to grow up, we seem to be proof against any kind of sickness. Something like Jenner's vaccination to prevent smallpox, I reckon. So when fever broke out in the upper third-floor row of cells in the women's division, and the poor creatures were dying like flies, I volunteered to nurse 'em. For—two reasons: if I caught whatever the dickens it was they had, and passed on, the good Lord couldn't hold me accountable for deliberate suicide. And if I didn't catch it, maybe I could do some good. I—didn't catch it. Then the poor things started getting better, largely because I managed to give 'em a little of the two things no human being can live without . . ."

He said, "And those two things are?"

"Love and—hope," Rose Ann McKenzie said.

So Raymond Carr had his story. Or almost. In the next two or three days, he obtained from the warden and his staff permission to interview, in half-hour sessions, fully thirty of the women who had survived what even the prison authorities admitted had been a really serious epidemic of some kind of swamp fever among the inmates of the third floor. He found himself almost overwhelmed by the depth, passion, and tenderness of the love—no other word would do—those poor bedraggled slatterns declared for Rose Ann. They had recognized, with the solidly ingrained snobbery of the very poor, here was a lady. A very great lady. And that she had fed them, bathed them with her two tender, freckled hands, combed their matted, lice-infested hair, held the basin for them to vomit black-streaked and bloody bile into, supported them upon bedpans and chamber pots so they wouldn't fall off, wept disconsolately over the ones who died, was a thing that none of them would ever forget.

"I'd die for 'er!" more than one of them declared. "I'd let meself be chopped into mincemeat 'n' roasted over hot coals fur 'er sweet sake!"

"I wuz slippin' erway," another hardened denizen of the streets told him, "but she took me hand, that li'l red-headed angel outa glory, and squeezed it 'n' hung on to it 'n' sez to me, cryin' like I wuz her sister o' her ma, 'Don't go, Jenny-Jo'—them's me names, Mr. Carr, Jane Josephine, o' leastwise they wuz when I wuz decent —'please don't go! I couldn't stand it if you died!' 'N' why? Jist 'cause I kept some of them bitch-kitties from the South Side from plaguing her the first time they heard the way she talks—like a grand duchess, like a queen—and she wuz grateful fur a li'l ol' thing like that. 'N' she *meant* it, sah! D'ye know how it feels to have sumbody *care* erbout you, *reeely* care, after thirty years o' kicks 'n' cusses? 'N' that sumbody as far above you as the blinkin' sky? So I

made up me mind *not* to croak. Two days after that, I wuz helpin'
her wit' the others . . ."

He had his story. And he put all that passion into it. All that
tenderness. The paper he wrote for was one of the capital's oldest
and best; it was read by senators, congressmen, high military offi-
cialdom, members of the Cabinet, and the wives of all of these; it
reached even into the White House itself.

Fat little Mary Todd, Southern-born, slammed a copy down beside long Abe's supper plate. He was the President of the United
States to all the world, but he was only her husband to little Mary,
and she had no compunction about making him toe the line, keeping him straight. She'd already put a stop to that tomfool notion
that her darling boy Robert ought to be allowed to go to the front
and get himself killed, because keeping him out of action was "embarrassing" to the President. Well, "the President" could be as em-
barrassed as he wanted to be, but her *husband* sure Lord had better
stop 'em from sending her twenty-one-year-old baby anywhere
near where people were shooting off guns, or by the Almighty
she'd make him rue the day! So Captain Robert Todd Lincoln
never heard a rifle fired in anger—at considerable political cost to
his father. Long Abe ran the country, but short Mary ran Abe.
Ragged, at that.

"Abe," she said now, "you've got to do something about this
girl."

"Such as, honey?" little Mary's husband said.

"Free her. Let her out of that jail. Turn her loose."

"But, Mary, this is the same girl you said *ought* to be hanged!"

"Well, I've changed my mind. Woman's prerogative. Abe, you
turn this girl loose, you hear!"

"Yes, honey," Mary Todd's husband said.

By the next night, La Fayette C. Baker, head of the Secret Service (for by then President Lincoln had long since found out that
Allan Pinkerton might well be the greatest detective extant, but as
head of the Secret Service he existed in a state of permanent confusion, so he'd replaced him with this tall, handsome, bearded, exceedingly dirty fighter), dropped by long after office hours to tell
the President that the case of Rose Ann McKenzie was happily
arranged.

"We've got her in a respectable boardinghouse, sir," Baker said.
"And day after tomorrow, we'll send her home . . ."

"How, La Fayette?" Abraham Lincoln said.

"By boat, sir. Down the coast and up the James to our deep-water port at City Point. Then, under a flag of truce, to their lines. I'm sure the Rebels will treat her well. She's something of a hero-ine to them, you know, sir . . ."

"All right," the President sighed. "Glad that's one thing settled. Give the little lady my best wishes, and tell her I hope to one day greet her—as a loyal citizen of the Union, of course . . ."

"Sir, speaking of that, she's asked me to ask you whether you couldn't spare her five minutes, say. She wants to thank you in person for setting her free . . ."

The President of the United States looked at the head of the Secret Service.

"What's she like?" the President said.

"Extraordinary," Baker said. "Small, delicate, even fragile—but —beautiful, in a haunting sort of way. I'd wager that no man who's ever spent five minutes in her company will ever forget her. I know *I* won't. And I'm not especially susceptible to the charms of the fair sex. In my line, I can't afford to be."

"You surprise me, La Fayette," the President said. "There are a good many beautiful women in Washington; even, I reckon, a few such in jail. Why does this one impress you so?"

"Not because of her beauty," the Secret Serviceman said. "Or rather not because of her beauty alone, though it too is extraordi-nary. But when you add to it wit, personality, charm, the heart of a lioness, the nerve of a brass monkey, a more than adequate degree of cultivation, a voice—low, husky, sweet—that talks like a grand duchess one minute and like a nigger field hand the next, and that makes you wonder, sir, why she hasn't used it as instrument of excavation to escape from prison since it could quite literally melt rocks—"

Abraham Lincoln threw back his craggy head and laughed aloud.

"La Fayette," he chuckled, "you sound just like a man in love!"

"Don't doubt it, sir. And I suspect that nearly every human male that little Miss McKenzie sets out to influence emerges from her company with his pulse racing and his head awhirl. That young woman is the closest approximation to the adjective 'irresistible' I have ever encountered in all my professional experience . . ." He paused, then added drily, "Or in my private life as well, for that matter . . ."

The President stared at him, but soberly now.

"You think I shouldn't grant her that five-minute interview, then?" he said.

"I think you *can't*, sir," the nation's number one spy said quietly. "Oh, I'm not talking about the advisability or not of having a pleasant chat with this young person. That's for you to decide, Mr. President. But the logistics of such a meeting are—or have become —a nightmare—"

"Why?" Abraham Lincoln said.

"Before she was released from prison, I might have arranged a visit on your part, Mr. President, to the Old Capitol; say, an inspection tour—as evidence of presidential concern for conditions there. But now? I am the head of your Secret Service, sir; with all due modesty, I can honestly state I'm good at my work. I can hoodwink the Rebel Spy Service every day in the week and twice on Sundays. But if I paid a visit to such a stunning young thing at her boardinghouse, Mrs. Baker would be advised by the *world's* best intelligence agency, the sisterhood of Washington gossips, before I even got back home. Whereupon both our dinnerware and my poor head would suffer, sir!"

"Women!" the President said with a wry chuckle. "But there is an alternative, my friend. I could have little Miss McKenzie brought here, y'know . . ."

"Of course, sir," La Fayette Baker said, "thus presenting yourself with two alternatives: That said visit be concealed from Mrs. Lincoln, in which case she'll only find out about it later, whereupon I humbly request to be made ambassador to *China*, sir, and sped immediately upon my way; or you can invite the First Lady to be present at the interview—"

"Exactly what I meant to do," the President said.

"Then, sir, you'd better be prepared to face a demand from Mrs. Lincoln that little Miss McKenzie be immediately returned to prison, long enough for an extra-high gallows to be erected in the jail yard below. While it is perfectly true that her fellow inmates literally adored that delightful little creature, nothing male— neither lovers nor husbands—entered into the equation, Mr. President. I strongly suspect that the reaction of the genus *wives* to our charming ex-jailbird would be both negative and explosive, sir!"

"I see," the President sighed. "You're perfectly right, La Fayette, and I'm sorry. I was sort of looking forward to meeting the Rebels' most famous female spy . . ."

"And you would have enjoyed the visit, I assure you, sir, but in this case it seems to me the price to be paid for a bit of innocent pleasure might be too high. I'll tell little Miss McKenzie that the pressure of affairs of state prevented your being able to—"

The President lifted a big, bony hand.

"No," he said. "Don't tell her that, La Fayette."

"Then what shall I tell her, sir?"

"That the First Lady would object. Strongly. Or violently. I leave the qualifying modifier up to you, my friend."

The head of the Secret Service looked at the President of the United States. Then, very slowly, he smiled. Shook his head in almost envious admiration.

"She'll be—enormously flattered. You really do know women, don't you, sir?" he said.

From the moment she climbed out of that rowboat, with one lone carpetbag, and it weighing practically nothing, on the north bank of the James, opposite the Union base at City Point, Rose Ann began to sense that the war was lost. Her escort—her second escort, for her first had gone back with the rowboat to the south bank of the James—was a detachment of Union cavalry. And, as the first had been, as were all the Union troops she saw, they were beautifully uniformed, bursting with health, sure of themselves, confident that it was all going to be over soon now, and that they were going to win. Of course, the only Johnny Rebs she'd seen so far had been a bunch of prisoners at City Point, and they—looked like walking corpses, like death warmed over enough to move, their rags fluttering about their skeletal figures, too beaten down to even try to flirt with her. And when a Southerner won't flirt with anything in skirts, even if she looks like homemade sin, as I do now, likely, he's sure Lord whipped, she thought sadly.

She rode behind the young lieutenant who led the cavalry detachment, with her arms around his waist, "Which makes this the first worthwhile duty I've drawn since I got mixed up in this man's war," he told her happily. Passing Malvern Hill, the one she'd got shot through the middle trying to save, they cantered north, skirting the edges of White Oak Swamp, until they got to Seven Pines, where her husband of one night, Giuseppe Lucarelli, her Joe-Joe, had got himself killed a million years ago back in 1861, after lying about his age so that they would let him join the Union Army, just as he'd lied about it before that justice of the peace up there in Massachusetts so they would let him marry her. I should change my name, she thought bitterly. To—Bubonic Plague McKenzie, maybe. 'Cause a fellow who climbs into the hay with me is—long gone, brother! Giuseppe. Greg. Kurt. Even—Colin. His body stayed alive. But his spirit, his heart, his manhood—what happened to them?

She closed her mind against those thoughts, stopped thinking altogether. By then they had turned into the old Williamsburg Stage Road and were riding straight toward the Confederate lines. Those lines, the Yankee lieutenant had told her, were all of thirty-seven miles long. They extended from the Chickahominy, all the way past Richmond, to down below, and more than halfway around Petersburg, in a huge semicircle. Once they had closed it into a full circle, all the railroad lines, the South Side, the Danville, the Weldon, bringing supplies into the two cities up from the south —"That is, if Sherman's left 'em any supplies to bring!" the young lieutenant exulted—would be cut, and the war would be over. With her capital in Union hands, the young lieutenant was sure, the South wouldn't have the heart to fight anymore.

"You just don't know us Southerners," Rose Ann told him.

And now he took from his first sergeant the lance staff bearing the company colors. Above them he attached a huge banner of white. "Wait for me here, boys," he ordered. "Those Rebs get nervous and trigger-happy if they see more than one horseman riding toward them at the same time . . ."

As he slow-trotted toward the Confederate lines, the pickets sang out: "Flag o' truce, Yank? Whatcha want to dicker about? Y'all planning to call this damn war off 'n' skedaddle back up Nawth like y'all oughta?"

"Not on your life, Johnny!" the lieutenant laughed. "What we aim to do is chase you into the Gulf of Mexico. But right now, I've brought you fellows a present: a little Josephine Reb who says she's from near Richmond. Caught her spying, but she's so blamed pretty we didn't have the heart to hang her. So we charged her a fine of two hundred kisses instead. That's why those honeydew lips of hers are a mite swollen, but other than that, she's just fine . . ."

Rose Ann leaned halfway around from behind his broad back and said sweetly, "Howdy, boys . . ."

"Jesus God! The Yank ain't lying! He's done gone 'n' brung us a angel outa glory! Somebody catch a holt on to me! O' else I'm a-gonna run hog wild, I tell you! Honey, is you fur reeel? Or am I jist dreamin' wide awake?"

"I'm real enough," Rose Ann sighed. "But is that the way you

boys usually greet a lady? A body would think you hadn't seen a
girl in the last twenty years . . ."

"One what looks like *you*, honey chile—never!" they chorused.
"When your pappy 'n' your mama made you, they throwed away
the patent 'n' busted the mold! C'mon, lemme help you down from
that there damnyankee hoss, and you come set a spell wit' we'uns,
angel baby, sugar pie. 'N' after that, you tell us which chunk o'
Yankee Land you wants 'n' we'll take it for you! Washington, Boston, New Yawk—name it and it's yourn!"

"I want you to thank the lieutenant mighty kindly for bringing
me home," Rose Ann said primly. "And after that, take me to your
commanding officer—"

"Aw, honey," they groaned, "he's mighty *old*. Now jest you take
a look at us. Mighty pretty boys, the fillies all allow. Full o' piss 'n'
ginger, why—"

"I'll bet," Rose Ann said sternly. "Take me to your commander,
please!"

When she drove up to McKenzie's Manse in that hired rig, none
of the blacks was in sight. The Hundred looked—run-down, un-
kempt, as though it hadn't been attended to properly in months.
Up in Richmond, she had already heard that the Negroes were
running away in droves, making their way to the encircling Union
lines, where they were enrolled in labor battalions—at, the bitter
word had it, absolutely no pay. Richmond was jam-packed with
refugees, both from the valley, where Early was trying to wreck at
first, then hold, and finally stop Phil Sheridan, and up from the
country around Petersburg, where life was even grimmer than it
was in Richmond, and growing more so by the hour. There were
men over sixty and boys barely fourteen holding those thin lines
around Petersburg now. Cripples. The lame, the halt, everything
except the blind. So changed was the capital that she rented the
horse and buggy from a total stranger, and got out of town without
talking to a single person whom she knew. In fact, she saw only
one old acquaintance: Father Erwell, of St. Paul's. But when, being
unwilling in her anxiety-driven haste to get out to the Hundred to
stop and chat, she waved at him cheerfully, the priest rubbed his
eyes with what seemed to be sheer disbelief, frowned, and turned
away.

The door was locked and barred, which didn't surprise her. She
had already heard tales of deserters and skulkers who preyed upon
outlying plantations. So she pounded on it with her fist for long

minutes. So long, in fact, that her hand was getting red and sore, but still nobody came to answer it.

Damned good-for-nothing niggers! she thought. Of course, A'nt Cindy could be asleep by now, late as it is. And if she is, not even artillery fire can wake her up. But that lazy Venus off kitty-catting around with the hands from some other place. Fairdale, likely. As for Caesar, Brutus, and Cassius—who knows? Caesar wouldn't run off; he's too old. But those other two? Lord! S'pose Gwen's in there all by her lonesome, except for Pa, who's three sheets to the wind by now, and is just plain *scared* to open the door?

She took a backward step, cupped her hand alongside her mouth, and called out: "Gwen! Gwen! Are you home, honey? It's me, Rose Ann!"

She listened. Slowly, tiredly, she heard those footsteps coming on. Then Gwen's voice came, faintly, tremulously, fearfully through the door.

"Who—did you—say you were?" she said.

"Rose Ann, silly! Open this door, will you? I just got back, from Washington! Took me nearly three weeks to do it, but here I am! Oh, Gwen honey, I—"

Gwen's voice came through the door, dead stopped, choked off, raging: "Go away. I don't know what your game is, Miss whoever you are. But you can't be my poor sister, because—she's dead!"

"Ohhhhh, Lord!" Rose Ann moaned. "In that case, Gwen honey, you're talking to the liveliest damn corpse you ever saw! Ohhhhh, Lord, twice! I know, I know! You likely read in the paper that the Yankees had gone and hanged me! Gwen sugar, they *didn't!* It was all a trick! Propaganda to scare other she-spies off! Oh, Jesus, Gwen, open this door, will you?"

She heard the bolts slide back, the hinges creak. The door opened an inch, two, five, then flew open wide. Gwen put out her arms to her little sister. Rose Ann grabbed her, squeezing hard, kissing her all over her pale face, and crying, crying, crying . . .

It took both of them a full ten minutes to calm down enough to talk. And then, very obviously, Gwen didn't want to.

"I'll make you some sassafras tea," she said nervously. "But if you're hungry, you'll have to make do with corn bread. *Cold* corn bread. A'nt Cindy is poorly. And Venus ran away, soon after Brutus and Cassius did . . ."

"With Cassius, I hope!" Rose Ann said. Cassius and Venus had jumped over the broomstick years ago. But they had never got along. Human nature was human nature, no matter what color hide it came wrapped in.

"I doubt it," Gwen said. "The darkies don't take their marriage vows very seriously, y'know. But as for that—" She stopped short, said. "Do you want the tea?"

"Yes," Rose Ann said. "But no corn pone, please! I couldn't stand it. Jail rations ruined my stomach, so eating has become quite a chore for me . . ."

"You are as thin as rail," Gwen sighed. "But you can't hope to fatten up down here. We're practically starving . . ." She got up, tiredly, heavily. As she did so, the cotton nightgown she had on caught briefly on the arm of the chair she had been sitting in, so that it tightened against her slender form. Rose Ann gave a little choked-off gasp. But she didn't say anything. She wanted to—contain her own feelings about this—abrupt turn in the ebbing tide of the family's fortunes. She couldn't trust herself to dominate them fully. Not yet. She needed time.

So—Cabe got leave, she thought bitterly. And luck was with him —with them—at last. I hope they'll be happy now, finally. I do, truly. So be it, Lord. When the war is over, I'll—just leave. There's —nothing here for me, is there? But then there's never been . . .

She dashed the back of a freckled hand across suddenly scalded eyes, called out in the direction of Gwen's retreating form: "I reckon Pa's calling hogs by now, isn't he, Gwen? Oh, well, I can wait 'til tomorrow to muss his hair up and tickle him. 'Cause when he's put himself to sleep with a bottle, waking him up is too big a chore . . . He is asleep, isn't he?"

"Yes, Father's—sleeping," Gwen said. Her voice sounded—odd. Ice cold. Toneless. Dead.

Rose Ann bounced up, scurried on back to the kitchen. Took out of her sister's snowy hand the poker that Gwen was using to stir the embers of the fire in the great fireplace in which the Mc-Kenzies—temperamentally incapable of doing anything either on time or exactly right, even living in their own century—still did their cooking, never having got around to installing a cast-iron range.

"Here," she said tenderly, "let me do that, honey. You really shouldn't exert yourself from here on in, y'know—"

Gwen's shell-pink lips went snowy. Disappeared against the general pallor of her face.

"Oh, my God!" she whispered. "You mean—it shows? That people can tell—already?"

"Not if you wear loose-fitting clothes and hold your breath most of the time," Rose Ann teased her solemnly. "But, aw shucks, Gwen sugar—what's the odds? You 'n' old Cabe have a real pretty piece o' paper with all kinds of seals and ribbons on it, granting y'all the right to commit matrimony, any old time y'all feel the spirit moving, 'pears to me. And since Cabe just can't resist whooping it up a mite in town with the boys every time he gets leave, all the long-nosed witches will have a nice, cozy date to start counting on their fingers from. By the way, how's that horny little sawed-off rascal, anyhow?"

Gwen stared into the fireplace. The now-renewed flames—for Rose Ann had already thrown several pieces of fat, resinous pine onto those smoldering embers—lent warm, orange-yellow highlights to her almost silvery, ash-blond hair. Then she turned, faced Rose Ann, said, flatly, slowly, calmly, "I don't know. He may be dead." She paused, added with the same eerie calm: "I *hope* he's dead—"

"Jesus Christ!" Rose Ann whispered very softly.

"Since he hasn't been home since the twenty-fifth of April 1863, which will be a year and five months day after tomorrow, it would be better for everybody. Even, very likely, for—him."

Rose Ann nodded in the general direction of her sister's midriff.

"Colin's?" she asked.

"Yes," Gwen said.

Rose Ann stood there, Lot's wife looking back over the Cities of the Plain. When she moved at last, that motion blurred sight. She brought her right hand whistling around open-palmed, to explode its impact into sound, pistol-shot loud, against her sister's face.

Gwen staggered, might—almost surely *would*—have fallen, if Rose Ann had not leaped forward and caught her in her arms.

"That slap," she rasped, "was on Cabe's behalf. He's not the kind of man who ought to be cheated on. And specially not by the sort o' fellow you chose to do it with. But *this*," she went on, her tone softening, "is from *me* . . ." She leaned swiftly closer, planted a soft, wet kiss on Gwendolyn McKenzie Henry's cheek, where the dead-white imprint of her own hard, hot little palm was slowly turning crimson.

"Welcome to the sisterhood of poor bedraggled bitches, Gwen," she said. "Oh, to heck with that sassafras tea. C'mon, let's sit down someplace while you tell me *all* about it . . ."

Gwen smiled then, a slow and secret smile, inward-turning.

"There's nothing to tell," she said softly. "I love Colin. I always have. I always will, until the day I die. Say that—one night, last June—the whole earth was—drenched—in the scent of honey-suckle—sick and reeling with it—and he came riding out here—under a yellow moon that filled up half the sky. What more is there to be said than that, Ramb? Or even needs to be?"

"Nothing," Rose Ann sighed. "That wraps the whole matter up, I reckon. And in pretty pink ribbons, at that. Anyhow, c'mon, let's go sit in the little parlor. Or upstairs in your bedroom. Reckon you ought to be lying down, anyhow. We got to take good care of my little unlawful niece. Lord, but she's going to be gorgeous! A com-bination of you 'n' Colin—that's almost a written guarantee of beauty . . ."

"Your—definitely unlawful—*nephew,*" Gwen said. "I've prom-ised Colin—a son, Ramb."

"Honey, forgive me for speaking out of turn, but then I always do, don't I?" Rose Ann sighed. "But from where I sit, the combina-tion—the spiritual combination, 'stead of the physical one, I mean, this time—of Colin and you would work out a heck of a lot better in a female. Colin is a really nice boy, but he frankly admitted to the world that he's a wee bit shy of one of the essential elements—of manhood, Gwen darling, which is valor, by shooting off his own kneecap. Now, a she critter doesn't have to brave—"

"*You* are," Gwen said drily.

"I'm the off hoss, always kicking over my traces. I should have been drowned as a pup. How's that for mixing my metaphors, Gwen sugar? That's just what I am, come to think of it: a mixed metaphor. An off horse. A poor bedraggled she pup. A disgrace to femininity and the human race both. And—"

"Very lovable. *The* most lovable person I've ever known," Gwen said quietly. "But you're wrong about Colin, y'know. The very morning after—we'd made love, for the very first time, believe me—"

"How was he?" Rose Ann quipped. "A short-fused dud, I'll bet!"

"With you, perhaps," Gwen said evenly. "Oh, I'd gathered that the two of you had had an *affaire,* though he was far too much of a gentleman to admit it. But with me, for me—he was—glorious. Masterful, and masterly, and I don't even care whether you per-ceive the distinction I'm trying to make—"

"I do," Rose Ann said soberly.

"In love—it's the *who* that counts, much more than the how, Ramb. When your senses reel at your lover's mere presence, when simple proximity—untouching nearness—can set you aflame, a kiss can achieve what it costs poor Caleb an hour's labor to bring me to, all the nearly diabolical black arts that my coldness, my indifference have forced my poor, and probably late, husband to become a past master of—are quite unnecessary, sister mine. Short-fused, you say? How am I to judge, when *mine* are shorter?"

"Sweet Baby Jesus!" Rose Ann whispered prayerfully.

"Amen. But what I was trying to tell you was that that next morning we quarreled. Oh, no! Not over the most sublime, the most unforgettable night of my whole life, but rather over his insistence that I run away with him. To Kansas, where the ease with which bills of divorcement can be pushed through the legislature is a public scandal. I refused—on the score that I couldn't institute a divorce suit against a man I wasn't sure was alive or dead. For if Caleb has been killed, the divorce proceeding would be unnecessary, and if he's alive, I owed it to him, as a decent man, a soldier, even a hero in our country's service, to put the matter to him fairly, asking for his consent, and his cooperation—with the warning, of course, that I'd proceed without them if he didn't see fit to grant them . . ."

"Gwen honey, you're signing Colin's death warrant, y'know. Cabe will *kill* him. And put you in the hospital for six months on top of it . . ."

"I think not," Gwen said coolly. "Cabe has a deep vein of—sheer civilization in him, despite all his bluster. I can appeal to it quite easily. I have, many times, in the past. And as for Colin's death warrant, I may have *already* signed it—"

"How?" Rose Ann asked.

"I told him bitterly that since I was in love with a man who was obviously the lesser of the two men in my life, I owed it to the better not to sneak off behind his back, not to have him come back from some Yankee prison camp and find me gone—"

"You think Cabe's been—captured?" Rose Ann interrupted her, the hope in her voice a brush fire, crackling, standing tall.

"No. I think Cabe's—dead, Rose. The circumstances under which he disappeared almost demand that conclusion, but since I don't *know* he is, it seems only fair to wait until the war's over, and give him the chance to come back, if he lives . . ."

"And those circumstances were?" Rose Ann breathed.

"Later. Let me finish telling you about Colin. It's important to me that you stop believing him a coward. He's actually the bravest of the brave, the man who functions nobly, perfectly by dominating his own acknowledged fear . . ."

"That's quite a trick, honey," Rose Ann said.

"It is. But he's done it. On June the sixteenth, the day after Colin and I had our bitter quarrel, General Grant, having flanked General Lee completely in four days and nights, and done it so silently and skillfully that our Commander in Chief simply wouldn't believe the desperate telegrams General Beauregard kept sending him from Petersburg, threw more than sixty-five thousand men against the lines that Beauregard was trying to hold with a mere ten thousand soldiers. Colin found it out that same night, God knows how. By the next morning, wounded unto death by my cruel words, he'd led a cavalry troop he'd organized out of the employees of his arms factory down to Petersburg, determined, as he now admits, to show me, or die . . ."

"A *cavalry* troop?" Rose Ann protested. "But, Gwennie darling, Colin can't even get up on a horse, so how the dickens could he have ever—"

"Led a troop of horsemen? In a *buggy*, Rose, with the dashboard cut down to let his stiff leg stick straight out. And with *six* breech-loading carbines, of the model that he and that Swedish engineer who works for him jointly designed, lying beside him on the seat so he could fire six times before he had to stop to reload. So here you have *my* hero, Ramb—who admits he was crying and praying and even wetting his pants he was so scared—charging, with a troop of old men and beardless boys, mounted on *mules* mostly because horses were too hard to come by, against, among other items which included shrapnel, grapeshot, chain shot, bomb bursts, breechloading and repeating rifles—the ones our boys swear the Yankees load on Sundays and shoot all week—a Gatling gun. You know what a Gatling gun is?"

"Yep. Sure Lord do. It's a rapid-fire gun that has ten revolving barrels, and uses brass-cased rimfire cartridges that are gravity-fed into the chambers of the barrels when you turn a crank. Nobody knows how fast the damned things will shoot. But fast enough to kill off *fifty* cavalry troops charging into its field of fire, not just one. So, begging your pardon mighty humbly, Gwen o' my heart, Colin's lying—ag'in. Ain't *nobody*, but *nobody* charged no Gatling gun and lived to tell about it!"

"Except Colin. He has the one he and his troop captured in his factory, where Lindsholm is trying to adapt it to using ordinary ammunition because according to Colin it's impossible for us to manufacture the kind it does use . . ."

"I know. You need one kind of machine to stamp the cartridges out of sheet brass, another to crimp the end plates, which look like little flat dishes, full of fulminate onto the back ends of 'em, another to—"

"Ramb, how on earth do you, a woman, know so much about *guns?*"

"I was a spy, honey. I really was. I got all that highly technical information out of engineering fellows in Connecticut and New York whom I was mighty, mighty sweet to 'til they softened up and started talking. And don't ask me how I went about doing that. Or you might find out that the exact synonym for 'female spy' is a word that begins with a capital 'w' . . ."

"In short—a whore? I'd heard as much. But in your case, my dearest sister, I refuse to believe it. But to finish my *chanson du beau geste*, Colin cheerfully admits that he captured that Gatling gun by a pure fluke. It seems that old Benjamin Beast and/or Silver Spoons Butler, late of the occupation forces at New Orleans, bought no fewer than twelve Gatling guns and twelve thousand rounds of ammunition out of the funds of his own division, and brought them to City Point in time to try a couple of them at Petersburg. Our artillery destroyed the first one. And Colin and his troop captured the other one, after Colin noticed that it fired away all its ammunition in a couple of minutes and then took almost ten to be reloaded. So he and his old granddads and baby boys charged it while they were trying to fit another of those doohickies full of cartridges to the top of it . . ."

"Hoppers," Rose Ann supplied. "Or magazines. That wasn't a fluke, sugar; that was plumb downright smart. So now I've got to apologize to Colin. You're right. He's not a coward. Cowards don't stop to think things out. They run first, and think later. Honey, believe me, I'm glad . . ."

"And I," Gwen sighed. "Truthfully, Colin's arrant cowardice bothered me. But he and his troop, after all their mules and both Colin's horses had been killed, stayed in the lines and fought as infantrymen all the rest of the sixteenth, the seventeenth, and the eighteenth until General Lee was finally convinced that Grant had slipped away past him and came down to Petersburg himself. By then, half of Colin's little troop were dead, and all the rest of them, including Colin himself, wounded—"

"Bad?" Rose Ann croaked.

"No, thank goodness! A minié ball in his upper right arm. He's going to be a trifle lame from now on, or rather, a trifle *more* than he already was, but—"

"Gwen sugar, you better bring that boy home before he loses something *useful*," Rose Ann drawled.

Gwen laughed merrily at that, which proved, Rose Ann realized, how much being in love had changed her. Makes her downright *human* at last, Rose thought.

"Oh, he ought to be out of danger for a while," Gwen said. "General Beauregard gave him and all his troopers a most handsome citation for valor. Which General Lee countersigned when he got there. Then he told Colin off, very thoroughly. He thanked him first, with that exquisite courtesy of his, for his efforts and the courage he and his 'irregulars' had displayed, but then—poor man, his nerves are distinctly frayed by now—he said, rather sharply, 'Lieutenant Claiborne, I have a fine excess of heroes who always seem to manage to get themselves most heroically killed, which both distresses me and ends, permanently, their usefulness to the cause. Right now, one expert arms manufacturer, which it seems you are, is worth more to me than a division of heroes. So go home and start turning out the guns and ammunition we need so badly. And that, Lieutenant, irregular or not, is an order!' "

"That's a relief," Rose Ann sighed. "I'll drop by his gunsmithy the next time I'm up in town—that is, if you don't mind, honey?"

"Of course not! Colin's—in love with *me* now, Ramb. Truly in love. I don't think you could take him away from me, even if you wanted to, and it's very apparent that you don't. Is—Kurt planning to join you soon?"

"Kurt's—dead, Gwen. He got killed when they captured me."

"I'm—sorry. No, that's a lie. Half a one anyhow. I *am* sorry he's dead, but I'm glad you're free of him. He seemed a perfectly dreadful creature to me . . ."

"He *was*. Gwen—tell me about—Cabe. What makes you so sure he's—dead?"

"I'm not sure. But it's—all too likely, unfortunately. You know what happened to General Jackson, don't you?"

"No," Rose Ann whispered.

"He was accidentally killed by our own troops. He and his entire staff—Caleb among them—rode out to see what the Yankees were up to, the first day at Chancellorsville. While they were out, some new troops from North Carolina moved into line. And when Stonewall and his aides came back, it was almost night—at the time you can't see colors very well. So those North Carolinians thought they were Yankee cavalry, and opened fire. Most of General Jackson's staff were killed outright, the general himself so badly wounded that he died two days later. His last words were rather beautiful . . ."

"What were they?" Rose Ann said.

" 'No, no,' " Gwen quoted softly, " 'let us pass over the river, and rest under the shade of the trees . . .' "

"Amen," Rose Ann murmured. "And—Cabe?"

"They never found his—body. And they found all the others. They even found the carcass of Caleb's horse. It was—riddled. Almost dismembered. But—Caleb's wasn't found . . ."

"Maybe," Rose Ann got out, "maybe—"

"And maybe not. It may have been—unrecognizable. Or totally destroyed by artillery fire. Many bodies are, y'know. Especially in the kind of battles we fight now . . ."

"Oh, Jesus!" Rose Ann said. "Jesus, Jesus, Jesus."

"Rose Ann—you're in love with Caleb, aren't you?"

Rose Ann lifted her head defiantly.

"Yes," she said simply, "I am. Any objections?"

"No," Gwen said softly. "None at all. I think the two of you are perfect for each other. Perhaps, after this terrible war, people will outgrow the stupid social prejudices that make it practically impossible for a couple to break free of a bad marriage and—remake their lives. At least I hope so."

"Me too," Rose Ann said. "Everybody else I know is all right?"

"Except Jeb Stuart. He was killed at a place called Yellow Tavern on the twenty-fifth of May . . ."

"Ohhhhhh, Lord!" Rose Ann wailed, and started to cry. Then suddenly she stopped, stiffened. "Gwen!" she breathed. "What about—*Jeff?*"

"Oh, Jeff's just fine. He's in London on some kind of procurement mission for our government. Seems to be having the time of his life . . ."

"And—Mary Sue?"

"Almost deliriously happy—since their baby came . . ."

"Their—*baby!*" Rose Ann gasped. "How—wonderful! How marvelous! Oh, Jesus, I'm so happy I've just got to cry!"

"Yes. Four months ago. A little red-haired she imp who looks more like you with every passing day. They've even named her Rose Ann in your honor. Of course, they thought you were dead, when they did that, but all the same . . ."

"Gwennnnn—" Rose Ann said darkly. "Jeffie was away from home an awful lot. Like most fellows, these days. And you and I have both proved just how modern we modern women can be. I sure Lord hope that Simpie Pie didn't hasn't wouldn't—"

"Cheat on our darling brother? Of course not. Besides, Jeff was home at exactly nine months before that blessed event. He came to Father's funeral—and—"

Rose Ann stood up. Her green eyes became the eyes of Pallas Athena's sacred owls, saucerlike and huge. They grew and grew until they eclipsed her face. Became twin emerald pools, light-blazed. Bottomless with horror.

"You—you told me Pa was—sleeping," she croaked.

"He is," Gwen said sadly. "Forever. Look, Rose Ann, I just wasn't up to—telling you about *that* tonight. About Father's—death, I mean. You see, he—"

"Read in the paper or somebody told him that I—was dead. That I'd been—*hanged*. So—he—he dropped down dead, didn't he?"

Gwen stared past the roundness of her pregnancy at her slippered feet. Looked up again. Her tears blazed star tracks down her face.

"Yes, Rose Ann," she said.

Those huge green eyes went out. Dissolved. Melted. Flooded that small, now almost skeletal face with the essence, the distillation of anguish.

"Ramb—please!" Gwendolyn moaned.

But by then Rose Ann had whirled, was already running.

Gwen knew just where to find her. McKenzie's Hundred was too far from town to permit burial in St. Paul's graveyard or in either of the public cemeteries—especially if a death occurred during the heat of summer. So, as such old plantations do, it had its own burying ground. When Gwen, wrapped in a quilted robe, got there, she found her sister lying face down upon their father's grave. But Rose Ann was unconscious by then.

She had beaten her two fists bloody against the earth that covered all that was mortal of David McKenzie, and ground her face into the mud beneath it.

That mud which she herself had made there with her tears.

Chapter Eighteen

"You sho' Lawd didn't bring no luck wit' you when you come home, did ya, honey?" A'nt Cindy growled.

"When have I ever?" Rose Ann said tiredly. "Where on earth is Caesar? I sent him out hours ago to cut some more firewood. And if he doesn't get back soon, we won't have enough to keep this water hot! The baby won't wait, you know. They come when they're ready to, whether you're ready for 'em or not . . ."

"The fust chile," A'nt Cindy said drily, "most in general teks he own sweet time. Hit's the others, after li'l fat 'n' sassy number one wit' he big bull head has done gone 'n' busted yo' insides plumb loose, whut comes a-flyin'. Ain't no hurry, missy. Caesar git back when he kin. He mighty ol', y'know. 'N' he gotta find wood whut's halfway dry. That ain't gonna be easy, col' 'n' wet as hit be. This heah's the middle o' February, y'knows, Missy Rose Ann—'n' we's done had ourselves the wust winter in living memory. Them po' fellas out there in them trenches, they dyin', them. Come spring, the damnyankees ain't gonna have to fight no mo'; they jes' march in 'n' gather them fine young Suth'n gentlemuns up lak cordwood. Be too weak to stand up by then, let alone shoot off they guns . . ."

"A'nt Cindy, if you don't shut up," Rose Ann cried, "I'm going to have you whipped, so help me!"

A'nt Cindy loosed a contralto chuckle that hung like midnight velvet on the kitchen's steamy air.

"You 'n' whut army, missy?" she purred. "Fust place, the Suth'n Army ain't up to holdin' on to a big black she b'ar like me, not t'mention whuppin' on my rusty hide, kase they's so starved out they plumb ain't got the strength. 'N' them Yankees has done give they Bible word they gonna sot us po' niggers free. 'Sides, even effen they doan do hit, Marse Robert his own self jes' las' month come right out 'n' 'lowed in the papers hit's the onliest thing whut y'all high 'n' mighty Suth'n white folks *kin* do now . . ."

Rose Ann stared at her aghast. She remembered her own astonishment at reading General Lee's words in the January 11 edition of the Richmond *Dispatch:*

It is the enemy's avowed policy to convert the able-bodied men among them into soldiers, and to emancipate all. His progress will destroy slavery in a manner most pernicious to the welfare of our people. Whatever may be the effect of our employing negro troops, it cannot be as mischievous as this. I think, therefore, we must decide whether slavery shall be extinguished by our enemies and the slaves be used against us, or use them ourselves at the risk of the effects which may be produced upon our social institutions . . .

The best means of securing the efficiency and fidelity of this auxiliary force would be to accompany the measure with a well-digested plan of gradual and general emancipation. As that will be the result of the continuance of this war, and will certainly occur if the enemy succeed, it seems to me most advisable to adopt it at once, and thereby obtain all the benefits that will accrue to our cause . . .

But how on earth had A'nt Cindy found out about it? She asked the big black woman that.

"Us kin read, honey," A'nt Cindy said proudly. "Yo' own grandpa, whut the Lawd has got wit' Him in glory, learned us how. Course, we had to study all them big words out a mighty heap afore the meanin' come clear. That wuz whut Gen'l Lee said meant, now wuzn't it, honey?"

"Yes," Rose Ann whispered. It did mean that. And also that the world—her world—was coming to an end. For William Smith, the governor of Virginia, had proposed exactly the same thing before the state legislature at Christmastime, pointing out there were already more than two hundred thousand black troops in the Union armies, and that their numbers were increasing with every passing day. All right, she thought wryly, I don't give a fig for preserving slavery; I never have, I reckon. But if we're going to concede that much, why don't we just quit? Why get more of our boys killed when we're bled white now? Why add the poor niggers to the slaughter pile? To stay—independent of the North? We can't. They'll make a colony out of us through banking, trade, heavy industry, reduce us to hewers of wood, drawers of water, tillers of the fields, at their beck and call—so why not admit we were wrong, go back into the Union as gracefully as possible and make the best of it?

She said then, nettled by A'nt Cindy's clearly growing insolence —a phenomenon that slaveholders were being confronted with quite frequently by mid-February 1865—"Before that happens, I can still have all your black hide off in strips, and I will too, if you don't watch that flip tongue of yours, A'nt Cindy! Just because Pa's dead, and Jeff and Master Caleb are away, doesn't mean you say anything you want to, old woman!"

"No'm," A'nt Cindy said with almost deadly quiet. "You right. Hit doan mean that. But they's another thing whut do, missy. 'N' tha's that the good Lawd His own self doan love ugly. You kilt yo' po' pa daid wit' yo' fas' 'n' fo'ward ways, messin' aroun' up Nawth 'n' mos' gittin' yo' fool self hung. Did him a favor tho', I reckons, kase he didn't have to live to see he oldest gal chile disgrace he name forever by cheatin' on her lawful husban' 'n' turnin' ho'. I done my bes', when y'all wuz left wit'out yo' ma. I tried ever' which a way I knowed to keep y'all gal chillun straight. But I ain't nuthin' but a po' ol' ignorant nigger woman, so y'all two swishy-tails figgered y'all din't hafta pay *me* no mind. 'N' now look! A yard child is gonna be birthed in yo' own good, sweet mama's bed. A *white* yard chile. I jes' hope the good Lawd won't hold it 'ginst the po' li'l fella, kase 'tain't he fault how he was got. But you"—A'nt Cindy bowed her head, looked up again, and now the tears were there, black diamonds and moon mist against her inky cheeks—"you talks erbout whuppin' on my po' tired ol' hide. Ain't no need fur that, Miss Rose Ann—kase you's done done hit already. You 'n' Miss Gwen—y'alls done took all the meat off my po' sorrowful soul, by mekin' me so awful shamed o' my own two baby gal chillun whut I nursed at my own big black breasts that I feels lak I wanna die!"

Rose Ann bounced up at that, flew across the room, threw her arms around A'nt Cindy, the only real mother she had ever had or known, and clung to her, sobbing.

"I'm sorry, A'nt Cindy!" she wailed. "I'm so sorry! You shouldn't have saved me when I was born! When Pa said I looked like a drowned red rat 'n' didn't even weigh a whole pound and—"

"Hush, baby. Hush yo' po' li'l mouf," A'nt Cindy crooned. "You crazy-wild, but you ain't *bad.* You married up wit' that good-for-nuthin' furrin gentlemun, whut warn't smart, but hit warn't *wrong,* so—"

"What's going on here?" that high, strained, nerve-tightened male voice said.

"Oh, Colin!" Rose Ann gasped. "You shouldn't have come out here! You shouldn't have! I knew I couldn't keep folks from finding out about the baby, but they didn't need to know who his daddy was! They didn't! And now—"

"And now," Mary Sue Hunter McKenzie said bitterly from the

doorway, "you 'n' A'nt Cindy better come give me a hand. 'N' right now. 'Cause it's on its way . . ."

While they waited, in the intervals when Rose Ann was not dashing into the bedroom with more pails of hot water, towels, cloths, pausing momentarily to stare at her sister's silent, utterly gallant struggle to bring the wages of her sin into this world, she and Colin talked. In slow, hesitant words, with many pauses, as they looked, not at each other, but at the fire in the grate before them.

"What are y'all gonna do?" Rose Ann said.

"Leave," Colin said quietly. "Go West. Kansas. Nebraska. Oregon. Or even California, maybe. We can't stay here after this; you know that, Ramb . . ."

"No. Don't reckon you can. Means the end of Fairdale, though. A pity."

"Fairdale is already finished," Colin said. "The South is, Ramb. Can you imagine trying to run a place that size with hired labor? Say the niggers stay on, and agree to work for wages—who'll ever be able to get a decent day's work out of 'em without a whip? Maybe you—and Cabe, surely—will be able to make a go of the Hundred. It's small enough so that with some really intensive farming, which means money for fertilizers, of course—"

"I've got it," Rose Ann said. "Or I will have it once this war is over . . ."

"How?" Colin said.

"Letters of credit. Union money. I sold the jewels Kurt gave me, in New York. Twenty thousand dollars. Only I can't draw on 'em until Virginia's back in the Union and greenbacks are legal tender again down here . . ."

Colin smiled at her then, ironically.

"So you've given up?" he said.

"Yes," she said. "Haven't you?"

"Long ago," he sighed. "All I was fighting for was an honorable peace. The war was suicide for the South from the start. It was lost the day that Edmund Ruffin jerked the lanyard—or, more likely, applied the torch to the touchhole—of that cannon and fired the first shot at Fort Sumter. We were a bunch of hotheads, and though the Yankees aren't all that smart, they're very long and cool of head, and know how to organize. While all we know how to do is disorganize and split apart. Look at Governor Vance of North Carolina and Governor Brown of Georgia . . ."

"A fair pair of disgraces, aren't they?" Rose Ann said.

"No. They're merely carrying states' rights to its logical conclusion, forgetting that no nation without a strong central government ever won a war . . . Good Lord! Isn't that poor little bastard ever going to get here?"

"Give him time. And you calm down. The first one always takes hours, A'nt Cindy says. Talk to me. You haven't in years, you know. What makes you so damn sure we've lost the war? Smart as General Lee is, he just might pull a real fast one and—"

"With what?" Colin said bitterly. "When Phil Sheridan comes down from the valley, as he can anytime Grant calls him, because he can just plain march over Early's forces in parade-ground formation, the Union Army will have one hundred twenty thousand men around Richmond and Petersburg. And when Sherman gets here from Savannah, which he left on the first of this month, fifteen days ago now, Rose, we'll be outnumbered *four* to one, instead of the three to one we are now . . . Grant doesn't even need to call Thomas in from Tennessee . . ."

"Well, you boys were always bragging about as to how three Yankees to one Sothoron was the proper proportion, 'cause you could lick that many with ease," Rose Ann said. She thought: Keep him talking. He can't even pace the floor like the rest of expectant daddies, the poor thing!

"I quit bragging at First Manassas," Colin said with a wry gesture toward his board-stiff knee, making that gesture with his left hand, because his right arm could only be moved slowly and carefully still, or the pain from it would almost floor him. "Look, Rose honey, an industrial nation can always whip an agricultural one, given the men, the money, and the time, all three of which the Yankees have. And granted the will, as well. Which they've found since Sherman made Lincoln a present of Atlanta and thereby ensured his reelection, not to mention when Abe put that block of ice-cold granite named Grant at the head of their armies. So to beat 'em, we had to create an armament industry. And we did it. It's poor and backward technically, but it works. Since, as a lady spy, you know all about guns—"

"Cut out the 'lady,' Colin. I did everything necessary, using all the available equipment. Notice I haven't tossed even a pebble in Gwen's direction, or yours, let alone a rock?"

"Don't tell me about it," Colin said bitterly. "I don't want to know. And when Cabe gets back, for God's sake don't start an old-

355

time, down-home, country-revival confession session with *him*. Cabe's a good old boy, but self-control ain't one of his virtues—"

"I know. I have no desire to spend six months in the hospital. But speaking of Cabe, what are you—"

"Going to do? I don't know. If I could follow my born coward's instincts, I'd take Gwen and the kid and clear out before he got here, leaving it up to you to persuade him not to come chasing after us with an eighteen-gun battery of artillery at the very least. But Gwen insists that we do the honorable things, which means I'm very likely going to wind up honorably dead, and she—"

"A cripple. And me an old maid. No, an old widow. A double widow, at that."

"Yes, I heard that Kurt was killed. I'm sorry. I rather liked him . . ."

"I'm not. 'Cause *I* didn't. Go on with what you were telling me. It's mighty interesting, Colin . . ."

"It doesn't, for your information, sweet Rambling Rose," Colin said drily, "keep my mind off what's going on in there . . ." He nodded his head brusquely in the direction of the bedroom door. "I'd go and hold Gwen's hand, and try to comfort her, if I were sure I wouldn't faint. But since I'm *not* sure, and dragging my mutilated carcass out would be quite a chore, I reckon I had better go on talking, at that. Where was I?"

"You were discussing our armament industry . . ."

"Yes. An example of which is that, right now, Lindsholm is desperately trying to make a double magazine that will feed paper cartridges and percussion caps separately but simultaneously into that Gatling gun my boys captured, the same system Dr. Gatling himself tried two years ago and gave up as impractical. Only, since we can't make brass cartridges, we've *got* to make it work, if God— and General Grant—will give us the time. Another example is that Grant has achieved complete mobility, since, these days, he can leave parts of his lines held only by a corporal's guard, knowing we dare not try to punch through what two years ago would have been practically a hole in his defenses, because that corporal's guard are now armed with Spencers and Henrys, and can lay down a volume of fire it would have taken twenty times their number to maintain in '61. While we're still making and using muzzleloaders, paper cartridges, and percussion caps. Still, our armament industry is a success, of sorts. Our boys haven't yet run out of ammunition in any major battle. But what's really lost us this war, Ramb honey, is that we don't know, and haven't the time, money, and materials to learn, how to make—shoes."

"Shoes!" Rose Ann gasped.

"Yep. Know why we had to fight at Gettysburg, giving the Yankees the sweetest defensive setup in this world? Because Major General Harry Heth found out the Bluebellies had a warehouse crock full of *shoes* there, and set out on a full-scale raid to get our poor barefooted bastards some. And ran into the whole blamed Yankee Army . . ."

"Good Lord!" Rose said.

"Amen. Coming back from Nashville, after George Thomas, the damn best general in the Union Army, with which, as another Virginian who dirties his drawers every time he hears gunfire, I won't claim his being from the Old Dominion has anything to do, had inflicted not only the first major defeat but absolutely the first rout ever pinned on a Confederate Army—"

"I didn't know that," Rose Ann breathed.

"The papers tried to soften the impact, but that's what it was," Colin said grimly. "Anyhow, with Nat Forrest's cavalry covering their retreat—I got the idea of cutting down the dashboard of my buggy from reading about Nat; that's what he did after he got shot through the foot—Hood piled those of our troops who didn't have shoes into wagons and hauled 'em south, so their bare feet wouldn't stick to the ground. And every time Wilson's Union cavalry—and let me tell you, Ramb, that after Nat Forrest, Wilson is the greatest cavalry leader of this war, 'cause your Jeb Stuart was a romantic fool, always off on spectacular raids instead of being around to scout for Lee, as at Gettysburg, for instance—"

"I know that. But I loved Jeb. All us girls did—"

"Including his wife. Now his widow. Daughter of Major General Philip St. George Cooke, of the *Union* cavalry. Hell of a war, this one, isn't it?"

"It is. Colin honey, you lost me quite a while back. What were we talking about?"

"Shoes—or the lack of them. What I was saying was that every time Wilson's cavalry caught up with them, Hood's boys would climb out of those wagons and hobble into battle, with their poor freezing feet sticking to the ground and leaving bloody footprints. And after that, every time they'd pass a dead horse or a mule, they'd hop down, skin it, and make moccasins out of its hide. Or they'd cut up their hats and wrap their poor blue-frozen feet in that. This here war, baby girl, is one of the first in history that was ever lost for the lack of shoes. Even as far back as Antietam, Lee had to order that no barefooted soldier be punished for failing to keep up with his company . . .."

"And—now?" Rose Ann whispered.

"Worse. Now—our morale's going, Rose. General Hill—D.H., not Ambrose—says the Southern foot soldier's morale cracked forever at Chickamauga, because that's where he discovered he couldn't win. Last summer General Lee told our men to gather sassafras shoots and the buds from wild grapevines to serve as 'small rations' or greens, so they wouldn't get the scurvy. But right now, they're getting it, and worse. Men have starved to death in the trenches around Petersburg, Ramb. Half rations are considered a feast. Quarter rations is what they get—a quarter of a pound of meat—usually *mule*—and a handful of cornmeal, for one full day, baby. So now they desert, even though we've started actually shooting deserters—posted before their own open graves so they poor riddled carcasses will fall into 'em. We started this war with nothing, and we're ending it with less. How we ever expected to win it, I just don't see—"

"Expected to, and almost did. Because we had generals like Robert E. Lee, Stonewall Jackson, the two Hills, Longstreet, Hood, Bishop Polk, and a dozen more. And the bravest soldiers in human history—including a self-proclaimed coward called Colin Claiborne, who charged a goddamn Gatling gun in a *buggy*, with his gimpy leg sticking straight out before him," Rose Ann said, the tears pouring down her cheeks. "And whom I'm going to kiss right now and real hard, no matter what my cheatin' hussy of a sister thinks about it!"

"Rose—" he said, his voice deep, anguished.

And it was at that very moment that they heard the sound of a slap, then a tiny gasp, a thin, high, piping wail.

"I hopes you's 'shamed o' yo'self, Marse Colin!" A'nt Cindy growled as she laid his firstborn in his good but wildly trembling left arm.

"Here, you give him to me, you poor old shot-up wreck!" Rose Ann hooted. "Or else you're going to drop him, sure as hell!"

"No, to me!" Mary Sue said firmly. "What do *you* know about holding babies, Rose Ann?"

"Honey, I had three whilst I was away from home," Rose Ann said solemnly. "Only I was busy about my spying, which meant I couldn't afford to lose my figure, or have my tits dragged down below my knees, so I put 'em out for adoption . . ."

"Wal, I never!" A'nt Cindy bassed, or rather contraltoed. "Missy, ain't you got no shame?"

"Is it—human?" Colin said wonderingly. "And if it is, what is it? Besides a monkey, anyhow. I mean, is it a boy or a girl?"

"Why—Colin!" Gwen said, and started to cry.

"Here," Colin said, "take little Darwin's proof positive, will you, Ramb? I've got to say something to Gwen—"

He placed his one good hand on the headboard of the bed, and bending from the waist, since he absolutely could not kneel, kissed her tear-wet face.

"Thank you, Gwen darling," he said huskily. "It's—just beautiful, whatever it is . . ."

"A—boy," Gwen whispered. "Your son—and image, Colin. But heir—only to the shame and sorrow we, the two of us, have brought down on his head . . ."

"We'll make it up to him," Colin said firmly, then looking up, he met Mary Sue Hunter McKenzie's eyes.

"I want to thank you, Mary Sue," he said, then: "Mighty, mighty humbly. I'd get down on my knees before you if I could. I know your folks. And Virginians prouder than the Hunters of Hunter's Point have yet to be born. So I know what it cost you to come over here. Bet you Brad Hunter's on the verge of a stroke, and your mama's in bed with a bottle of smellin' salts pressed up her nose right now. But you put—friendship above some mighty straitlaced conventions, which never have taken into consideration plain human nature, and hold that even a mismatched pair in a long-gone marriage should be locked together forever. Which is a slavery worse than any we ever kept the niggers in. But anyhow, I thank you, and if you'll condescend to take the hand of a sinner, here's my hand on it . . ."

Mary Sue put out a small, quivering white hand.

"It's not condescension, Colin," she said in her clear, sweet voice. "Found out a long time ago that a good woman is one who's been lucky—or unlucky—enough not ever to have been left alone with the right man—or, maybe, the real, honest to God *wrong* one —on a warm June night with a full moon up, and the whip'o'wills a-crying. Besides, rock chunking's no fitting occupation for a Christian, anyhow. My li'l Rambler's lawful, and for that I've got Jeff's gentlemanly ways to thank, 'cause I wouldn't bet a plugged lead nickel on what would have happened if he had ever really tried. Beforehand, I mean . . . Sure hope y'all will be able to straighten the whole thing out when—and if—Caleb comes home . . ."

Colin looked at the supreme authority present, the guardian dragon of that dishonored house.

"A'nt Cindy," he said plaintively, "couldn't I stay over tonight? You could put me in the guest room, or—oh, heck—even in the hayloft over the stable . . . I just want to make sure that Gwen and my kid are—all right—"

"Naw!" A'nt Cindy boomed. "Why, hell naw, Marse Colin! Ain't you done this heah fambly 'nuff harm already? You stays heah overnight 'n' folks be swearin' you's tomcatting round Miz Gwen 'n' Missy Rose Ann bof! Git along wit' you, suh, afore I teks my broomstick to yuh!"

"All right," Colin sighed. "You're the boss, A'nt Cindy!" He bent and kissed Gwen again, lingeringly, tenderly. Straightening up, he said, "Walk me to my buggy, Ramb? I need somebody to lean on to get up into it, y'know . . ."

"I'll bet!" Gwen said bitterly.

"Ah, heck, honey. I mean to be faithful until death. Besides, the Rambler threw me over a long time ago . . ."

"She's been known to change her flighty mind before now," Gwen said darkly.

"Only, this time, I have no intention to, Gwen o' my heart," Rose Ann said. "C'mon along, Colin. Time we sent you packing!"

On the way to the buggy, she said, "Colin, what about your mother? If you and Gwen have to leave here, I mean? She's always been so devoted to you and all—"

"Oh, Mama'll be all right. She's just like a cat—always lands on her feet. She and Judge Tyler Ellis of the Supreme Court have a big romance going. They plan to be wed any day now. I made the mistake of giving my consent too quickly, and maybe showing my relief that she'd be taken care of by such a fine gentleman of her own age. He's sixty, y'know. So now she's got the sulks, swearing that I don't love her. But she'll get over that . . ."

"And this business about Gwen—how is she taking it?"

"The subject's taboo, by mutual accord. Or else she goes into the most awe-inspiring hysterical fits you ever saw," Colin said with a rueful grin. "Much ado about nothing. What's done is done, and that's that—"

"Colin, about Caleb—how long are y'all planning to—wait?"

"Gwen says—six months. Which seems to me fair. I'm sure the

Yankee government will provide railroad transportation for prisoners of war after this is finally over. I'd say that any man, even one who's badly crippled, who isn't back home, or hasn't got a letter to his family, in a month or two can be safely assumed to be dead . . ."

"Safely—dead?" Rose Ann whispered. "Cabe?"

She came up very close to Colin then. In the moonlight her face was very white. When she spoke, her voice had a little grate in it, a scrape.

"Hasn't it occurred to *anybody* I know that a little thought's in order before jaw waggling's indulged in? Oh, all right, forget it. Put your hand on my shoulder. Boost yourself up. Thaaat's it. 'Good night, sweet prince, and flights of angels sing thee to thy rest!' " she said.

Chapter Nineteen

When it was over, it was over very quickly. Spring burst like lovely, flowering death over a stricken land. On April 2, 1865, Rose Ann McKenzie went to church at St. Paul's. She wanted to pray. She had a need, a craving to talk humbly with her God that was like a brand burning in her breast. Kneeling there in the McKenzies' pew, she let the unashamed tears pour down her face in sight of the whole congregation. Gwen's disgrace was known to all Richmond by then, so in that jam-packed church Rose Ann had a full three yards of clear space around her in every direction, as the pious dames of Richmond crowded one another into close and uncomfortable physical contact to avoid moral contamination. Some of them admitted they were being unfair. About Rose Ann's own sins, if any, what really was known? She had married a foreigner, gone away, been charged with spying by the Yankees, sentenced to be hanged. Nor could the stubborn popular suspicion that a female spy had necessarily to be a woman of loose morals be always sustained. Rose O'Neal Greenhow had been a thoroughly decent woman, a widow, the mother of a lovely daughter—and she had been a spy. What's more, she had capped her devotion to the Southern cause by achieving martyrdom in her country's service; in September 1864, she had drowned off Wilmington, North Carolina, while carrying, on a blockade runner, dispatches for the Confederacy.

But although they couldn't *prove* anything against poor Rose Ann, the theory of guilt by association held full sway in St. Paul's on that lovely Sunday morning. If she hadn't done anything wrong, why was she crying that way? Because she was ashamed of, and for, her sister? That would be scanned! All they knew of female human nature—based upon a too acute and intimate knowledge of their own!—made them doubt that degree of pristine unselfishness profoundly. And it was here, precisely, that they were wrong, because they couldn't hear Rose Ann's anguished, but silent pleas:

Dear Lord, let Cabe be still alive. And after that, let him come back home. And when he gets home, let me or Gwen or both of us be able to talk some sense into his head. Failing that, if You demand a blood sacrifice for all the sin this crazy, wild McKenzie family has been wallowing in, let *me* be that sacrifice, Lord. 'Cause if you punish Colin, punish Gwen for the sin they did, the ultimate sufferer is going to be an innocent child, oh, Lord, and that just isn't fair no matter how fine Your mills grind, or how unfathomable are Your ways. Don't, please don't, let Cabe kill Colin. Never saw one word in Your Holy Writ that puts a qualification or a condition on the Commandment what says: "Thou shalt not kill!" Thou shalt not kill *anybody*, not even blue-nosed Yankees who oppose your right to keep a passel of burr-headed, liver-lipped good-for-nothing niggers in slavery, nor, for that matter, a man who's committed adultery with your wife. You hear that, Cabe? And you, Colin, for you to kill Cabe—even if self-defense—would be just too awful. To lie with the wife, then pistol the husband would be— Oh, Jesus, what? A combining of abominations, a piling up of—brutishness. So me, Lord, take me. I offer you my life, my blood, my pain—to save my loved ones. If my dead body is what it takes to make 'em fear You, keep Your Commandments, and walk in the ways of righteousness all their days, then smite me hip and thigh with the sword of Your Divine Wrath, 'cause it appears to me I'm the only one who can be spared—

That was as far as she got. Because by then the rising rustle of whispers in the church had disturbed even her intense concentration. Turning, she saw a man standing worriedly beside President Jefferson Davis's pew. The man, although somewhat apologetically, was clearly insisting that the President of the Confederacy take the note he held in his hand.

Mr. Davis took the note, read it swiftly. His thin, hawklike face flushed dark red, then went as white as snow. Without a word to Father Erwell in the pulpit box, or indeed to anyone, including his wife, he clutched his hat in convulsive hands and rushed out the door. Of course, Mrs. Davis immediately followed him.

There was nothing for the old priest to do but to abruptly dismiss services, for all the worshippers streamed out of the door behind the President. They dared not ask him what was wrong, and besides, there was no chance to. The President and the First Lady of the Confederacy had already climbed into their carriage, and their black coachman was whipping up the horses in quite evident haste.

They were all standing there in wonder when the first ear-rocking boom from the river came. Windows crashed in all around them from the force of that explosion. People milled about, some heading for the river, some running, as if for their lives, away from it. Then borne as if by magic on a tide of voices from the city's docksides to the very square before the church, the cries rang:

"The rams! They're blowing up the ironclad rams!"

Someone ventured a timid or an incredulous "Why? In God's name, why?"

And back with chilling certitude the answer came:

"Petersburg has fallen! All the railroad lines are cut! Richmond is cut off—and doomed!"

The crowd whirled away, chaff in the breeze, dead leaves in moving air. Each to his dwelling to grab what easily transportable valuables lay to hand and start out toward the railroad stations. To go where? The Union Army lay across all the lines running south and west; to the northwest, Phil Sheridan's boast that he had left the Shenandoah Valley so devastated that a crow flying across it would need to carry its own rations was almost literal fact; and to the northeast lay—Washington. Did they plan to take refuge in Yankee Land? The crowds milled about aimlessly. They had not yet degenerated into mobs, but, by night, they would. Already groups of men, whose lank-jawed faces, tight-lipped mouths, except where a plug of chewing tobacco loosened them, made them dribble, and beady, rapidly shifting eyes betrayed them as "sharpies," were beginning to gather in front of the commissary stores, some of them with wagons ready to haul away what loot as might lie to hand . . .

The explosions, due south, down the river, went on. Sighing, Rose Ann went to where she'd left her father's ancient, dilapidated buggy, the only vehicle, besides a couple of almost equally worn-out farm wagons, that the McKenzies now had left, and untied old Dobbin, a swayback grayish-white gelding who, Caleb had sworn, must have arrived in Virginia from Mount Ararat on the Ark, which was the reason they still had him, for all their other horses, including her beloved Prince Rupert, had long since been requisitioned by the Confederate cavalry. Then she climbed up into the buggy and drove westward toward the bridges that went over the James to the suburb called Manchester.

As she drove along at the pace of a crippled snail, which was all old Dobbin could manage, she saw plumes of smoke rising here and there, behind her in Richmond and before her in Manchester, as government arsenals and warehouses were put to the torch to prevent their stores from falling into the hands of the enemy. Fortunately for her, they fired the warehouses first, and only much later, toward night, the arsenals. Or else her snail's pace through the streets of Manchester would have been hideously dangerous.

But she didn't know that. All she was thinking, slowly, peacefully was: Now I can go see my little namesake . . .

Up until now, she hadn't been able to go see her baby niece, whom Jeff and Mary Sue had named in her honor, because Hunter's Point lay to the southeast, where the James broadens almost into an arm of the sea and the Appomattox River joins it, which meant that it had been on the other side of the Yankee lines for almost a year now. And although the Union officers permitted civilian passage—especially of lone women with convincing excuses—across the extreme lower and upper ends of their lines, where fighting was unlikely to break out, the journey from Hunter's Point to McKenzie's Hundred had become so roundabout, even so uncertain, and to some degree dangerous, that Mary Sue had wisely left little Rose Ann II with her mother when she'd ridden, against her parents' grim disapproval, on horseback, to the Hundred to attend Gwen in her hour of need.

So it's over now, finally over, Rose Ann thought. No more nice boys in blue, nor even nicer ones—or at least more full o' hell—in gray—gray, my eye! In butternut-brown nigger cloth, and it in rags—are going to get killed from here on in. For which I thank you, Lord! Now, if I can only persuade Cabe to call off his private war against poor Colin when and if—no, not if, *when;* that's right, isn't it, Lord?—he gets here . . .

She had herself a wait. So did poor Gwen, whose calm confidence that she could handle her wild, crazy husband had largely evaporated by then, and was getting closer to the vanishing point with every passing day.

One of the troubles was that the Civil War—though, in later years, Cabe was to growl, "What the hell was there so *civil* about it?"—didn't end when Lee surrendered to Grant at the home of Wilmer McLean in the little town called Appomattox Court House, Virginia (probably because there was a courthouse there), on April 9, 1865. There remained the problem of letting the scattered forces of both contenders know that hostilities officially had ceased. Of course, Samuel Morse's telegraph was a mighty fine invention, but it had the major defect that you had to be where a telegraph office was to get a message over it, or else wait until a man on horseback brought you that message from said telegraph office to wherever the hell you were. The result of that was that a brisk little engagement was fought, and men got killed, at West Point, Georgia, one week after Lee's surrender, and almost one month after that, at Palmetto Ranch, near Brownsville, Texas, on

May 13, quite a few volleys were exchanged in the last engagement on land of the Civil War.

At sea, matters were even worse. Marconi's wireless telegraph lay years in the future. So it was that some unknown ensign, acting upon the direct orders of Lieutenant Commander Geoffrey McKenzie, chief gunnery officer, under Captain Waddell, on the Confederate commerce raider *Shenandoah*, fired the last shot of the Civil War, somewhere in the northern part of the Pacific Ocean on June 28. That shot was sent screaming across the bows of a steamer flying the Stars and Stripes, as a warning to heave to. And the only reason it was the last was that when Captain Waddell sent a lieutenant junior grade with a whaleboat to pick up the now-hoved-to Yankee's papers, he brought back not only a protest from the Yankee's captain that what they were doing now constituted piracy, because the war was damned well over, but a bunch of San Francisco newspapers to prove it. So Captain Waddell let the Yankee vessel go, got up steam, and headed south toward the distant *Cabo de Hornos*, the Cape of the Ovens, the extreme tip of South America, which Anglo-Saxons, with their sublime indifference to what anything means in any language but their own, call Cape Horn, because that's what *Hornos* (Ovens) sounded like to them, and because the southernmost tip of the Americas does look like a ragged bull's horn anyhow. From there, once he had rounded the Cape into the South Atlantic, he meant to beat northeastward against and across the trade winds to England, where possibly the *Shenandoah* could be sold. That voyage was a mere bagatelle of seventeen thousand nautical miles, which explains why, when Jeff McKenzie, sporting an enormous spread of whiskers that made him look, if not like Bluebeard, at least like Frederick Barbarossa, got back to the Hundred finally, on Christmas Day 1865, his firstborn was able not only to walk but to run, screaming her terrified little head off, to her mother at the sight of him.

On July 4, 1865, Lieutenant Colonel Caleb Henry came staggering into the front yard of McKenzie's Hundred. He was staggering, not because he was drunk, but because he was so weak from hunger, prison-camp fever, and the lice that were literally devouring him from head to heel that he could hardly stand. He could have got drunk if he had wanted to, because the Yankees had a monster Independence Day celebration going up in Richmond when he got off the train, and by the time Cabe stumbled from his tail-end car, they had gone far beyond the stage of feeling absolutely no pain at all, to that of a bemused and complacent euphoria that inclined them to entertain most fraternal sentiments toward their former enemies. Cabe had to turn down two dozen offered drinks, some of them from black Union cavalrymen, out parading with some of the sleekest, flossiest black girls Cabe had ever seen, which almost broke his heart because it demonstrated to him, as nothing else could have done, the degree to which the world had been turned upside down.

But he refused all the drinks, because he quite reasonably figured he'd never make it out to the Hundred if he were even a little drunk, since he hadn't a red copper in his pockets and had to walk all the way. Besides, as dizzy as his head was, he wasn't all that sure he could explain to Gwen why she just had to present a bill of divorcement against him in the state legislature as soon as Virginia was readmitted to the Union so they could live in peace. After that, she could marry anybody she wanted to, even her pretty coward, Colin Claiborne, as long as she left him free to marry Rose Ann— once he had carved up, shot, or otherwise disposed of that greasy furriner his darlin' Ramb had gone 'n' got hitched to, of course. So taking on a drap o' two would have only made matters worse.

As he staggered into the yard, he was honing his arguments by adding to them the historically accurate contention that divorce, while rare, was hardly unknown in the United States. Why, even a President, Andrew Jackson, had married a divorced woman. In fact, he'd married her twice, because the first ceremony had taken place before the bill of divorcement had even been certified as legal, so Old Hickory and his Rachel had had to commit matrimony all over again to make it stick. A more recent case he could bring up was the divorce of British aristocrat Fanny Kemble from the high and mighty Pierce Butler, of the distinguished Georgia Butlers, just before the war. There were quite a few such cases, and if need be, he could ask one of his lawyer friends to dig them up and prepare him a list to convince Gwen with . . .

So far, Cabe was proceeding with impeccable logic. Gwen didn't love him. She had told him that many times. What puzzled and troubled him was the fact that they got along surprisingly well in bed. Cabe couldn't shake the notion that there was something intrinsically immoral about very nearly first-class intimate matrimonial relations (he had to use that circumlocution because in his times the word "sex" was used only to distinguish men from women and always went preceded by the word "male" or "female" as the case might be. To have used it as a synonym for the act itself, to his generation was not only unthinkable but inconceivable) between two people who fought like cats and dogs whenever they were standing up and fully clothed. But there it was. He had a shrewd suspicion that between him and Rose Ann, whom he *loved* as well as had a monumental yen for, bedding was going to be nothing short of miraculous, because, among other things, if Rose Ann didn't love him she was so close to it that it really didn't make any never mind, having refrained thus far from giving way to how she really felt about him only out of respect for her sister.

That was as far as he got. And, from that very moment, every thing went wrong.

For Rose Ann saw him first. She let out a squeal calculated to the decibel to shatter crystal, came flying out of the house, and hurled herself into his arms. Now, not even the ninety-three pounds soaking wet she was back up to by then would ordinarily have been enough to knock poor Cabe down, but he had been almost a week en route from the prisoner-of-war camp near Jersey City, New Jersey, and the meals he'd been able to scrounge up on the way had been few and far between. Besides, it could be reasonably argued that, at least until Grant took command and tried to steamroller over Lee by main force, a man wasn't *much* worse off in the front lines at places like Antietam, Fredericksburg, and Chickamauga than he was in any prisoner-of-war camp whatsoever, North or South. The North hanged Major Henry Wirz because of the horrors of The Andersonville prison camp in Georgia, for which the major was not responsible and was powerless to ameliorate, but of the 190,000 Northern POWs held in the South, 30,000 died, while of the 200,000 Southern captives held in the North, 26,000 died of cold, malnutrition, and disease. "A discussion of the comparative obscurity of their respective complexions among kitchen utensils is a mighty futile business," was the way Cabe put it.

So she knocked him flat on a tailbone that had precious little hide left to cover it, and lay there on top of him greedily kissing his mouth in spite of the facts that he was crawling with vermin and his stench would have given any self-respecting billy goat the heaves.

And Gwen came out of the house and saw that. It made her, for some reason twisted deep into the recesses of the human psyche, fighting mad. She had, it is fair to recall, committed some first-class and flagrant adultery, and had a fine, fat, bouncing little bastard who was the very image of his long-tall cheating hound dawg of a pappy to prove it, but the sight of her sister kissing her husband like a female cannibal working her way head first through the *pièce de résistance* at an anthropophagous banquet got her wild. She forgot she didn't love said husband, that she was planning to ask him to be both reasonable and civilized and grant her a divorce so that she could marry the father of her child, whom, very truly, she loved. She forgot everything except that he was *hers.*

So she came up with the perfect method of punishing him for allowing her arrant little female canine of a sister to commit what she bitterly described in her mind as "dry fornication" upon him, then immediately amended to "Dry, hell! Say—clothed!" She marched back into the house and came out with little Colin II in her arms.

"Here, Cabe!" she grated. "Have a look!"

As much as he was enjoying himself, that tone got through to Caleb Henry. He pushed Rose Ann off and away from him with surprising strength. He sat up. Stared at Gwen. At that beautiful male child who was Colin's very image, a long, slow, dead-stopped time.

Then Caleb Henry, hero in his country's service, the man who had won every decoration for valor the Confederacy had to offer, did the last thing on earth that anyone who knew him would ever have expected him to do.

He bent his head and cried.

It was, quite simply, unbearable. He sat there and shook. A nest of vipers crawled visibly along all his nerves, his veins. Then he raised his grimy face, streaked jaggedly with white where the freshets of his tears had plowed through, toward heaven, and said in a terrible, hoarse-voiced whisper that carried beyond the rim edges of forever out to the end of the visible universe where time and space are one entity, and it totally meaningless:

"Dear God, please let me die!"

After that, he leaned forward in the direction of Gwen and the child, bowing to them with grave reverence, loosened all over, and lay there on the grass before McKenzie's Manse, his starved-out figure very slight and very small and very, very still.

Rose Ann couldn't decide what she wanted to do most, save Cabe or kill her sister Gwen. But looking up, she saw how Gwen was crying, which was, if anything, even worse than the way Cabe had wept, and she melted. Rose Ann McKenzie's major weakness was that, as Cabe later swore, "she hasn't a mean bone in her body," and that fact defeated her now.

She said, "Oh, Lord, Gwen, forget it! Go put that kid down and come help me get Cabe inside the house and to bed, will you?"

Between them, they managed that task with no trouble at all, for by then poor Cabe weighed no more than an average-sized boy of ten or twelve. The troubles—Rose Ann's, anyhow—started once they'd got him there. For Gwen faced her with streaming eyes, and said, seriously, meaning it, "You'll—take my baby, won't you, Ramb? You—and Cabe, if he lives? Because—I'm going to kill myself. I can't live after this. Nobody could, with this much—shame . . ."

"Then what am I supposed to do with Colin and Cabe both?" Rose Ann snapped. "Turn Mormon? Oh, for God's sake, Gwen, go get me some scissors, and his razor, and some soap, and tell A'nt Cindy to heat as much water as she can manage as hot as she can get it. And— Oh, Jesus! Look at his hair!"

"What about his hair?" Gwen whispered.

"It's crawling, honey, crawling," Rose Ann sighed. "Go get me a shovelful of hot coals and bring 'em here, or else we'll have to burn down the house!"

Between them, they clipped off Caleb's hair down to the scalp and afterward they shaved both his head and his face. The clipped locks and the shavings they shriveled instantly on the hot coals in the shovel, which was standard treatment for returning veterans in the spring and summer of 1865, or else they'd have had to move out of McKenzie's Manse. After that they cut the rags of his uniform and what was left of his practically nonexistent underwear off him with the scissors, and burned them in the grate, thereby almost inventing chemical warfare forty-nine years before 1914.

"I'll bathe him," Gwen volunteered. "After all, you—"

"Have been married too," Rose Ann drawled, "and have seen a damn sight more naked men than you have, Gwen o' my heart! Or d'you want to run up a tally, winner takes the prize? Besides, it'll take both of us to turn him over . . ."

They had, finally, to shave his whole body, leaving him almost as bare as a newborn baby, and bathe him in a weak solution of carbolic acid, in order to free him of the lice that were devouring him. Before they got through with that, Cabe opened his eyes.

"What the hell are you brace o' Salem witches doing?" he roared. Then his eye fell on his razor in the basin of water, which was tinged with red from all the places they had accidentally cut him in their nervousness and haste.

"Jesus God!" he gasped. "These here broomstick jockeys have gone and gelded me!"

He put down his hand and gingerly felt the assaulted territory. A smile of pure, blissful relief stole over his lean, ugly face.

"All right, all right," he said. "You refrained, even when y'all had me helpless. Gwen, can I trust you not to pizen me if I ask you to go fix me some rations?"

"Don't know," Gwen said bitterly. "I just might get tempted beyond my strength . . ."

"I'll chance it," Cabe said. "Rose Ann, go get me that young'un, and bring him here."

"What!" Gwen gasped.

"Want to see if he's heavy enough hung," Caleb said solemnly. "Got a fine enough pair on him, I'll keep him, bring him up. Apply my razor strop to his li'l tail every day, 'til I make a man out of him, even if his pappy was a ball-less wonder. I'll even let him lay a lily on his lily-livered old man's grave every other Easter Sunday—"

"Caleb Henry, you—" Gwen cried.

"Go wrastle me up some grub, woman," Caleb said. "Since I mean to whup on your nice little round pink behind every day for a month o' Sundays, I'm gonna need my strength. Now get out here. You heard me—scat! The Rambler 'n' I have got talking to do . . ."

Gwen stared at him. Her mouth twisted into a bitter grimace. But whatever she had been about to say, she thought the better of it, for, head down and shoulders shaking, she left the room.

"Cabe," Rose Ann whispered, "you really want me to bring you the baby?"

"Sure Lord do, Ramb honey," Caleb said.

Rose Ann got up, went down the hall to the back porch, where little Colin was sleeping peacefully in a wicker cradle with mosquito netting over it to protect him from the flies. She pushed the netting back, picked the baby up. As she did so, she heard Gwen's outraged—or terrified?—gasp.

"Rose Ann!" Gwen cried. "You put my baby down! Don't take him anywhere near that wild man! He just might—"

"Kiss him and shed a tear," Rose Ann said flatly. "Good Lord, Gwen, don't you know Cabe by now? He's as tender as a woman, and twice as gentle. Reason he was so all-fired brave. He was a wee mite scareder of letting the other fellows see how scared he was than he was of risking his poor skinny hide. Bet he had to knot his guts back together before every battle. Come on, get out of the way; there's no harm in letting him see this kid . . ."

"Oh, Lord, Rose, if he—"

"He won't. That's Caleb Henry in there, Gwen sugar. A gentleman and, in many ways, a scholar. You ever heard him when he feels like talkin' sense?"

"All right," Gwen said tonelessly, "but if he were to—"

"He won't," Rose Ann said, and went back up the hall.

"Lemme hold him," Cabe said. "Bible word I won't drop him, not even accidental-like. Come here, you li'l wild wood shoat you! Lemme have a look at a livin' wonder: a young'un got without the use of balls. 'Cause your pappy sure Lord ain't got none, y'know!"

"Cabe," Rose Ann said, "that isn't so."

"The hell it ain't! At First Manassas, he—"

"I know. He told me about that himself—like it was, neither lying nor excusing himself. But he fought at Petersburg, three whole days, self-crippled leg and all, from June sixteenth through the nineteenth, last year. Until they carried him away from there with half of the troop of volunteers that he raised dead, and him with a crippled arm, to keep that leg of his company. And if you don't believe me, go look at the citation he's got hanging, not in his office, but in his shop in honor of the old grandpas and baby boys from there who got killed during those three days. Signed by both Beauregard *and* General Lee. For extraordinary heroism, that piece of paper says, if I'm remembering right . . ."

"Jesus Christ!" Cabe whispered, staring at her. "You," he croaked finally, "ain't lying. In a case like this, lying don't make no sense, 'cause I kin check the facts too easy . . ." He looked down at the baby, who was awake now and gurgling happily in his arms. "What did you do, li'l fella?" he crooned. "Lend him one o' yourn? Ohhhh, Jesus! It just ain't fair! Look at him! Finest, fattest, sassiest young'un I ever did see! 'N' I can't even take him by these nice li'l rosy feet and bust his cute li'l head up agin a fence post! Him—he gits a kid like this'un, and I ain't got none at *all!* It ain't fair, Ramb; it purely ain't!"

The baby looked up at him wonderingly, at the tears pouring down that craggy face. Rose Ann crossed to the bed and took the baby from his arms.

"That's because you haven't ever tried—with me," she said with a wry little chuckle. "Satisfaction guaranteed, or double your money back . . ."

"Satisfaction, yes, Lord! Tha's for sure. But—results, Ramblin' Rose? The fault could be mine, y'know . . ."

"Oh, I don't think so," Rose Ann said. "Be back in a minute."

"Where you takin' that li'l buster? I ain't even had a chance to whup on him yet!"

"The day you ever do," Gwen said as she came through the door with the tray, "you'd better have a lily ready for me to put in your hand, for God knows, it'll be your last! Here you are. Seasoned with Paris green and salted down with ground glass. You want Father Erwell to preach over your carcass?"

"Yep. Might as well. He'll send me off in fine style, won't he? Jesus—real, honest to God potatoes, piping hot! Gwen, it's a shame I gotta beat you t'death. And—a hunk o' side meat! Y'know whut? I ain't gonna stripe your tail more'n twenty times a session. That way you'll last longer . . ."

"Caleb Henry, if you ever so much as lift a finger in my direction," Gwen began wrathfully, but then she saw how he was wolfing down that quite good food she had prepared him, and in spite of herself she had to smile. "Wait," she said. "I'll go fix you a little more . . ."

"Go heavy on the Paris green!" he called after her. "And don't spare the powdered glass neither. Lord God, I ain't et like this since before the damn war . . ."

Rose Ann came back and sat down beside the bed, watching him eat. The sight of his terrible thinness sent a great wave of maternal tenderness stealing over her.

"Cabe," she drawled, "what d'you aim to do about—me?"

"Mondays, Wednesdays, and Fridays are your turn, sugar. For seat warming and tenderizing both, I mean. You got it coming too, y'know. Don't mean to let you off none at all, girl baby . . ."

"You lift a hand, or your belt, in my direction, and you'll end up in a wheelchair," Rose Ann said grimly. "Cabe, you damn fool, you don't mean to call Colin out, do you?"

"Jesus God! Listen to the woman! Honey, what fool questions you do ask! Of course I mean to call him out. He tumbled not only my wife but, by her own confession, the sweet baby girl I *love*. Or were you just plaguing me back then, Ramb sugar? Want to retract?"

"No. I don't. He—as you so delicately put it—tumbled me all right. With my willing consent and enthusiastic cooperation. Which wasn't, and isn't, any of your goddamned business, Caleb

Henry. Let's say that this—ugly business of Gwen and the child is —in a way—"

"You can bet all that livin' glory you're sitting on it is!" Caleb howled. "And I'm gonna—"

"Wait, and let me have my say. Colin—is crippled, Cabe. He can hardly lift his right hand. He'd have to shoot with his left. And he's right-handed. It wouldn't be—a duel. It would be an execution . . ."

"He should have thought about that before he started pulling down *my* wimmen's drawers!" Caleb said grimly.

"Which he didn't. We both took 'em off, voluntarily. At least I know I did. Don't make us innocent bystanders in the case."

"I don't mean to, Ramb. The minute I get my strength back, I'm gonna take off my belt and make the two of you look like a pair of she zebras! That is, if I don't feel *real* mean one day and use an honest to God nigger whip on your straying tails!"

"You'll get yourself a couple of ounces of lead in your skinny guts, as a present from *me*, if you try it," Rose Ann drawled. "Oh, for God's sake, Cabe. Forget you're a backward idiot of a Southerner, and try to function as, and think like, a human being for a change. Say you *could* do all that—I'll waive the obvious fact that you damned well can't, for a good many reasons, starting with the main one, that you'd have to walk over my dead body to even begin acting like such a howling savage in the first place—but say you could. Are you prepared to accept the consequences of your actions? And stop talking like a field hand, will you?"

"The consequences?" Caleb croaked.

"Yes. Losing Gwen, to start with. You don't think she'll stay with you after you've—murdered her baby's father, d'you?"

"Jesus God!" Caleb all but screamed; then he sobered. "All right, Ramb," he said evenly, flatly, "hear this: I can live—without Gwen. Whom I couldn't live *with* would be myself, if I accepted this kind of affront to my honor . . ."

"To assuage which, you'll—murder a helpless man?" Rose Ann said quietly. "Break a woman's—heart? And perhaps even her mind as well? Leave an innocent baby—God knows, he had no vote in the way he was got, Caleb!—fatherless, and very likely motherless as well? High-priced honor you've got, boy!"

"Jesus, but you're a great hand at crowding a fellow up into corners, aren't you, Ramb? The kid—he'd be all right. I'd adopt him. Make him my own. Teach him to ride, and shoot, and speak the truth. And—"

"To read, I hope!" Rose Ann quipped.

"Of course. And to down his liquor like a gentleman, hold his cards close to his nose, respect good women, and pin billy blue hell on the other kind!"

"The code of a Southerner," Rose Ann said despairingly. "No wonder we lost the war! You wouldn't adopt that kid, because *I* wouldn't let you. I simply wouldn't permit you to drive yourself out of your so-called and alleged mind watching that boy growing to look, and probably act, more like Colin with every passing day. I wouldn't allow you to torment him—as you would—as you couldn't help doing—into a whining nervous wreck. So forget that there proposition right now. He's a darling baby, and at the moment, you love him, but later on, you wouldn't, because you couldn't, and a boy *needs* his father's love. But forget all that for the time being. Let's take up consequence number two. Are you prepared to also give up—me?"

Caleb stared at her, and his eyes were utterly bleak.

"Ramb honey, I purely ain't got you, y'know," he sighed.

"Sometimes I think you have absolutely no brains in your head at all, Cabe boy. You don't even ask the right questions. For instance, aren't you even slightly interested in finding out what's become of—Kurt?"

"That's right! Knew I was forgetting something. Where's that greasy furrin boar hog? Mean to mess him up right smart before I finish him off! Where is he, Rambling Rose?"

"Dead," Rose said sadly. "The Yankees killed him . . ."

"Who would of thunk it! That the damnyankees is actually good for sumpin', I mean. Praise God, from whom all blessings flow! Ramb sugar—"

"Cabe," she said then, "tell me something: Are you—light-headed? Delirious? You could be, you know. And if you are, I'll come back to see you tomorrow. What you and I have to talk about is too serious for me to want to waste my time—"

"And that thing is, Rose baby?" he said.

"You. Me. Us. I—love you, Cabe. You should have gathered as much by the way I greeted you—"

"Well," he quipped, "far be it from me to be presumptuous, but—"

"All right. Then hear this: Tomorrow, I'm going to go get Colin, bring him here. On your solemn oath that you'll—accept his apology—"

"Jesus God Almighty! No! That bastard's got to die! He tumbled *both* my women! Gwen and *you.* Maybe I could forget about—Gwen. But you, sweet Rambling Rose, never! I couldn't live knowing that there's a two-legged pants-wearing critter, walking around breathing air, who's—had—who can smile to himself gloatingly, the very cockles of his miserable heart warmed by the memory that he's lain all night in the arms of the girl I love—"

"Lain all night between the naked thighs of the girl you claim to love, you mean," she said bitterly. "A spade's not an instrument of husbandry, Marse Caleb Henry! Look, I could put this as a threat, tell you that if you don't let Colin alone, you'll never see hide nor hair of me again, which is more in the nature of a promise than a threat, because that would be just what I'd do, because I couldn't help it. I lived with one—murderer, Cabe; I couldn't stand another—"

"Jesus!" he moaned. "Rose, you don't mean to tell me I just got to take low, tuck my tail betwixt my legs like a yellow puppy dog, 'cause if I don't, you'll—"

"No, I won't tell you that, at least not right now. Later I will, if you force me to. I'd rather put the matter on a higher plane, Cabe. I won't even point out to you that unless you let Gwen go, allow her to move out to Kansas with Colin where she can get a divorce, there's no way on earth you *can* marry me anyhow, nor add to that the simple truth I just won't live in sin with you or any man. I'll go get myself a job teaching school, and die an old maid—hell!—a spinster first. As I said, I'd rather put the matter on a higher, more solidly intellectual and moral basis, backward Southern boy!"

"Such as?" he croaked.

"Such as the fact that you're talking about—possession, the usurpation of bought or granted rights. So let me ask you this: What nigger dealer did you buy me from, Caleb? You say I'm your woman, that Gwen is. How much did you pay for your pair of riding fillies, friend? Where's your bill of sale? Your certificate of ownership? This body is—mine. I have a perfect right to lend it to any man I damned well please, for an hour or a night. Or to pledge it for a lifetime, if I ever find the one man in all the world who can convince me he's worthy of such a promise. Gwen is—*yours?* Say rather that she entered into a partnership with you that both she and you have passed a nullification act against. Rendered void. You say you love *me.* Which smashes that forsaking-all-others clause all to hell. I won't ask you if you've ever cheated on Gwen, because you're both a Southerner and a Virginian, which means you have. So hear this, Mr. Self-Appointed God, you who think you've got the right to beat women bloody for committing the selfsame sin you men wallow in every day in the week, and twice on Sundays—and with black wenches, at that. I don't want to lie beside—or with —a murderer for the rest of my life. I don't want a husband who arrogates to himself the possession of my body and my soul. Only I can grant him both, and I will—in return for—complete understanding, tenderness—love—that he be as faithful to me as I pledge upon my sacred honor to be to him, until the day we both shall die. You want that, Cabe? Less, you can't have—from me. And more, doesn't exist. Do you want that—and me?"

He stared at her, and his dark eyes filled up with light. With glory.

"Yes, Ramb, I want—both," he said.

"Then let Gwen go. Out West with Colin, and their child. To make a new life. While we—you and I—make one here. Upon this dark and bitter land drenched with the blood of boys slaughtered over questions of—ownership. Over the reduction of men—black men, if you will, but men for all that—into things. I won't be your thing, Caleb. I can't. I'm me. I can only be your equal, and—your wife. May I bring Colin here tomorrow, so that you can take his hand and prove, once and for always, that you have the only kind of courage that counts?"

"Which is?" he whispered.

"To be—a man. As distinguished from, and opposed to—a beast. Which implies—understanding, compassion, the willingness to—forgive. All those qualities which add up to—civilization, call it. To repeat: May I bring Colin here tomorrow, Cabe?"

The silence between them pooled, fathoms deep.

He bowed his head. Looked up again. Said, "Yes. God, yes! Bring him."

He took her small, freckled, wildly trembling hand. Sat there holding it, and gazing at her with almost owlish wonder. Then, very slowly, he grinned all across his starved-out ruin of a face.

"Nope," he drawled judiciously. "Ain't got no whiskers. Don't hit the bottle, nor smoke no stogies. But all the same—"

"Cabe, what on *earth* are you talking about?" Rose Ann demanded.

"You've got it. Unconditional surrender. Done moved in on my works. Learned me how to spell Appomattox. But—thank Jesus!—you're a *little* prettier'n Gen'l Grant," he said.

28797